EXTRAORDINARY PRAISE FOR
SARA BLAEDEL AND
THE LOUISE RICK SERIES

"Blaedel is one of the best I've come across."

—Michael Connelly

"Crime-writer superstar Sara Blaedel's great skill is in weaving a heartbreaking social history into an edge-of-your-chair thriller while at the same time creating a detective who's as emotionally rich and real as a close friend."

—Oprah.com

"She's a remarkable crime writer who time and again delivers a solid, engaging story that any reader in the world can enjoy."

—Karin Slaughter

"One can count on emotional engagement, spine-tingling suspense, and taut storytelling from Sara Blaedel. Her smart and sensitive character, investigator Louise Rick, will leave readers enthralled and entertained."

—Sandra Brown

"I loved spending time with the tough, smart, and all-too-human heroine Louise Rick—and I can't wait to see her again."

—Lisa Unger

For Adam

AUTHOR'S NOTE

For readers who have been following Louise's story all along, *The Night Women* takes us back to an earlier time in Louise's life, before the events of *The Forgotten Girls*. Louise is still a lowly homicide detective as well as a single woman living on her own, and she hasn't yet joined the Missing Persons Department of the Special Search Agency.

The Night Women was first published in English many years ago under the title *Farewell to Freedom*, though this new edition has been revised and updated.

To my readers new and old...I hope you enjoy it!

THE
NIGHT
WOMEN

Copyright © 2010 by Sara Blaedel
Translated by Erik J. Macki and Tara F. Chace; translation © 2012 by Sara Blaedel.
Excerpt from *The Daughter* © 2018 by Sara Blaedel
Cover photograph by Steen Brogaard
Cover copyright © 2018 by Hachette Book Group

Grand Central Publishing
Hachette Book Group
1290 Avenue of the Americas
New York, NY 10104
Hachettebookgroup.com

First published in the United States as *Farewell to Freedom* by Pegasus Books in 2012.
Previously published as a trade paperback in January 2018 by Grand Central Publishing
First mass market edition: September 2018

Grand Central Publishing is a division of Hachette Book Group, Inc.
The Grand Central Publishing name and logo is a trademark of Hachette Book Group, Inc.

The Hachette Speakers Bureau provides a wide range of authors for speaking events. To find out more, go to www.hachettespeakersbureau.com or call (866) 376-6591.

The publisher is not responsible for websites (or their content) that are not owned by the publisher.

ISBNs: 978-1-5387-5970-7 (trade paperback); 978-1-5387-5969-1 (mass market);
978-1-5387-5971-4 (ebook)

Printed in the United States of America

OPM

10 9 8 7 6 5 4 3 2 1

THE
NIGHT
WOMEN

SARA BLAEDEL

Translated by Erik J. Macki and Tara F. Chace

Previously published as *Farewell to Freedom*

GRAND CENTRAL
PUBLISHING

NEW YORK   BOSTON

BOOKS BY SARA BLAEDEL

THE LOUISE RICK SERIES

The Missing Persons Trilogy

The Forgotten Girls

The Killing Forest

The Lost Woman

The Camilla Trilogy

The Night Women

The Running Girl

The Stolen Angel

The Homicide Trilogy

The Midnight Witness

The Silent Women

The Drowned Girl

The Family Secrets Series

The Daughter

1

The woman was lying on her back, her arms out to her sides, her head tilted toward one shoulder. Her throat had been slashed in one long, straight slice, her blood saturating her blond hair, which spread in a sticky mass over the left side of her torso.

Assistant Detective Louise Rick straightened back up from her kneel and took a deep breath. Did anyone ever get used to this? God, she hoped not.

Darkness lay heavily over Copenhagen's Meatpacking District, the vast industrial tract between the train station and the harbor, where the city's slaughterhouses and meatpackers had sold their wares for centuries. It was almost two in the morning, so Sunday had already given way to Monday. Damp April air lingered over the Vesterbro District just west of the inner city, although the previous evening's rain had subsided. The flashing lights and police barricade that had been erected out on Skelbækgade were keeping most people away, but a few curious bystanders chatted as they watched the officers work.

A lone drunk sat on the doorstep of Høker Café, seemingly oblivious to the large police presence. He sang and occasionally screamed out whenever someone drove by. The girls who usually worked this street were nowhere in sight, likely having retreated to Sønder Boulevard or around the corner to Ingerslevsgade.

The bright glare of the large crime-scene spotlights created sharp contrasts of light and dark. One of the first things the team had done was to go over the surface of the body with tape to secure any fibers and loose hairs before swabbing for DNA with slightly moistened cotton swabs. Forensic pathologist Flemming Larsen turned to Louise and the chief of the Homicide Division, Hans Suhr.

"The incision is approximately twenty centimeters long, leaving a large, gaping wound across the entire throat. It's a deep cut with clean edges, which means the knife was drawn across the throat quickly, and only once."

Pulling off his rubber gloves and face mask, he nodded at the techs to signal that he was done so they could investigate the area around the murdered woman.

"There are no other signs of violence, so it happened fast. She didn't see it coming; there are no defensive wounds on her hands or arms. I would bet that it went down within the last three hours," he said.

"Do you have any clues as to who she might be?" Louise asked. They hadn't found any ID on the body.

"Well, don't you think we can assume we're dealing with a prostitute?" Flemming asked, his eyes resting on the victim's skimpy cotton skirt and tight top, before adding that he doubted she was Danish, given the poor state of her teeth.

"It's not a bad guess," Suhr agreed, taking a step back so that the techs could get by.

They moved the floodlight Flemming had been working under farther down the street so they could search the entire area for evidence.

Louise squatted down next to the woman again. The wound was high on her throat and went all the way around to her cervical vertebrae. It was difficult to make out the facial features in the dark, but she was obviously young—probably about twenty, Louise guessed.

She heard footsteps behind her, but before she could stand up, her colleague Michael Stig came to a stop right behind her and placed both hands on her shoulders as if for support. He leaned forward to inspect the body.

"Eastern European whore" was his swift assessment before removing his hands and allowing Louise to stand up again.

"What makes you so certain?" she asked, taking a step away from him to disrupt the physical intimacy he had forced upon her.

"Her makeup. They still do their faces the way Danish women did back in the eighties. The colors are too bright and there's too much of it. So, what do we know about her?" Stig asked, his hands into the pockets of his baggy jeans.

Louise caught the scent of her newly washed hair and fresh deodorant. She had been asleep for less than an hour when Suhr had woken her with his call, and she had left her Frederiksberg apartment and made it to the murder scene within twenty minutes. After almost five years as a homicide detective, she had a speedy routine for nighttime calls like this one.

"Not a thing," she replied tersely. "The local precinct received an anonymous tip about a dead body on Kødboderne Street behind the Hotel and Restaurant Management School, and then the caller hung up."

"So the caller must have had pretty thorough knowledge of this less than savory section of Copenhagen," Stig concluded. "Like someone who's a regular in this part of town."

Louise raised one eyebrow, and he explained:

"Only people who know the Meatpacking District fairly well would use one of the specific street names: Kødboderne, Høkerboderne, and Slagterboderne."

I wonder why you're so familiar with the area, Louise thought as she turned to join the others. Her partner, Lars Jørgensen, was off with some of their colleagues from the local precinct knocking on the doors in the apartment buildings on Skelbækgade whose windows faced the Meatpacking District. Another team was dealing with the people on the street as well as in the buildings immediately surrounding the scene. Even though the call had gone to the main precinct, formerly known as Precinct 1 on Halmtorvet, the case had been quickly turned over to the Homicide Division at Police Headquarters. Suhr had decided to call some of his own people in so they could be in on the investigation right from the start, but he had spared Toft, who had spent the weekend out in Jutland celebrating his sister's silver wedding anniversary. The chief said he'd figured he ought to let Toft sleep in after all the glasses of port and hours of brass band music that such an event would have required.

"Nobody has anything to tell us," Jørgensen reported. "Either that or they don't dare open their mouths. And strangely, it seems like no one has been anywhere near Skelbækgade in the past twenty-four hours. Not even the people Mikkelsen saw here earlier with his own eyes." He shook his head and yawned.

Mikkelsen was the local officer from the Halmtorvet station who was most knowledgeable about what went on in the Istedgade neighborhood with its prostitutes, pushers, and drug addicts. He was a short, stocky man in his mid-fifties, and he'd spent almost all of his many years on the force working this area. He had served one three-year tour with the riot squad before putting in for a transfer and getting his old office back.

"What about that guy over on those steps?" Louise asked.

"He said he hasn't seen anything except for the bottom of the last bottle he downed," her partner replied, repeating the remark a moment later when the chief came over and asked the same question.

"OK, nobody wants to say anything, so it's business as usual around here," Suhr said as he waved for Stig to come over and join them. "There's nothing more we can do right now. Mikkelsen and his people will continue interviewing passersby, but I doubt we'll get anybody to talk tonight. If any of the regulars around here saw anything, we know from experience that it will take time for them to share. So let's all get some sleep. We'll pick this up again in the morning."

"What about Willumsen?" Louise asked as they headed toward their cars. It surprised her that she hadn't seen the detective superintendent here yet.

"I'll brief him first thing in the morning," said the homicide chief, giving her a wry smile. "It's better to let him get his beauty sleep."

Louise nodded. They all knew what Willumsen was like when he got up on the wrong side of the bed. He had a bad habit of infecting everyone else with his lousy mood.

* * *

When Louise Rick woke again after four hours of sleep, she had a sore throat and her whole body felt sluggish. She had gotten up several times in the night, the image of the dead woman implanted in her mind's eye. She wondered why she had been killed that way. The deep wound in her throat seemed so aggressive, but the killer had come up on her from behind, so the woman likely hadn't had a chance to fight back. Thoughts drifted through Louise's mind, coalescing into more visuals from the night's murder scene. Again and again, she saw the nighttime shadows on the low, white-brick façades of the Meatpacking District, where butchers and delicatessen wholesalers served customers in the daytime.

Louise went to the kitchen to put some water on to boil before she climbed into the shower. She stood under the hot spray for so long that the whole bathroom was filled with steam before she felt ready to get out. Afterward, she sank onto a kitchen chair with a cup of tea cradled in her hands.

Suhr had announced just before they'd parted that there would be a briefing on the case at nine o'clock. Things had finally settled down again in their department after the big reorganization that had sent powerful shock waves through Police Headquarters. They had closed down both Division A, which had been in charge of homicides, and Division

C, which had handled burglary investigations. Now everything had been reshuffled, dividing lines had been erased, and some of the most senior detectives had been moved elsewhere. And there was no longer room for all the assistant detective superintendents who had previously acted as team leaders. Which was why Louise had lost Henny Heilmann. Henny had been offered a job as lead detective at HQ and was now up in radio dispatch, stuck directing squad cars. Louise knew it had taken Henny quite a while to see the upside to her transfer.

Louise went into the bedroom and pulled a heavy sweater out of her closet. She was tempted to take the bus from Gammel Kongevej, but at the last minute mustered the energy to ride her bike.

The traffic on the bike path was heavy, full of morning commuters. Even so, she moved over into the passing lane as she crossed H. C. Ørstedsvej. Pedaling hard, she pulled her helmet down low to shield her eyes from the glaring spring sunshine that had suddenly appeared now that the rain clouds had drifted away.

* * *

"Just have the downtown precinct keep doing the interviews in the neighborhood, especially in the red-light areas that the johns frequent. It's likelier we'll get something out of a regular client who happened to know the victim than out of any of the hookers. Meanwhile, we'll focus on identifying the victim and processing the forensic evidence. You're probably not planning on allocating too many resources to this case, right?" Detective Superintendent Willumsen asked, shooting Suhr an inquisitive look.

The homicide chief seemed to deliberately pause before responding. Louise leaned her chair back against the wall. It had been a year since Suhr had appointed Willumsen lead detective for Louise's group. Willumsen was widely disliked for his arrogance and rudeness; he didn't give a damn about anything or anyone, and he made no distinction between superiors and colleagues. All the same, Louise was actually quite fond of him. Willumsen had taught her to just say "Yes," "No," or "Kiss my ass," to say things clearly without a lot of screwing around.

His other trademark line was "Is that understood, or not, or do you not give a shit about what I'm telling you?" He was also the one who had signed Louise up a few years back to train in hostage negotiations.

Suhr took a step back and propped his arm against the wall, as if gathering strength to reply.

"You have all the resources you need right now—all four of the detectives in your group: Rick and Jørgensen, Toft and Stig. Plus the assistance we're already getting from Mikkelsen and his folks at Halmtorvet precinct." Suhr let his arm drop again after firing off this remark.

Willumsen lowered his eyes to focus on his right thumbnail. He meticulously cleaned it with the tip of his pencil. Finally, he tossed the pencil aside and announced that he'd decided Toft and Stig would keep tabs on the forensic techs and keep everyone up-to-date on the latest evidence. They would also attend the victim's autopsy.

Then Willumsen's eyes shifted to Louise and her partner.

"I want the two of you to go down to see Mikkelsen and concentrate on the investigation in the neighborhood." With that, he wrapped up the meeting.

2

The alarm clock went off at six thirty. It had rained hard through the night and into the early morning hours, so Camilla Lind decided to skip her morning run, which was supposed to be the first stage of her new exercise regimen. Instead, she decided to walk over to the Frederiksberg public pool two blocks from her apartment. There, she would force herself to swim at least twenty laps and follow that up with some time in the sauna. Hopefully, that would work off the effects of her weekend with a few too many mojitos and far too little sleep. Her son had been at his father's from Thursday through Sunday, and from there he'd gone straight to the home of a classmate, where he was going to spend the night. On Monday morning, his class was taking a field trip to the Open Air Museum, and they were supposed to meet at Nørreport Station at ten. But his friend's father was a pastor and worked at home, and the man had assured Camilla that he'd be happy to see the boys off for the field trip. So at ten o'clock on this Monday morning she was going to attend the weekly editorial meeting for the *Morgenavisen* crime beat.

With great purpose, Camilla took out her swimsuit and a towel. She didn't go to the pool often, but she was determined to get some exercise today. It was pathetic how many times she had resolved to start exercising more, only to have her best intentions fizzle out, resulting in half-hearted attempts at best. She always felt extremely guilty when ultimately forced to admit to herself that she just really didn't want to do it.

* * *

The newspaper's crime desk was deserted when she unlocked the door to her office two hours later, her cheeks flushed, ready to tackle the new week. Thirty laps and a good sweat in the sauna had filled her with renewed energy. She had an hour before their meeting started with no leads on anything worth writing about. Out of the news loop, she hadn't read a newspaper or watched any TV because of her date Saturday with Kristian—who didn't mention until Sunday that he'd promised his girlfriend he'd pick her up at the airport when she got back from her girls-only trip to London.

Camilla had just happened to run into Kristian at Magasin, the department store. They had gone to elementary school together, but she didn't recognize him when he stopped her at the bottom of the escalator. It wasn't until he rattled off a bunch of names of other classmates that it dawned on her who he was, and it turned out he lived in Frederiksberg, too. So she had accepted when he asked her out to Belis Bar on Saturday night, and they ended up at her place after a couple of strong drinks. She had been fine with it the next morning when he said he had to take off.

Camilla booted up her computer and went out to put on some coffee. At the same time, she gathered up the pile of morning papers from the floor in front of the door to the crime division's modest conference room. She had time to leaf through them before the meeting started, and she also logged in to the website for the Ritzau news agency to see what sort of crime stories they were running from the weekend. A serious stabbing incident in Ålborg and a major car crash on the island of Fyn with three dead. She was jotting these down on her notepad when she heard the door open, and she nodded to the intern, who said hello.

She kept searching, quickly scanning the other papers' news services and checking Radio Denmark and TV2, but there wasn't much. The stories she did find weren't going to end up on the front page. Camilla reached for the phone as she glanced at the clock. It was already quarter past nine, and the editor in chief, Terkel Høyer, nodded to her as he walked by. Camilla closed the door to the conference room before placing a few calls to the major police departments to find out what they had in their blotters from the weekend.

* * *

"OK, what've we got?" Terkel began once Camilla and her colleague, Ole Kvist, were seated along with Jakob the intern. Jakob offered them the cinnamon rolls that he'd picked up. It was his last week on the job before he returned to the School of Media and Journalism to finish his degree.

Camilla looked down at the one story she hadn't crossed off her notepad yet; neither the stabbing nor the car crash had made the cut. Kvist leafed through the clippings in front of him. He made a habit of stopping by the news desk every Monday morning on his way up to their editorial offices on the second floor. Like most large news desks, they subscribed to all the smaller newspapers in Denmark, and Kvist quickly tossed any crime stories. He didn't actually evaluate which items were worth discussing until it was time for him to pitch his own stories. His stack of clippings always looked so impressive, even though only a couple of them would actually merit any follow-up; by the time they reached the crime pages of *Morgenavisen*, they were considered old news.

"There's a gang of art thieves at work in the Silkeborg area," Kvist said, reading the lede of the first clipping and glancing sideways at his boss, as if to make sure the man's interest was piqued, before continuing.

"Apparently, the thieves go straight for the expensive art on the wall, and this weekend they took a pricey Per Kirkeby painting and two other works by a Norwegian artist in the same price range from some mansion. The police estimate the mansion has several million kroners' worth of art in it. And they've had similar types of break-ins over the past couple of months."

The tone of his voice grew more eager as he worked up enthusiasm for the story. "I don't think that's really anything for us," Camilla ventured. "That story's already old news."

"It'd be worth doing if we could help them nail the gang by publicizing the case a lot more," Kvist pointed out, adding a pleading look to his face for their boss's benefit.

"Which newspaper did you get that from?" the editor in chief asked, reaching for the clipping.

"It's from central Jutland, so the story probably hasn't run in any of the bigger papers yet," Kvist replied, then proposed that he at least take time to make some calls about it.

Camilla broke off part of her cinnamon roll. There wouldn't be anything to that story until the police made some sort of breakthrough, but it wouldn't surprise her if Kvist got away with it anyway.

"It's right out where all those car dealers live, with a fabulous view over the Silkeborg lakes. They can all afford to have that kind of art on their walls," Kvist reminded them. "So it wouldn't be that hard for the thieves to figure out someone's home address, case the joint, and then make their move when the occupants go out for cocktails with their neighbors."

Camilla thought about the officers handling the case. Surely that scenario must have occurred to them, too.

"Well, look into it then," said Terkel, interrupting her thoughts. "Have you got anything else?"

Kvist shook his head, shoving the other clippings under the story that had been accepted. He glanced over at Camilla, who quickly wiped the crumbs from her mouth.

"Lind, what have you got?" Høyer asked.

"I've got a homicide. A young woman was found murdered in Vesterbro last night."

Høyer raised an eyebrow to show his interest.

"There's not much to tell you right now. An anonymous

tip to the police. They found her down by Skelbækgade somewhere near the entrance to the Hotel and Restaurant Management School."

"So, it's a prostitute," Kvist said, leaning back.

Camilla ignored him. "The woman's throat was slit, and Suhr has a team on the case," she continued. "They haven't ID'd her yet. But they're willing to say, off the record, that they suspect she was from Eastern Europe."

"Yeah, well, plenty of them are these days," Kvist said. Then he cut her off, suggesting that he go to Silkeborg to talk to some of the victims who had had their expensive artwork stolen. "I'd really like to follow up on this story," he said.

Trying to hold her boss's attention, Camilla raised her voice. "She was no more than twenty."

The editor in chief sat in silence for a moment, nodding. "Go ahead and write it up, Camilla, but keep it to two columns."

"It sounds like a really brutal killing," Camilla went on, frustrated that Høyer didn't think the story deserved more space. "It could be a big story, especially if we haven't got anything else."

"But we do have something else," Kvist interrupted from his other side of the table, and it looked as if Høyer agreed with him.

"I'll call the forensic pathologist who examined the body last night. If it was a professional hit—"

Camilla was interrupted by her cell phone ringing. She was just about to switch it off to continue her argument when she saw it was Markus calling. She pushed her chair back from the table, quietly answered, and told her son to make it quick. At the same time, she kept her eyes on

Høyer, who was asking Lind to present his suggestions for the paper.

"What do you mean 'a baby'?" Camilla asked, speaking into her cell and asking her son to speak up a bit. "In the church? When you were on your way to Nørreport Station?"

Camilla could hear the irritation in her own voice. As her son's words continued to spill out, she took a deep breath and calmly asked him to repeat everything he'd just said, but this time a little slower. Even though she could hear Kvist pushing his art heist some more, she turned to face the wall so she could concentrate on what her son was saying. Only now did she notice the quaver in his voice and how upset he seemed amid all his disjointed sentences. She let him go on until he'd gotten everything out that he needed to say.

"I'll be right there," she said, ending the call.

The others at the conference table could see the change in Camilla and looked at her with obvious curiosity as she returned her attention to their editorial meeting.

"I've got to go. My son and his friend found an abandoned baby on the floor of Stenhøj Church."

3

Down on Gothersgade, Camilla waved her hand for a taxi. The first three were occupied and drove right past, so she started jogging along Rosenborg Castle Gardens toward Copenhagen's Nørreport Station, keeping her eye out for a cab.

"Stenhøj Allé," she said after a minivan with its taxi light on veered over to the curb to pick her up. The morning traffic had subsided as they headed out toward Frederiksberg, the well-to-do suburb of Copenhagen where she lived, but she thought they were still moving too slowly. She knew she ought to be using this time to put in a call with the Institute of Forensic Medicine and locate the forensic pathologist who had been out to Skelbækgade last night, but she couldn't concentrate with all the adrenaline that Markus's distress had triggered coursing through her veins. She pictured his cheerful face, his short, spiky hair that he styled every morning with gel and hair spray. He was quite grown up for an eleven-year-old, but still enough of a child to call his mother when something upset him.

She had her wallet in her lap as they reached the white Lutheran church with the red-tile roof.

The cabdriver flashed her a look of irritation in the rearview mirror as she passed him her card. "You should have told me that you were going to pay with a credit card before we started."

"Look, do you want to get paid or not?" she asked, gathering up her handbag from the floor.

A moment later, she was out of the cab, making her way down the side of the church.

A police car drove past and turned into the parking lot next to the cemetery. Camilla followed the path to the back of the church and the courtyard in front of the parsonage. The pastor, Henrik Holm, greeted her in the doorway, holding a little bundle in his arms. Markus ran over to Camilla from the kitchen chair where he had been sitting, with his friend Jonas close on his heels. Jonas greeted her with that slightly hoarse voice of his that Markus thought was so cool.

The pastor tried to hush them as they both started talking at once, telling Louise that they had been on their way out that morning when they heard a baby crying. But their eager explanation was interrupted by the piercing chime of the doorbell. The boys raced excitedly out of the kitchen and through the rooms to the front door to let the police in.

"What exactly is going on?" Camilla asked hurriedly once she was alone with the pastor.

He sat down, rocking the bundle back and forth. "I sent the boys off just before nine thirty and was standing in the doorway watching them cross the courtyard. Suddenly they stopped and stood still for a moment, and then they started running toward the church. I went out to tell them they needed to get going or they'd be late for the field trip. And that's when they came rushing back, yelling something about a baby crying."

Camilla leaned in over the infant in the pastor's arms. The tiny face was sleeping calmly, the thick, dark hair plastered to the baby's head.

"Is it a boy or a girl?" she asked.

"It's a baby girl," he replied, turning to look toward the living room as they heard footsteps crossing the parquet floor.

"Let me put some water on for coffee while you talk to the police," Camilla suggested, then greeted the two officers who came into the kitchen.

"Hello," the pastor said in a voice close to a whisper. "She just fell asleep, but otherwise she's been crying nonstop ever since the boys found her."

The officers nodded sympathetically, which signaled to Camilla they must have children of their own and knew firsthand how important it was to avoid waking her.

"Where did you find her?" one of the officers asked as he turned to look at Jonas and Markus, who suddenly seemed nervous and shy.

"By the front entrance to the church," they said, but when they didn't say anything else, the pastor took over.

"The boys were on their way to school when they heard her," he explained and then nodded to Camilla, who was gesturing at a kitchen cupboard as she searched for the coffee.

"She was lying on the stone floor just inside the door,

wrapped in this." The pastor fingered the dark blue terry cloth towel that was wrapped around the infant's body.

The baby girl stirred uneasily as the officer began unwrapping the blue terry cloth bundle, but she didn't wake up.

"I think she's exhausted from all the crying," the pastor said. Then he explained that he'd finally gotten her to calm down when he remembered how, many years ago, he used to soothe Jonas by stroking his face in little circular motions.

"She's probably hungry. She calmed down when her nursing reflex kicked in, and she was sucking like crazy on my little finger until she fell asleep just now," he said, moving back a bit so that he could lay the baby on his lap as the officers moved in closer to get a good look at her.

Camilla went over and stood behind them to look, too.

A day old, at most, maybe even less. She looked like a newborn, and she was naked except for a long, bloody umbilical cord dangling from her body, which was smeared with amniotic fluid and blood.

"She certainly hasn't been cleaned up since she was born. It kind of looks like she was born under rough conditions, maybe even without the help of a midwife," one of the officers concluded as he studied the umbilical cord. "I suspect the cord was ripped in two—it looks frayed, so they didn't use a knife or scissors to separate her from her mother."

The officer looked at the pastor.

"Could she have been born inside the church?" he asked.

Pastor Holm shook his head but then shrugged. "I couldn't really say," he admitted. "There was no sign of anything like that, but I haven't inspected the rest of the church."

Camilla put the coffeepot and cups on the table, hesitating a bit when the officer asked whether she would hold the baby until the ambulance arrived.

Turning to Pastor Holm, the officer added, "It'll only be for a few minutes, and we'd like to take you and the boys over to the church so you can show us where you found her." The pastor wrapped the child back up in the towel before carefully picking her up and placing her in Camilla's arms.

* * *

As the kitchen door closed behind them, Camilla sat down on the bench against the wall. She didn't dare pour herself any coffee while she was holding the baby. Instead, she sat motionless, looking down at the little girl. Something hard to put into words was swelling up inside of her. The tiny newborn radiated such enormous vulnerability, Camilla recognized the same emotion swelling up in the two policemen.

With her free hand, she pulled her handbag closer and took out her cell phone. She turned on the camera function and managed to take a couple of pictures of the sleeping infant, but when she heard a knock on the door, she tossed the cell back in her bag and called out: "Come in." A moment later the EMTs were in the kitchen asking her if the baby was still asleep.

"We'll go get the portable bassinet," one of them said.

Camilla nodded and carefully stood up. While she waited for them to come back, she hugged the baby close, noticing how calm her breathing was. She stood still, letting the feeling of calm pervade her body until she heard footsteps crossing the courtyard, and Holm returned with one of the officers.

Through the window, she saw that Markus and Jonas had stopped next to the ambulance, watching with obvious interest as the back door was pulled open and the bassinet was brought out.

They retreated a bit as the EMTs came back inside, and Holm quickly cleared off one end of the kitchen table to set the bassinet there. It was the same kind that Camilla had had when Markus was a newborn, made of see-through plastic; this one was lined with a thick white blanket and a clean towel.

"We're going to take her to Frederiksberg Hospital, and they'll feed her before she's examined and cleaned up," said the officer. "They'll take some blood samples so we can run a DNA test on her, and then they'll keep her under observation."

Out in the courtyard, the crime-scene techs had arrived, and the officer explained to the pastor that they would take the blue terry cloth towel to the forensics lab for further testing after they were done with their work inside and around the church.

The portable bassinet was ready, and Camilla took one last look at the tiny girl before handing her over. The moment she let her go, the baby started crying again. It was loud and heartrending. Her little face contorted, and she began waving her little fists in the air. The young medic stepped back in alarm and asked Camilla if she wouldn't mind placing the baby in the bassinet.

"I'm sure they'll take good care of her at the hospital," he added, his voice reassuring.

Camilla looked at her son and his friend as the paramedics carried the bassinet out to the ambulance. They stood there distressed, clearly upset by the child's piercing cries, and they watched until the ambulance pulled out into traffic.

Then they all sat down at the table. Camilla poured coffee into the mugs and served them, while the police asked the pastor and the boys to recount what had happened.

"None of you heard or saw anyone around the church this morning?" the officer began.

All three of them shook their heads.

He looked at the pastor. "What time did you come downstairs to the kitchen?"

"I got up at six forty-five and was here in the kitchen by seven to make breakfast and pack their lunches," Holm explained, nodding at the counter. "From the window, I can see right across to the church."

The officer nodded. He'd already been over to the window and noticed that there was a good view of the church and the entire courtyard.

"The boys said that the church door was slightly ajar when they heard the baby. Did you see whether it was open when you came down to the kitchen to make breakfast?"

Camilla kept listening as she took a carton of milk out of the refrigerator and set it on the table. She sent Høyer a quick text message to say that she was going to be a little longer, but that he would definitely be getting a story for the next day's paper. Then she sat down on the bench next to Markus and put her arm around his shoulder.

"I really couldn't say," Holm admitted. "I didn't notice."

"But you would have noticed if someone went inside?"

"I'm sure I would have, but I wasn't looking at the

church the whole time. I had to get the boys up and fed before they left for their field trip."

The officer nodded and shrugged. "Well, I guess we don't have much to go on if you didn't notice anyone in the vicinity of the parsonage or the church," he said.

"What will you do to find the mother?" Camilla asked when the officer looked like he was about to get up from the table.

"Mainly, we'll hope she turns up on her own," he replied, once again picking up his coffee mug. "In most cases like this, the mother usually does show up. And all indications are that the child was meant to be found, since she was left here in the church. Otherwise she might have been left anywhere at all, or even been killed."

Camilla pulled Markus close as she felt his body tense.

"But won't you do anything to try to locate her?" exclaimed Holm.

"There's really not much we can do if she doesn't want to be found. But, of course, we'll go to the media and make an appeal for the mother to contact us. And we'll interview people here in the neighborhood to find out if anyone saw anything."

The officer sounded a bit tired, and he leaned back in his chair. "But if nothing comes of our efforts," he added, "the child will be put up for adoption. Until adoptive parents can be found for her, I assume that she'll be placed in an orphanage, presumably Skodsborg."

"Isn't someone going to take care of her?" asked Jonas, who had stood up as the officer was talking.

"They absolutely will. Some very nice ladies will take good care of her until she gets new parents."

"But there must be something else you can do. Maybe

the towel could give you a lead," Camilla interjected, removing her arm from Markus's shoulder as he, too, stood up.

"We'll certainly do everything we can. But at least the baby's alive, and if the mother doesn't want her, it's probably best for the girl to be placed with some couple who really wants a child," said the officer. Then he asked the pastor for a phone number where he could be reached.

As the officer stood up to leave, he gave his business card to Holm and handed one to Camilla as well. She noted that his name was Officer Rasmus Hem, and she automatically nodded when he said that she was welcome to call him if her son happened to remember anything else. Standard procedure, she thought, sticking the card in her pocket.

The boys disappeared upstairs to Jonas's room. Camilla shifted her gaze away from the stairs and nodded to accept the pastor's offer of another cup of coffee. A pall had fallen over the kitchen, and the silence weighed heavily between them.

"What a mess," said Pastor Holm, sinking onto a chair by the table and reaching for the sugar.

Camilla tried to imagine what would drive a mother to abandon a newborn to an uncertain fate, but in all the scenarios and feelings she considered, she couldn't find a single credible explanation.

"Can you think of any pregnant women who have been here?" she asked instead. "I've been racking my brain like crazy, but the only pregnant woman who comes here on a regular basis is Mette, and she hasn't delivered yet."

He shook his head and glanced at the clock on the wall.

"I have to go write a column for the paper this week,"

he said, gazing out the window at the church. "But I don't suppose they'll be needing me for the next couple of hours."

Camilla shook her head and got up. It was almost eleven thirty, and she called Markus downstairs to tell him she was leaving.

"I've got to get back to the paper," she said, running her fingers through his hair, flattening out a couple of tufts that he immediately retousled so it stuck out all over the place.

She smiled at him and placed her hands on his shoulders as she looked into his eyes, trying to determine whether he was still upset. But she started to relax, realizing he was likely impatient for her to leave so he could go back up to Jonas.

"I'll call as soon as I can get away," she promised, giving him a kiss on the cheek and another on his forehead before he writhed out of her grasp. Shouting "Sure, fine," he disappeared up the stairs.

Camilla turned to face Pastor Holm and smiled. "Well, it looks like they've moved on," she said, and after thanking him for the coffee, she left.

4

"A t this hour of the day, you won't find a single person
on the street who might have seen anything,"
Mikkelsen informed Louise and Lars when they arrived at
the local precinct. A clerk had shown them to Mikkelsen's
office, which had a window overlooking Halmtorvet,
Copenhagen's old Haymarket Square, which was now
somewhat gentrified and lined with cafés and restaurants.
The detective, who had gray hair and wore small horn-
rimmed glasses, crossed his arms and glanced outside
before telling them he'd already chatted up a few individu-
als last night who usually knew a thing or two about events
in the area.

"Were they able to tell you anything?" Louise asked.
She wondered whether Mikkelsen had even been home to
sleep, having immediately noticed the utilitarian daybed
pushed up against one wall of his office when she came in.

Currently it was covered with piles of papers and folders, but underneath was a cotton blanket with a floral pattern.

He shook his head but shrugged at the same time, as if to say that it wasn't always easy to know how much weight to place on their statements.

"I showed the picture around," he said, pointing to the photograph taken the night before of the woman's face from the chin up. "Several people said they'd seen her, but they claimed not to know who she was. Or who she works for."

"And you're positive she's a prostitute?" Lars asked.

Mikkelsen reclined in his high-backed office chair, pausing for a moment with his hands clasped over his round belly.

"We might never get that fact confirmed a hundred percent," he said, fixing his gaze on the wall behind them. "But I think we can proceed based on that theory."

"A colleague claimed he could tell by looking at her teeth that she was from Eastern Europe. Does that sound right?" Louise asked, noticing at once how Mikkelsen's face tensed up and his expression darkened.

He leaned forward again, placed his hands on the desk, and said, "It's always nice to have colleagues who are smart enough to observe everything in a single glance, and who are ready to lump all the girls together. But it's not that simple. We're not dealing with brand-name goods here. We can't just assume that if they look a certain way, they must come from a specific region. These are human beings we're talking about, not some cultivar of a flower that you can look up."

His tone was acerbic. This was clearly a pet peeve of his that apparently came up a lot.

"So, what's your best guess?" asked Louise once he'd calmed down.

"She could very well be from Eastern Europe," Mikkelsen admitted, but then he smiled. "I'm not basing just that on her appearance. That's based on what happened to her and where she was found. Plus, I'd be more likely to know her a little if she were one of the Danish prostitutes. And lately I've also been getting the impression that things have been getting difficult in Eastern Europe for these girls, so more and more of them have been showing up in Denmark in the past couple of years. Some of them work for pimps, others work for themselves, but ultimately they all have to pay to use the street."

"Use the street?" Louise interrupted with a puzzled look. "What exactly does that mean?"

"Some of the nastier pimps think they're in charge of the street, and they make the girls pay between 300 and 500 kroner a day for permission to use it."

"How the hell can they do that? If anyone 'owns' Istedgade, surely it's not a bunch of foreign pimps," Lars exclaimed indignantly.

"Do the women get anything in return after they pay?" Louise asked, staring at a large city map hanging next to Mikkelsen's desk that showed the Vesterbro District. There were also some photos on the wall of Istedgade and its side streets from an era when the shop fronts looked completely different, Louise guessed from the fifties. In one of the pictures a police officer was riding a bicycle, and another showed three men raising bottles of beer at the photographer in a toast. All of the photos were in black and white.

Mikkelsen shrugged. "Sure, they promise them protection," he said with a nod as he scratched his unshaven cheeks.

Louise understood this to imply that the prostitutes couldn't really count on this protection.

"They believe it because they have no other choice. They're told that the pimps are in cahoots with the police, and that they have to pay if they don't want to be thrown out of the country."

"But don't the girls find the truth when they talk to each other?" Louise asked. Mikkelsen shook his head and pushed his black-framed glasses up onto his forehead.

There was something retro about their styling, but she was sure that he hadn't chosen them for fashion but because he'd actually owned them since the sixties.

"Keep in mind that many of the girls who end up here don't necessarily have the world's best education. Where they come from, bribes aren't uncommon to get the authorities to leave you alone. At the same time, these girls aren't used to having much of a say about anything. So, when someone who talks louder than they do, so to speak, explains that these are the rules, they fall in line accordingly."

"So who's controlling the girls this way?" Louise asked next.

"The crime bosses. The ones who work with the Nigerian prostitutes, the Roma, and the ones from Eastern Europe. There are girls walking around out there"—he tilted his head toward the window—"who have no idea how many months there are in a year, or how many hours in a day. Those kinds of girls aren't going to rebel against someone who gives them an order. They do whatever they're told.

"They're here for only one reason, and that's to make money," Mikkelsen continued. "Either for themselves or for the crime bosses who force them into prostitution. But whether they're here of their own free will or they've been forced into it, most of them dream of being able to put a little aside or to send money home to their families. When there's a middleman involved, there's not much money left over, so sometimes a few of them try to go it on their own."

"Do you think that's what happened here?" asked Louise, leaning forward a bit.

"It's possible," Mikkelsen said, nodding.

Louise sat in silence for a moment, lost in her own thoughts, trying to put together a scenario that would explain the killing.

"Well, should we head out and see if anyone has shown up who might recognize the woman?" Lars suggested, interrupting her thoughts.

Mikkelsen stood up. "Let's do that," he said. "But just think of it as getting some exercise, because I don't think our odds are all that good. If this is what I think, the girl didn't want to follow orders. So, the only motive for the murder is to send a signal or a warning to the other girls, to show them what happens if they don't obey and do what they're told. And those guys do their job so thoroughly that there won't be any evidence for us to find, not even if we roll out our entire technical arsenal."

Mikkelsen put on a black leather jacket, pulled a pack of cigarettes out of his desk drawer, and stuffed it in his inside pocket.

"And if anyone happens to be unlucky enough to have seen something, you can bet they're not going to feel like picking the perpetrators out of a lineup later on," he added.

* * *

"But it is still possible that the victim was Danish and that the perp was a john, don't you think?" Lars asked as they made their way downstairs.

"I doubt it." Mikkelsen's voice was quite firm. "If so, there would have been some indication of emotion. Not the kind of emotion that makes married people kill each other, but the more ambiguous kind that can pop up suddenly between a man and a prostitute: feelings of domination, rage, or possessiveness. We see it all the time when we pick up hookers who've been beaten. But there was no emotion in this case. She was slaughtered like an animal."

Out on Halmtorvet, Louise squinted in the bright sunlight as they started walking down Sønder Boulevard. There were fewer cars now that the street had been closed to through traffic, but there weren't many pedestrians or bikers out, either. Louise spotted a young drug addict leaning against the door in an entryway. The woman's purse had slipped out of her grasp and was lying on the sidewalk. Louise guessed she was in her midtwenties. She was wearing stylish clothes: tight jeans and a short, light-colored leather jacket. Her short brown hair was disheveled, and at the moment she seemed to be going through hell. Violent spasms appeared to be racking her body. She leaned her head against the rough bricks of the building and clung to the door, her fingers jabbing at the doorbells. She doubled over, gasping for air.

Mikkelsen went over to her and cautiously placed his hand on her shoulder. "What is it, Sanne? What's wrong?" he asked.

The woman didn't turn to look at him, instead raising her arm and trying to push him away. He pressed one of the doorbells, and a moment later the door buzzed. He gallantly held it open for her as she staggered unsteadily into the stairwell, fumbling along the wall with one hand. Then she disappeared from Louise's view. Mikkelsen had picked up her bag and hung the strap over the woman's shoulder before pulling the door closed.

Rejoining his colleagues, Mikkelsen made no comment about the incident and just kept walking.

"It's always deserted around here in the early afternoon. But in an hour or two the johns will start heading home from work, and then the girls will show up," he told them as he waved to a couple of middle-aged men sitting on a bench, each holding a beer. Louise fell in behind Jørgensen as a group of school kids passed them, taking up most of the sidewalk as they made their way toward DGI-byen, the enormous conference center complex that included a gym, spa, and restaurant.

Mikkelsen was headed for Skelbækgade, which felt different to Louise in the daytime.

There had been much more life on the street the night before than there was now.

"Let's just go over and ask Nesip what sort of rumors are going around," Mikkelsen said, sounding like a local. He motioned for them to follow as he went down four steps into a basement grocery store, calling out: "Hello, is the little shrimp working today?"

Louise saw a young immigrant boy behind the counter give him a high five over the candy bins and the neat stacks of morning newspapers.

"He's in back," the boy said in the thick, local neighborhood accent.

Mikkelsen led the way through the shop, and Louise noticed the boy following them with his eyes, curious looking. He didn't seem concerned about a group of police officers tromping through the place.

* * *

In the back room, Mikkelsen sat down next to a small man who was apparently the shop owner. The tea was sweet, and the music was so loud that Louise had a hard time following the conversation, but it seemed as if Mikkelsen were a friend of the house, and Louise and Lars were merely along for the ride.

Mikkelsen placed the photo of the dead woman on the table, and Louise didn't need to hear what they were saying to see that Nesip didn't know her. She leaned forward to listen as Mikkelsen tried to ferret out what people in the neighborhood had been saying, and whether there was anything the police hadn't caught wind of yet. Occasionally the Turkish man would have a highly emotional outburst, his voice rising in passion and temporarily drowning out the Middle Eastern music as he expressed his great sorrow that the harsh reality of street life had claimed yet another soul.

Mikkelsen glanced over at them and winked as he paused in his questioning, until the shopkeeper had calmed down a bit.

Ten minutes later, they were back on the street. They hadn't learned anything new, and the sweet tea had left a cloying taste in their mouths.

"So he didn't know her name, but he saw her walk by a few times recently, although he couldn't say whether it was a week ago or a month ago."

They started walking back toward Halmtorvet. When

Louise looked across the street, she suddenly grabbed Lars's arm—she had seen the same drunk who had been sitting on the steps outside the Høker Café when the body was found.

"Isn't that the guy?" she asked, pointing at the opposite sidewalk.

"It sure is, and it looks like he's finally on his feet," her partner said. He told Mikkelsen that the man was one of the first witnesses he'd talked to. "But the guy was so far gone he hadn't even noticed anything was happening."

"Oh, that's Kaj," Mikkelsen said. "He lost his grip on reality years ago. He does better when he keeps to his own world. He puts away a liter or more a day, but he wouldn't hurt a fly. Sometimes he even makes his sofa available if someone needs a place to stay."

The man was walking in their direction on the sidewalk on the other side of the street and stopped to lean against the wall of a building as he rummaged through his pants pocket. He finally pulled out a pack of cigarettes, and with great difficulty removed one from the pack and then found his lighter.

Louise watched him as he started staggering forward again.

"He was sitting right across from the place where the body was lying. He must have seen her," she said. Then she asked Mikkelsen if he'd consider having a word with the man. "Maybe he'd be more willing to recall something if you were the one who asked."

Mikkelsen stopped abruptly and glanced over at Kaj, but then he started walking again. "OK, I'll do it, but not here. I'd rather catch him at home. Kaj would catch hell if people think he might have seen something. People consider a guy like him worthless, and the ones we're dealing with wouldn't blink at shutting him up for good."

Kaj was almost directly across from them now. He crossed the street, heading for the basement grocery store. When he got close, he recognized Mikkelsen and raised his hand in greeting.

"*Ça va, monsieur?*" Mikkelsen asked, going over to shake his hand.

"*Très bien, mon ami. Très bien,*" Kaj slurred, a smile passing over his ravaged face. He let go of the officer's hand, pointed down at the store, and then raised his hand to his mouth as if he were tipping a bottle to his lips.

Mikkelsen smiled and gave him a slap on the back before Kaj headed down the basement steps.

"He's OK. He was the chef at the Plaza Hotel until his wife dumped him, and then his son was killed in a car accident, or maybe it happened the other way around. In any case, his whole world fell apart, and he said good-bye to his old life," Mikkelsen explained. "Let's take a stroll over to Istedgade. I want to show the photo to the folks at Club Intim. If this woman worked here in the neighborhood, she probably used their booths. Although I doubt the guys over there will feel particularly motivated to share, either."

Rounding the corner onto Istedgade, Louise smelled the spicy aroma of grilling shawarma, and her stomach instantly contracted with hunger. She found a piece of chewing gum in her pocket and hoped that it would tide her over until she could get back to the office and the box of crackers waiting in her desk drawer.

A group of men was standing in front of the homeless shelter in the spring sunshine, clutching their beer bottles and chatting. A big dog had stretched out lazily in the middle of the sidewalk so that people had to walk in a big circle around him. The street scene was a motley mixture, with everyone from bums and schoolchildren to the parents of toddlers who didn't bat an eye at the sex shops, maneuvering their strollers home around the African prostitutes who were strolling in small groups.

* * *

Club Intim was three steps below street level. The three officers edged their way single file past racks of porn DVDs in the crammed shop.

Louise could tell that the guy behind the counter recognized Mikkelsen, and it took him only a quick glance at Lars and her to make clear he knew they weren't new customers. On the contrary, they were the sort of people he wanted out of the shop as fast as possible.

Club Intim promoted itself as Denmark's leading porn theater, with four separate screens and signs advertising topless service and draft beer for 30 kroner. But only a certain clientele knew about the business transacted in the numerous private booths where prostitutes serviced their customers. The prostitutes paid 90 kroner per visit to rent a booth, and according to Mikkelsen, they could turn over three or four customers an hour.

Louise and her partner hung back as Mikkelsen stepped over to the counter to show the guy the photo of the murdered woman found on Skelbækgade. Louise perused the DVD titles. Bare breasts and spread legs—the packaging was basically the same on all of them.

Two men in their early twenties came out of the back room, which Louise later learned was a bar. Topless and bottomless, as Mikkelsen described it. She stepped aside to let the men pass. They gave her a knowing smile, and she made sure she had a response ready if they tried to proposition her. But just then a middle-aged man in a work jacket and white mason's cap came barging out of the other corridor where the theaters and sex booths were. He was clearly in a hurry, and on his way to the door he happened to bump into one of the younger guys, pushing him into a rack. A couple of DVDs fell to the floor. Without even pausing, the man rushed up the three steps to the street, but before he got any farther, the young guys were on him. A punch slammed the middle-aged man into the shop's front window with a loud bang.

Louise was up the stairs by the time he had taken the second blow, and she grabbed hold of the assailant. With a quick twist, she had his arm pinned behind his back and her police badge out before Lars had even reached the entrance.

"All right, that's enough," she said, nodding at the older man to let him know he could go. She was just about to ask the young guys their names when a loud scream was heard through the open door. Lars quickly turned back, and Louise let go of the man's arm to follow Lars as he ran back into the shop and down the corridor with the booths, toward the direction of the screams. Mikkelsen had remained inside while his colleagues dealt with the young men, but now he followed them into the corridor.

Inside the hallway, Lars stopped abruptly. Louise ran into him with such force that he lost his balance and fell against the wall.

The African girl was naked. Small and slender, with her feet dangling thirty centimeters off the floor, she hung from a row of coat pegs on the wall with her arms stretched through the coat hangers like a female version of Jesus on the cross. Her head hung limply to one side, her eyes were closed, and a thin stream of blood trickled down her cheek from a cut over her left eyebrow.

The screams stopped, replaced by faint sobs coming from a blond girl standing in the doorway next to the coat pegs. She was wearing black lace underwear and she rocked from side to side as she wept.

Mikkelsen and Lars lifted the girl down from the coat pegs. Her legs trembled, but she was conscious. Louise took a blanket that someone handed her from a door that opened but then quickly closed again. Then she helped the girl sit down on the bed in a little booth that stank of sweat, semen, and poor ventilation.

"Do you speak Danish?" Louise asked, wrapping the blanket around the girl's shoulders.

The African girl shook her head listlessly as she reached for a paper towel that she tore off a roll on a small table. The cut over her eye was bleeding heavily now, and she dabbed at her cheek first, then pressed the paper towel to her eyebrow to stop the bleeding. She looked like she'd taken more blows than the one that had split open her brow, but she looked away every time Louise tried to talk. Finally, Louise got up and left the woman alone to collect herself.

Mikkelsen was with the blonde who had summoned them with her screams. He knew her. The girl's name was Anita, and the needle tracks on her arms were so visible that it was obvious she had been using for a long time. Her sobs subsided, and she blew her nose loudly on the tissue Mikkelsen handed to her.

"I heard him hitting her, but I had to finish with my customer before I could see if she was all right," Anita said with a hacking cough. "And there she was, hanging there. Not making a sound. I thought she was fucking dead."

"Did you see who did it?" asked Mikkelsen. Anita shook her head.

"Was he middle-aged and a bit heavyset, in a white mason's cap?" Louise asked, jumping into the conversation.

Anita looked at her and then shook her head again.

"No, that was the guy with me," she replied. "He took off when his wife sent him a text message reminding him to buy some milk on the way home."

She gave a hollow laugh as she turned around and started getting dressed with the door still open.

"He gave me an extra hundred," she said, pulling her blouse over her head. "I'm sure he heard the guy punching her too. He probably thought the big tip would get him out of any obligation to find out if she was all right."

* * *

"It happened before we got there," Mikkelsen said once they were again standing outside on Istedgade. "So it's impossible to know who did that to her."

Louise refrained from pointing out he hadn't asked the African girl to produce any ID. They had walked the woman over to the Nest—a shelter for prostitutes where they could rest, take a shower, and get a hot meal—so she could recover. The volunteers would also be able to find her a doctor if she needed to have the cut over her eyebrow stitched up. "Some johns think they can get away with damn near anything just because they shell out 300 kroner for a lay,"

Mikkelsen said after they dropped off the battered girl. "If the man can't get it up, then it's the girl's fault, and she has to be punished for failing to deliver."

He shook his head and they began walking back toward Halmtorvet, which was where they'd decided to start searching for witnesses who might have seen the murder victim in the area or noticed anything unusual around Skelbækgade the previous night.

5

On her way back to the *Morgenavisen* building, Camilla called her editor to expand on the brief text message she'd sent earlier. She promised there was enough material on the abandoned-baby story for it to carry the next day's front page, what with the pastor and the two boys' statements, and she told him she also wanted to go ahead with the story on the murdered prostitute in the Meatpacking District.

"I wonder why the baby was left in that church," Høyer said fifteen minutes later as he sat down on the extra chair in Camilla's office. "You would assume it was someone from the area, someone who was already familiar with the church, wouldn't you?"

Camilla shrugged and said the pastor hadn't been able to think of anyone who was pregnant and due around this time who was associated with the church in any way.

"The police are questioning people in the neighborhood, but neither Pastor Holm nor the boys saw anyone. I'm waiting to hear back from the hospital to find out what they have to say about the time of birth or any other details about the birth. Personally, I'm guessing the baby wasn't more than a few hours old. The techs are investigating whether the woman gave birth in the church or if she maybe just left the baby there."

"You should head out there and find out what people in the area have to say. I think there's a day care or a nursery school a little farther down the road. We should do the rounds. Also, talk to a couple of pregnant women who are due to give birth soon. See what they have to say about someone abandoning a baby right after birth."

Camilla could tell that he was looking for the right way to put it before he added that, of course, they should also take advantage of the fact that they had a sort of inside scoop.

"We ought to be way ahead of everyone else when we run the story tomorrow," he said, standing up.

Camilla nodded. Of course he would see it that way. For her part, she wasn't sure how she felt about having her own son suddenly in the public eye like this, but of course at the same time she could see that it would be hypocritical to insist that he be kept out of it since she spent most of her time trying to get eyewitnesses to talk.

"I'll start with writing about how they found her, and then we'll see what the police have to say about the towel she was wrapped in."

After Høyer left, Camilla took out her cell phone and looked at the pictures she'd managed to snap of the newborn. She hadn't told anyone she had them, nor was she planning to. She could still feel the baby's tiny body against her chest and was trying to remember what the mood in the pastor's kitchen had been like when she arrived. Markus described how the baby cried and cried, and Pastor Holm had said the cries went straight to his heart.

Well, she couldn't have been crying like that all night, Camilla thought as she browsed through the pictures she'd taken. Such a tiny baby wouldn't have the energy for that.

She hung up and then dialed Rasmus Hem at the Bellahøj precinct, whom she had met at the pastor's residence that morning.

"Have you determined the time of birth?" Camilla asked immediately after explaining that she was Markus's mother and they had met each other that morning.

"I don't recall your mentioning you were a reporter," he said frostily.

"Well, I really didn't think it was the right time to get into that. The only reason I was at the pastor's residence this morning was because my son was upset about what he had just seen. If I had been planning to exploit the situation, I would have been pressing you for details this morning. I held that little girl in my arms and I would really like to help reunite her with her mother."

The officer sighed and grumbled a little before finally continuing.

"As I believe I also told you this morning, I have no idea if being reunited with a mother who abandoned her would be the best thing for her. Perhaps it would be better for the baby to be adopted as soon as possible, so she can get a fresh start on life," he said. After a brief pause he added that that last part was off the record.

"Of course," Camilla said. For a second she agreed with

him, but then she admitted to herself that despite a rough start, she still thought it was best for a child to be with the woman who gave birth to her. After all, she thought, the child should have a sense of being rooted in her identity later in life.

Officer Hem hissed tersely. "Most women can give birth to a child, but that is absolutely not the same thing as knowing how to be a mother."

Camilla didn't touch that, but she did jot the expression down in her notebook.

Instead, she repeated her question about the time of birth, and she wasn't surprised when he said the doctors estimated late last night or early that same morning.

"Did it happen in the church?"

"Too soon to say."

"Do you have anything on the towel?" she continued.

"Afraid not. It's from one of the big national chain stores, Føtex, we think. They sell hundreds of them every year, so it'll be impossible to find the buyer."

"But you are going to have it analyzed to possibly ID the mother?"

"Of course, but obviously the technicians need a little time, and then they'll have to run whatever DNA they find on it. We won't get the results back until next week at the earliest."

"How is she doing?" Camilla finally asked.

The officer's voice perked up. "I just came from over there, and she's spending most of her time sleeping like most newborns, so I'm guessing she's doing quite well." He added that the little girl had gotten something to eat and been cleaned up.

Camilla thanked him and gave him her number, even

though she didn't expect he would call if anything new turned up on the case. She would follow up on it later, and in the meantime she would try to find out what they'd learned about the murder on Skelbækgade.

She called the chief of homicide at Police Headquarters, who impatiently referred her to Willumsen, but so far that was still a dead end. Willumsen and Camilla had butted heads on several occasions in the past. The first time was when a coworker of hers at the paper had been murdered because of a drug story the coworker was working on. It hadn't improved Camilla and Willumsen's relationship, either, when she quoted Willumsen in an article and made prominent mention that his title had recently changed from "detective superintendent" to the lesser-sounding "police superintendent" as a part of the police reorganization.

So now she sat here with her hand on the receiver, wondering whom she could call instead of Willumsen. She decided to start with Louise to find out who else had been assigned to the case.

Camilla and Louise had known each other since high school in Roskilde, and even though they were quite different in many ways, they had become best friends over the years. She dialed Louise's personal cell number.

"Actually, I'm on that case," Louise said.

Camilla could hear traffic noise in the background. "Am I bothering you? You sound like you're outside."

"It's fine. I'm on Sønder Boulevard. We're trying to find out who the girl was. I'll just step into a doorway so I can hear you better."

"Is there anything new? Have you found out where she was from?"

"No," Louise replied. "Apparently, no one saw anything."

"What happened out there in the Meatpacking District?"

Camilla realized Louise was stalling to avoid giving privileged information to the press, so she tried reassuring Louise that she was of course aware that the lead case investigator should actually be the source for all the information about the case, and it worked.

"Her throat was slit in the middle of the night," Louise continued, "but you won't get much further on the story right now. We're going to spend the rest of the day and evening canvassing for witnesses, and obviously, we're hoping that someone can help us ID her. I'm under the impression Willumsen is planning on releasing a picture of the victim sometime tomorrow, but you'll have to talk to him about that."

Camilla nodded at the phone, knowing she would have to accept going through official channels if she wanted more information, so she changed topics and told Louise about the abandoned baby that Markus and his friend had found.

"I think what shook Markus the most was that a mother just abandoned a newborn baby like that, leaving her lying there all alone. If they hadn't found her, she could have died."

"It must have been a terrible experience for him," Louise said, suddenly warm again, and concerned. She asked how Markus was doing now.

Although Louise didn't have any children of her own—and had maintained for years that one could easily have a happy and meaningful life without them—she was very close to Camilla's son. Sometimes Camilla even felt a little excluded when Markus and Louise were together.

"I think he's all right, but I suspect it'll stick with him for a while."

"Is there anything I can do?" Louise said, full of concern.

Camilla said he was still over at his friend's house.

"Then I'll call him tomorrow and tell him he's welcome to call me if there's anything I can do. Also, I'll try and see if I can find out how the baby girl is doing. Another division would be handling that case, so I haven't even heard about it—and clearly we have plenty of our own cases to keep us busy."

6

H omicide Division, Louise Rick speaking."
She stifled a yawn. She and Lars had been out until one the night before, working with Mikkelsen and a couple of his people. As darkness had slowly fallen over the city, they had made contact with every living thing in the vicinity of the murder that could crawl or walk.

"This is the duty desk. Are you working on that murder down in the Meatpacking District?"

"Yeah, me and several other detectives," Louise said, leaning back in her chair.

"There's a man down here who'd like to talk to you. He says he has information that might pertain to the murder."

Louise was on her feet before she'd hung up the phone. The new security procedures at Copenhagen Police Headquarters meant that no one was allowed to walk around freely in the building without identification. They were so strict about it that even the chief superintendent had been asked to show ID, because the desk clerk didn't recognize him—or maybe he did recognize him but didn't think he should be given any special treatment.

She took the stairs down and then a shortcut through the memorial garden for fallen officers before crossing the round courtyard in front of the building.

The man who was waiting for her had his hands in his pockets. She quickly estimated him to be somewhere in his midthirties. He was leaning against the wall, but when he saw her approaching, he started over to meet her. He had his red visitor's badge clipped to the pocket of his light blue, short-sleeved shirt under his leather jacket. His dark hair was neatly combed back.

Louise noted that his eyes wandered a bit as she approached. She introduced herself, and they walked back across the courtyard.

"You had something you wanted to tell me?" she prompted.

He nodded in silence. Only now did it occur to her that she wasn't sure he spoke Danish, but when she asked he smiled.

"Some," he said. He had a definite accent, but they wouldn't need an interpreter.

Lars had been out making a fresh pot of coffee when the front desk called, and so he cocked his head with a puzzled look when they came into the office and Louise asked the visitor to take a seat.

"Would you like a cup of coffee?" she offered, gesturing to the coffeepot. "Or some water?"

The man politely declined both.

Louise briefly explained to her partner that their visitor was here because he might have information about the woman in the Meatpacking District.

Lars eyed the man with curiosity. "Sounds good." He turned and looked back at Louise. "Would you like some privacy?"

She shook her head. It was fine if he stayed.

"Then I'll take notes," he offered and turned to his computer screen.

To put it mildly, Willumsen had not been particularly thrilled with the lack of progress in the case at the morning briefing. Louise had caught Lars's eyes during Willumsen's rant, and she could tell Lars agreed with her. Willumsen could shout and scream. They'd figured out a long time ago why his cases always got off to such a good start. It was quite simply because he selfishly dragged detectives in from the other groups without asking for permission, so his team had triple the usual manpower or more for the first few days. In this case, however, he had not commandeered people, which was obviously a sign that a prostitute's murder didn't rank very high on his priority list.

She put aside her thoughts of Willumsen and looked at her visitor, who was sitting with his hands folded in his lap.

"Let's start by getting your name and address," Louise said. She was eager to find out what had brought him in. You didn't get many freebies in cases like these, and so far, they hadn't had a single one.

"Miloš Vituk," he said and then helped Lars with the spelling. He said he was thirty-six and Serbian, but he'd been living in Denmark since 1995, when he had come to get away from the civil war.

Lars's coffee got cold while his fingers were busy pecking on his keyboard. Once the formalities were taken care of, he and Louise waited for the visitor to start, listening patiently as he cleared his throat a couple of times before he spoke.

"In the beginning of January, I was stopped on the street by a young woman when I came out of a shop down on Halmtorvet. She was very unhappy, crying, and said she was scared and needed help."

"Did you know her or had you ever seen her before?" Louise asked, raising an eyebrow.

After a moment's hesitation, he shrugged his shoulders. "I may have seen her a time or two, but I didn't know her name and I didn't know where she was from."

Louise nodded and asked him to continue.

"She seemed really shaken. She didn't speak any Danish, and I had a hard time understanding her English, but I said we could go get something warm to drink. She was shivering and definitely wasn't wearing enough clothing for how cold it was. But she didn't want to do that. She was very afraid. She kept looking around the whole time."

He spoke quickly, concentrating, clearly trying to remember all the details.

"She wanted me to drive her somewhere where they couldn't keep their eye on her." Louise refrained from interrupting, but jotted "who?" on her notepad.

"My car was parked on Valdemarsgade, so we drove out toward the Fishmarket, down that street that runs over the Sjælland Bridge and out to that big parking lot at Bella Center. The whole way there she just sat there crying."

"Did she tell you what she wanted?" Louise asked after the man stopped talking.

"Yes, she said she was being forced to work as a prostitute and was desperate to buy her way out so she could go home."

"What was her name?"

"Pavlína Branková. She was twenty-two and came from Ústí nad Labem in the Czech Republic. She said she was working as a prostitute against her will. They forced her with violence and threats, and she showed me some of the marks on her upper arms and the back of her neck from their beatings."

Louise wrote "they" this time.

"And now she's been murdered," Lars stated, pushing his cup of cold coffee away. Miloš Vituk quickly shook his head.

"No, God almighty!" he exclaimed and held up his hands as if to ward off bad news. So, Louise asked him to explain what the connection was between Pavlína and the crime on Skelbækgade. Instead of answering, he started explaining the rest of what she'd told him out in the Bella Center parking lot.

"Pavlína never knew her parents; she grew up in an orphanage with her sister who's two years younger. When she turned sixteen, she was too old to stay in the orphanage and she's been on the streets since then. Her sister followed her two years later, and they got by on their own until Pavlína was forced into the backseat of a car late one night and brought to Copenhagen."

"Who forced her?" Lars interrupted, trying to get a sense of whom Miloš was accusing of kidnapping the woman.

"Arian and Hamdi, both Albanians," Miloš Vituk said curtly. He explained that there had been two other girls from the Czech Republic in the car to Copenhagen, but Pavlína hadn't known either of them before.

"The man in the front seat didn't want them talking to each other. She doesn't remember much from the ride, but that's probably because they were drugged most of the way."

Now Louise was starting to wonder what Miloš's role in this story was, since he'd decided to go to the police. So she asked if he was still in touch with Pavlína.

He nodded and then stopped to think for a moment, as if considering how much he ought to tell her.

"I met her a few times," he said, and added that was only when she'd been able to slip away without being discovered. "She was under surveillance most of the time, at the hotel where they put her up with another girl and whenever the girls were sent out onto the street. I said I wanted to help her, but didn't know what I should do. She said that she was under a lot of pressure because she couldn't earn as much as they demanded. She was paying for her room and board and for permission to use the street. At that point, she was about to collapse under the pressure, and I got the sense that that was her handlers' intention, to push her to the limit, to a point where she no longer had the energy to put up any resistance. One night I met her in front of Café Yrsa. In tears, she begged me to help her find the money to pay her way free, and she promised to pay it all back."

There was a pause that made the mood in the office feel somber, and each of them sat quietly until Louise broke the silence.

"Do you have any sense of why she stopped you that first time on the street?"

Miloš Vituk shook his head slightly, as if that question had been bothering him for a while.

"Maybe there just wasn't anyone else around right then as she was reaching the breaking point," he finally said, clearing his throat so his voice sounded more solid. "I don't believe in coincidences. People usually meet each other for a reason. That's also why I wanted to help her."

Louise studied him for a moment. He seemed a little naïve, she thought, but at least he was being honest.

"I told her to find out how much they wanted to let her go, so we met again a few days later. They were demanding 50,000 kroner to release her. I didn't have that much, but I agreed to meet them at a bar on Victoriagade and we negotiated that I could have her for 15,000 kroner."

"That's a fair amount of money considering that you didn't know much about her and only had her word that she'd pay you back," Louise interjected.

At the same time, it was a shockingly small amount to pay for a woman, but Mikkelsen had told them the night before that you could buy a foreign woman for 1,000 euros.

That was less than Louise paid for her mortgage every month.

Miloš nodded and shrugged. "I was starting to grow fond of her," he admitted. "So I paid the money and she moved into my apartment with me."

"Is she still working as a prostitute?" Louise wanted to know.

He shook his head vehemently and said they were dating now. "She wanted to go back to the Czech Republic and find her little sister and tell her about me. Everything happened so quickly the night she was abducted. Her sister didn't even know where she was," he reminded them. He then explained that Pavlína had taken a bus to Prague on March 10, and from there she had continued by train to Ústí nad Labem.

"And?" Louise prompted, waiting for Miloš to continue. "Weren't you worried that you would never see her again? After you'd paid all that money?"

He smiled and shook his head. "We talked to each other every day. But two weeks ago, she called me one night crying and yelling that they'd found her. One of Arian's contacts was following her, and she didn't dare go outside. She was afraid that they might take her sister this time if they saw the two of them together. She wanted me to come and get her."

Miloš Vituk seemed to deflate a little, preoccupied by his own account, and then he was overcome with a rage that made his voice rise.

"Last week, she disappeared from my apartment. I'd been out the whole day," he said. His voice suddenly sounded tired, and he took a deep breath before continuing. "When I got home, she was gone. Then later that night I got a brief call from her. She was sobbing and asked me to pay 80,000 kroner. She said they were going to send her back out onto the streets again to earn the money if she couldn't come up with it and they threatened to cut her throat if she tried to run away."

Finally, Louise thought, an indication of how this related to the case, just as she had been starting to think they would never get there. But considering that they didn't have any other leads and still had nothing else to go on, she realized that Miloš Vituk was currently the best chance they had at solving the case.

Lars asked Miloš what had happened after he'd left

Pavlína in his apartment. Louise could picture the whole thing as Miloš explained how they'd tricked the young woman into opening the door and then forced her to go down to the Albanian club on Saxogade, where they locked her up in a little room in back after punching her several times.

"After I explained that I didn't have that much money, I spent the next few nights driving around looking for her. I thought that if I found her maybe we could talk our way out of the situation. The third night I spotted her down in front of the conference center, but at first, she refused to even talk to me. They'd told her that I refused to help her again and that I was responsible for her being sent back out onto the street."

"As far as I know, slavery was abolished two hundred years ago," Lars interjected drily into the conversation.

Miloš shrugged.

"Some people say there have never been as many slaves as there are today," Louise said. She then asked Miloš if he had heard from the two Albanians again.

"They ambushed me down on Istedgade later that same night. They knew I'd talked to her, and now they were demanding 100,000 kroner, but in return they promised that that would be their last demand for her. But they keep women like slaves, abuse them, and extort money from anyone who tries to help them, so I don't believe them," he concluded.

Well, you're certainly wise not to, Louise thought. She sat for a moment letting the story sink in. It wasn't news to her that women were being bought and sold in Copenhagen, but realistically speaking, you couldn't do as much about it as you might think because the few cases they'd seen had been hard to clear up. The women were typically in Denmark only for the three months they were legally allowed to stay without a residence permit, and then they were off again, usually shipped on to some other country. And Louise had no doubt that most of the girls had been coerced into saying they were doing it voluntarily.

"I had just been in touch with someone who was going to help me get the money, so I said I would pay, but then this morning they sent me a message that the price had gone up to 120,000 kroner because it had taken me so long to show any interest."

"Does this have anything to do with the woman we found on Skelbækgade?" Louise asked, eyeing him earnestly.

He hesitated a bit before responding that, of course, he couldn't say for sure, but the threats the Albanians had made regarding Pavlína sounded the same as what had happened to the victim.

"And now you're asking us to catch these two men, Arian and Hamdi?" Lars concluded.

Miloš nodded and looked uncertain for the first time, as if he'd just sicced some pit bulls on a couple of little boys.

"How do we find them?" Louise asked. "And what are you planning to do?"

"I'm not sure—you might be able to find them at the club on Saxogade. I guess for me, I've decided to trust that they'll let her go this time, so I'll pay what they're asking," he said. "But I've told them that she has to be there when I get there, otherwise I won't pay. And I have to get her before they can have the money."

"When?" Lars asked.

"Tonight at six p.m.," he replied.

"What do the two Albanians look like?" Louise asked.

"Arian has shoulder-length hair"—Miloš gestured with his hands—"and he wears glasses. Hamdi has short hair and is short and thin."

A slight smile crossed Lars's lips as he jotted down the descriptions. Half the people they encountered on Istedgade would match that description.

"We're going to have to talk to Pavlína as well and find out if she knows anything about the woman who was killed. We'll need her help if we're going to try to put a stop to those two and their trade in Czech women," Louise said.

"Of course," Miloš said, "but I think she'd prefer to be free to come in on her own."

"We could meet in the parking lot at Bella Center, where the two of you went that time, if that would make her feel safer," Lars suggested.

Miloš nodded and promised to get back to them once he'd paid the money and she was hopefully back home again.

He didn't say anything as Louise escorted him back downstairs, but when they parted he thanked her for taking on the case and helping him so the Albanians couldn't continue with their outrageous extortion.

* * *

Willumsen was standing in their office when she got back upstairs. Lars had filled him in about their visitor and was just explaining how the Albanians had kidnapped Pavlína and sent her back out onto the street after Miloš paid for her freedom.

"Shouldn't we move in as he hands over the money?" Louise asked, eyeing Willumsen.

Toft stopped on his way down the hall and leaned against the doorframe to listen in.

He had one of those plastic nicotine inhalers in his mouth that he always used, a sorry substitute for the cigarettes he used to smoke until the total ban on indoor smoking went into effect at Police HQ. In the beginning, Louise had thought they were to help him quit smoking, but as time went by she realized her colleague had simply replaced his cigarettes with the nicotine from the Nicorette product so he wouldn't have to keep running outside every time he wanted to smoke.

Willumsen stroked his chin, clearly lost in thought.

"So he thinks the two Albanians might have some connection to the woman we found? I don't think there's enough here for us to get involved yet," Willumsen opined. "Instead let's try to figure out what's going on and how big a network we're talking about. Try to get a sense for the organization the Albanians are part of so we're sure we wrap up the whole syndicate when we do strike."

"Where was the girl living until the Serb bought her and she moved in with him?" Toft asked, stuffing his hands into the angled front pockets of his corduroy pants and looking at Louise.

"At one of the cheap hotels on one of the side streets coming off Istedgade," she replied.

"Maybe we should do a round of the hotels in the area with a picture of our murdered woman and find out if anyone knew her," Toft suggested.

Willumsen nodded to him. "Do that. If that doesn't give us any leads, we'll go back again after Rick and Lars have talked to the Czech woman. Surely she can show us where she was staying," he added.

"If she can recognize it. You hear about how these women are kept on such a short leash they never see anything other than the inside of the room they're kept locked in and the stretch of street where they earn the money," Toft interjected.

"We could also take a little look at the Albanian club," Lars suggested, but Willumsen waved Lars off the idea.

"For now, let's focus our attention on the Skelbækgade woman," he decided. "Once we get through with that, you can look into this other situation."

He lowered his hand again.

"I'm not ruling out a possible connection between the two. But I want to know who the dead woman is first, and until we have a name we're not going to get very far."

Willumsen adjourned the meeting and quickly departed.

7

Camilla had spent most of the day following up on her story about the baby abandoned in the church, even though she didn't make it into her office until after eleven.

Markus had woken up several times with terrifying nightmares about her abandoning him and never coming back, and Camilla had no idea what time he had stumbled into her room with his blanket under his arm, sobbing. He lay down beside her, and she stroked his hair until he settled down again.

"If we'd left for school earlier, we might have seen the mother," Markus said while they were eating breakfast. "And then we could have stopped it from happening."

Camilla had tried to explain to him that there were many reasons why a mother might choose to leave her child.

"Maybe she did it for the sake of the child, because she knew she would never be able to give the little girl the life she thought the child ought to have. And that she would be better off if she were adopted by someone else."

Camilla could see from Markus's expression that he didn't understand how it could be better for the little girl to wind up with strangers instead of her actual mother.

"You do know that it's very hard for a grown-up to be accepted as a foster parent, let alone an adoptive parent, don't you?" Camilla asked him. "You have to be preapproved so everyone is sure that you're suited to taking care of a child. And that you'll make sure the child has a loving, secure place to grow up in. It's a big responsibility. Maybe this was the best thing that could happen to that little girl if her own mother couldn't handle that responsibility."

Camilla hoped she sounded convincing enough to put the worst of her son's fears to rest.

They sat at the breakfast table for a long time. Finally, she got up and cleared away the Nutella and cardamom rolls and put the butter back in the fridge. Then she called the pastor to ask if he and Jonas wanted to come over for dinner so the boys could talk a little more about what they'd been through. She explained that the previous day's experiences had made quite an impression on Markus, and it turned out that Pastor Holm had decided to keep Jonas home from school for the same reason. He invited Camilla and Markus to come over to his place for dinner. When he said that Markus was welcome to come over right away if he wanted, Camilla decided to let her son play hooky along with his buddy.

They biked over to the pastor's residence together. Camilla put Markus's laptop with *World of Warcraft* in the basket on the front of her bike and followed him on the bike path. When they reached the church, she walked out back to the attached pastor's residence with Markus and knocked twice with the heavy door knocker before kissing him on both cheeks and promising that she would try to finish work at a reasonable hour. She smiled at Markus's friend when he yanked open the door and dragged Markus inside so they could start playing. She could see the pastor sitting at his computer in the living room and waved to him before shutting the door again and pushing her bike back down the drive to head to *Morgenavisen*.

* * *

When she called Frederiksberg Hospital, Camilla learned that the baby girl was still in the hospital; the doctor thought the infant would be there for a week or two longer until she was sent on to Skodsborg Orphanage.

"Unless the mother turns up before then," he added.

Then she called the social services office and spoke to a woman who was also really hoping the mother would come forward. She made it clear that they would be lenient on a woman who had left her child that way. She didn't need to be afraid of prosecution, because what was important now was looking toward the future, and they would offer her whatever help she might need.

When she finally got hold of the right social worker who could tell her how the system worked, Camilla asked, "If the mother comes forward now, will she be allowed to take the child home with her?"

"No," Tanya Jensen replied without hesitation. "First there will be a period for the two of them to get to know each other, and the child will remain with the orphanage during that time. Obviously, we must be convinced the mother can take care of the little girl now."

"And what if she can't?"

"Well, then we absolutely couldn't allow her to take the child home," she replied after a moment's contemplation.

Camilla wondered how they evaluated that. The story of a mentally disabled woman who received assistance from the Danish government to be artificially inseminated only to have the same government authorities turn right around and take her child away the minute it was born was still fresh in her mind. Who decided who was suitable, and what was the decision based on?

Camilla took a deep breath and decided not to ask that question.

"Let's say the mother doesn't show up," she said instead. "Then the child will be put up for adoption. When will that happen?"

Camilla had the sense that Tanya Jensen suddenly became a little less forthcoming. "Hard to say. The biological mother should always have the chance to change her mind. She may be suffering from postpartum depression, and she may need a while to come out of that."

Camilla interrupted her. "Well, surely there must be a limit to how long the little girl has to wait in limbo to see if her mother is going to change her mind?"

"Of course. We're not talking about limbo, as you call it. There's always a waiting period for any adoption, even ones that have been planned for the whole pregnancy, and that's true in this case, too."

"How long is it?" Camilla wanted to know.

"We figure it will take a couple of months before the child can be placed into her new family," the social worker explained.

* * *

After that, Camilla talked to a psychologist who strongly rejected the notion that a child who had been abandoned by its mother would suffer any permanent sense of loss.

"Of course, a newborn is affected when something is missing—eye contact, for example," Camilla wrote and further quoted the psychologist: "This is why it is essential for other people to start caring for an abandoned child quickly. But the most important thing is for the child to establish fundamental, basic trust either in her biological parents or in other people. The vast majority of children, four-fifths, will do well so long as that trust is there early on. The last fifth will have some problems, and a very small number will suffer serious harm. In those cases, a good outcome will depend on finding a family that can create a secure enough environment for the child."

Camilla's own writing suddenly struck her as too impersonal. She pictured the little girl in her mind. What about that last fifth? Oh, she wished she knew if the baby would end up in that group; she thought she would end the article with the psychologist's statement that there was really only one researcher out there who claimed people could recall their own births—so this little girl's loss should by no means cause irreparable harm.

Earlier she had stopped by the church with the paper's photographer in tow and watched police using tracking dogs in the area. But when she called Rasmus Hem about the dogs, he said the police still didn't have anything to go on.

Once Camilla finished her article and submitted it to her editor, she packed up her bag. She checked with the police to see if there was any news in the search for the mother. She had also been trying to get in touch with the coroner who'd been out to the Meatpacking District Sunday night. In sheer irritation at the lack of interest her proposal had aroused at the editorial meeting, she was going to pick the case of the murdered woman back up and pursue it until she had enough material to run the story by her boss again. Kvist was staying in a hotel out in Silkeborg and had an interview lined up with one of the well-to-do married couples the art-theft ring had targeted.

"Detective Larsen still isn't in, and to be quite honest, I don't think he will be in today. He gave a lecture at National Hospital today and then went straight home from there, I believe," said the receptionist at the pathology lab, where Camilla had given one last try before she headed home. "He'll be off for the rest of the week."

"Could you give me his cell number so I can contact him?" Camilla asked.

"Unfortunately, I can't give that to you," the woman said.

Camilla tried again. "Well, could I have you call him and leave a message to contact me?"

Sometimes that worked. Other times it annoyed people that she was assuming they had time to waste helping her.

"I can't promise I can get hold of him, but I'd be happy to leave a message," the woman agreed, and Camilla thanked her profusely.

8

Camilla had offered to pick up some dinner and bring it over to the pastor's residence, but Henrik Holm wouldn't hear of it. Instead, she brought a few bottles of soda in her bike basket.

"The boys are up in Jonas's room. They have a visitor," Henrik told her with a grin as she walked in and set her basket on the kitchen table.

She looked at him in surprise. He was standing at the stove stirring a pot that smelled of chicken and spices. She asked who the guest was.

"A good friend of yours, I understood. Markus asked very politely if it would be OK if she came over to talk to Jonas and him."

The pastor smiled when he saw Camilla's face stiffen.

"It's not a journalist," he reassured her quickly. "And your son seemed very happy to see her."

She relaxed and went upstairs to see if it was who she suspected.

Louise was sitting on the thick cushions on the floor with one boy on either side, and when Camilla stuck her head in, Louise was explaining what the police usually did about abandoned babies.

Louise flashed a smile at Camilla and then continued explaining the procedure, how the police would search for the mother in hospitals.

"We go through lists of women who are due to give birth around that time. Using the lists, we contact those women. Some of them have already had their babies and are busy taking care of them, while others are still walking around with their big bellies, looking forward to the birth."

Markus was holding Louise's hand as she spoke, and Jonas's eyes didn't leave her face.

"And then once in a while we find a woman who no longer has a big belly and who isn't busy with a new baby—and those are the mothers we're interested in, of course," Louise said. "But there can be lots of reasons why they don't have the child. Usually it's because the baby died before the birth or maybe right afterward."

Both boys' eyes were wide and they seemed to be holding their breath.

Typical Louise, Camilla thought with a little smile. She was not dumbing it down for the kids. She was telling it like it is. And it usually turned out that was actually what they liked best, even though the reality sometimes shocked them.

She went back down to the kitchen to help with dinner, and before she quite realized it she was telling the pastor about the previous night.

"I wasn't prepared for the fact that it had made such a strong impression on Markus," she admitted, then offered to set the table.

"Jonas woke up, too, and came into my room. I suppose an experience like that will affect them for a while," he said, then added that Louise was welcome to stay for dinner if she wanted. "There's plenty of food."

Camilla smiled at him and explained that she and Louise had known each other since high school in Roskilde.

"She works in homicide with the Copenhagen PD, and she's also Markus's godmother. Maybe I should have thought of it myself, asking her to come over and have a chat with them. But it's good that they figure these things out on their own without my help."

As Camilla set out the plates, she admitted that the event had also affected her more than she would have thought. "I keep feeling that tiny little body against me."

The pastor poured wine and lit the candles. Then he gestured to the bench, and they sat across from each other and waited for the rice to finish cooking.

"Little kids who are suddenly left without parents always make a big impression," he said. "They're so tremendously vulnerable."

He explained that many years before he had worked in a refugee camp in Bosnia.

"I had just become a pastor and really wanted to make a difference somewhere before I found a permanent parish position. My wife and I went and worked at the camp for two years, and it's never quite left me. Especially the children who'd lost their families in the war."

Camilla didn't have any trouble picturing him in a place

like that, but this was the first time he'd mentioned his wife.

"My wife died when Jonas was four," Henrik continued, interrupting her train of thought. "She was born with a rare blood disease, which in the best-case scenario she might have lived her whole life with. But she wasn't that lucky."

The timer went off for the rice and Henrik got up.

Camilla watched him. He seemed as though he'd put the worst of it behind him. She felt safe in his company as she took the pot he passed across the table to her and he called the boys down.

Louise was in the lead when they came downstairs.

"We set a place for you," Henrik said, gesturing to the table. Louise smiled at Jonas when he invited her to sit next to him.

"That's so nice of you," she said, "but I have to get home. I haven't gotten much sleep the last couple of nights, so I'm planning to turn in early tonight."

Both boys stood in the kitchen doorway waving as she left.

"She's supercool," Jonas said, clearly filled with admiration as he moved over to the table. "She knew all about how the police work and what they do when they find a little baby that's been abandoned like that. Plus, she was really nice."

Camilla could tell how proud her son was that Louise had made such a good impression on his buddy.

"Maybe we should watch the news?" Jonas suggested, looking at his dad. "Maybe there's some news about the baby."

Camilla got the sense that Henrik was about to say no, but instead he shrugged his shoulders and then asked her if she minded.

Jonas took that as a yes and turned on the TV that was mounted on the wall. It showed commercials at first, but then the news came on, leading with the abandoned-baby story for the second day in a row. The first image shown was of the blue towel; the police deputy superintendent was holding it up as he explained that the baby had been wrapped in a towel just like it when she was found at Stenhøj Church.

The news crew had done their job well—they had taken plenty of footage of the pastor's residence and street while the CSI techs were working at the church the day before.

"As we indicated yesterday, the towel is sold at Føtex, so we have little expectation of identifying the mother that way," the superintendent said, answering the reporter's question with a discouraged smile, before he changed topics and turned serious again.

Camilla watched her son dish chicken and rice onto his plate, his eyes glued to the screen, hanging on every word as the deputy superintendent explained that they had been assuming the baby was born inside the church itself, because they believed it was a relatively short time between the birth and the baby's discovery. But without technical evidence to support this theory, they couldn't be sure, so the police were eager to hear from any witnesses who had seen or heard anything around Stenhøj Church in the early-morning hours that day.

"Well, they didn't say anything about that when I talked to them this afternoon!" Camilla exclaimed in irritation.

"Aren't they going to show a picture of the baby?" Jonas asked, looking at his dad. "So her parents can see how cute she is?"

A second later, a large picture filled the screen. Sound

asleep, she was lying on a white pillow with all her dark hair surrounding her tiny head like a wreath.

Camilla felt her eyes mist over and hurriedly looked away when the cameraman zoomed out a little so the viewers could see that the girl was lying in the arms of a nurse who was saying the abandoned baby was doing well but missed her mother.

Camilla was annoyed the police hadn't told her that they were going to run the baby's picture on the news. Now she was going to have to go back to the paper and make sure they had a picture from the hospital to print alongside her article in the next day's paper. And she was also going to have to rework the article to mention the police now thought the baby might not have been born in the church where she was found. If Camilla didn't get these latest developments in, she would be way behind the other press coverage when the paper hit the streets.

Just then, the doorbell rang.

"Oh yeah," Henrik said, standing up. "I should have anticipated visitors what with the church on the news and all."

He went to answer the door, and a second later he came back with a tall young woman who wore her dark hair in a pageboy cut and a lot of mascara around her eyes. She was pale and she seemed a little nervous.

She was in her late twenties, Camilla guessed. She started to clear the table while the boys got up, thanked the pastor for the meal, put their plates in the sink, and disappeared back upstairs to their computer game.

She heard Henrik invite the woman inside and then ask what he could do for her. Camilla was assuming the visit had to do with Baby Girl, as the press had started calling the abandoned newborn, but the woman had come looking for work, obviously under the impression the pastor was looking for a housekeeper.

"No," Henrik said in English, "there must be a misunderstanding." He held out his hands apologetically. "I don't know who gave you that impression. But I will be happy to let you know if I hear of someone looking for one," he offered.

The woman quickly shook her head and explained she had been referred to him by a friend of her family.

She pulled out a slip of paper that, sure enough, had Henrik Holm's name and address printed neatly on it.

The pastor sat down with the slip of paper in his hand. It didn't say anything else, and the woman didn't have the name of the friend who had sent her to him.

"I don't know who gave you my name, and I'm very sorry not to be able to help. It's just my son and me living here, and I can manage the housekeeping on my own. But please give me your phone number. If you stop by again next week, I'll ask around to see if I know anyone who's looking for help with their housework."

She shook her head again and looked disappointed as he stood up to show her out. Meanwhile, Camilla called Markus to say she had to go back to the office.

"He's welcome to spend the night," Henrik offered when he returned from the door. "You can just swing by and drop off his backpack before school tomorrow."

He thanked her for loading and starting the dishwasher and apologized for leaving the cleanup to her.

"Do people often stop by the way that woman did?" Camilla asked, nodding at the front door.

"No, not often," Henrik said, explaining that the people who did stop by usually needed to talk and didn't have anyone else to talk to. Sometimes someone would spend a night or two if they didn't have anywhere else to go, such as a husband or wife going through a divorce, or people who were grieving.

Camilla looked at him and felt a flicker of admiration. She had a hard time finding the energy for that sort of thing herself.

"But this is the first time since I've been here that someone has come thinking I needed a housekeeper," he said with a smile.

Markus kissed his mother good-bye, and Jonas hollered a hoarse "Bye" down the stairs.

"The hoarseness is chronic," Henrik explained with a smile. "In the beginning, we thought he would just get over it and then when it didn't go away, we assumed it was asthma, but he doesn't have any trouble breathing. It turned out to be a condition called multiple laryngeal papillomas, which are little bumps on his vocal cords." He added that you could have them removed with a laser if you didn't want to wait until puberty, when they would probably disappear on their own.

"No, well, then I don't suppose there's any reason to do it if they're not bothering him," Camilla protested.

Once Markus had planted yet another kiss on her cheek and she was in the kitchen doorway with her jacket on, she thanked Henrik for letting Markus spend the night.

"If anything at all comes up, just call," she told Henrik. Her son had assured her that he was totally cool with spending the night, even though he'd had a rough time the night before. "Markus says he's put the whole thing behind him."

"I'll keep an eye on him," the pastor promised. He pointed out that his bedroom was right next to Jonas's. Then Henrik held the door for her and waved as she left.

9

M iloš just got Pavlína released," Lars said, as Louise stepped into their office on Wednesday morning, carrying the basket from the front of her bike.

She stopped abruptly in the doorway. Her thoughts had been somewhere else entirely. She had just managed to catch Markus on his cell phone while he and Jonas were on their way to school. She asked if they'd slept well, and both boys had assured her they were doing fine and that they had put their fears behind them. That had made her smile, but now she stared at her partner in surprise.

"Did you talk to him?" she asked.

Lars shook his head and explained that he'd just been out to the witness's address and found Miloš had been about to leave.

"He went into Spunk, a bar down on Istedgade, and it didn't take long before he came out again with a girl on his arm. Then they went back to his apartment."

Louise watched him for a second from her desk chair before she said anything. "Why didn't you say you were going to drive over there? I would've come with you."

"Yeah, well, I wasn't planning on it. It just hit me as I was sitting in the car about to head home," Lars said in his own defense. "If I'd planned on going, of course I would have told you."

"And then what?" Louise asked.

"Then? Then nothing. I drove home once they'd gone in the front door. But it is totally repugnant that you can just go out and buy a woman like that."

Louise agreed with him wholeheartedly and looked up at the clock. They had an office lunch every Wednesday, and it was their team's turn to provide the food this week, so she'd stopped by Hauen Bakery on her way in and filled her bike basket with Danish bread and rolls.

"We'd better go put some coffee on," she said, getting up.

"Done," Lars said. "I also tidied up the kitchen and emptied the dishwasher."

Louise sat down again. "What the hell's up with you? Is something wrong at home?" she asked. Not that Lars usually shirked his share of kitchen duty, but they usually did the less than appealing cleanup together. Each team was responsible for making sure the lunchroom was clean and for running the dishwasher during their assigned week.

"It's nothing serious," Lars said. "I just needed a little space from home." He got up and retrieved the bread from her bike basket.

"Let's go in and hear what they have to say."

Louise got up and followed him, deciding not to pry any further into his home life for now. She was all too familiar with that feeling, and she respected him for taking the space he needed for himself.

* * *

"I understand there's news in the Skelbækgade case," Suhr began once everyone had helped themselves to bread and their coffee cups were full.

He looked at Louise and Lars, who both nodded and explained that they had received a visit from Miloš Vituk. Lars added that afterward he had driven by the witness's address and followed him and seen that he had a girl with him.

Louise saw Willumsen furrow his brow, and it looked like he was going to say something, but Suhr beat him to it.

"Interesting," Suhr said. "We'll have to run a check on the two Albanians. But maybe that's already been initiated?"

Willumsen shook his head and confessed that he had decided they should observe for a little longer before they put anything bigger in motion, but in light of what Lars had seen, there was probable cause to believe there was something to the Serb's story.

"Let's identify the two people we're talking about—Arian and Hamdi—with their full names so we can get a court order and set up a wiretap," Willumsen said. He asked Toft and Michael Stig to take care of that.

Suhr nodded and pulled a hand through his short gray hair. He turned to Louise and Lars and asked if they thought they needed a court order for Miloš Vituk also, or if they believed his story.

"We probably ought to, since he intentionally caused trouble for the two Albanians by putting them in our crosshairs," Louise admitted with a nod. "But it seemed more like he came in because he was starting to fear that they were just going to keep raising their extortion price."

"First of all, we have to determine if any laws have actually been broken," Willumsen said. "We all know how hard it can be to figure out if something is common procuring or if it is in fact a case of trafficking in women. Meanwhile, if the two Albanians might be connected to the murder in some way, then we're interested in them."

His eyes wandered around the table and stopped on Stig, who signaled that he wanted to say something.

"Then we have to keep the pressure on that whole scene and try to get someone to start to move," Stig suggested.

Louise followed him with her eyes as he tipped forward in his chair and started rapidly tapping his pen against the table, filling the room with loud clicking sounds. It was a bad habit he had that had bugged Louise for years. Now she looked away, forcing herself to ignore the pen.

"And they say," Stig continued, pausing for dramatic effect, "that the girls, the Eastern European ones, have to pay about 400 kroner a day. Someone cons them into thinking they own the street and the girls have to pay to work there."

He leaned back and tossed his pen onto the table.

Louise sighed, glad that Mikkelsen wasn't here to hear him. That would have sent his blood pressure through the roof.

"We should keep that in the backs of our minds," Stig added, looking from Willumsen to Suhr. "Because if the same men are working with the trafficked girls, we ought to be able to spot them by keeping an eye on the money when it's handed over. There must be a discernable pattern."

Louise couldn't hold her tongue any longer. "It is absolutely true that someone has made a sham business of extorting money from the people on the bottom of the food chain on the street, but there are also quite a few Danish prostitutes who've figured out that there's money to be earned that way, so they are also demanding money from some of their fellow prostitutes. It's turned into a regular business practice. Everyone's cashing in on it in their struggles to make money," she said, her eye trained on Stig's pen, which was about to roll off the edge of the table.

Stig flashed her an irritated look. He squinted his eyes a little and was about to respond, but Willumsen beat him to it and assigned the next task to Stig with a subtle gesture of his index finger.

"That is exactly what I want you to check out. Set up surveillance on the area and keep an eye on the girls. Don't do anything. Just find out if there's a pattern."

Louise glanced away to avoid the look she was sure Stig was giving her. What Willumsen was asking of him was going to require some real legwork, but she didn't feel sorry for him. He'd brought it on himself.

* * *

After the meeting, they milled about in the hallway for a bit outside Louise and Lars's office. "Do we know anything about the two Albanian men yet?" Toft asked, looking at Louise and her partner. They both shook their heads.

"I'd be surprised if Mikkelsen couldn't tell us who they

are," Toft said, offering to call his old friend. He and Mikkelsen had been partners for the brief period Mikkelsen worked as a plainclothes officer keeping an eye out for disorderly conduct.

"I'd really like to have a chat with Pavlína," Louise said, looking at Lars, who concurred.

Willumsen nodded and said, "Do that as quickly as possible. It'll be interesting to hear her version."

"I'll contact Miloš Vituk and set up a meeting." Louise nodded. "And then I was thinking that we ought to do a round of all the brothels and massage parlors in the neighborhood and see if the woman might have worked in any of them."

Willumsen nodded at the latter suggestion before turning back to Stig.

"We can certainly start putting pressure on the street scene, as you suggested," Willumsen said, "but make sure it's not too obvious, because then our folks will be way too easy to spot later if we seriously need to keep an eye on them."

He looked around at everyone again to make sure they understood he was serious. The bottom line, really, was that they wouldn't have an unlimited amount of manpower to call on if there happened to be a major break in the case.

10

Camilla felt sad and empty inside as she set her bag of beer bottles on the counter. She pulled one leg up under her, removed the first lid, and took a swig out of the bottle. Markus had gone to his dad's house after school and was going to be with him for the weekend; it was his grandmother's birthday, and the whole family was staying at an inn. Camilla was planning to spend the rest of the day and evening enjoying all the beer she could drink while she sniffed around Skelbækgade and Halmtorvet, and took a stroll up Istedgade. She changed from her skirt and high heels into jeans and rain boots. She wasn't planning for this to be an investigative reporting trip. She was just curious to see what Copenhagen's prostitution scene looked like at the street level.

She had had yet another run-in with her editor. It had all started when Terkel Høyer arrived that morning and slammed his office door behind him. A minute later the phone on Camilla's desk rang.

He was yelling when he told her that the free alternative paper had run a big interview with a woman—featuring her name and picture—who had come forward to say she had seen a young mother outside the church with a bundle in her arms. The woman also claimed she saw her open the door to the church and after a moment come back out empty-handed, then disappear down Stenhøj Allé.

Høyer lowered his voice a little and asked her to come to his office.

It turned out the article, which continued inside the paper, described what the mother looked like in detail, with long blond hair pulled back into a ponytail. Not very old, maybe just a teenager. No, she hadn't been with anyone, and she had gone quickly into the church and quickly come back out. And no, the woman didn't think she'd seen her before. So it couldn't be someone who lived on the street, because she thought she'd recognize most of the women who lived along this section of the wide suburban avenue in Frederiksberg, actually a separate city surrounded by Copenhagen on all sides. The witness stated that she even knew "the ones in the large mansion on the corner at the end of the street. Well, don't know them socially, that is," she was quoted as saying, "just what they looked like."

Camilla threw the newspaper onto Høyer's desk after skimming the story and beat him to it by asking why they hadn't scooped the story.

"Don't you wonder why she chose to take such an important witness statement to a free paper instead of telling the police what she saw?"

Høyer twitched in his chair and spluttered angrily into

her face that he couldn't be bothered to wonder about things like that, because that wasn't what sold real newspapers like theirs. She turned her back to him and returned to her office.

First, she called the Bellahøj precinct to find out if they knew about this witness and ask why they hadn't mentioned it to her the day before when she last spoke to them. The officer on duty claimed he hadn't heard about any new witnesses. Then she called her own source, Rasmus Hem, whom she'd met at the pastor's residence when the baby was found. The officer sounded sincere when he vehemently insisted he had never heard of the woman who'd given her statement in the free paper. He flatly denied it was because they hadn't been persistent enough looking for witnesses.

"But we did bring her in for questioning this morning," he added begrudgingly.

Camilla decided to head over to the precinct to hear the woman's explanation firsthand and—as she had to admit— to steer clear of Høyer, who was still pissed off. Before she could leave the building, however, Camilla's morning got even worse when the paper's longtime photo editor suddenly appeared in her office doorway. He asked her how the hell a journalism student from one of the smallest papers in the country had scooped them on this angle while Camilla kept claiming there was no new information to run about the case.

Holck, as he was called, said she should know this was exactly the type of case that appealed to their readers: Children and dogs! That's what sells papers! And then he took a few steps into her office, glaring at her the whole time, saying he was starting to doubt she could handle the story professionally since her own son was involved.

* * *

What a day it had been. Camilla drank half of her beer in one gulp. It had been a long time since she'd sat on a bench drinking beer out of a bottle—and maybe it was a mistake, she thought as she emptied it. But there was something that felt liberating and reckless about sitting out here alone without having to be accountable to anyone.

She had lost it with Holck, yelling at him that first of all, it most certainly was not a journalism student but an extremely well-paid, established journalist that the free paper had hired from Denmark's premier newspaper, *Berlingske*; and second of all, she was way fucking closer to the story than any of these other reporters, because she had held that little baby in her arms. She was not done making her point when Holck walked right over to her, leaned in over her desk, picked up her cell phone, and pointed to its camera lens.

"Well, if you think you're such a great damn journalist, then why didn't you so much as snap one single measly picture of Baby Girl with your handy-dandy little phone?"

She hadn't been able to stop herself before she snatched the phone out of his hand and showed him the picture. He accused her of being disloyal to the paper, possessing poor judgment, and being incompetent—which was when she stormed out.

But before she made it out of the building, she called Høyer and told him it was true. Then she recused herself and said she couldn't cover the story since Markus was one of the witnesses. She said good-bye before he could respond, but could just hear Holck starting to rant in the background as she hung up.

* * *

Camilla jumped slightly as a man sat down on the other side of the bench.

After she had stormed out, she ended up heading out to the Bellahøj precinct anyway and had waited for three hours until she learned that there wasn't anything to the woman's statement. Then Officer Hem invited her to coffee. He seemed tired as he explained that a reporter had rung the witness's doorbell right after the nine o'clock news on TV. The witness had let the reporter in, a charming, attractive man who seemed polite and interested. And without really knowing what had happened, the witness told him she'd seen a young woman with the bundle in her arms. The reporter had seemed so disappointed the first time when she said she hadn't seen anything. And then he took her out for a stroll past the church and then one word had just sort of followed another.

"Are you sure she's telling the truth now?" Camilla asked Hem.

Hem nodded, adding they knew the mother had not opened the church door as the witness claimed, because the CSI techs had dusted the handle thoroughly for prints, and there were no fingerprints or even smudged prints from someone wearing gloves—which meant someone had gone out of their way to remove them.

* * *

Camilla had the feeling that the man sitting at the other end of her bench was watching her, and for a second she felt the unease of trespassing into a world where she didn't belong. But what the fuck. She had as much right as anyone to sit here on a public bench drinking a beer, even if this wasn't her neighborhood.

When she turned to look at him, she realized he wasn't looking at her but at her bag of beer bottles. She smiled and offered him one.

"Thanks," he said, taking it. They sat together in silence watching the traffic and passersby.

"That guy there is the Meat Meister," the man said, raising his beer in the air in salute as a large Jaguar drove past them out of the Meatpacking District. The car returned his salute with a quick honk.

The Jaguar was certainly opulent compared to the man beside her in his gabardine pants, which must have been fashionable at some point in the distant past, but now they were threadbare. His shirt collar curled up through his worn blue sweater, and he seemed generally old-fashioned and unkempt.

Camilla turned toward him in curiosity. "How do you know the guy in the Jag?" she asked, pulling two more beers out of the bag.

He gallantly offered to open them and stuck the lids in his pocket instead of tossing them on the ground as so many before them had obviously done.

"I used to be one of his biggest customers. He was new back then and a little too expensive, but his product was better than anything else that was out there. So, I had faith in him, and that laid the foundation for the business that has made him rich."

Suddenly, Camilla thought back to the drug kingpin with whom she herself had crossed paths—Klaus West trafficked a drug known on the streets as "green dust."

He might also have been driving around in a Jaguar if he hadn't wound up behind bars.

"Nice car," Camilla said, watching it as it disappeared.

The man was lost in thought for a bit, but then he finished his beer and mumbled, "That was some fucking good meat that one time. We drove a van with forty servings of tournedos Rossini with foie gras, truffles, and everything else down to the French Riviera for a big fête for Roger Vergé himself. Oh, the Moulin de Mougins!"

Suddenly the man turned to look at Camilla and his eyes seemed present again. "What a chef," he said, waiting to see if she had any idea who he was talking about.

"I'm talking about Paul Bocuse, the Troigros brothers, they were all there. But that night the Danish Gastronomic Academy was honoring Roger Vergé because his new cookbook had just been released in Danish translation. They even awarded him some sort of honorary degree."

The man reached over and pulled another beer out of Camilla's bag. Again, she could see that his mind was lost in the past.

"Monsieur Vergé came down to the kitchen afterward and admitted that he'd never had such good meat before."

He drank a practiced swig of his beer.

"There's a picture of the two of us together," he remembered, smiling.

Out of the corner of her eye, Camilla spotted two men talking to a young woman. She was fairly sure one of the men was Detective Michael Stig from Louise's division, and she recognized two more police officers standing a little farther over toward Halmtorvet.

The man next to her kept talking and drank more of her beer while she kept her eyes trained on the street. She could see a fair number of people from her vantage point on Sønder Boulevard, with practically the whole Meatpacking District in front of her, and she had a good view up Skelbækgade. Istedgade ran parallel behind her and Halmtorvet was to her left.

A car stopped and quickly picked up a girl before disappearing again. Camilla didn't stop watching until she noticed that the man next to her was holding out his hand.

"I'm Kaj," he said, introducing himself, his hand wrapping around hers in a firm handshake.

"Camilla," she said with a sigh. When he asked what she did, she replied, "I'm a reporter, and right now I'm so sick of it that I just might start making food or selling meat and getting rich myself."

Kaj pulled out another beer. This time he passed it over to Camilla without taking one for himself.

"That's not something you just do," he said with a sudden seriousness, turning toward her. "That's something you need a knack for. Like anything else you want to be good at. You need a knack for it, and skill. And then you need to put your heart into it. There are far too many young chefs who think it's just a matter of getting your name out there."

He made a face and Camilla couldn't help but smile.

"They make a little bit of food and then they do all they can to become famous and then they make a little more food while they wallow in their fame. I mean, look at someone like Erwin Lauterbach—that's a totally different story. He made a hell of a lot of good food and became known for that and then he continued to make a lot of fucking good food and now he is respected for that. That's how it should be. And just because those young chefs talk up a storm and attract a bunch of attention, they'll never be the next Søren Gericke. There's only one of him. And you should have seen him back in his glory days," Kaj said, his thoughts slipping back in time. "They'll never even measure up to his sock suspenders. Not even if they're on the morning talk shows every other day."

Camilla grinned and gave in. Here she'd been thinking the rest of the day would be full of prostitutes and pickpockets, but instead she'd gotten a regular rundown on major contemporary French and Danish chefs.

The bag had run out of beer, and Camilla asked if Kaj would stick around if she went and bought them another round.

"With the greatest of pleasure," he called to her as she got up and walked over to a basement grocery store.

She noticed a Citroën C3 stopped and was waiting to turn off Absalonsgade onto Skelbækgade. She recognized the prostitute in the passenger's seat from before, and when the driver turned his head, she made brief eye contact with Holck, the photo editor at the paper who had laid into her at work earlier. He quickly glanced away and zipped across Sønder Boulevard between a truck and a bus.

It took Camilla a moment to process what she'd just seen.

* * *

"You'll never guess," she said when she returned to the bench with a full bag and reported what and whom she'd just seen.

"Yes, well, everyone comes here. You're a reporter—it shouldn't surprise you. We regularly have the pleasure of high-level media people and then there are the politicians. Everyone needs to let off some steam," Kaj pointed out.

Now Holck was not exactly all that high-level, but given

the situation she was way too distracted to ask Kaj who else he'd seen.

"What the hell?" she snapped. "He has a wife, children, grandchildren, and I don't even know what all else!"

Kaj grinned, revealing his darkened teeth.

Day had faded into evening, but Stig was still on the street talking to the girls as they showed up for work one by one. Camilla didn't see the other pair of officers who had been there before, but as she scanned the area for them, her eyes settled on a head of long, curly dark hair that was pulled into a loose ponytail. The person was standing farther up toward Halmtorvet with her back to Camilla.

Camilla had consumed too many beers to want Louise to run into her here, sitting on a park bench next to an aging alcoholic, who she otherwise had to admit was remarkably good company. As a couple of large clouds slid in front of the low evening sun and she felt the first drops start to fall heavily, she got up.

"Come on," Camilla said. "Let's go to the pub instead of sitting here and getting cold."

At first, Kaj tried to get her to sit back down, pointing to the bag, which wasn't empty yet, but Camilla remained standing.

"You can take those home," she suggested. When he still seemed reluctant, she added that it'd be her treat, of course.

Stig had vanished by the time they started walking up Skelbækgade. When Kaj pointed at Høker Café, she followed him.

Camilla went up to the bar to order. Kaj changed to a double whisky, but remained in the background until she passed the glass to him. They looked around for an empty table and found a spot by the window. They were right across from the gate at the entrance into the Meatpacking District and the Hotel and Restaurant Management School.

11

Louise stopped. She spotted Kaj standing up from a bench farther down the street and walking away, followed by a blond woman in loose jeans, who was carrying a plastic grocery bag. Louise watched them stagger through the Meatpacking District.

"Hey, do you know if Mikkelsen ever talked to Kaj?" Louise asked, walking over to Lars, who shrugged and said he hadn't spoken with Mikkelsen since they'd seen him last. "Toft might have talked to Kaj, instead. Otherwise we'll have to remind Mikkelsen to make sure he follows through on that," Louise said, as they walked back toward their unmarked car parked around the corner.

They had fifteen minutes until their meeting with Miloš Vituk and Pavlína at Bella Center. They'd just finished a lengthy tour of the neighborhood's brothels, with some of their colleagues from downtown, following Mikkelsen's meticulous notes. Some of the brothels were not that easy to find, and the police were not particularly welcome at many of them, either, but the brothel operators eased up when they realized the police wanted only to see if anyone recognized the still-unidentified dead woman.

Their Czech interpreter was waiting for them on the corner of Sommerstedgade. She apologized for not having been able to meet them sooner.

"I was in court all day," she explained. "Then I had to make dinner for my kids at home before I could come back out again."

"No problem," Lars said, unlocking the car.

Once again, Louise sensed that Lars didn't mind in the least spending his evening at work. Not that she had anyone sitting at home waiting impatiently for her, either. She hadn't since Peter left her three years ago, precisely because he had gotten tired of sitting around waiting. And to tell the truth, Louise thought it had been very much for the best.

* * *

The rain hammered on the roof and windshield of the car as they drove toward Bella Center. Earlier in the month they had had a long spell of sunshine and warm weather, lulling Copenhageners into feeling summer had come to stay, but now the weather was constantly changing. As they drove over the Sjælland Bridge, a flash of lightning tore across the night sky, and the subsequent clap of thunder was so powerful that it shook the car for a moment.

The rain picked up, battering them. Lars slowed down and turned the windshield wipers up as fast as they would go.

"They're not going to come in this weather," Louise said, as they crawled along through the dense blanket of rain.

"It'll stop. It's just a front coming through," her partner replied calmly, sounding just like her father had whenever she didn't want to go outside as a kid because it was raining. "Of course they'll come. After all, they're the ones who want to be able to move around on the street without having people extort huge sums of money from them."

And Lars was right. When they turned off Center Boulevard, the rain stopped as suddenly as it had started. Lars turned off the windshield wipers, and Louise spotted a lone red car in parking lot P7.

"Where did you tell them we'd meet?" Lars asked.

"I think that's them," Louise replied, and he drove over and parked.

* * *

Pavlína Branková was short and slender. From a distance, she looked more like a high school student than an adult, but as Louise got closer she could tell that the woman must be in her early twenties. Her thick bangs ended in a sharp edge just above her dark eyebrows. Her hair was black and smooth and hung down just past her shoulders.

Her handshake was limp and her eyes hesitant, but she nodded when she was asked to follow them over to the benches along the side of the parking lot.

"Let's just begin with your name and date of birth," Louise told the female interpreter. She opened the trunk of the car to see if there was anything in there she could spread out on the bench so they wouldn't get wet when they sat down. Luckily there were a few wadded-up plastic bags.

Louise sat down across from Pavlína; the interpreter sat down next to the Czech woman and started talking. At first Pavlína's answers were very curt, but gradually the conversation began to flow more smoothly.

Miloš Vituk jumped in several times, and Louise sensed Pavlína was keeping her eye on him whenever she said anything, so she suggested that Lars take Miloš back to the car. Maybe the witness would speak more freely if there were only women involved. Miloš's presence was obviously making Pavlína clam up.

Once they were alone, at Louise's instruction, the interpreter began to probe in greater depth, asking Pavlína to talk about what she had been through since she had been stopped on the street back home in the Czech Republic, stuffed into a car, and brought to Denmark.

"Had you seen the driver before?" the interpreter asked.

Pavlína shook her head and said that she had been with a guy she knew from the street scene back home. She didn't know him well, but they'd been out a few times even though he wasn't part of the clique she normally hung out with. He turned up every now and then, and that last time he invited her to a party in an abandoned train station building.

"He brought drinks and cigarettes," Pavlína said as if to explain herself. Then she added that it had been so cold outside and her sister was with friends, so she'd gone with him.

On the way there, he had grabbed her shoulders as a dark car pulled over to the curb, and before she knew how it happened, she was suddenly sitting next to a foreign girl in the back seat of a car speeding away through the evening rush hour.

It took some doing for the interpreter to get the rest of the story out of her.

Pavlína didn't remember crossing into Germany or Denmark and said she must have slept a lot of the way. She sounded upset and watched the interpreter intently with each sentence that was said.

"At one point, another girl joined them in the car," the interpreter said, turning to Louise. "She says she's sure they drugged them with the drink they offered because she only has a foggy memory of the whole trip and had no idea where she was when they arrived—not even what country she was in. They put the girls up in a hotel where they were greeted by two men, who later turned out to be Arian and Hamdi."

"The rooms were small and dark, and the bathroom was down the hall," Pavlína said through the interpreter, explaining she had shared a room with one of the girls from the car.

She started crying as she recounted how Arian had raped her after Hamdi took the other girl out of the room. Afterward, the men switched places, and they sat her on a chair outside the door while Arian kept an eye on her.

The next morning the two men came back and took the women out on the town to buy new clothes and makeup. They were very generous. But then that same night, they sent the girls out onto the street, ordering them to earn back all the money the trip, the clothes, and the hotel had cost.

Pavlína stared urgently at the interpreter while she spoke, and then the interpreter told Louise that Pavlína had never worked as a prostitute before and had asked the two men several times that first week for permission to return home to her sister, who didn't know where she was and was all by herself now.

"First, they threatened to cut her face if she refused," the interpreter translated, "and when she persisted, they threatened to cut her sister. After that, she didn't dare disobey.

"They demanded she pay 3,000 kroner a day. Some days she wasn't able to earn that much and then she would have to pay extra the next day and even more the day after if she were still behind. There were days when she did up to twenty tricks or more in a day to pay off her debt."

Pavlína had stopped crying, but there was an absent look in her eyes as she mentioned eight girls who gave money to the Albanians.

Louise quickly began calculating how much money the girls had been bringing in each week. Pavlína answered the interpreter's question by saying that they were forced to work six days a week. Louise closed her eyes and did the math. With eight girls that must have been about 144,000 kroner a week.

"There's a lot of turnover among the girls. Most of them only stay for the three months they're legally allowed to remain in Denmark as tourists. If they want to be here longer than that, they have to apply for a residence permit, which they won't get," the interpreter said, as Pavlína confirmed what Miloš Vituk had already explained.

"Several of the girls have been here multiple times," she added through the interpreter. "Some are sent home for a while, but then are brought back the following year. Some of the girls are also sent on to Norway or Sweden. If they move around from country to country, it's hard to keep track of them."

"That's what the Roma are known for doing," Louise

said. She asked if Pavlína was sure the men were Albanian and not Roma, because the Roma were well known in Denmark for their brutal human trafficking and successful methods at evading detection: They were called "shepherds" for a reason. They moved their girls around Europe as if they were livestock, cleverly directing them from meadow to meadow to avoid attention from the various governments or police.

"What if the girls earned more than 3,000 kroner in one day? What would happen to the extra money?" Louise asked and watched the interpreter while she waited for the question to be translated.

"They got to keep that. That was the carrot," the interpreter reported after having passed the question on. "But that very rarely happened."

"Ask her if she could have gone home if she had enough money for the ticket," Louise asked, but the girl shook her head once she understood the question. "No, once you're with them you can say farewell to freedom. There's no way out again."

Louise nodded sympathetically and pondered it all for a moment before changing the topic. "I understand from Miloš that at one point you were forced out of his apartment and taken to a club on Saxogade."

Pavlína listened carefully to the interpreter, who then let her talk for a long time before she started translating. Louise couldn't tell from Pavlína's voice whether she was angry or afraid.

"She was raped again while she was locked in a small room in the back of the club. Someone hit her because she said they couldn't force her back out onto the street now that they had their money."

Pavlína's voice had become high-pitched and frenzied.

"They taunted Miloš, saying he couldn't look after me properly. Just look how easy it was for them to come and take me. They thought it would be better for me to stay and work for them because then I would have security."

That last part made Louise shake her head.

"Ask her if she knows the girl we found on Skelbæk-gade," Louise said, looking at the interpreter.

There was a longer pause during which a string of reactions flickered like a slide show over the woman's face in rapid succession. Finally, Pavlína nodded and looked down at her hands.

"She was one of the girls who was in the car," she said quietly, but quickly added that it wasn't the girl she'd shared a room with.

Louise tried to catch the young woman's eye. She could have chosen to ask this right off the bat, but she'd thought it better to wait until they were done so it didn't get in the way of the woman's own story.

"Do you know what her name was, or where in the Czech Republic she was picked up?"

Pavlína said she didn't know anything other than that her name was Iveta—or at least, that was what she'd said her name was. Pavlína estimated they were the same age, but she didn't know where Iveta was from.

"Ask if she knows who murdered her, if she knows why Iveta was killed."

Louise followed along intently as her questions were translated and tried to discern some of the answers.

"She thinks Iveta fell victim to the threats the men were always making if the girls didn't obey," the interpreter said. "Once they arrived at the hotel, Iveta had begged incessantly to go home again because her mother was seriously ill and needed her. She wanted to go home and earn money so she could help her mother."

The interpreter added that unlike Pavlína, the murdered girl had worked as a prostitute back home, as well.

"But she found out that either she had to raise the money to buy her way out of the debt she was already in or she would have to find someone else to pay for her. A few days before she died, she received a message that her mother was in the hospital and in a final attempt to get permission to go home, she went to see Arian and told him that she was pregnant and couldn't work anymore because it hurt."

Pavlína started crying again. This time it took a long time before she was ready to continue.

"That was just something she said," the interpreter continued once Pavlína started talking again, "because she hoped that they would take pity on her. The next day she disappeared and Pavlína didn't see her again until Miloš showed her Iveta's picture in the paper, where it said she was dead. He had also asked if it were someone Pavlína knew. But she was afraid, so she just shook her head."

A heavy silence lay over them until Louise got up and thanked Pavlína for telling her story.

* * *

They walked back over to Lars and Miloš, who were sitting in the police car waiting. As soon as he saw them, the Serb leaped out of the car's front seat and rushed over to meet Pavlína with his arms outstretched. He put them around her shoulders and pulled her into an embrace.

"The girls have to show up at the main train station every morning and pay the two Albanians. They do that at the entrance onto Istedgade," Louise said when she reached her partner.

Lars walked the couple steps over to Miloš and thanked him for arranging the meeting with Pavlína.

"We promise we'll keep an eye on those two," Lars said. He explained that the police needed evidence to support Pavlína's story before they could do any more.

Before they parted, Louise requested that the interpreter ask if Pavlína would stop by the pathology lab and identify the dead woman, because no one had confirmed her identity yet.

"We'll also make sure to issue the Czech police a request to locate her ailing mother so she can be notified of her daughter's death," Louise said, shaking the hand Pavlína held out to her.

12

The waitress had just come and set another double in front of Kaj when Camilla's cell phone rang. It was almost ten p.m. and she didn't recognize the number on the display.

"Yes?" she said, holding a hand over her other ear to help her hear better. She pulled her chair back a little and sank further into the corner, trying to shield herself from the jukebox music.

Flemming Larsen, the pathologist, began by apologizing for calling so late.

"But to be honest, I forgot I had the message in my pocket and didn't happen to think of it until now," he admitted.

"That's perfectly OK," Camilla said. "I'm in a pub in Vesterbro and may have had a little too much to drink...so maybe we'd better talk tomorrow. But there's still one thing I want to ask."

Flemming laughed and apologized again for interrupting her evening.

"I was trying to get hold of you because I wanted to do a piece on the murder that happened just across from where I'm sitting. But I'm having a hard time getting my boss to bite. He doesn't think we have enough to go on. All we have is that the victim is presumed to be a foreign prostitute. Do you have any more information on what happened to her?"

Camilla nodded across the table in response to the waitress's question of whether she wanted another round. Meanwhile the pathologist hesitated a little on the other end of the line.

"It was a straightforward, execution-style killing," Flemming finally said, then made it clear that this information was off the record. "It was on the quite-brutal end of the scale—she never had a chance to defend herself," he went on. "During the autopsy, I identified a number of lesions on her body from blows, which she appears to have sustained before death. So this wasn't the first time someone had been after her."

"That sounds atrocious," Camilla said, her adrenaline surging through all the alcohol.

"I think there's every reason for you to follow up on this story," Flemming said.

Camilla totally agreed; she was determined to tackle the story whether Høyer wanted to run it or not. But it wasn't that easy, of course, she thought. Especially not since Holck was obviously more intimately acquainted with Copenhagen's prostitution scene than she had previously realized.

"There are so many prostitutes who are abused and

raped. No group of people is more vulnerable to violent assaults than they are. We treat them when they take refuge at the Nest, where they are routinely sent to the Center for Victims of Sexual Assault at the hospital."

Camilla had the sense that Flemming had more to say on this topic, but she was starting to zone out, so she suggested that she call him back so they could have this conversation when she had her notepad and was somewhere quieter.

"Sure, just give me a call," Flemming said and gave her his cell number, which she quickly wrote down on the back of a receipt.

* * *

Camilla pulled her chair back over to the table and took a sip of her beer while Kaj started telling her a story about another great French chef from the past, Auguste Escoffier, who had once been a visiting chef at Copenhagen's luxury Hôtel d'Angleterre.

"When he wanted to finish his menu off with poires belle Hélène, he got so angry he almost left the country," Kaj said, and a merry glint entered his bleary eyes.

"Why?" Camilla asked. She was eager to move on from thinking about the girl who'd had her throat slit across the street.

"Because they wanted to top it with whipped cream!"

Camilla had no idea what Kaj was talking about, so he had to explain that it was a deadly sin to put whipped cream on top of a dessert that consisted of vanilla ice cream, poached pears, and high-quality melted chocolate.

"Whipped cream!" Kaj scoffed indignantly. "That's

something cooks do when they don't know any better and can't be bothered to listen. But this was his dessert. He created it, and they wanted to pull it down to a more plebeian level, which is how so many people have served it since."

His words dripped with derision.

Camilla smiled at him, thinking she would have loved to eat in this man's restaurant.

Sadly, she had met him twenty years too late.

They sat in silence for a bit while an old Johnny Cash number played from the jukebox in the background:

"Because you're mine, I walk the line," Kaj sang along in a deep voice when they got to the chorus. His tired eyes had come to rest on the window and the doorway across the street.

Camilla realized that she wasn't angry at her boss anymore, and that she'd had her fill of beer.

"I saw her," Kaj said suddenly, turning his head to Camilla as the song finished.

"The murdered woman?" Camilla asked after a pause and then followed his gaze out the window to the doorway across the street.

Kaj nodded.

"Did you tell the police?"

He shook his head and said he didn't have any plans to, either.

"Yes, but it's important," Camilla began, and he interrupted her by reaching a hand across the table and taking hers so she stopped talking.

"That's not always how it works in the real world," he said, pulling his hand back again. "I really want to be able to come and go here in my own neighborhood without being afraid. Even though our local beat cop, Mikkelsen, is nice enough, eventually they'll ask me to testify in court, and that's not going to end well for me."

"No, now listen here," Camilla blurted out, suddenly ordering another round. "You can't just not go to the cops. That woman was executed. Her throat was slashed."

Kaj sat there eyeing her. His face was lined with deep wrinkles, his hair gray, but she guessed he couldn't be older than his midfifties. His eyes were dark and held the experiences of a long, hard life, which made her feel like a naïve schoolgirl.

"All right," she said. "I don't know shit about that. I only know that no one is willing to talk in this case. All I know is that she was really young and now she's dead. It's just completely...unbearable!"

Camilla knew she sounded ridiculous, but she'd meant it. In her beer-induced stupor, she really wished she could have saved the girl, but it was too late. She also wanted to save Kaj, and the killers shouldn't get away with what they'd done, either.

Kaj didn't say anything, so Camilla spoke again. "What did you see?"

He studied her for a minute, and she sensed the alcohol hadn't had anywhere near the effect on him as it had on her. But, of course, he was also probably more used to these quantities.

"I really want to tell you what I saw, and you should also feel free to write about it if you want. But you have to guarantee me that you won't reveal me as your source."

"Goes without saying," Camilla exclaimed. Then she went over to the bar for a mineral water and some paper from the waitress's notepad.

* * *

"I knew her personally—the girl who was murdered. Her name was Iveta, and she has a little daughter who lives with the grandmother back in the Czech Republic. Sometimes I helped Iveta send money home to them. I could tell she was having some problems, but she wouldn't tell me what was going on because she didn't want me to get messed up in something. She had gotten word her mother was sick, and the last time I talked to her she was quite worried about her daughter and really wanted to go home."

Camilla took her notes in tiny letters so she'd have room for the whole story on the small pieces of paper.

"Sunday night, I saw her turning onto Skelbækgade off Dybbøls Bridge. She was walking down the opposite side of the street from me. She spotted me and started waving when she answered her cell—I was close enough to hear the ringtone. I was sitting outside drinking a beer and relaxing right over there on the steps." He nodded toward the front door of the bar that opened onto the street. "At first I thought she was going to come over to me. Instead, she stepped into that gate over there." He pointed toward the entry into the Meatpacking District. "So I assumed the phone call was from a john who was en route. It took only about five minutes before a car stopped and a man got out of the backseat and followed her inside. But a few minutes later he came back out and jumped into the car, which sped away."

Camilla flipped the paper over and started writing on the back.

"I realized something was wrong, and I went over there as soon as they were gone. But when I saw her I knew there was nothing I could do. I called the police from that pay phone in back." He tilted his head toward the back of the bar, where there was a phone mounted on the wall.

"Did you see what make or model the car was?"

He nodded and said it was a dark Audi A4, and he was also sure that the driver was the Albanian Iveta worked for.

"You have to talk to the police," Camilla said. "They'll put you into witness protection and take good care of you."

"Yeah, yeah. They promise so much." He shook his head. "I've done what I need to do for Iveta and her little girl. It's up to you now whether this information makes it any further," he said and emptied his glass.

Camilla nodded.

"But I have no idea where you heard all that from. If anyone should happen to ask," he emphasized again.

"No, of course not," Camilla said and got up to go pay the tab. It was time for her to go home. Even though she'd already decided her boss could go fuck himself, Kaj's account had pushed her spat with her boss aside. Considering the eyewitness report she was going to write up for the next day's edition, she would serve the story to her editor on a silver platter first thing when he showed up for work.

"Are you going to stay for a bit?" she asked when she returned to the table.

"*Oui, encore une minute, madame*," Kaj replied in his Danish-accented French and nodded.

Camilla added 200 kroner to the tab and told the wait-staff it was for Kaj, in case he wanted another round.

13

It took Louise a long time to return his call, but when she found another message on her answering machine after returning from Bella Center, she finally sat down on the sofa and dialed Mik Rasmussen's home number.

"A foreign prostitute was murdered," she said apologetically, then felt guilty for making an excuse for not calling sooner. "We've been looking for witnesses the last several nights and are still hoping to find someone who saw something."

They had been dating since the fall. The relationship had started when Louise was on a case in Holbæk while assigned to the Danish National Police Mobile Task Force.

She and Mik were partners on that case, and Louise had fallen in love and let herself be whisked off her feet and into Mik's world—with his idyllic farmhouse and his passion for sea kayaking. They'd also taken a dreamy vacation to Växjö in Sweden, where they kayaked on lakes and rivers, gathered mushrooms, cooked over a campfire, and had sex under the open sky. And for a while she thought a long-distance relationship was the ideal answer for her, with Mik in Holbæk and her in Copenhagen. Things had been wonderful at Christmas when they went shopping together along Strøget, Copenhagen's downtown pedestrian shopping street. Hand in hand, they sipped warm mulled wine. But with the distance, they hadn't ended up seeing each other quite as often since then.

"Do you want to come up for the weekend?" Mik asked without commenting on her case. "A few of us from the club are going to take the kayaks out along Cape Tuse on Saturday. We're going to bring food and set up camp when we feel like it."

"I'm going to be working. Unfortunately," Louise added as she suddenly realized just how much she wanted to see him, with his gangly limbs and crooked front teeth. "But maybe we could take a trip when this case is over?"

He laughed into the phone. "Don't you think there'll be a new case then?"

"Oh, stop," she cried, hoping he could hear that she was smiling. "If you start driving now you could actually be here in Frederiksberg within the hour."

"Deal," he quickly replied, snatching the invitation. "You put the coffee on and I'll bring the rest. I just have to take the dogs for a quick walk before I leave."

He hung up. Irish coffee had been a staple of theirs ever since their night together sitting on a bench enjoying the view from his farm. He had just happened to offer her one after they'd finished their beer. Now it was "their" drink, and they had since explored the difference between whiskey with an *e*—which is Irish and not quite as smoky—and whisky with no *e*—also known as Scotch and totally out of place in an Irish coffee.

She smiled and pulled her legs up onto the sofa. She was far too tired to skip a night's sleep. On the other hand, a good, thorough roll in the hay would surely reinvigorate her and give her more energy than eight hours of deep sleep.

14

Camilla was sitting at her computer when her boss walked into the office at nine thirty. His blond hair was still wet from his shower, and she guessed he'd run his standard fifteen kilometers before coming in. Her own head felt heavy, and the light from her screen glared in her eyes. She would have just stayed home if she hadn't stormed out of the office so dramatically the day before and if she hadn't been so eager to serve up Kaj's eyewitness statement for her boss along with his morning coffee.

He stopped in her doorway and watched her collect the pages of her article. "What's going on with you?" His tone was caring, and he sounded concerned. "You look sick."

She nodded and was surprised that he didn't start by commenting on their argument.

Maybe they were starting to butt heads often enough that he no longer noticed.

"Yeah, I'm going to go home in a bit," Camilla said with a nod before holding out the printed pages to him. "I've been looking into that murdered Czech girl on Skelbæk-gade. She was evidently snuffed by her own pimp, and I have something here you should read."

Høyer stepped into her office and walked over to her desk to take the papers from her.

"The police don't have any witnesses or leads yet," Camilla continued. "But this is a person who knew the woman. He saw her go through the gate into the Meatpacking District off Skelbækgade, and he also saw the guy who followed her in shortly after."

Høyer stood there for a second just looking at her before reaching for the article. He was about to say something, but she cut him off.

"You should consider me out sick today. Which in practical terms means I'm not here and I'm not turning anything in for the paper. But if you want to print this article—and will respect the fact that I want to keep my source 100 percent confidential—then you can blow this story wide open, because this witness hasn't talked to any other members of the press besides me. And you can also be sure that this isn't just something he made up," she said, knowing that Kaj hadn't told anyone else.

Høyer sat across from her and skimmed over the two pages she'd handed him.

"But you also need to understand that I'm going to contact the police and pass on the information contained in this article," Camilla said.

Her editor set the pages down and leaned back resting

on the arms of the chair. "Well, I should say so. How sure are you that this witness is telling the truth?"

"As sure as I am that it's a travesty to put whipped cream on top of authentic poires belle Hélène," she replied, enjoying the confusion in Høyer's eyes.

"Well, all right. I'll look at it. Kvist's report from Silkeborg won't be ready to run until tomorrow, anyway."

Fatigue suddenly washed over Camilla.

"Let me tell you one more thing," she said, mustering her courage. "Human trafficking is one of the most lucrative crimes out there. And here you are with a hard-on over some rich people's paintings worth a lousy couple million."

She stood up.

"I'm going to go home and nurse my cold," she said. "Call me if you decide to run it."

Camilla's voice was calm and she managed to keep her irritation under wraps. "But first I'm going to go hand over the witness statement to the police. I'll get them to sit on the new information and keep it from the rest of the press until tomorrow, then you can have the scoop if you decide to run it. But I can't ask them to withhold it any longer than that."

She ran into Holck in the hallway. She was wearing her sunglasses, but pushed them up onto her head as he approached her. He averted his gaze and before he had quite reached her and would be forced to look her in the eye, he turned and vanished into an empty office. But even that was enough for Camilla. She now knew that seeing him with a prostitute the day before would add a whole new dimension to their already tense relationship—meaning he wouldn't be able to walk all over her the way he wanted to anymore.

* * *

Camilla biked a printout of her article over to Copenhagen Police Headquarters. She parked outside the building, called Louise, and asked for five minutes. She had to wait for a bit at access control before the guard had time for her, and when she said that she was there to see Assistant Detective Louise Rick, he gave her a blank look.

"Where does this person work?" the guard asked.

Camilla explained that Louise had worked in Unit A before the re-org, and the guard flipped in confusion through a binder and asked Camilla for an office number, which of course Camilla couldn't remember. Finally, Camilla gave up on waiting and called Louise herself and asked her to come down and escort her up.

Her hangover was becoming more and more obtrusive, and Camilla guessed that the only reason she had been able to get up that morning and write her article was that, in all probability, she hadn't actually been sober yet. She had filled herself with black coffee before sitting down at her keyboard to write, and once done, she'd read her piece through several times to be sure it didn't ramble too much. But with the article written and her mission almost complete, she realized she was about to lose all her steam as her head started to throb.

15

Louise gave Camilla a quick hug, and when they got up to Louise's office, she grabbed the thermos on the desk and went off to the kitchen to fill it up.

"You look a little ragged around the edges," Louise commented when she returned.

Camilla nodded and smiled. "Not that you look all that chipper yourself," she retorted. "But you're right. I had a couple of beers last night. Mmm, or maybe seven...which is actually why I'm here."

Louise sat down, full of curiosity, and watched as Camilla pulled a few sheets of paper out of her purse.

"I ran into a man who was practically a witness to the murder in the Meatpacking District. He knew the murdered woman a little and saw her walk onto Skelbækgade right before she received a call on her cell phone. When she was done with the conversation, she went through the gate in front of the Hotel and Restaurant Management School, and immediately after that a dark Audi A4 pulled up, then a man got out and followed her in.

Lars Jørgensen had been sitting at his desk talking on his phone when they entered the office. Now he hung up and listened. He knew Camilla well and had worked with her several times on cases she had covered.

"A moment later the man came back out again and jumped into the car, which sped off."

Camilla took off her jacket.

"Is this a witness we can talk to?" Lars asked from his desk, which faced Louise's.

Camilla shook her head. "No. You have to use me for this witness statement."

Louise had suspected as much when Camilla had started telling the story.

"Before you continue, I just want to see if we can't get the rest of the group in here. I know that Mikkelsen is here today talking with Toft and Stig. We ID'd the woman yesterday, and they're informing the Czech police so they can locate her family and make sure they're notified," Louise said. Then she turned to Lars and asked, "Will you find Willumsen and the rest and ask them to come in here?"

Camilla stood up when everyone else walked in a few moments later. Louise introduced her to Mikkelsen. Camilla already knew everyone else.

"What's so important?" Willumsen asked brusquely as he entered the doorway and looked around at his investigative team. His eyes came to rest on Camilla and he took another step forward.

"God, are we here because of some reporter?"

Camilla stood up again and only then did Louise notice

that the hair in her friend's ponytail seemed unwashed. And, she was barely wearing any makeup, which was quite unusual for Camilla. She must have hurried out the door faster than she usually did. Not that Louise was one to talk, because she looked the same way after a night with only a couple hours of sleep and countless cups of coffee with whiskey and whipped cream. But it was sort of more normal for her; she didn't always manage to do that thorough of a job with her makeup or tame her wild, dark hair. It just wasn't a burning issue for her.

"No, it's only a humble journalist here to provide law enforcement with some important information," Camilla responded, flashing Willumsen her sweetest smile.

Louise leaned back a little with her coffee mug in her hands, ceding control to the others.

Willumsen nodded a couple of times, looking around for a place to sit down. Stig was standing in the doorway with his pen in his hand, and only grudgingly did he give his place to Suhr when his superior asked him to make a little room.

Camilla repeated what she had already told Louise and Lars.

"That sounds like the two Albanians," said Mikkelsen, who had his leather jacket over his shoulder and his glasses up on top of his head. "And Arian drives a new Audi A4."

"Arian is also the name Pavlína knows him by," Louise added, saying that before Pavlína had ID'd Iveta in the morgue, she told them Iveta had a mother back home she was sending money to. "But she didn't say anything about a child."

Camilla shrugged and could only pass on what Kaj had told her.

"We must be able to trace the call she received," Lars suggested and was countered by Suhr, who shook his head.

"She didn't have a cell phone on her when CSI went over the body."

"Then it must have been removed," Lars concluded, and no one objected.

"Can we use this for anything?" Willumsen wanted to know.

"Of course, damn it," Mikkelsen exclaimed. "You can't expect to get much more than this." He turned to Camilla. "But are you sure your source isn't someone we could talk to? He can remain anonymous and we can do the questioning off the books so he won't risk being called in later as a witness."

Willumsen was about to protest but was interrupted by Toft, who reminded them that the source's statements meshed well with Pavlína's.

"So now there's an extra reason for us to keep a sharp eye on those two Albanians."

Superintendent Willumsen stood there for a moment with his arms crossed, nodding thoughtfully, but as he was about to leave the office Camilla stopped him with her hand.

"In exchange for this, you must promise me you'll hold off until tomorrow telling any other reporters about what my source said, unless I call and tell you otherwise this afternoon," she asked, giving Willumsen a pleading look. His skepticism softened more when Suhr sent him a just-say-yes look.

"All right, we'll leave it at that. We really appreciate your going to the trouble to come to us with your information so we don't have to read it in the paper tomorrow," he said, sounding satisfied, before turning his attention to the others.

"Locate that Audi and then we can put a tail on it," he ordered to no one in particular. "And install a tracker once it's found." That was for Toft. "Spend today and tomorrow tracking down any witness statements to support Ms. Lind's anonymous source, and find out who those Albanians are and what they do. Once we have an idea about that, you can go to the main railway station and see whether girls really do meet there daily to settle their accounts with their pimps."

Then he gave Camilla a nod and left the office, while Homicide Chief Suhr took the time to thank her properly.

Stig lingered after the others left.

"Funny, I thought for a second I had seen you down on Sønder Boulevard last night," he said, his eyes running down Camilla's Malene Birger designer dress and high-heeled shoes. "But it must've just been someone who looked like you, because this lady was sitting on a bench drinking beer with an old alcoholic."

Camilla smiled at him, saying that sounded pleasant enough, but she'd taken her son to his break-dancing class.

Louise knew that was a lie. Markus had had break dancing on Monday—and that had been his last class. And then Louise recalled the same woman Lars was talking about. She wouldn't be surprised if Stig had seen correctly. Louise walked her friend back to the main entrance, and when Camilla said she was going home to bed, Louise gave her a hug.

"I'm going to do the same just as soon as I can," Louise said, waving after her.

16

On Saturday morning, Camilla was in her jogging clothes and on the way out the door when her phone rang. For a second, she considered ignoring it. She and Louise had a brunch date, and she was determined to get her run in beforehand.

Her story had filled the entire front page and two pages inside the paper the day before. The intern's last assignment before he went back to school was to put together a fact box on prostitutes murdered in the last few years in Vesterbro and also in the rest of the country. There were several brutal killings in Ringsted and Ålborg. Not that they seemed connected; it was mostly just evidence of the brutal violence that these marginalized women were subjected to, an angle Camilla was perfectly satisfied with.

"I'm going to have to cancel," Louise said after Camilla

walked back into the living room and picked up after all. "There's been another murder."

Camilla could hear people talking in the background and a car driving by. "Where are you?" she asked.

"I'm standing down on Sønder Boulevard. The victim is in the courtyard in one of the buildings off the street."

"Is it a prostitute?" Camilla asked, already fearing a recurrence.

"No." The answer seemed calming in a way. "It's one of the drunks," Louise continued. "Mikkelsen ID'd him before I got on scene. It was pretty brutal, not something you want the families who have a view into the courtyard seeing."

Camilla sank down on her sofa's armrest. "Is it Kaj?" she asked softly, feeling an iron fist clench in her stomach.

"How the hell do you know him?" Louise asked, surprised.

"I just know him," Camilla responded tersely. "I'm coming down there."

"I don't think that's wise. They won't let you see him."

"God damn it! I don't want to see him, either. But don't you get it? He was the one who told me about Iveta and the Audi. How the hell did they find out it was him?"

Camilla's voice broke as the iron fist grew bigger and was now so large that she had a hard time getting up off the sofa arm. Suddenly she started shivering as the room seemed to contract around the sofa.

"Ah," Louise said. "Well then, you'd better come. We've cordoned off the courtyard and our cars are parked out front, so it ought to be easy for you to find us."

* * *

Camilla saw the investigators from far away, as well as the ring of curious bystanders gathered on the sidewalk outside. As she moved closer, she could hear people discussing and speculating about what had happened. She recognized a couple from the pub and the guy from the grocery shop on the corner.

Louise was standing by one of the blue vans talking to Niels Frandsen, the head of the Forensics Department. The barrier tape was strung across the entrance to the courtyard.

"He's still in there," Louise said, after Camilla parked her bicycle and greeted Frandsen, "so we'll stay out here."

An ambulance with tinted windows came around the corner. Louise took Camilla by the elbow and pulled her to the side a bit.

"Flemming just finished examining the site and doing the preliminary postmortem exam," she said. "They're getting ready to move the body."

"It's been a long time since we've seen anything this bad," Frandsen admitted when he heard that Camilla knew the deceased. "We speculate he was knocked down here in the archway before being pulled into the courtyard."

The ambulance stopped and Frandsen walked over and undid the police tape on one side so it could drive in.

He followed it over to talk to a couple of his people. Their faces were strained, and they were talking together quietly as they passed by. Behind them came the homicide chief followed by Willumsen.

Camilla confirmed that Kaj had been the source for her story and vigorously shook her head when asked who could have known that.

"What happened to him?" she whispered to Louise once

they were alone. She noticed her heart racing while the rest of her body felt completely stiff.

She could tell that Louise didn't know how to respond.

Just then the pathologist ducked under the police tape and Camilla took her eyes off the gurney, which had just been pulled out of the ambulance.

"It's nasty," Flemming confirmed with a grim look. "Not something I've seen before."

"What happened to him?" Camilla repeated, now with a shrill desperation in her voice that she couldn't suppress.

Flemming and Louise exchanged a quick glance.

"The killers stretched out his four limbs and tied each between four benches. Then, they gave him a variation on the 'Colombian necktie,'" Flemming said, watching her.

"And what's that?" Camilla asked, uncomprehending and not sure she really wanted to understand.

* * *

"The Colombian necktie is something the Mafia does to people who rat to the police," Louise explained, taking hold of Camilla as she began to sway.

"Normally what you see is the throat slit ear to ear and the tongue pulled through the gash. But in this case, his throat was cut vertically and his tongue stuck to the roof of his mouth with a knife inserted through the incision."

"So, this variant could be called a Balkan necktie," Camilla said, thinking about the two Albanians and leaning against the wall for support.

Louise had just suggested Camilla go back home when Suhr emerged from the courtyard, putting his arm around Camilla's shoulder when he reached her.

"I would really like to have you take a look at his face before the ambulance takes him away," the homicide chief requested. "We need to know for sure that we're talking about the same man who was your source."

Camilla nodded mutely and followed him under the police tape.

"Everything here will make sense if it is him," Willumsen said once they were in the courtyard.

Make sense, Camilla thought, spotting the body of the former chef ahead of her. Now the iron fist was so enormous it pushed its way up into her throat and obstructed her breathing. She could inhale only in brief gasps.

"We'll show you only the top of his face," Suhr said reassuringly when Camilla's footsteps started to stiffen in reluctance.

There were a fair number of people in the courtyard. The first person Camilla recognized was Mikkelsen, who was sitting slumped over on a bench, his face ashen, his eyes staring vacantly at the asphalt. Above him, a green tarp had been stretched out as a shelter to keep people in the building above from seeing the body. The CSI techs had made a white outline on the ground underneath the tarp to show where the body was found. Kaj was on a gurney now, the ropes with which he had been bound to the benches still dangling off the sides. The four benches had been pulled together from the courtyard's two seating areas and arranged like the vanes of a windmill, jutting outward from the spot where the body was left. His arms and legs had been fully stretched out at right angles from his torso, so he looked like a capital H on its side.

Camilla forced herself to look at Kaj's body on the gurney. It had been zipped inside a white body bag. The homicide chief now cautiously pulled the zipper down a little.

She recognized Kaj just from his hair and the deep wrinkles on his face, and she cried as she nodded in confirmation. Suhr didn't unzip the body bag any farther than the mouth so Camilla couldn't see the deep incisions that ran from the Adam's apple, where the knife had entered, down to his chest where it had been stopped by the breastbone. The homicide chief held her by the elbow, supporting her when she turned and started to walk away.

"I suggest that we drive over to HQ and have a chat," he said, as they started to make their way out to the sidewalk back out on the street.

Camilla heard the rear doors of the ambulance close, and leaned against the wall as it pulled away, heading toward National Hospital, where the pathology lab was.

Flemming squeezed her arm as he walked by, and Louise said they were ready to go.

Toft, Mikkelsen, and Stig stayed behind with Willumsen while Lars and Louise went with Suhr and Camilla.

"I just don't get it. How could it end like that?" Camilla asked, as Louise opened the back door of the car and helped her in. "No one could have known he was the one who told me what happened."

Camilla leaned her head against Louise's shoulder and kept her eyes closed for the short drive in to Police Headquarters. Camilla was reliving glimpses of the afternoon and evening she had spent with Kaj, thinking about her article as well. She'd gone through it several times—including after she was sure she was totally sober again. But there was nothing in it, nothing that could identify him in any way. She didn't get it.

But she had no doubt it was her fault he had been murdered so viciously and left in plain view in his own courtyard. Humiliated and chastised.

17

They were sitting in Louise and Lars's office. Suhr had brought in an extra chair and Camilla had downed two cups of black coffee before she suddenly leaped up and raced down the hall to the bathroom with her hand over her mouth.

A copy of the paper with her article was sitting out when she came back and they agreed that nothing in the story could have identified Kaj Antonsen as her source.

"The only thing I can see right off the bat that might have helped someone figure it out is the picture of you in your byline," Louise said, pointing to the small photo of Camilla that appeared next to her name under the title of the article.

Suhr reached for the paper as Louise pointed this out.

"If someone recognized you after seeing you with Kaj the day before the article ran, then they could have guessed your source," Louise explained, watching Camilla struggle with more nausea on realizing that she'd so carefully obscured anything that would point to Kaj while ignoring the possibility her own identity might give him away.

Suhr nodded. "It certainly could have happened that way," he agreed. Then he asked Camilla where she and Kaj had talked and who might have seen them together.

"Everyone," Camilla replied honestly. "Obviously, I had no idea it would turn into a story like this. I was only there to get a little feel for the neighborhood. I'm not really that familiar with Istedgade and that area. I also didn't know how visible the prostitutes were in the street scene. I was interested in the case of the murdered prostitute, but then I met Kaj and we got to talking, had a few beers together, and lost track of time."

Louise wrote as Camilla talked.

"Afterward, we went over to the pub, Høker Café, and we were there for a few hours while he filled me in on how a proper poires belle Hélène should be made—without whipped cream, of course," she added, unable to hold back the tears.

* * *

There was a knock on the office door. Toft apologized for the interruption, and then stepped in along with a tech.

"We found the Audi late yesterday afternoon," he told Suhr. "And last night, I installed a tracker on it. It's parked out in Valby, and we just went and checked if it had been anywhere near Sønder Boulevard and the courtyard where the body was found. But it's still in the same location and hasn't been driven."

Louise learned that they had obtained a four-week wiretap warrant, and with the electronic chip Toft had mounted on the car they could now follow the dark Audi A4 via a screen in the surveillance room.

"One of the boys is monitoring it in there, so we'll know the second he puts the key in the ignition. And we're working on getting an interpreter to help with the wiretap," Toft said, mostly to Suhr. "I hope it's Igli. He does Albanian, Serbo-Croatian, Slovak, and Czech. He's going to call in around lunchtime and let us know if he's in. I just talked to him, but he was at some little league soccer game out in Hvidovre, and his son had just scored a goal. He had to go home and look at his calendar before he could make any promises."

Suhr nodded, satisfied. Igli was one of their best interpreters when it came to cases that involved people from the Balkans. He used to be a police officer in the former Yugoslavia, and the Homicide Division often benefited from his experience now whenever he worked with them on a case. Suhr asked Lars and Louise to go through Camilla's account, from when she met Kaj to when they parted ways. Especially whether she had noticed anyone keeping an eye on them.

Louise promised they would let him know.

"I can't bear it," Camilla exclaimed after Suhr left. "It just occurred to me now that I put a couple hundred extra kroner on our tab for Kaj to use when I paid at the pub and then they had my name on the receipt for that. I just didn't even think about it. I wanted to do something nice for him, as a kind of thank-you for the story. Plus, I'd had a few too many beers to be thinking about things on that level."

Camilla hid her face in her hands, and Louise thought

Mikkelsen must have had his reasons for not wanting to talk to Kaj until he could go visit him at his home, where no one could see them. But she didn't say anything, just put her hand on Camilla's shoulder while Lars called Mikkelsen and told him about the 200 kroner and the debit card receipt. When he hung up, Lars said someone would go talk to the waitress so they could find out if anyone had asked to see the receipt after Camilla had left.

"So Michael Stig did see you out there that night," Lars said, and Camilla nodded dully.

* * *

"I just feel so awful about it," Camilla said Sunday evening when they were sitting on Louise's sofa, a bottle of red wine between them. "It feels every bit as bad as if I'd murdered him with my own hands. Anyway, it's my fault he's not alive anymore and that they killed him in that gruesome way."

Louise listened and let her friend talk. At first, she'd tried to contradict her and assuage her guilt a little, but Camilla had told her to stop that.

"There's no getting around it. I have to own up to what I did."

"Yeah, but for Pete's sake, you were just doing your job. Neither you nor Kaj for that matter could have predicted that your conversation could have led to this."

"I mean, he was talking to me to protect himself," Camilla reminded herself. "Otherwise he could have just gone to you guys. If he'd done that he might still be alive."

Louise filled her glass but held back on Camilla's.

"You were protecting him," Louise said and got up to

light a few candles in the living room. She went over to the stereo and put Big Fat Snake on repeat before sinking back down onto the sofa. "But you didn't need to go in to the paper today and write that article about your own role in the killing. Why are you putting all the blame on yourself? And so publicly?"

Camilla looked at her, her eyes unflinching as if Louise were the edge of a cliff between her and the abyss.

"There's no doubt what triggered everything yesterday," Camilla said plainly. "It's horrific every way you look at it, but I have to stand by it. And the readers deserve to know the kind of ruthless sickos we're dealing with here. Besides, I've seen way too many reporters stick their tails between their legs and refuse to take responsibility when they push their sources over the edge by leaking information and digging up dirt. I mean, you can't sink any lower than that."

* * *

They stopped by Camilla's place and packed her a bag of clothes and toiletries to take to Louise's apartment; contrary to expectations, Camilla didn't protest.

"I told the paper I wanted to take a leave of absence," Camilla said suddenly with her toothbrush in her hand after Louise had made up the guest room. "And if they don't give it to me, I'm going to quit. But I think I'm going to quit anyway," she added after a moment's thought.

Louise nodded. She had spoken with Camilla's boss herself. He was deeply concerned about one of his top reporters and told Louise he was prepared to support her. In the end, he was the one who'd run her byline photo with the article without thinking about it.

"I'd really like your permission to call a crisis psychologist I know at National Hospital," Louise said from the guest room doorway once Camilla was tucked into bed. "His name's Jakobsen. He's really good. And there's no point in your beating yourself up with all this guilt. There's really a risk all this will overwhelm you."

Louise expected a bunch of protests, so when they didn't come, she could almost hear her preplanned, must-convince-Camilla speech crash and burn.

"That's probably a good idea," Camilla said, turning off the light.

18

"I'm guessing they wanted to secure his tongue so he couldn't scream," Flemming Larsen said as he and Louise sat in his office on the Monday morning following the autopsy. "Given the configuration of the courtyard, the killer or killers were probably standing in the archway waiting for him. They grabbed him from behind and plunged the knife under his chin so it attached his tongue to his palate. That silenced him while they dragged him into the courtyard and splayed him out between the four benches."

"Which is why no one heard anything."

Louise took one of the two sodas Flemming had brought up to his office from the vending machine. She was heartened that he, too, valued their friendship enough to take a little extra time to discuss the autopsy with her.

Her mind filled with images of the courtyard off Sønder

Boulevard. There had been a number of bikes along the wall of the building in front of the garbage cans. So some-one could easily have entered the courtyard while the mur-der was taking place, she thought, picturing the location of Kaj's body.

"I wonder how long it took for him to die," she said, looking over at Flemming, who was almost done with his Fanta.

"We know he was still alive when he was tied to the benches. You yourself saw that his hands were dark and filled with blood," Flemming said, then added that they were also a little swollen. "That tells us there was still cir-culation in his body."

Louise nodded as he spoke, peering down at the crime-scene photos showing enlargements of the details on the hands and throat.

"He has red foam around his mouth," Flemming ex-plained. "Which means he started aspirating his own blood. The blood that goes down the trachea froths up as the victim breathes rapidly out of fear. I'm certain he lived for a while before he asphyxiated."

Louise closed her eyes for a moment, acknowledging the shiver of horror that traveled through her body.

"In other words, he choked on his own blood," she said, opening her eyes again.

The gravity of the situation had drawn a deep wrinkle across the tall pathologist's forehead. He nodded, a thoughtful expression on his face.

"As long as his tongue was stuck, he couldn't swallow. After that, it looks like they turned the knife around and pulled it, creating a long incision which sliced open his throat and trachea longitudinally all the way down to his breastbone, where the incision fades away on the left side of the anterior thorax."

Louise couldn't hide the shudder that coursed through her. She knew Flemming well enough to tell that he, too, was profoundly affected by the depravity of this murder.

"They knew exactly what they wanted to do with this execution," she said, blocking out the light and sounds for a second while the pieces of this portrait of bestiality fell completely into place.

"To show everyone in that world that you keep your mouth shut if you see something," Flemming said, finishing her idea.

Their eyes met.

"And all the same, they took the time to tie him up and do the job thoroughly, before leaving him there in the courtyard. Which shows that whoever did this couldn't have cared less if anyone happened to walk into the courtyard and catch him in the act," Flemming concluded.

Louise got up and stuck the crime-scene techs' pictures back into the bag. Flemming came over and put his arms around her shoulders, looking into her eyes the whole time. "Are you OK?" he asked her.

Louise sighed and shrugged. "Mostly it's Camilla who's not OK," she responded. "I just really want to find out who's evil enough to subject a harmless elderly man to this. I mean, here's the evidence of how pointlessly brutal Eastern European crime gangs are—and apparently, we've got them right here in Copenhagen now, too."

"Yeah, you have to admit these people are more ruthless than the criminals we're used to," Flemming admitted, pulling Louise into a quick hug as they reached the elevator.

"Take care of yourself," he told her, as the elevator door opened in front of them.

Louise gave his hand a squeeze and thanked him for the soda, before stepping in and pressing the lobby button to return to Police Headquarters and her Monday briefing, which had been pushed back until after the autopsy.

* * *

"This morning our interpreter, Igli, intercepted information that Arian is going to go pick someone up at the airport this afternoon," Willumsen reported once everyone was gathered around the circular conference table in Suhr's office. "It's Starling flight NB564 scheduled to arrive from Prague at 1:55 p.m. And I want all four of you out there. We're going to get to the fucking bottom of what's going on now. Before they slaughter anyone else."

Toft nodded. "Do you want us to follow his car out there? Or not make contact until the arrivals hall?" he asked, looking from Willumsen to Suhr.

"You two go wait at the airport," Willumsen responded, pointing to Toft and Stig. "Rick and Lars will tail them out there. But stay well back; don't let them see you."

"We're just going to be watching," Suhr added.

The group's collective mood had been tense ever since Kaj Antonsen's murder. Everyone had realized that they were going up against people who did not value human life in the slightest, and it was still rare to encounter this type of criminal in Denmark, even in the capital.

"Get out there and get into position. It's less than two hours until the plane lands, and I don't want you running through the airport at the last minute," Willumsen commanded. "From now on we're going to be right on their asses."

Then, as if he realized he was sending mixed signals, he started up again. This time, he spoke plainly, making clear that everything should take place without their being detected.

"And when you leave the airport, Toft and Stig will come back here and focus on the wiretap, and Rick and Jørgensen will stay on the two Albanians so we know where they go. Then everyone come back here. We have to find out what they're up to before we can plan our next move."

* * *

Louise and Lars were parked at opposite ends of the underground parking lot when Arian and his passenger drove their Audi down to P6 under Terminal 3.

They walked over to the elevator slowly, but there was a crowd of people with suitcases waiting to go up, so Louise pulled her partner over to the stairs instead. Up in the arrivals hall, they quickly spotted Toft and Stig, one of them with a newspaper, the other with a cup of coffee, expectantly eyeing the passengers as they emerged through customs. Louise nodded at the elevator and walked over to the arrivals screen, where she confirmed that the flight from Prague had just landed, five minutes ahead of schedule.

The two Albanians emerged from the elevator. Checking on the arrival status, they went to stand by the opening where the travelers came out.

"Do we guess the short-haired one is Hamdi? He matches

the description Pavlína gave, and there is certainly no doubt that the driver is identical to the owner of the car," Louise told her partner, who nodded without taking his eyes off Arian, who had shoulder-length, slicked-back hair and glasses.

After waiting ten minutes with only a trickle of people clearing customs, a large group of travelers pulling suitcases appeared. Hamdi held up a white sign, but Louise couldn't see what it said from where she was standing. Stig walked right in front of her then, heading for a trash can to throw away his empty coffee cup.

Louise watched him.

"Ilana," he said on his way back past them as he returned from the trash can.

None of the new arrivals reacted to the sign, nor any from the next group, who came streaming out of customs and spread out in all directions. Louise walked over to the arrivals screen and saw that the baggage had already been assigned to a carousel. Which meant that the passengers could be out at any point. When she turned around to walk back over to her partner, she stopped and suddenly took a step to the left to avoid a column.

All the way over along the opposite wall she had caught a glimpse of bangs that had been cut just over the eyebrows. It was Pavlína, and Miloš Vituk was next to her. Both of them had their eyes trained on the two Albanians, who were steadily watching the stream of emerging travelers.

Louise walked back over to Lars and nodded in their direction. "Did you see when they arrived?"

He shook his head. "But they obviously aren't particularly eager to be seen," he remarked, returning his focus once again to the arriving passengers.

Louise agreed with him and followed along curiously as

Pavlína suddenly took a few steps toward a young woman with long blond hair, who was carrying a big bag over her shoulder. The woman was almost all the way to the door and out to where the cabs were before Pavlína and Miloš made their presence known. After the two women greeted each other, Miloš gallantly offered to carry her bag, and they quickly walked toward the entrance to the train station underneath the arrivals hall.

"Who was that?" Lars asked after the three of them disappeared down the stairs to platforms 3 and 4.

"Maybe her sister," Louise suggested, shrugging her shoulders. She then added that of course it could also have been a friend coming to visit.

The two Albanians hadn't seemed to notice the other reunion, and were still standing there scanning the stream of people coming out of customs. The little luggage icon wasn't flashing on the screen anymore, which meant that all the bags had been picked up.

After ten minutes, they saw Arian take out his cell, and a moment later he stepped back from the crowd and spoke, gesticulating vigorously with his free arm. He walked over to the window that looked out over the luggage return carousels and scanned the area, but then came back and said something to Hamdi. It wasn't hard to tell from their body language that they were impatient and that something hadn't gone according to plan. They were pacing back and forth in front of the exit from customs.

Twenty minutes later, Arian made another call.

"I'm going to go over to the police service desk," Louise said. "From there, I can call Documentation and find out if there were any problems with the flight arriving from Prague. You hold the fort here, OK?"

Louise walked over to the office, which was in the corridor between arrivals and departures. She had a hard time imagining that the Documentation Group with the Danish National Police would be interested in an arrival from the Czech Republic, since anyone traveling between European Union member states that were covered by the Schengen Agreement could just walk right through without showing a passport—obviously, though, security might have flagged the flight, in which case passengers would have to show their passports.

Maybe they had detained Ilana for something like that.

Louise greeted a young officer and showed her police badge before asking if he could put her in touch with a person from Documentation and whoever was currently in charge of Concourse C, where the flight had been directed, to see if the flight had had any security flags.

"Ask him if they detained anyone, and to check and see if there was a passenger with the first name 'Ilana' on the flight manifest for Starling NB564 from Prague."

Louise waited patiently while he checked on this. Documentation didn't have anything. It took a little longer to access the flight manifest, but when the officer on duty called him back five minutes later, he was able to report that an Ilana Procházková was on the manifest but that she had never checked in.

Louise thanked him for his help. It wasn't hard to see that the young officer was intrigued, but he refrained from asking what was wrong when she didn't volunteer anything.

"Let's see what happens," Lars said when Louise returned. "I'm sure they'll give up at some point and drive back into town. At least now we've put faces to the two names," he said, trying to look at the bright side of a trip that hadn't turned up anything useful.

Louise nodded and glanced over at the men, wondering which one had done the knife work in the Meatpacking District. Since Arian owned the car and apparently also did the driving, she guessed it was Hamdi who had jumped out of the backseat.

* * *

The two Albanians gave up an hour later and drove back to Copenhagen. The whole way back in from Kastrup Airport, Louise and Lars took turns tailing the dark Audi with their two colleagues.

"Remember to maintain eye contact if he looks at you," Lars warned when they pulled right up next to the car at a stop light in Amager at one point.

Louise nodded. She knew looking away was an easy way to tip people off. They made room for Toft and Stig as they passed Hotel Scandinavia, and they agreed that their colleagues would turn off at Police HQ while they followed the Audi for the rest of the trip.

They continued along Tietgensgade behind Central Station with the sun glaring on the windshield, then drove down past the conference center.

There was a lot of traffic. It was a quarter after five, and the cars were inching along over Halmtorvet. If they lost the Audi, they could fall back on the electronic chip Toft had mounted underneath it, but they wanted to be able to follow them in person to see where they went after they parked.

With two cars between, they continued down past the

Meatpacking District. Traffic was much less heavy here, and when they turned up Saxogade, Louise started to relax.

"They're going to the club," she said and started looking for a parking spot. They'd had the Albanian club under surveillance since Pavlína told them about it, but they hadn't seen any sign of Arian or Hamdi going there. The Audi parked two buildings farther up the street.

"Let me out," Louise said quickly. "I'll stay here while you find a parking spot."

She hopped out of the car just outside the club and busied herself by rooting around in her bag while she watched the two Albanians approaching her.

They were talking and didn't look her way. All the same, she pulled back in against the wall of the building and turned her face away. Arian sounded angry, as if it were Hamdi's fault the girl hadn't shown up. They took the four steps down into the basement club in two bounds and disappeared through the door.

In the brief instant the door was open, Louise saw that there was a fair number of people inside. She smelled smoke and heard conversations. She stood a bit waiting for Lars, who'd found a spot not too far away.

They stepped into a doorway with a good view of the entrance to the basement club, but Louise realized the view was just as good from inside the club. So, every time the club door opened, they were sure to back farther into the shadow of their doorway.

"They've made us," Louise confirmed after she noticed a head pop up over the side of the stairwell to look in their direction. "Let's move over to the other side of the street."

Three older men deep in conversation walked down the sidewalk and went down the stairs into the club side by side.

"I wonder what they do down there?" Louise said, considering the basement windows covered with faded yellowish curtains.

"Play cards, talk, smoke," Lars said.

Louise smiled. "Sounds like just the place for you," she said.

Lars nodded. "Doesn't sound so bad to me. Nice to have a place to hang out," he said. "A woman-free zone with a bar and gambling."

"They're playing for money?"

Her partner started laughing. "What, did you think they were playing Go Fish? I'm betting that sometimes they play for quite a bit, but they're clever enough to use all kinds of codes so there'll never be money there in the clubs if the police stop by."

He shook his head. "But that's true of all clubs, not just the Albanian one," he hastened to add. "It's like that in most of the expat clubs we've raided."

"Damn," Louise exclaimed. "And here I thought they were drinking sweet tea and chatting about old friends and memories. In reality it's organized gambling with a bar."

Two hours had elapsed without any sign of Arian or Hamdi. At a little past six, they agreed to return to HQ, where Willumsen was still waiting for them.

* * *

They found him in his office, collecting all the information that was still coming in about Kaj Antonsen's murder. A large team from the downtown precinct was working on questioning the residents of the buildings surrounding the courtyard, and the first reports from the crime-scene techs had just been turned in. He stood up and cleared the meeting table while Louise went to get Toft and his partner.

"There's no doubt that those two were up to something that didn't work out for them," Toft stated. "We traced the calls made from Arian's cell phone during the time we were at the airport and they all went to a foreign number, which we weren't able to identify. But the country code was the Czech Republic, so I think we could assume that he was trying to get hold of the Czech contact who was supposed to see the girl off."

Willumsen nodded. "That's a good guess, anyway," he said, eyeing Toft and Stig. "I suggest you do another round at the hotels off Istedgade this evening and see if anyone knows the two Albanians, but stay on top of what Igli gets out of the wiretap so we make sure we're keeping up with them."

They both nodded, and Willumsen glanced quickly at Louise and Lars.

"You two are going to Istedgade," he ordered. "Get the rundown on the scene so we have some idea how many Eastern European prostitutes are working out there these days."

He asked Lars to set up one of the department's small video cameras in his backpack. "Stroll around and listen to the solicitations you get from the hookers. Keep the camera hidden, obviously, but make sure the lens is unimpeded when the girls talk to you."

Once Lars nodded that he understood, Willumsen added he could get someone to help him set it up in his backpack if he had any trouble.

"I'm sure I can figure it out on my own," Lars was quick to say. Louise knew he hated going to the techies for help, because they tended to scoff anytime there was something the "desk officers" couldn't handle.

Willumsen had already moved on to Louise.

"You keep an eye on the girls who use the rooms in that porn theater for their customers. We need to identify all those using the booths and, by elimination, the ones who are working for the Albanians. As of now, we still don't know if the Albanians' girls operate off the street or through a brothel— where they'll be harder to keep an eye on."

"They're working off the street," Louise said, reminding him what Pavlína had told them. "But, I'd still like to take a closer look at Club Intim and see whether Arian and Hamdi turn up."

Willumsen seemed to ignore her correction; he plowed ahead undeterred.

"First thing tomorrow, you guys are going to head over to Central Station. We're going to verify whether the girls meet there every morning to settle their tabs," he said, still to Louise and her partner.

"If what Pavlína claims is true, then there's definitely a pattern to it," Louise said.

"Exactly," Willumsen said. He added that Mikkelsen had put a few extra uniforms on the streets to keep a lookout for meetings of prostitutes and their potential pimps.

Earlier at the airport, Louise heard that Suhr had asked the downtown precinct for assistance detecting any pattern to identify locations on the Albanians' "route"—what Arian had called a few specific places in the neighborhood in one of the conversations Igli had translated. Mikkelsen had confirmed that the route included at least Istedgade, the streets around Halmtorvet, Sønder Boulevard, and Skelbækgade.

"How about if I start out at Arian's address early to-morrow morning?" Lars suggested. "Then I'll be on him as soon as he leaves his apartment, and Louise can head straight to Central Station and be ready if anyone shows up."

Willumsen nodded and looked at the time before getting up and retrieving his jacket from the coat hook on the back of the door.

"Let me know if anything interesting turns up," he said, closing his briefcase after he put his jacket on. "I'll see you two in here early tomorrow," he said to Toft and Stig. "You should also keep up-to-date on how far the CSI techs have gotten with the evidence from the murder site."

As the four detectives stood up, the chief was already on his way down the hall with a farewell wave.

Stig and Toft offered Louise a ride to Halmtorvet.

"Great," she said, popping back into her office where her partner was setting up his video camera in a backpack.

"Let's meet at Central Station later, OK?" she asked Lars.

19

In the pastor's kitchen, Camilla watched him operate the espresso machine. She was sitting on the bench at the table in an oversize T-shirt and a pair of faded jeans, with no makeup.

"I'm sure they'll find the people who did it," Jonas promised in his gravelly voice after he came into the kitchen to say hi to Markus and his mother. "Detective Louise told us that."

Camilla smiled at Jonas, tenderly running her hand over his hair while he kept his dark, serious eyes trained on her. She knew that Louise was still in touch with the two boys, and she was just as happy to have her friend handle that area of conversation. At the moment, she had her hands full just keeping herself above water.

"Louise also told us to take care of you because you're so sad about the murder," her son's best friend continued, which made Camilla choke up. Otherwise, she had mostly finished crying by this point. She felt a little more relaxed after talking to the psychologist at National Hospital and hearing she'd been granted the leave she had requested at work.

"Thanks," she said, giving the hand Jonas had placed on her shoulder a little squeeze, before the boy disappeared upstairs with Markus.

Høyer had given her a month off when they'd met at the paper earlier. He served her coffee as they sat on the sofas in the visitors' interview room and emphasized the leave was just long enough for her to get back up on her feet.

Camilla had sat across from him, staring as he spoke—it wasn't what she wanted. "The leave should be for an unspecified length of time," she said. "And if I'm not back in three months, I will totally understand if you hire someone else."

She had already heard he'd pulled someone off the news desk to replace her while she was away, and there would be a new intern starting next week as well.

Høyer had stood up and stepped over to the window with his back to her for several minutes before finally turning around and giving her a look she had trouble interpreting. It was a confusing combination of concern, helplessness, and burgeoning irritation. In the end he gave in, dropping his head in exasperation. But he wanted her permission to call her while she was on leave to check up on her.

She hugged him before leaving, because she was brimming over with relief.

* * *

"I read about Kaj Antonsen in the paper yesterday," Henrik said, setting a cup of espresso in front of her. "*Morgen-avisen* wrote that you were seeking his next of kin, but from today's article I take it no one has come forward yet. Did you get hold of his ex, the one who left him when their son died?"

Camilla nodded. "But she didn't want anything to do with him—as far as she was concerned, he had died years ago—when she lost her son. She said he doesn't have any family but made it abundantly clear she wanted nothing to do with the funeral, so I thought I'd take care of it myself."

The pastor sat down across from her. "You don't need to do that," he said. "If there isn't any next of kin, then the Danish government will take care of it."

Camilla shook her head and said that she didn't want that. Kaj should have a proper funeral.

"Which is why I wanted to ask if we could hold it here at your church."

"Certainly," he said warmly but with a look that meant he wondered if she was sure she'd thought her decision through.

Camilla knew she was going against the sad contemporary trend in Denmark where the next of kin try to get out of arranging funerals for family members to avoid the bill. But she'd thought a great deal about Kaj, and even though they had known each other for only a few hours, she knew she wasn't doing it merely out of compassion. It was also to ease her own conscience.

"What do you think about a funeral service, and then afterward we can inter his urn in the unmarked graves?" Pastor Henrik suggested.

Camilla shrugged. She hadn't made any decisions on

the details and was happy to go along with whatever the pastor recommended, as long as Kaj got a proper sendoff. She didn't think a proper sendoff would fix anything, really—but it just felt right.

Her eyes drifted over to the TV, which was on but muted. The evening news was in the middle of its report on Baby Girl, who had been brought to Skodsborg Orphanage. It had been a week since the boys had found her, and the mother still hadn't come forward. That meant the baby would probably be put up for adoption. In other words, Skodsborg was just a layover on the little girl's journey.

One week, Camilla thought. The abandoned baby felt like the distant past already.

She wished she could forget everything that had happened since she was found.

"Can we play Johnny Cash in church?" she asked, turning from the TV to the pastor and gulping the rest of her espresso.

He smiled and said that since no one else was helping plan the service, there was no one to object to that.

Camilla felt herself grinning; it was totally liberating to feel something other than the hurt of the past two and a half days.

"There will be a ton of flowers," she said. "But I don't think we need to do any singing."

She sat for a moment, staring off into space.

"I guess I didn't know him," she said. "Maybe it's too much stuff." There was a little pause.

"I don't know if I'm going to go back to writing," she said softly, leaving the topic of the funeral for a bit. "Before all this, I felt like writing had a kind of legitimacy and gave meaning to the things I did. But it's pretty darn hard to see it that way now. No news story justifies what happened to Kaj."

She could see the pastor weighing what he wanted to say next, but she just wasn't up to listening to anyone else encouraging her to stop feeling guilty. So she was glad for the interruption when the kitchen door knocker made three loud clunks.

Camilla glanced up at the clock over the sink. Nine fifteen. The boys were still up in Jonas's room watching a movie or playing computer games. Markus had insisted that it wasn't too late for him, even though, at this rate, they might not be home until ten.

* * *

There was a young foreign woman standing outside, the same one who had been by the day the boys found the little girl inside the entrance to the church. The last time she came she'd rung the bell at the front door of the pastor's residence. Now she was standing at the back door, holding out a slip of paper to Pastor Holm.

He glanced at it and shrugged.

"I don't understand," he said, and invited her in.

It was a warm spring evening outside, and yet a cold draft rushed through the kitchen. Henrik pointed to the coffee cups, but the woman stood just inside the door and politely declined.

Camilla didn't remember the woman being so tall, and this time she had a more insistent look, which was trained on the pastor. Then Camilla remembered that Henrik had asked the woman to come back again after a week.

He apologized and explained that unfortunately he

hadn't been able to find her any work, but offered to keep an eye out and let her know if anything turned up.

The woman shook her head vigorously and pointed at the slip of paper.

He studied it again, before passing it to Camilla and asking if she could make out any of what it said.

Daj ovoj devojci posao u tvojoj kući, i tvoj dug je plaćen.

Camilla shook her head. She couldn't make sense of even a single word.

"Looks like Croatian; if it were Serbian it'd be in Cyrillic," Henrik said. "It's going to take me some time to translate it. Luckily, I have a dictionary from my time in Bosnia."

He started explaining to the woman again that he couldn't help her right now. "Give me your number, and I'll call you if anything comes up," he said.

She shook her head and kept pointing at the slip of paper.

Finally, the pastor asked her to wait a moment. He turned on the light in the living room next to the bookshelf and he returned a moment later with a worn dictionary and a pair of reading glasses.

Slowly, word by word, he translated the first sentence:

"Give this girl a job in your home, and your debt is paid," he read after writing the words down on the back of a shopping list. He started on the next sentence, but after a couple of words he pushed the paper away and apologetically shook his head, once again explaining to her that he didn't need any help with his housework, he preferred to do it himself.

He watched her reluctantly leave the kitchen and start

down the back steps. "What else did it say?" Camilla asked once he was seated at the table again. Henrik emptied his little coffee cup and pulled the piece of paper over to him, scanning the tall, thin letters.

"It says: 'Greetings from a friend.' But, of course, that could be anyone who knew I used to work down there."

Camilla asked what it had been like working in Srebrenica.

"Awful and wonderful," he said, smiling at her. "Some of the worst things I've ever experienced, but also some of the most life-affirming. Once you got used to the darkness, the food, and the mud, you started to see the people. Although it took me quite a while to get to know the people, because they were hiding under so many layers of pain and displacement. It was hard to say who they were—or who they had been."

Camilla nodded. His words had struck a chord, reminding her of something she'd experienced in the spring of 1998. The year after she had Markus, the *Roskilde Dagblad* had sent her to Kosovo to write a story about a young Danish woman from Lejre who was cleaning up land mines. After the young woman took Camilla and her photographer out into the minefield, they spent that evening in a bar where the woman introduced them to a young man Camilla guessed she was interested in, although she never actually admitted as much.

The young man told them a little about his story, which began four years earlier when he returned home one day to find his family's house ablaze. After neighbors helped put out the fire, they found his father and two brothers on the floor of the kitchen, each shot in the back of the head, and his mother and two little sisters were down in the basement. The basement door had been locked from outside.

The pastor nodded as she shared her story.

"We'll never fully understand the kind of trauma something like that marks a person with," he said. "I have a lot of good memories, too. Of really bonding with people, and helping people create new lives, even though their minds and bodies bore the scars. Small Muslim children would come in by night, rescued from Serbian areas where their families had been exterminated—but inexplicably the children had escaped."

Henrik paused, lost in thought, and Camilla watched the subtle expressions flicker across his face as he relived the memories.

"One Serb came by several times, always after dark, after most people were in bed."

The pastor absentmindedly tore the shopping list into small strips, his eyes following the motions of his fingers.

"He knew no one would take care of a Muslim baby in a Serbian zone, so he brought the baby to us at great peril to himself should anyone have caught him."

Henrik looked up.

"So, there were inspirational stories, too," he added, pushing aside the memories as he brushed the little pieces of ripped paper into a small pile. "But it was definitely an experience I'll always remember. Even though I see a very intimate side of people and their lives in my everyday work here, my time in Srebrenica left an indelible impression on me."

"Didn't it help, doing the work with your wife? A shared experience?"

Henrik nodded. "Definitely. And we had Jonas while we

were there," he said, trying to brighten his voice and discard the gloominess.

Now it was Camilla's turn to nod.

"But then Alice died, and Jonas and I were on our own. I may have been a bit naïve, but I tried to create a home life for my son and me where our relationship is as close as possible—so he won't suffer so much from growing up without his mother. Of course, I know that I can never make up for her," he said with a wry little laugh and then a moment of silence before he spoke again.

"Neither my wife nor I had any family left, so it's just Jonas and me." He hesitated a little before continuing. "I suppose that's also why the idea of a housekeeper seems so alien to me. There's no room for a stranger in the life Jonas and I have together."

Camilla understood what he meant. But at the same time, she felt sorry for him, because it would probably prevent him from ever falling in love again.

"Do you think the service could be Thursday or Friday? Or should we wait until the weekend?" she asked, turning the conversation back to Kaj's funeral.

"That depends on when the police will release the body," Henrik responded.

Camilla ran her hand over her hair, resting her face in her hands for a second. "Right," she said. "We'll have to wait and see what they say."

"Can we have some ice cream?"

The boys startled her, suddenly rushing into the kitchen.

She watched Henrik ruffle his son's hair as he nodded at the freezer. She warned Markus that they ought to be getting home.

"We can leave as soon as we're done with the ice

cream," he said, and she nodded obligingly. She held out her cup when Henrik offered her more coffee, knowing it would keep her up all night. At least that way the thoughts and guilt that had kept her on the brink of sleep for the past two nights wouldn't haunt her tonight.

"Call me after you talk to the police. Do you have my cell number?" Henrik asked.

She reached for the scraps of the shopping list and wrote his number down on a free corner, thanking him for the coffee and especially the conversation.

20

"Suck and fuck, 500 kroner!"

Lars played the recording back for Louise on the video camera's tiny screen.

It was ten fifteen, and Mikkelsen had just called Louise's cell to let her know he was on his way over as well.

Lars explained that he began his tour by walking down Istedgade. He continued onto the surrounding streets and headed over on Skelbækgade, where he'd gone up to Dybbølsbro Station and back, before calling Louise and telling her he was ready to meet up at Central Station.

She grabbed another chair and pulled it over to their high table outside the only snack kiosk still open that late, just as Mikkelsen walked up with his hands in his pockets and his leather jacket open, revealing a bright red shirt that lit up the sleepy train station.

Mikkelsen laughed when he listened to the recording. "How could you resist such an appealing offer?"

Lars blushed, and Louise smiled.

"Nah, but a guy who works with my wife did walk by while I was talking to one of the women—so there may be some conversation over the watercooler at my wife's company tomorrow," Lars said, not looking particularly worried.

"What was he doing in that neighborhood?"

Louise briefly considered the possibility that Lars's wife might think her husband had been seeking comfort from a prostitute because they were having trouble at home.

"Oh, he had just come out of one of the restaurants."

She nodded. She, too, had been struck by the strange mix of crowds created as Copenhagen's red-light district had turned trendy in recent years, and there were a number of destination restaurants and cafés there now that drew in a whole new clientele compared to the people on the margins of life who lived there.

"How many of the women do you think were Czech?" Mikkelsen asked.

"A good number," Lars replied. He paused a moment, then admitted that he had a hard time telling exactly which country the Eastern European women were from.

"You can tell which ones are from Africa just by looking at them, and you can hear which ones are from Denmark by listening to them. But I really couldn't tell you if a woman was from the Czech Republic, Slovakia, Poland, or Romania, for that matter. Maybe Igli can help us narrow it down if he looks at the tapes?"

Mikkelsen nodded and said he got the impression a lot of them were Czech, actually. "Although we have taken a bunch of Czech women into custody lately in raids, and then they stay scarce on the street for a while after that. Of course, they come pouring right back in again soon enough."

Lars grabbed one of the kiosk's limited, laminated menus and decided on two Danish-style hot dogs. Mikkelsen got a Polish sausage in a bun, while Louise opted for the croque monsieur. After they paid, Louise told them that an elderly lady who lived on Istedgade across from Club Intim had been nice enough to let her sit in her living room for the last two hours of her stakeout on the club.

"I also saw Arian in the dark Audi. He drove up a little after eight and parked farther down the street," Louise reported. "And Hamdi was working. He walked up and down the stretch of sidewalk in front of Club Intim with an armful of dark red roses that he was trying to sell to passing drivers. He apparently supplements his income that way."

She looked at Mikkelsen to see if this were something he was aware of. Her colleague ran a hand over his stubble, a smile lighting up his face.

"Well, you may be giving him a bit too much credit," he said and then grew serious again. "The roses are just an excuse. When he walks around like that, he's really just keeping his eye on the women. If he doesn't think they're doing enough, he goes after them."

One of Louise's eyebrows shot up as she nodded thoughtfully. Of course, she thought, suddenly remembering an old case from Southern Jutland where several foreign pimps had assigned their women numbers and ranked them by earnings, that is, how much they brought in per hour and how much per day. The information was useful when they later sold the women—maybe that was why they kept such a close watch on these women, Louise thought. They needed a way to estimate productivity and keep track of each woman's value. Someone at the Nest had explained how harsh the punishment was if the women didn't live up to what was expected of them. God, it must cause tremendous stress to have their pimps' eyes on them all the time like that, she thought.

"I saw Pavlína," Louise said, after her partner set food and drinks on the table in front of them. "She was walking with the girl she and Miloš picked up at the airport, but I didn't have a chance to ask if that was her sister."

Mikkelsen reported that he'd stopped in at the basement grocery and chatted with his other informants.

"People are worried," he said, explaining he'd heard from a number of sources that there were more new girls. "They've been reorganized a little, and the fee they have to pay to use the street has gone up."

"How the hell can they raise the price?" Louise exclaimed, accepting the cup of coffee Lars handed her.

"It happens any time there are suddenly a lot of women walking the street. Someone will offer to keep the sidewalk 'clean' for the prostitutes who pay. Then the neighborhood gets divided up into sort of zones where some areas are more attractive than others."

"I don't get why the women go along with this," Lars objected, looking at Mikkelsen.

"Yeah, I know," Mikkelsen agreed. "But if you think about the long lines of women standing along the old rural highways out by the border between the Czech Republic and Austria, and then they find out that they could be earning a lot more if they just went to Copenhagen, well then maybe it's not so strange. I mean, don't forget, quite a few of the women are here of their own free will, because they can make a lot more money here than where they come from. They're not just here because greedy men have forced them up here with violence," he added. "The percentage of prostitutes who are victims of human trafficking is surprisingly quite small."

Louise nodded but argued that human trafficking would increase if the police didn't start coming down harder on the traffickers.

"True enough," Mikkelsen said. "But as long as we have a minister of justice with no compassion for these women, it'll be damn hard to prevent. If she ever mentions the police stepping up their efforts against trafficking in women and pandering, I suspect it will have more to do with political strategy than because she really wants to fix the problem."

Mikkelsen smiled sarcastically. "If she can go to the press and say that she's increasing the sentences for violent crimes, that will do her some real good. That's the kind of thing that gets you votes," he continued, snapping Louise out of her reverie. "Not prostitutes."

"Well, we certainly can't praise our own higher-ups for being particularly committed to the cause, either," Louise pointed out. Lars immediately backed her up on that.

"Until we put more resources into cleaning up the pimps and traffickers, they can pretty much continue to operate with impunity," Lars said.

"Except of course when they start murdering people," Louise added and finished off her coffee.

Mikkelsen nodded and stood up. "I'll meet you guys here in the morning and we can see what's going on." He yawned. "Should we say around nine?" he suggested, looking at Louise.

"It's a date," she said. Then she and Lars strolled down the length of the train station's main concourse out to the bus stop, while Mikkelsen headed off for the rear exit.

* * *

The next morning Lars called Louise's cell just before ten to report that Arian had just left his apartment. He hadn't taken the Audi and was instead walking toward the Valby train station.

"I'm at Central Station now," Louise said. She'd been standing in the bookstore but had stepped out when her phone rang.

"I'll call you again when we get close, so you'll be ready," Lars said. "Sounds good."

Morning rush hour was over. The people in the station were more relaxed now, taking time to stop and study the departure screens before heading down to the various platforms. Mikkelsen had gone to get himself a cup of coffee and a croissant, and Louise was studying the bookstore's sale table, browsing through the books from one end to the other. Some caught her interest, others she rejected just for their covers. After Lars called back a little later to say Arian and he were on the light rail B line heading toward Holte, Louise found Mikkelsen and told him that Arian would arrive about 10:27.

That was three minutes away, and Mikkelsen nodded toward a woman with short, blond hair.

"I think she's the first one," he said softly. "It looks like she's hanging around, waiting, and I don't think it's for a train."

The woman sat down on the very edge of the bench in front of the Danish National Railways' fast food window.

She looked at her watch and clutched her little purse tightly under her arm.

Arian came up from the platform below with his hands in his pockets. His hair was slicked back, and he had an ambling gait. As he passed the woman, she got up and quickly slipped him something. The next second she was gone. They didn't exchange a word.

Lars was still over by the escalators, while Mikkelsen had pulled back in case Arian recognized him. Although they'd never had anything to do with each other, people talked, and a lot of people in the prostitution world knew the folks from the local police station. Louise walked over and sat down on the bench. She set her purse in her lap and slowly opened a newspaper in front of her.

She watched the Albanian buy a cup of coffee and a roll. After that he sat down at the table Mikkelsen had just left, and started flipping through one of the free newspapers Mikkelsen had left behind.

* * *

They came, one at a time. Handing over their money and leaving. They looked like friends happening to bump into each other; a short greeting and then the women moved on. Arian only took a couple of bites of his food, and Louise had the sense he was dragging it out, killing time like every other person who was waiting for the next train.

A young woman approached him hesitantly, her eyes trained on the floor. Intermittently, she raised her face and glanced at him fleetingly, while everything about her body language suggested she did not want to walk over to him.

Louise instinctively knew that Arian had seen the

woman, even though his eyes were still focused on his newspaper. When she finally made it up to his café table, Louise watched her lips forming the words while she gestured in despair with her arms. Louise also saw how quickly Arian was up out of his chair and how aggressively he pulled the woman to him so they were standing face-to-face. He leaned in threateningly as he chewed her out.

Several people walking by saw the incident but quickly looked away, opting to hurry on toward their destinations.

Just then someone came running toward Arian and the woman. Louise saw Mikkelsen step forward as Lars approached from the escalators.

Hamdi brutally pushed the woman away and pulled Arian aside as he angrily and nervously delivered a message. Whatever he had said drove the men to leave, running toward the station's rear exit and then down the stairs toward Reventlowsgade.

Lars followed them, and Mikkelsen walked over to the young woman, who had sat down, shaken.

Louise guessed Mikkelsen asked her if she was all right, because the woman quickly nodded, brushed aside his expression of concern, and hurried off.

There were two options, and Louise wavered between keeping an eye on the young woman or following her partner. But when Mikkelsen started to head for the escalator, Louise decided to stay, watching the woman's nervous looks and the scared expression on her face.

It took a little while before Louise realized her cell phone was ringing in her purse, and by the time she noticed it she was afraid it was too late.

Willumsen's voice was clear and precise; he didn't waste any time on hellos. "A German tourist just pulled a young foreign woman out of Copenhagen Harbor, alive," he reported succinctly. "I want you to go down to National Hospital right away and talk to her."

"Do we know what happened?" Louise asked.

"The tourist spotted her while he was pulled over, figuring out where he was on his map. She was lying in the water with both hands tied behind her back. A pouch hanging under her shirt against her stomach contained a Czech passport listing her name as Hana Simrová, born in 1990. There was also some cash. We're trying to get the female interpreter in right now, the one we used with Pavlína. We'll send her straight to the hospital when we get hold of her. Toft and Stig are on their way down to the harbor; their tracker shows that the Audi A4 left the Albanian's Valby address at 10:13 a.m. and, strangely enough, was at Kalvebod Wharf on Copenhagen Harbor only half an hour ago," Willumsen said.

"Wow, that's quite brazen, throwing her into the water in broad daylight," Louise commented once he'd finished. "I'm sure you won't be surprised that the Audi showed up at Central Station less than ten minutes ago. At least— Hamdi came running in and got Arian."

Louise leaped to her feet and asked if he'd reserved patrol cars for the detectives so she could head straight to the motor pool, or if she had to go upstairs and sign a car out first.

"Just go straight there. I'll make sure there's a car waiting for you."

From the sidewalk out front she called Lars to update him on Willumsen's information.

"I'm on my way to National Hospital now, but I'd really like to know what the wiretap picks up for the next couple hours," Louise said as she crossed Bernstorffsgade and continued past Tivoli toward the police parking garage.

21

A young woman, pale and wrapped in a large bathrobe, was sitting on a chair in the examining room. She had a towel around her hair, so her face was exposed only from eyes to chin, to which she had pulled up the bathrobe like a collar. She was holding a plastic mug of hot chocolate, and her eyes wandered a little as Louise held out her hand and introduced herself.

The interpreter wasn't there yet, so Louise tried English and asked if the woman understood.

"A little," she replied, eyeing Louise uncertainly before confirming that her name was Hana Simrová.

The door opened and a nurse peeked in. She told Louise that she had been the first one to see the woman when she arrived in the ambulance.

"At first glance it doesn't appear that she's suffered any serious harm, but she is suffering from exposure and is of course in shock," she said. "I'll send the doctor in as soon as she's done with the patient in the next room."

Louise nodded and turned back to the young woman, but she didn't have a chance to say anything before the interpreter opened the door.

The interpreter smiled at Louise and walked over to the chair and said hello to Hana.

The girl crept further into the bathrobe every time a new person stepped into the hospital room, but when the interpreter started speaking Czech, Hana's shoulders seemed to relax a little.

"Have you spoken with Pavlína since that day?" the interpreter asked Louise as she took off her jacket and laid it over the back of the chair.

"Pavlína!" Hana exclaimed, and she seemed desperate as she spoke a long stream of Czech words directly to the interpreter.

Louise leaned forward in her chair and listened, even though she didn't understand the slightest bit of what was being said. To her, it sounded like chains of words being pulled through the room, rising and falling in strength. Hana gesticulated madly, and the interpreter's face turned serious. She pulled her chair all the way over to Hana while Louise stayed back. Finally, the flood of words ebbed, and the woman started shaking, and now Louise stepped over to the crying woman and introduced herself. The doctor slipped in quietly.

"I'm Karen," the doctor said quickly. "Would you mind waiting outside while I examine her?" She looked at Louise through small, gold-rimmed glasses. "But I'm sure I'll be needing your help," she said to the interpreter.

* * *

It took fifteen minutes before the door opened again.
Louise asked if she could come in.

The towel around Hana's head had come loose, and her
long blond hair hung like a fraying rope down her back.

"It turns out that Hana here knows a Pavlína, and I think
it must be the same Pavlína we talked to because she also
mentioned a Miloš," the interpreter explained.

Louise raised an eyebrow and looked at the young Czech
woman. Her head was bent as she studied her own hands,
folded in her lap. It wasn't until Hana raised her face, holding
out her empty cup to the nurse who came in to offer her more
hot chocolate, that Louise recognized Hana from the airport
and their brief encounter on the street.

"Ask her if she's Pavlína's sister," Louise said.

The Czech woman shook her head, and the interpreter
explained that they were just friends. "She lost her cell
phone in the water, so she can't call Miloš Vituk and tell
him what happened. She wants to know if we can call them
so they'll come get her. She doesn't know where they live."

"Of course," Louise said. "But let's go down to Police
Headquarters first so we can take her statement. That's where
Miloš's phone number is, anyway. If you didn't bring your
own car, you can ride with us. You'll have to come so I can
ask her about what really happened out by the harbor."

* * *

At HQ, they ran into Toft in the hallway. He had just returned from the harbor and was on his way into the small
room where they were monitoring the wiretap.

He greeted Hana politely and told Louise that several witnesses had seen the Audi at the wharf, but no one had seen the woman being thrown into the water.

Louise nodded toward the office where Igli was sitting, listening in on the wiretap. "Has there been anything?" Louise asked.

"Surprisingly little," Toft admitted.

"I'm on my way in to call Miloš Vituk and tell him what happened. Then he or Pavlína can bring Hana some dry clothes. I'll come see you after I've taken her statement," Louise said, disappearing into her office and shutting her door behind her.

22

It didn't take long. Hana Simrová was eighteen and from Ústí nad Labem in the Czech Republic, just like Pavlína. She had come to Denmark to visit Pavlína and was staying with her at Miloš Vituk's apartment. That morning, just as she and Pavlína had reached the front hallway of the building on their way outside, a car suddenly pulled up to the curb in front of them.

"When did this happen?" Louise asked, watching her.

Hana didn't know. Maybe ten o'clock or a little after.

"It all happened so quickly," the interpreter explained. "She thinks they must have been watching them. Two big, muscular guys jumped out of the back seat and grabbed hold of her. Pavlína screamed, but they hit her so hard she fell down. And then they drove away, leaving Pavlína behind. Hana doesn't remember anything else."

Louise asked about the plastic ties Hana's wrists were bound with.

"They twisted her arms behind her back before she had a chance to fight. They put them on in the car, and it hurt. But she was so scared that she just closed her eyes, because she didn't know what was going to happen or what they were going to do with her."

"What did they look like?"

Hana shook her head and sniffled a little as she apologized for not paying closer attention. She was just so scared.

"What about the guy driving the car? Was he big and muscular, too?" Louise asked, focusing intently on the Czech woman.

Hana shook her head and said that only the other two men were. "The third guy just sat behind the wheel."

Hamdi, Louise thought.

"She never really noticed him; she saw him only from behind, but his hair was short and straight, and he drove really fast the whole way."

The car had driven down to C. But even there the woman didn't understand what was happening until she was in the water and the car was speeding off, its tires screeching.

"Tell us what happened after they drove away," Louise asked. "How long did it take before the German man rescued you?"

Hana closed her eyes for a second, as if she were trying to run through the whole scenario for details, but then she faintly shrugged her skinny shoulders and shook her head.

"Not that long," the interpreter said. "She says she kept her mouth closed and focused on trying to stay afloat. But she has no idea how long it was before she heard someone jump into the water and felt herself being pulled in toward the wharf.

Louise accepted that Hana couldn't provide any more information. The young woman still seemed quite shaken and was pale and weak from exposure.

"How long will she be in Denmark?" Louise asked, looking back and forth between the interpreter and Hana as the question was translated. Again now, the woman shrugged, her skinny shoulders moving up to her ears.

"That hadn't been nailed down yet. They invited her in the first place because Pavlína was missing her girlfriends from home, and Hana was thrilled to get the invitation and the airplane ticket they sent. This trip was her first step away from a life on the streets, and once here she could see how well things had gone for her friend."

Louise watched Hana, wondering how much the woman knew about Pavlína's ordeal before she met Miloš.

"Ask her if she's here just on vacation," Louise instructed the interpreter.

Hana nodded and looked at her a little uncertainly.

Louise smiled apologetically at her. Just then the front desk called and announced she had a visitor. Louise got up to go meet them so Hana could get her clothes.

* * *

Miloš Vituk was alone as he approached with a white plastic bag in one hand. His mouth narrowed, and Louise could see that he was angry about the assault on Pavlína, even though he was mostly preoccupied with Hana right now.

"What happened?" he asked after greeting Louise. "Is Hana hurt?"

Louise shook her head and said she was mostly in shock. "Why do you think this happened?" Louise asked, looking at him for a long time.

It took him quite a while to respond.

"Could it be anyone other than the Albanians?" he finally said. "I don't really have any enemies in Denmark, but I'm guessing those two have it in for me because I'm taking such good care of Pavlína."

"Have they asked you for more money?" Louise wanted to know.

He shook his head, his shoulders drooping.

Louise refrained from pointing out that the Albanians probably thought he was a long-term source of money now, since they'd already pressured him into paying far more than their original demand. Now they were setting the limits, not Miloš.

"They don't have anything to do with Hana, but still they hurt her," he said. "Pavlína is really upset and scared."

Hana stayed in her seat when they came into Louise's office, but Hana smiled cautiously at him, pulling her bathrobe even tighter around her, as if she suddenly realized that all her wet clothes were in a bag.

Miloš walked over and kissed her head, where her hair was now mostly dry. He held out the dry clothes, and the interpreter offered to accompany her to the bathroom, where she could get dressed.

Louise studied Miloš when they were alone.

He had taken a seat and looked miles away. His thoughts were obviously elsewhere. "They're not going to leave us alone," he finally said, looking at her despondently. "This will continue as long as Pavlína and I stay in Copenhagen. But I won't stand for it. They have all the control, and they're violent with the girls. Pavlína was badly hurt today—I think they broke her nose. I'm going to take her to the doctor after we're through here."

When Hana returned, she was wearing a light dress that revealed her skinny body, which could have belonged to a child. There were no breasts or hips evident under the material.

Miloš offered her his sweater when he noticed her shivering again. His sweater was almost longer than her dress, a little bit of yellow peeking out from beneath the bottom of the sweater. Miloš took Hana's arm, and they walked close together as Louise followed them out.

* * *

"We'll put tails on the Albanians," Willumsen began once the whole group was present. He nodded at Toft and Stig, then moved his eyes onto Louise and her partner before he continued:

"You two keep an eye on Miloš Vituk and the girls. We don't want to risk anything else happening to them, and it doesn't seem like these guys are going to leave them alone until they're sure they can't get any more money out of Miloš. Mikkelsen's got his people on the street, and our interpreter Igli is monitoring the wiretap."

He nodded to the room behind him.

"And then I think it's time we drag those two Albanians in here for questioning. It's about fucking time we find out where they were when those two murders took place and confront them with the fact that they were seen at the wharf, right?" continued Willumsen, raising his voice as he spoke and looking at each of his detectives in turn.

"The car was there, but we don't know for sure who was in it," Toft corrected. He pointed out that no one had seen Arian or Hamdi, just the two gorillas who'd roughed the girls up so badly. "Until we have some evidence that they're somehow involved in prostitution, it's just going to hurt the investigation if we start talking to them now about their connection with those two killings."

Willumsen was about to say something, but Toft beat him to it.

"We can't bring them in for questioning until we have enough evidence," he said. "If we strike too soon, they'll close up shop. And right now, we don't have enough."

Willumsen grumbled a little as he contemplated the situation.

"Fine. But I want to see photo documentation of them receiving money from the girls. Pictures of conversations on the street and of the girls heading off with their johns, whether to cars or down into the booths at Club Intim. And they'd better be fucking close-ups."

* * *

The next day, they were standing in a doorway on Valdemarsgade, each with a to-go coffee and a sandwich. They'd been waiting a long time when Miloš finally came down the stairs in the early afternoon. He opened the door and stood with his back to the street, waiting. Pavlína emerged shortly thereafter. She was walking slowly, her head bent. Out on the sidewalk he took her under the arm and started walking so fast that she was having a hard time keeping up. Her eyes were trained to the ground, but Louise saw bruises on her face.

"I'll follow them. You stay here and keep an eye on Hana," Lars offered, crumpling up his sandwich wrapper, having taken his last bite.

Louise stepped out into the street a couple of times and looked up at the apartment's windows. One had been opened a crack before Miloš and Pavlína came down, but otherwise there were no signs of life to be seen behind the dark panes. She assumed Hana was still up there, and she figured they would be back soon so their young guest wouldn't be left on her own for too long following her experiences that morning.

Louise ate the rest of her sandwich leaning against the wall, and smiled at a woman who walked her bicycle up to the building with a baby in the seat on the back. Several people gave her curious looks as they came and went, but no one asked what she was doing. People were starting to come home from work, so there was a little more life on Valdemarsgade than earlier in the day, when it had been practically deserted.

Louise was lost in her own thoughts, still waiting, when she noticed a young couple who had stopped at the front door to Miloš's building. The man was carrying a couple of cloth shopping bags, and the woman was looking for something in her big shoulder bag, finally pulling out a key ring. They had just gotten the door open and the bags inside when a man in a dark, neat crew cut walked out. He was wearing a light gray suit. Louise watched them nod politely to each other before the man stopped abruptly on the sidewalk and looked at her. She thought he was going to come over, but then he started walking toward Vesterbrogade. Backing deeper into the doorway where she was standing, she typed a text message into her phone, wanting to find out where her partner was.

"Western Union," he texted back.

They must have gone to send some money abroad. People often did it that way: money transfers outside the banking system.

"On my way back," the next text said.

She strolled down the street a while until the man with the crew cut returned. He stopped at the front door to the building and rang the buzzer. As Louise waited, the man turned around; this time, she didn't have a chance to look away before their eyes met. Someone buzzed him in a second later.

Instead of returning to her doorway, Louise crossed the street and leaned against the front wall of Miloš's building to assure she wasn't visible from the windows above.

* * *

"It was nothing. They went and took care of their money matters and then went home again. No one contacted them along the way and they didn't seem particularly distracted."

Lars had come back shortly after Miloš and Pavlína.

"I'll just give Miloš a call and ask him how Hana's doing. Then I can also ask him if he's heard from the Albanians," Louise decided.

Miloš answered right away, as if he had been waiting for a call, and he sounded pleased that she was showing an interest. He assured her that Hana was doing better. He said she'd slept most of the day. And, no, no one had been in touch with him.

Louise could hear the TV and a quiet conversation in the background.

"I just ordered pizza," Miloš said, "and then we'll probably all go to bed early."

Louise said that sounded like a good idea, and he promised to call if anything happened.

"Well, have a good night," Louise said, jogging off to catch up with Lars, who was already walking down Valdemarsgade.

23

The funeral home was on Falkoner Allé, and when Camilla called to ask Louise if she would come, Louise assured her that it would be no problem.

"We spent the whole day yesterday keeping an eye on the building, and today Lars and I have been standing out here again since nine thirty this morning. Nothing has actually happened, so I'm sure he won't mind handling the surveillance on his own for a couple of hours," she said.

Camilla had found out earlier in the day that the police were ready to release Kaj Antonsen's body. No distant relatives had come forward yet. His ex-wife hadn't been in touch, either, and since she had declined to have any further involvement, Camilla was given permission to handle the practical details. She put in an obituary for tomorrow's paper saying the funeral would be at Stenhøj Church on Saturday.

"No, I don't have the deceased's birth certificate or baptismal records," she repeated patiently to the funeral director after she'd handed him the paperwork she'd gotten when the police released the body to her. "No, I don't have his spouse's birth certificate or their marriage certificate. But they've been divorced for years now."

Even though she'd already told him everything over the phone, the funeral director had wanted to run through the standard questions with her again in person.

Camilla gave Louise a pleading look. Camilla's smile was a little stiff, but she was trying to stay calm, and she just nodded briefly when the funeral director decided they would just have to do without the separation papers.

But when the funeral director repeated his question about a birth certificate, Camilla had finally had enough.

"Look, I assume you're aware that the deceased was the victim of a spectacular and extremely violent murder. The police are hard at work right now trying to locate his murderer, which is why they have not yet had the opportunity to provide me with all of his personal papers. But, of course, we could ask the police to switch around their priorities a little so they have time to get the paperwork in place before we plan the rest," Camilla said angelically.

Louise stayed back, pretending to study a framed poster listing most of the routine questions the funeral director would likely ask.

"And your relationship to the deceased?" the funeral director asked, looking up from his form. He had obviously decided to ignore Camilla's sarcastic outburst. "Ah, yes. You're the reporter who wrote the story in *Morgenavisen*, right?"

Camilla made do with a nod.

"Good," the funeral director finally said. "So, I'm going to assume you don't have a burial permit or a deed to a burial plot?"

"Correct," Camilla said tersely. "I don't think he was prepared to have someone slit his neck just then."

Louise turned and gave her a look.

The man behind the desk let her remark slide once again and instead walked over to the wall where the urns were displayed. "Have you had a chance to think about which urn you're interested in?"

Camilla took a step back to look at the selection. "It doesn't need to be anything special," she said. "A standard one, if that's a thing."

The funeral director raised his eyebrow for a second and looked at Camilla. "That's not 'a thing.' But you can certainly get one without too many frills." He pointed up at a black vessel with a flat lid. The tag underneath said, "Simple." Next to that there was a "Simple Exclusive," and then the rest of them became progressively more ornate.

Camilla pointed to the no-frills urn and asked if everything could be arranged in time for the funeral on Saturday.

"We have the pastor scheduled for one p.m.," she said.

The funeral director nodded; he was obviously interested in wrapping up his business with Camilla Lind as quickly and efficiently as possible.

24

The afternoon sun shone from a spring sky practically devoid of clouds. They were lucky that Belis Bar had a free table out on the square in front of Frederiksberg Town Hall.

Louise ordered two beers in the hopes they'd help to shake off the funereal mood a little. Taking her first sip, she realized she didn't feel the least bit guilty about letting her partner hold the fort alone down on Valdemarsgade. At the morning briefing, Willumsen had made it clear he didn't think there was any reason to keep an eye on Miloš Vituk and the Czech girls anymore, but Suhr hadn't agreed. So they had decided to continue the surveillance at least for the rest of the day.

The only thing they'd noted so far was that Pavlína had brought a guest home with her—a young woman about the same age who had with her a bouquet of flowers that Louise figured were for Hana.

Louise watched Camilla sip at the thick foam at the top of her beer. She was worried about her friend, but not as much as she had been the first couple of days after the murder.

Camilla's chat with the crisis psychologist had apparently allowed her to acknowledge that some things were out of her control, even if she might have helped trigger them. Camilla was still weighed down in self-recrimination and guilt, but right now at least she was planning on using her leave of absence to reevaluate her goals in life and the steps she needed to achieve them.

"Right now, I don't have the slightest desire to go back to the paper," Camilla admitted when Louise asked what she was thinking.

"What do you want to do then?" Louise asked, holding her beer in her hands and tilting her head back, enjoying the sunlight.

"I don't know," Camilla said after a pause. "I might start writing books."

Louise smiled. What journalist wouldn't want to do that?

"Well, I recommend you write a murder mystery and become world-famous—then you'll be rolling in money," she said with her eyes closed, the warmth spreading from her face to the rest of her body. "Plus, it'll get you away from *Morgenavisen*."

She heard Camilla scoot her chair slightly, but Camilla didn't say anything for quite a while.

"Maybe. But first I want to have a baby."

This news was so abrupt that Louise opened her eyes and gaped at her friend, who was watching a young woman pushing a stroller down the sidewalk in front of them.

Louise leaned forward over the table and set down her beer.

"You have a child," she reminded Camilla, who was watching the stroller with a serious expression, which confused Louise.

"I've always dreamed of having a whole bunch of kids, actually. And ever since I had Markus, I've known that I wanted one or two more, but nothing ever came of it. So, I've decided to do something about that dream so I won't have to look back and regret not even having tried."

"For Christ's sake, Camilla. You have plenty of time—you're only thirty-eight! You make it sound like you're closer to fifty. But you're also going to have to find the guy you want to have these kids with. Children are still something people dream about having together, usually."

Louise hadn't intended to sound quite so nagging, but Camilla picked up on it right away. "Why do you always get so uptight whenever kids come up?" she asked, irritated. "You're so down on kids."

"Oh, come on. That's ridiculous. But you already have Markus, after all, and he's the best. Besides, I guess I think people sound spoiled when they say their 'whole life' is a failure just because they haven't had the number of children they wanted, or something."

Camilla took a swig of beer and looked at Louise, who vaguely suspected the abandoned baby from the church had put this notion in her friend's head.

"I don't understand how you can be so negative when you don't even know what you're missing," Camilla said. "It's not like you haven't had a chance to have kids, either. If it'd been up to Peter, you'd have five by now. I think you're running the risk, yourself, of waking up one day and realizing it's too late."

Louise felt the emotion before it showed in her eyes. She went completely cold inside.

Here she'd been thinking they would spend a couple of pleasant hours together, Camilla would be able to get things off her chest, and maybe that would help her relax about all her inner turmoil. Instead the conversation had wound up here—where there was no comfortable way out.

She sat up straight and tried to sound more upbeat, holding in the cutting remarks that were on the tip of her tongue.

"I came to terms a long time ago with the fact that I don't think having kids is a right," she said. "Some people have kids, some don't. It's not something you can expect. Or an indicator of your life's success. You know I don't go around wishing my life were different than it is, and it's just turned out that my life doesn't include kids. But that doesn't make it a bad life."

Louise leaned back, realizing her voice was sounding defensive in spite of her best efforts.

"I don't mean to annoy you," Camilla said, trying to calm Louise down. "But it's different for me. I'm not sure I have time to wait for the right person to come along, so I'm considering artificial insemination."

Louise was speechless but then she shook her head. "As long as you don't make the government pay for it, well, good luck. I'll take care of Markus when you're breastfeeding."

Louise got up to pay. She was disappointed that the mood had been ruined. What bugged her the most, though, was that children had become a criterion for a successful life; who cared whether they were born out of love as long as you had them? If that were it, she'd rather be free. She remembered an old case where she had visited a fortune-teller, who in all seriousness told her that a child's soul chose the mother it wanted before it was born. Personally, Louise was just fine with the fact that no child's soul had picked her.

* * *

Camilla and Louise walked across the square to Falkoner Allé in silence.

"I can tell you've already made up your mind," Louise said.

Camilla nodded. "You know how I feel about people who talk up a storm about all the things they want but never step up and make it reality. If I'm going to criticize other people for all their empty talk, well then, I'd better fucking step up and do something about my own life. Otherwise I ought to just shut up," she said.

Louise smiled. "Well, I know you well enough to be fairly sure this shutting-up phase won't last long." She gave Camilla a quick good-bye kiss on the cheek and hurried across the street when the light turned green.

On the other side, she stopped and watched as Camilla's back disappeared toward Falkoner Center.

25

This is going to take fucking months," Willumsen said, irritably, brushing cake crumbs off the papers on the table in front of him. The team was meeting around the conference table Friday afternoon before heading home for the weekend, and Willumsen was glaring at Stig, who had just said they still didn't have enough on the Albanians to take action.

"Obviously, we can haul them in for questioning and check their alibis, but that would make it pretty obvious that we've been watching them and we still don't have enough to hold them on," Stig continued. "We're going to have to wait until we have more. We just haven't gotten much out of the last couple of days of surveillance. We don't have any witnesses to the two murders, and after what happened to Kaj Antonsen, we shouldn't expect people to suddenly feel like talking to us, either. Instead, let's keep watching and gathering info. It's really not enough that they drive a car that's identical to the one that was seen on Skelbækgade the same evening that prostitute's throat was slit, or at the harbor, for that matter. And we have nothing at all to tie the Albanians to the location where Antonsen was killed."

"Yeah, which is exactly why we need to find out where they were when all that happened," Willumsen growled loudly, staring at Stig until he eventually looked away. "You've been following them. What have we gotten out of that?"

Toft set a stack of pictures on the table. They were all taken in the last couple of days and showed the Eastern European women on and around Istedgade. There were pictures of the prostitutes standing on the sidewalk with different men, walking into Club Intim with their johns, and leaning over to talk into rolled-down car windows.

"Things really pick up around closing time," commented Stig, who had accompanied the photographer. "And then there's another rush after dinner and kind of steady traffic until a good while past midnight, depending on the weather."

"Did you see any Roma women, or girls?" Toft asked, pulling a menthol cartridge for his plastic cigarette out of the shirt pocket under his sweater. "Some of the girls on the street aren't much more than thirteen or fourteen, and I've heard their families are the ones who send them to Denmark in the first place."

Louise realized Toft's own granddaughter, Ida, was just that age.

"The group on the streets right now apparently arrived a few months ago. They have to earn money for the grand houses their fathers are building. According to one of the girls down at the Nest, the girls were sent to Italy first but couldn't earn enough there, so they were sent up here, and now they're hanging out down at Halmtorvet in front of the convention center."

Louise had also recalled the Roma girls as she absentmindedly reached for the plastic mug in front of her. If someone didn't know any better, they'd have no idea the girls were actually for sale. They looked like any other teenagers in their loose, white, low-waisted pants and tight tops. Grinning and goofing around, they stood in a little cluster waiting for the next customer to stop and flash his lights. One of them had been wearing a headband and was nothing more than a child.

Louise tried to focus and put the Roma girls out of her mind.

"What do we know about the girls you saw the Albanians collecting money from?" Willumsen asked.

Toft, who was visibly moved by the sad fates of these girls, said they were being put up in a number of cheap hotels.

"They can get a room for 5,000 kroner a month, and then of course there's no telling how many people they cram into one room."

"We need to get these girls to talk," Willumsen decided, poking a couple of the pictures with his finger.

Mikkelsen was still for a moment before he finally nodded. "We could certainly arrest them," he began. "But prostitution isn't illegal per se, so we can really nab them only for working without a valid work permit and smack a 500-kroner fine on them. And in cases like this you need to have all your evidence spic and span, otherwise the courts won't have it. You can be sure if we ask the women if they were being forced to prostitute themselves that they will most definitely say no—not because they don't want us to help them, but because they dare not say otherwise. They don't get a simple scolding if they don't do what their pimps say, after all; the pimps break them down psychologically with threats of retaliation against their families back home. They'll kill their parents, burn down their houses, rape and sell their sisters. That kind of thing creates such a deep-seated fear that the girls choose to keep quiet and just obey the pimps, no matter what. And if we go to the pimps, they'll just claim they don't know a thing about extortion or human trafficking. They'll say the women are turning tricks because they want to. So I agree we need a little more," he finally concluded with an eye on the throbbing blood vessel on Willumsen's temple.

"We could also drag things out so long that they have time to really ramp up their business," Willumsen said testily. "Then they'll have a chance to abuse even more of their girls because no one is intervening."

Toft pulled the plastic cigarette out of his mouth and rolled it back and forth between his fingers but stayed out of Willumsen's vortex. Experience had taught him that he would do best by dropping the subject now and waiting to bring it up again later when Willumsen's blood vessels weren't throbbing quite so obviously.

"When we investigate human-trafficking and prostitution cases like this, the outcome always depends on how patient we can be," Mikkelsen said, leaning forward, ignoring Willumsen's tone. "I think we'd be wise to spend some time developing an overview and tying all the pieces of the case together before making our move."

Mikkelsen spoke calmly and rationally, and Louise watched Willumsen's blood vessels continue throbbing. Willumsen's active vocabulary really lacked words like *patience* or *overview*. And yet, he seemed like he was buying it this time. At any rate, his face grew less gruff; he nodded a couple of times, and for the time being at least he stopped interrupting with comments. Instead, he changed the topic by pulling a couple of photos out of the stack and sliding them out into the middle of the table.

"Overview," he repeated, dwelling on the feel of the word in his mouth, as he pointed to one of the pictures. "That's what we'll do then. But take a look at this, will you, and tell me what our friends are up to."

The pictures showed a small group of men, standing around a bench on Strøget, the famous pedestrian shopping street in the heart of Copenhagen. They were concentrating on something, but it was hard to see what. Arian was standing behind them. There were also pictures of money changing hands. Hamdi was in only a couple of the photos.

"The matchstick game," Stig said, and then Mikkelsen explained:

"It's a 'dexterity game' fairly common among Albanians—and it's not for small potatoes. They might make up to 4 or 5,000 kroner a day."

Willumsen nodded as Mikkelsen explained the police went after these games regularly.

"They are damn good with their hands. You have to guess which box the matchstick is under. Usually what happens is that the group gathers in a little crowd. One of them runs the game, a couple of them keep an eye out for police, and then there's one or two who pretend they're lucky winners. Then when some random person passing by stops to try his or her luck, the fraud begins. It's all sleight of hand and there's basically no chance of winning." Mikkelsen added that the downtown precinct regularly charged people with disturbing the peace or gathering without a permit. After a couple of those, they were usually banned from hanging out on Strøget at all. "But I don't know how much that impedes them, really, and it's certainly possible that they also use the distraction of the game to pick some pockets."

"I suppose Arian and Hamdi organize it and then give the guys who run the games a little cut for doing the work," Louise guessed, pointing out that both of the Albanians were welfare recipients. "Arian came to Denmark in 1997 when he was granted asylum and then a residence permit. He's thirty-one and lives alone in his apartment out in Valby. It's subsidized public housing. In addition to that, he receives 1,800 kroner a month in welfare benefits."

"Well, he must be doing quite well then since he can afford to buy an Audi A4!" Stig exclaimed with poorly concealed jealousy.

"Exactly," Louise said, noting that a few con games couldn't be financing his lifestyle. "Hamdi arrived in Denmark the following year. He's twenty-six and also has a permanent residence permit. He lives in a fairly large one-bedroom apartment on Vesterbrogade and gets the same benefit check each month."

Willumsen nodded, with his hands folded under his chin contemplatively. The room suddenly turned quiet, as everyone in the room pictured the possible scenarios and tried to figure out what their next move should be.

"Is anyone out on Valdemarsgade watching Miloš and

the girls right now?" Willumsen finally asked, breaking the silence.

Lars sat up a little straighter.

"The girls went out with a female friend in the late afternoon," he reported. "The friend picked them up at Miloš's apartment. He didn't leave the apartment until later in the evening when he met a male friend at a bar on Victoriagade."

"But he was already back home an hour after that, and I talked to him on the phone for a bit," said Louise, who had been watching the building from the doorway across the street. "It sounds like the girls have calmed back down again, and there haven't been any signs of commotion since the episode with Hana. No one has contacted them, and they said they didn't feel watched. Now their plan is for Hana to move to the friend's place tomorrow—the friend who came to visit. She apparently has a guest room. I understood from Miloš that the apartment was feeling a little too crowded, given Hana's long-term stay."

"How long?" Willumsen asked.

"Well, he says she's going to stay for the full three months she's allowed to stay in Denmark on her tourist visa."

Willumsen nodded. "All right. Let's call off the stakeout on Valdemarsgade," he decided, his eyes on Louise and Lars. "Make sure you give Miloš, Pavlína, and Hana your cell numbers so all three of them can get in touch with you if any problems should arise. And let's focus our efforts on the Albanians. We still need a list of the women working for them, and you're going to need to get photo documentation of money changing hands. If there's a demonstrable pattern, we'll be able to use that in court. Do we have anything else from Central Station?"

Mikkelsen nodded and said that Arian had shown up at the same location that morning and had accepted payments from the same girls as on Tuesday.

"We have pictures, but unfortunately they made me. Arian was really paying attention today, as if he knew he was being watched. Hamdi sat down on the bench so that he could see everyone who was anywhere nearby when the money changed hands. I expect they've already set a new location to accept payments in the future."

"Right. Get to work," Willumsen urged. "It's up to you guys to make sure we have enough to bring them in so we can find out if they have alibis for the evening of the Skelbækgade murder and the Kaj Antonsen murder Friday night. We'll find out next week if CSI got any useful DNA from the murder locations. Meanwhile, keep focusing on collecting evidence on the two Albanians."

Louise looked over at Stig to see if he had noticed that the boss had backed down and agreed to wait. Their eyes met and she smiled at him. They would never say it aloud, but it was kind of amazing to know that even Willumsen could be moved if you kept at it long enough.

26

There were no cars outside the church when Camilla arrived Saturday morning. Louise was supposed to meet her, and she knew that the sexton would arrive at any moment, as well. She opened the back hatch of her car where she had the flowers for Kaj Antonsen's funeral service, and the wreath was in the front seat. When the woman at the flower shop had asked her if she wanted to order a sash and what it should read, Camilla drew a blank at first until she settled on a basic "Rest in Peace," which was printed in gold. At the time she thought that would be better than "Forever in Our Hearts" or any of the other standard phrases, but walking out of the flower shop she had had second thoughts and regretted not just leaving the sash blank.

Now all the self-recrimination came rushing back. If only she hadn't sat down on that damn bench with a bag of beer and had for once just left a good story alone. Looking at the flowers in her car, she was overcome by tears, even though she hadn't thought she had any left.

Camilla sniffled and checked her watch, noting that there were still ten minutes until her appointment with the sexton, so she pulled the bucket of small bouquets for the front pew out of the trunk, and after she set it on the ground, she carefully picked up the large bouquet for the altar. With the bouquet under her arm and the bucket of flowers in her hand, she started walking up to the church, the gravel of the drive crunching below her high heels.

The sun was shining down on the white church with its red-tiled roof, and fluffy banks of white clouds slid lazily across the blue sky, but the cheerful spring weather didn't do anything to raise her spirits. She could sense the deep abyss just below the surface that had been threatening to swallow her up for the last week. Camilla knew that the only things holding it at bay right now were the careful makeup she'd applied that morning and the dark suit, which was very tight. They gave her the sense that she could hold herself together no matter what happened.

She set the bucket down and grabbed the door's iron handle. The pastor had prepared her, warning her that she would need to push with her shoulder if she had trouble pressing the handle down. But the door opened without any trouble, and she walked over to the bench just inside the entrance to set down the altar bouquet. It wasn't until she turned around to go back and get the bucket that she stumbled over something.

It felt solid and yet soft under the sole of her shoe. She jumped back reflexively and felt her pulse speed up, her heart pounding.

The towel was dark blue, exactly like before, but that

wasn't why she stood frozen, her eyes fixed on the bundle on the stone floor.

She was staring because it was totally silent. No movement, no sound. She still knew what was in the towel, but she couldn't make herself bend down and check, and it wasn't until it flickered through her mind as she ran for the pastor's kitchen door that it hit her that it could also be a dead animal. Maybe a cat, she thought, bounding up the five steps to the door and furiously banging the knocker hoping the pastor was home.

A cat, she thought again, hitting even harder as she yelled for Henrik.

And then everything started spinning as she admitted to herself that it wasn't a cat or some other animal, and that what was wrapped in that towel was no longer alive. She felt something fragile inside herself shatter as images of babies, dead and alive, flitted through her head along with Kaj, lying there alone in that courtyard in all his brutalized wretchedness. Everything got all mixed up, ultimately exploding in her mind like a sea of light.

"Help! Help me!" she sobbed, failing to support herself on the broad door, sliding down to the stoop, her façade cracking completely as the abyss engulfed her.

She didn't hear the footsteps running across the gravel courtyard, and didn't see the person who leaned over her and put a hand on her shoulder. Nor did she register the taste of blood that spread through her mouth from the wound in her cheek, from her own teeth.

Nothing reached her where she was.

In a swirling roar, she was pulled down into a black darkness that shut out the lights and sounds of reality.

27

Louise propped her bike up against the outside wall of the church. Swinging her bag over her shoulder, she unbuckled her helmet and strode toward Camilla's silver-gray VW Polo, its hatchback door wide open and the driver's-side door ajar. She figured Camilla must be bringing things in, and she decided to help out by carrying something when she walked over to the church.

The back was empty, so she shut the door and checked the backseat before carefully removing the wreath from the passenger-side door and pushing the driver-side door shut with her elbow.

The flag wasn't at half-mast yet, but there was still a little over an hour until the funeral. Louise knew that Mikkelsen was planning to come. He still seemed genuinely shaken up as though he'd lost a family member, Louise thought, but he hadn't chastised Camilla for her article even once.

To the contrary, he said that he ought to have talked to Kaj right away, that maybe he could have prevented the tragedy that way. And he had reminded Willumsen again that you couldn't blame people who weren't familiar with the world of prostitution if they broke some of the unwritten rules that people lived by in this part of town.

The scent of flowers filled Louise's nose as she made her way across the gravel courtyard. Louise saw the open door to the church and when she spotted the bucket filled with small bouquets outside, she assumed Camilla was already hard at work.

It took a second before she reacted to the voice and looked over toward the pastor's residence, where a heavy silhouette was squatting down over something that was lying on the stoop in front of the pastor's kitchen door. Louise recognized the blond hair right away and dropped the wreath and started running.

The man stood up and seemed a little confused as he pointed down at Camilla and explained, practically tripping over his words, that his name was Otto Birch and he was the sexton.

"She was lying here like this when we arrived a couple of minutes ago," he said. "She's crying and mumbling something about 'dead,' but she won't really respond," he said.

"Did something happen to her?" Louise thought of the brutality involved in Kaj Antonsen's death. "Is she bleeding? Does it look like someone hit her?"

Louise leaned over her friend and brushed her hair out of her face, which was frozen in an expression of stubborn denial, like you might see in a toddler throwing a tantrum.

Camilla's sobs were throaty and sounded more like a constant moan interrupted by muddled speech, from which

Louise could only pick out a few words like "dead," "funeral," "baby," and "church."

Louise took hold of her friend and tried to get her to sit up. She studied Camilla's face and ran a hand through her blond hair to check and see if there were any signs of physical trauma.

"She's in shock," Otto said, trying to light a cigar.

The pastor was walking over from the parking lot, and when he spotted them he sped up. Jonas was just behind him, but he hadn't noticed the commotion yet, because his eyes were glued to the Game Boy he was holding in his hands.

"What happened?" Henrik Holm yelled, breaking into a run.

"Baby, church, dead..." The words were unclear and running in a continuous loop.

Henrik gave Louise a puzzled look. Louise had managed to get Camilla up into a sitting position, her back leaning against the kitchen door.

Even though she didn't think it would matter, she still stepped out of range of Camilla's hearing before admitting that she'd been afraid of a mental breakdown ever since Kaj Antonsen's murder.

"But maybe it's not so strange that it didn't happen until now," Louise said, explaining that she'd tried to talk Camilla out of assuming responsibility for the funeral several times. Then Louise went back and sat down on the steps with an arm around her friend.

"The baby is dead," Camilla mumbled into her shoulder.

Now Louise felt her own tears coming. She knew there wasn't much she could do to alleviate her friend's incapacitating pain. She could try only to comfort her as best she could.

"What is she saying?" Henrik asked, moving in a little closer. "It's just a bunch of unconnected words."

Louise shook her head a little, and then looked over to Jonas and noticed how he lit up when he spotted her. But an instant later he stiffened when he spotted Camilla on the steps.

She turned back to Camilla, thinking that she was going to have to call Jakobsen, even though the crisis psychologist had the weekend off.

"Let me hear what she's saying," Henrik urged. He quickly glanced at the church and asked if the sexton had been over and finished getting things ready.

Otto shook his head and explained that he'd spotted Camilla before he'd ever made it over to the church.

Henrik got up abruptly and started running toward the church door. When the shout came, Louise was already on her legs.

The shape and size matched a tiny newborn, so Louise was prepared when she carefully loosened the towel after having pulled the bundle farther out onto the floor in the triangle of light the sun was making through the door opening.

The infant was dead, just as she had guessed. It was a little boy, she confirmed, as she slowly let her eyes move down over his body covered with dried blood and vernix caseosa, which had a faint greenish tinge.

Louise took a deep breath and looked up at Pastor Holm, who was watching from the open door. The stone floor of the church was cold and there was a draft along the floor. The little baby's eyes were closed, his face looked like a dried mask that had never had a chance to be shaped by movement and expressions. Neither his joints nor his muscles were stiff anymore, the way they would be right after death, and he had a rancid smell, not the pleasant baby smell you associated with a newborn. The greenish tinge could come from an amniotic fluid infection, Louise thought, clearing her throat before she said anything.

"He might have died right after the birth," she guessed and straightened up partway. Henrik had a deep furrow in his brow. Then he went and sat down on the bench next to Camilla's altar bouquet. At Louise's request, he dialed 114 and was connected directly to the local police station that served the neighborhood.

"Ask for the officer who was here when you found the little girl," Louise said, standing up. She heard Henrik ask for Officer Rasmus Hem, and heard him briefly explaining that they had found the body of an infant wrapped up in the church in the same location where they had found Baby Girl.

* * *

"I don't understand what's happening," he said, shaking his head as he spoke to the officer. He explained that Camilla Lind had apparently found the baby when she walked into the church bringing flowers for today's funeral; he and Jonas had been in downtown Frederiksberg doing some shopping.

"We left a little after ten, but I didn't go into the church before we left, and we went out the other way, so I didn't notice anything."

Louise looked at her watch. It was a little past twelve. She nodded as Henrik stuck his cell phone back in his pocket and said the police would be right there.

"Then we ought to go out and keep the door locked until they arrive," she said, taking one last glance at the bundle in the blue towel.

"That's just completely absurd to have two such similar events one right after the other," he said, heading for the door. "Officer Hem thought it was related to all the media coverage following the discovery of the abandoned baby here, that maybe that was the reason someone decided to copy that."

"That is also quite possible," Louise admitted. "Copycats aren't all that uncommon. My immediate guess is that the child has been dead for twenty-four hours and that it might have been stillborn to begin with. It doesn't look like the birth took place in a hospital. If it had he would have been cleaned up and his umbilical cord clamped."

"No, it looks more like a birth that happened without any professional assistance," the priest agreed, pulling the door to the church closed. Then he nodded a couple of times as if he were trying to convince himself of something.

* * *

When Louise emerged from the church, Camilla was still sitting on the steps with her eyes closed and her back against the kitchen door. Jonas was sitting cross-legged on the gravel in the courtyard with his Game Boy on the ground next to him.

Henrik walked over and helped him up, then picked up his Game Boy and they started slowly moving toward the residence.

"We'll go in the other way," he said. Then he stopped

and turned to the sexton, who was sitting on the stairs as if he weren't really sure what he should do.

"There's a baby in the church," the pastor said to Otto. "I called the police. We're going to keep the door closed until they arrive."

"What about the funeral?" Otto asked, standing up with difficulty. "It will have to be postponed."

A confused expression passed over the elderly sexton's face as his schedule for the whole day was instantly canceled, but then he nodded and glanced up at the church clock, which now said a quarter past twelve.

Louise watched Jonas as he disappeared with his father. Poor little guy, she thought, wondering if he shouldn't be offered a chance to talk to Jakobsen, too. That was twice in fourteen days that something so devastating had happened right outside his front door. Then Louise walked over to Camilla and leaned down over her.

"You're going to have to get up. The police will be here soon, and they're definitely going to want to talk to you."

Her friend was just staring into space. Then her eyelids shuddered a little, and she turned to look at Louise.

"I don't know if I'm up to that," she said so softly that Louise had to lean forward to hear. "It feels like somebody drained out everything that's usually inside me. Suddenly I'm the figure with the scythe who appears in people's backseats right before a traffic accident happens."

Camilla was as pale as a corpse, and her words emerged through lips that hardly moved, as if her face had grown stiff along with the rest of her body.

A dove had hopped up to the second step of the stairs and had its back to them, poking at something on the step. Louise watched it before taking a deep breath and psyching herself up to tell Camilla what they'd found in the church.

"You were right. The baby was dead. But it was probably a stillbirth, so it wouldn't have made any difference if you had gotten there sooner."

Louise was silent for a bit before finally taking her eyes off the dove and then adding, "If that's even the kind of thing you're thinking about?"

The dove flew away when Louise stood up. She held out a hand to Camilla and pulled her up.

There were cups out on the table and the kettle was on. It was warm in the kitchen, a little stuffy. The sun had been shining in the big windows over the long kitchen table.

Louise settled Camilla on the bench and took a seat while Henrik remained standing, a little hesitant.

"I have an op-ed column I need to finish writing, but I don't suppose there's any point starting on that before the police have been here," he said, setting milk and sugar out on the table.

His words hung in the air as silence took over the room, because no one was really sure how to respond.

Louise finished making the coffee and poured some into Camilla's cup before filling her own. She was familiar with Henrik Holm's columns in the paper. He was one of the people the media turned to when they needed a religious point of view—a "media priest," as he was sarcastically called by some of the slightly harsh satirists. For her part, Louise had always found him to be a good, plain-talking writer, and she enjoyed reading his weekly column.

"Why here?" Camilla asked, finally breaking the wordless vacuum.

"Basically, it just makes sense," Henrik said, explaining

that in Germany there were still churches that had little trapdoors to leave newborns in. "It's really not such a ludicrous idea to choose a church if you're in that situation." He added that he would much rather the unhappy mothers choose his church than toss the baby into a river.

"But who decides to give birth outside the system, without a doctor or a midwife or anything?" Camilla wondered out loud to herself.

They were interrupted by the sharp ring of the doorbell, and the pastor stood up to let the police in and accompany them over to the church.

Exactly. Who does decide to give birth completely alone? Louise thought. She hadn't heard anyone coming up the kitchen steps, so she jumped a little when there was a hard knock on the door.

It was the sexton, who stuck his gray-haired head in while the rest of him stayed out on the stoop.

"Someone is here for the funeral and insists on knowing why it's been postponed," he announced. "He says he's from the police, but he doesn't have his badge."

Louise got up and went out to fill Mikkelsen in on what had happened. Two police cars had just pulled up in the courtyard next to the church, almost as if they felt at home there. Louise heard one officer yell to another that the techs would be there within five minutes.

Mikkelsen was wearing dark trousers and a dark suit jacket, which was a little tight around the gut. She could tell he wasn't comfortable, not in the clothes and not with the situation, and his eyebrows shot up like two seagull wings when he spotted her.

"Oh, right, your friend," he said when Louise reached him.

Louise nodded and explained that the funeral had been canceled, because Camilla had found a dead baby when she arrived to decorate the church. Every time she finished a sentence, he nodded as if she were filing a report. Something about his posture told Louise that it had been a struggle for him just to show up. A lot of people had trouble with funerals, but in his case, it probably had more to do with how involved he was with the Istedgade neighborhood beat. It was rare for a death to happen in such a brutal fashion as the former chef's, and Mikkelsen wasn't hiding the fact that he feared this was something they were going to be seeing more of. No other funeral guests had arrived, not that Louise had been expecting any.

They stepped back a little out of the way as the crime scene investigators arrived and pulled their car in. Louise nodded at Frandsen, as he and his people started taking out their equipment.

Mikkelsen, who was from the downtown precinct and so wouldn't be involved in this particular investigation, looked at his watch.

"I suppose I might as well head home and have a little breakfast," he said. Louise walked him out to the parking lot, but stopped when Rasmus Hem from the Bellahøj precinct walked over and introduced himself before asking to see Camilla.

"She's in the kitchen," Louise replied, and then said goodbye to Mikkelsen so she could accompany Rasmus in.

* * *

Camilla was still sitting right where Louise had left her, and she just nodded when Rasmus greeted her.

"So you're the one who found him," Rasmus stated, and Camilla nodded again. When he didn't ask anything else and just sat down across from her, she started to explain on her own.

"I went into the church with some flowers for the funeral, and when I was on my way out again, I stumbled," she said in a voice that sounded mechanical.

"Did you see what had caused you to fall?" Officer Hem wanted to know. Then he asked if she had done anything else just inside the entrance of the church there besides set down the flowers.

Camilla shook her head and said no to both.

"I'm probably the only one who touched anything," Louise interjected, showing how she had moved the bundle before taking hold of the corners to unwrap the towel. "Besides Camilla, the only people who have been in the church since the baby was found were the pastor and myself."

Behind her, Louise heard Henrik coming down the stairs from the second floor. He'd brought Jonas a soda and a bowl of popcorn.

"He's reading *Harry Potter*," Henrik said when Louise asked how he was doing. "But it would be nice if we could avoid any more dramatic events," he said in a forced, upbeat tone. "People are going to end up being afraid to go to church for fear of finding an abandoned baby on the floor."

Officer Hem smiled at him and agreed that things couldn't continue like this.

"Would it be all right if I just sat off on the side and did a little work on my computer?" Henrik said, asking Officer Hem for permission. "I have a piece I need to finish writing for tomorrow, and I haven't quite decided yet how I'm going to approach it."

Hem nodded and said that would be fine. He was just going to write down what Camilla had told him.

It didn't look like anyone other than Louise had noticed that Jonas had come downstairs while they were talking. He was standing over next to his father, looking at the policeman, whom he obviously recognized from the last time.

Henrik absentmindedly stroked his son's hair before going into the living room, but he shook his head when Jonas whispered something to him. It was obvious that he was already thinking about how to word the introduction to his op-ed column.

Jonas stood there for a second, hesitantly, as if he couldn't quite decide if he should go back up to his room as his father had told him.

That made Louise stand up and go put her arm around him. They walked up to his room together.

Camilla watched them as they disappeared up the stairs. She wished she could go with them and avoid having to relive what happened in the church. Instead she dutifully responded to the questions, which were being asked in chronological order. When had she arrived at the church? Had she seen anyone as she walked across the courtyard? Was the door shut all the way when she entered the church?

Camilla thought about the last time they had been sitting in the pastor's kitchen and how the boys had said the door had been open.

"It was shut all the way," she assured the officer, pushing her cup of now-cold coffee away a little and putting her elbows on the table to rest her head in her hands.

After they'd run through the brief explanation, Camilla felt as though everyone was staring at her, and she noticed she was breathing heavily. Finally, he added one last thing.

"Could we agree that you'll hold off on writing anything about this until tomorrow?" he began. "I'd really like to have a chance to find out what's going on before we go to the press with this."

Camilla made a little face, which silenced him. "You don't need to worry about that." She let her hands drop down onto the table and shook her head slightly. "I'm not working right now."

Officer Hem raised one eyebrow.

"I'm on a leave of absence," Camilla explained briefly, adding wanly that he didn't need to worry that she would inform her editor, either.

"I would actually prefer not to have any contact with the paper at all while I'm on leave." She looked down at the table. "But of course, I can't guarantee that they won't find out about this on their own," she added after a brief pause. "*Morgenavisen* does have quite a track record of doing stuff like that."

Officer Hem nodded, and Camilla got the sense that he wanted to say something else, but he was interrupted by Louise coming back down the stairs.

* * *

Louise walked into the living room where Henrik was bent over his computer. She waited for a moment before she interrupted his writing.

"What would you say to Jonas coming with Camilla and me when we leave?" she asked. "I think it might be nice for him to get out of here for a little bit, while the crime-scene investigators are here working in the church. Then you can also finish writing your piece."

He ran his hand through his hair, and Louise could see that he found the offer tempting, but at the same time he didn't want to be any trouble.

"He's very welcome," Louise reassured him. "And he can stay until tomorrow, when Markus will be home from his dad's place."

"I really want to go," they heard Jonas say from the stairs, and Louise could see that that settled the matter.

"But remember your toothbrush," the pastor called and smiled at his son as he turned and ran back upstairs to pack.

"Thank you," he said. "If you don't have any family, you don't get many chances when a situation suddenly comes up and you need a little break." He looked at his computer screen. "Then I could use my evening cleaning up my sermon for tomorrow. Today certainly turned out a little different than I'd planned." He looked at his watch, as if he had been reminded yet again that a good portion of the afternoon was already gone.

"If they're even going to let me use the church tomorrow, that is," he added, giving Louise a questioning look. "There's a baptism tomorrow."

"We'll just have to see what Frandsen says, but I would imagine the investigators can get enough done today that they'll be gone before tomorrow."

"Although if the parents for the baptism hear that it happened again, they may decide not to come." He ran his hand through his thick blond hair again.

"Well, but that doesn't have anything to do with the church or you," Louise said, trying to allay his concerns.

The pastor nodded and got up to give his son a hug before he left.

Officer Hem had gone, and it looked like Camilla had

pulled herself together enough that she was ready to get going.

Louise told her they would be having an extra overnight guest and bent down to pick up her friend's bag, which had slid down onto the floor.

"Did you remember your cell phone?" Henrik asked Jonas, after one more hug good-bye.

"Yes, and the charger," Jonas said, sounding impatient to get going.

Camilla was pale as she waved to Henrik but said that she would call him so they could set a new time for the funeral.

"I just don't know if I'm up to planning the whole thing another time," she admitted, as they crossed the courtyard away from the police cars. A couple of curious bystanders had taken up position by the wall of the cemetery, and Jonas shuddered faintly as they walked over to Camilla's car.

"Maybe we ought to drop the ceremony and have a beer and play a Johnny Cash number in his honor instead," Camilla mused.

Louise smiled at her and asked if she wanted to bring any of the flowers she had brought into the church home.

Camilla made a face. "What do you think? Do you have enough vases for them? Oh, how fun to be surrounded by them for the rest of the weekend!"

Louise left her bike there. She shut the passenger-side door after Camilla and Jonas got in Camilla's car. Feeling like she was responsible for two convalescents that she had to have on the mend before the weekend was over, she climbed in behind the wheel and started the car.

28

It took Willumsen less than a minute to yank Louise back to reality after he started the briefing Monday morning; he announced that the group researching the two murders had just been cut in half.

He was standing there holding his coffee cup in his hand, staring at each of them—Toft, Stig, Lars, and finally Louise, who was leaning back complacently in her chair, looking forward to a calm start to the week after a Sunday that had turned out to be quite pleasant.

* * *

Saturday afternoon, everything had been forced and tedious. Camilla lay down in Louise's guest room with some magazines, and Jonas had alternated between sitting in front of the PlayStation that was hooked up to the TV in her bedroom or being engrossed in his Harry Potter book.

It was funny that in a lot of ways he was the diametrical opposite of Markus. Camilla's son had short blond hair, and Jonas's was dark and hung way down over his eyes. Jonas was very focused and liked to concentrate on the things he did. He had played guitar since he was seven without losing interest, which left Louise pretty impressed.

Markus was more impulsive and got all excited about new things, but he still hadn't managed to find anything that really, truly, held his attention. The last thing had been break dancing. Louise wished that at least a little of Jonas's love of reading would rub off on Markus—and even though the pastor's son seemed a little introverted and shy, she couldn't help but notice that Markus really admired him.

Louise had spent her time in the kitchen with a newspaper until she offered to go pick up some pizzas around seven. After that they'd watched a 1970s Danish con-men movie about the Olsen Gang and turned in early.

Mik Rasmussen had called in the middle of the movie and asked if she wanted to come out to Holbæk on Sunday. He tempted her with sea kayaking, sex, barbecue—if the weather held—and maybe a single Irish coffee. She had been a little too curt when she turned him down, and she could tell right away that she'd hurt his feelings. She hadn't meant to do that, but she knew that what they had together was part of a totally different world right now. She spent most of the evening worrying that Jonas was regretting having accepted her invitation to spend the night. They hardly knew each other, so she'd told him several times that he should just let her know if he'd rather go home, but each time he said he wanted to stay.

They had all slept in on Sunday, and it wasn't until around eleven that they headed down to Belis Bar for brunch. Camilla was still a little quiet and withdrawn, but when Markus came back from his dad's place in the early afternoon, they had managed to convince her to go to the pool with them. In the beginning, she just sat there wrapped in a big bathrobe watching the boys as they jumped off the diving boards, but then they managed to lure her into going down the slide, which curved down into the pool from ceiling height, going in and out of the wall of the building. The two boys almost threw up from laughing so hard as Louise and Camilla thundered down into the water shrieking at the tops of their lungs.

When Louise took Jonas home that evening, she suddenly felt like she was part of a real family. Not that that was something she craved, but just then she had to admit it felt nice.

Her mission had also been a success. The convalescents seemed to be doing better.

* * *

"We have a new case, so we're splitting up our resources," Willumsen announced, his eyes on Louise as if he'd noticed that her thoughts were still elsewhere.

Louise straightened up and pulled her chair all the way in to the table.

"We'll have to make do with just two people continuing to work with Mikkelsen and his people on solving the Vesterbro case, while the other two move on to the new case."

Stig was about to protest but was stopped by Willumsen's hand.

"It's too early to move people off this," Toft said over the raised hand. "If we pull back, they get free reign again. You know there's no way we'll be able to get to the bottom of what they're up to and keep an eye on things without more people."

"Of course you can, and I'm going to need to see some progress soon. We're not getting anywhere and nothing's happening," he grumbled, staring grimly at them before straightening up and changing his tone. "This Saturday a dead infant was found out in Stenhøj Church in Frederiksberg, and this is something you're aware of, Rick."

It wasn't a question, and he wasn't expecting Louise to respond, because he continued himself.

"Our colleagues from the Bellahøj station were out there for a similar case a couple of weeks ago. In that case, the infant was found alive."

He pulled the top sheet of paper out of the case file he had on the table in front of him.

"They did an autopsy on the infant yesterday afternoon, and I have the provisional findings here. Flemming Larsen writes…"

He pulled his reading glasses out of his chest pocket. Louise felt the anxiety moving from her stomach toward her solar plexus. To anyone who knew anything about Willumsen, the sign was obvious. Something was wrong. They must have found something in the autopsy that changed the case from a family tragedy to a particular type of crime, otherwise the case wouldn't be assigned to them. The Bellahøj precinct was perfectly well equipped to handle most things on their own.

Louise considered Willumsen's face as he read the text, paraphrasing it in his own words. He ran through it quickly at first.

"The infant was wrapped, a newborn boy, no more than a couple of days old. The body had a faint greenish tinge as you might find with chorioamnionitis, or amniotic fluid infection, and it was still covered with dried blood and vernix caseosa."

Here, he slowed down slightly.

"Beyond that Flemming writes that the umbilical cord had been crudely severed from the mother and the skin had peeled off in several locations."

The door suddenly opened and Suhr came in and sat down with a face that made it clear he wanted to cause as little disruption as possible so they should just continue. The look was wasted on Willumsen, who didn't respond to the homicide chief's arrival at all.

"The peeling is a type called maceration and may indicate that the infant died prior to the birth. But the reason this case has landed on our desks now is..."

Finally, he looked up to make sure he had their attention.

"...that the infant is missing its pinky toe. And we're not talking about a birth defect. It was chopped off or cut off after the birth. The surface of the wound is smooth and even, so it was amputated with a sharp instrument. Flemming is sure the toe was removed after the boy's death, otherwise there would have been a reaction in the form of bleeding, and that is why he concludes with great certainty that we're talking about a stillbirth."

Now Willumsen looked directly at Lars and Louise.

"This is your case now. Bellahøj will continue to investigate the abandoned baby that was taken to Skodsborg Orphanage a week ago. At the moment, there is no reason to think that the two cases are connected, but obviously you should consider that. For the time being we'll run the two investigations separately and think of them as two separate cases. It's far more likely that the church was chosen because of all the media attention. The injury the infant boy incurred doesn't have anything to do with Baby Girl. She was in good condition when she was abandoned. This will definitely involve a ton of routine work, and I want you two to personally get in touch with all the mothers who were scheduled to give birth within the last two weeks, and the ones whose due dates are within the next fourteen days."

Suhr's forehead had contracted into deep wrinkles, but he remained silent.

"You'll have to go check out the maternity wards, and if there are cases that seem interesting, compare the DNA. If that doesn't give us anything, we'll have to broaden our search by asking the public for help and appealing to people to get in touch with us if they know a pregnant woman whose baby bump has disappeared but who doesn't have a baby in her arms."

Lars started shaking his head.

"Who are you going to assign to assist them?" Suhr asked, looking at his lead detective. Willumsen's eyebrows shot up as if he had no idea what Suhr was talking about.

"To begin with we'll handle this ourselves. We're going to have to be able to keep several balls in the air," Willumsen pronounced, once he finally detected the heavy silence that had settled over the room. "Working on one case at a time is a luxury we just don't have."

Louise nodded. This wasn't the first time and certainly wouldn't be the last when she wouldn't have a chance to follow a case through to its conclusion. She took the thin case folder Willumsen handed her and got up to follow Lars back to their office.

29

What does it say in the report we got from the pathology lab?" Lars asked, waiting patiently while Louise plugged in the electric kettle on the shelf and got a glass with a tea bag ready.

He opened the window and a mild spring breeze blew in, freshening up their dark office a little.

By the time the water was finally boiling, he had the phone to his ear and was waiting to talk to the court. They were going to need a warrant to obtain the patient lists from the various maternity wards.

Louise set down her glass of tea and opened the case file, which so far contained only two pieces of paper. She started reading but was interrupted when her partner hung up, having obtained the warrant.

"Read it aloud," he asked, unscrewing the lid to a bottle of mineral water and pulling his chair back so he had some support for his back when he put his legs up on the edge of the desk.

"Saturday, April 26, at approximately 10:55 a.m., a woman entered the front door of Stenhøj Church.

"That was Camilla," Louise interjected before continuing.

"There was a bundle wrapped in a towel lying on the floor immediately inside the door. The woman ran out of the church without touching anything. Approximately ten minutes later, Assistant Detective Louise Rick, Copenhagen PD, arrived; she was at the church on private business. The detective and Pastor Henrik Holm of Stenhøj Church examined the bundle together, which turned out to contain a naked newborn male infant who was dead at the time he was found.

"This doesn't really say that much," she said and skimmed the rest of the text before she continued.

"The area was cordoned off, and scent dogs were brought in to try and pick up a trail. They didn't find anything. Preliminary questioning: Negative.

"Nada," she commented and read on.

"A postmortem was conducted at the scene and an autopsy the following day. The male infant's weight was 3,750 grams and length was fifty centimeters."

"Well, that's completely normal, so the mother must have been to term," said Lars. He was the more knowledgeable of the two of them about babies, even though his own twins had been adopted from Bolivia when they were about six months old. They were seven now and had left a little of the craziness behind them. They used to be terrors, though, and on several occasions when their father brought them to work they had taken great satisfaction in scattering case files all over the office.

"The umbilical cord appeared to have been severed by biting or tearing and was not tied off," she continued, brushing the twins out of her mind. "It was seventeen centimeters long. The time of birth was estimated as one to two days prior to the discovery of the body. The child's race is Caucasian."

Louise glanced up from the report. "Well, that pretty much just means he's not black or Asian, but it doesn't narrow it down that much. Caucasian is still a pretty broad spectrum!"

Her partner nodded and asked if there was any more, but she shook her head and pushed the piece of paper away.

"Nothing aside from the fact that he had thick, dark brown hair."

They were interrupted when Suhr, after a quick knock, opened the door and sat down on the low shelf just inside the doorway.

"I talked to Sillebrandt from out at the Bellahøj precinct. He's still got four people on the case and is offering to expand the search for witnesses so that they're looking for people who might have seen something around the church from Friday night until Saturday morning. That's the time frame during which we assume the boy was left. They've found two witnesses who said independently that they saw an older-model light green car by the cemetery around six a.m. Saturday morning. One of the witnesses, an elderly man who was out for his morning walk with his Labrador retriever, was very sure that it was a Fiat Regata from the mid-1980s. He had a similar model himself, just in red. The other witness, a young guy, was on his way home to sleep off a night on the town, and all he remembered was that there was an old light green 'bucket of bolts,' which he peed on. And that description certainly fits pretty well if we're talking about a car that's over twenty years old."

The homicide chief smiled, probably because he never let his own Volvo get more than two or three years old before he swapped it out for a new one.

"Based on the witnesses' statements, our colleagues have been searching for a Fiat Regata in that color. They found seven registered in Sjælland, and they're looking at the owners. But otherwise they don't have anything," he continued, scratching his chin, which was thoroughly shaved every morning and slathered with expensive aftershave. "I recommend that we accept their offer to expand their search for witnesses."

Louise and Lars nodded. So she had been right when she'd thought she could tell what he was thinking in Willumsen's office. Obviously he was aware that the group leader couldn't leave this entire case to just two people, but since the homicide chief was a polite man he hadn't challenged his subordinate on this point in front of everyone else. He had bitten his tongue instead.

"Let's start by going after the most obvious. Concentrate on checking the hospital lists of women who are supposed to give birth soon or have just done so."

He looked at them to confirm that they agreed.

"Take the metro Copenhagen region," he continued after they both nodded in confirmation. "In other words, Hvidovre, Herlev, Glostrup, National Hospital, Frederiksberg, and Gentofte, and let's see what we get from that."

"We already requested a warrant, so we can get the hospitals to hand over the basic information on the women of interest," Lars said, receiving a satisfied nod.

"I'll send a press release to the Ritzau news service in a bit, and I've already arranged for us to meet a TV Avisen reporter at the church for the six thirty p.m. broadcast. In addition to that, I'm planning on appearing on the TV2 News at seven p.m. We're going to have to go public with this, and I don't understand why Bellahøj hasn't already been more aggressive. Sillebrandt hasn't really been very proactive."

Louise scrupulously avoided looking over at Lars. There wasn't that much gossip about the homicide chief, but people did joke about his frequent appearances on TV whenever they got the chance. Louise didn't actually think he overdid it. To the contrary, she was glad to have a boss who was respected by the general population, and no one could deny that when they hit a dead end with a case this approach was usually what brought them new leads.

"While we wait for the lists from the hospitals, I want to drive out and see Henrik Holm and run through the whole thing with him one more time," Louise said. "Maybe there's something he just hasn't thought of, and I also just want to mention the light green Fiat to him."

"Bellahøj already talked to him," Suhr said, as Louise was collecting her purse from the floor and stuffing her cell phone into her pocket.

"Yeah," she replied, "but now the case has been assigned to us, so we'll talk to him."

The homicide chief nodded and smiled at her. "Of course."

"We also need to tell him about the pathologist's report, before the whole story is splashed all over the media," she added. "But you're not planning to mention the toe when you talk to the press, are you?"

He seemed to consider this briefly, and then he shook his head.

"Not to begin with. As long as we don't know if that has any significance, we might as well spare people that detail. But mention it to the pastor. How the hell should I know—maybe there's some sort of religious significance to it that our limited insight into biblical history is causing us to miss."

"Well, that's a possibility," she conceded, and then told him that Pastor Holm was a little worried that the two tragic events would harm his church.

"You certainly can't blame him for that. I read his column yesterday," Suhr said as Louise was on her way out. "It was about the 'maternal instinct,' which doesn't always kick in right away, and he wrote about the scientific explanation, which is that the production of female sex hormones drops off dramatically after giving birth, and that can affect both a woman's attitude and her maternal instinct. His own theory was more that the infant's soul just needed time to settle into place before it was ready to bind itself to its mother and awaken those strong feelings in her. Some just took longer to move in than others, as he put it. It was very interesting, but the piece was obviously inspired by Baby Girl's mother, so he must have written it before the boy's body was found."

"Why did it happen two times, so close together?" Louise asked, her mind back on the stillborn little boy. "Years can go by without there being an abandoned baby."

"Every once in a while we have cases of abandoned stillborn infants just months apart, and in rare cases even just weeks. Unfortunately, it's not all that uncommon," Suhr corrected. He was interrupted by Stig, who had stopped to listen from the open doorway, as he unscrewed the cap from a half-liter bottle of cola.

"I'd hazard a guess that you won't be finding the mother in the upper echelon of society," he said with the same conviction in his voice as when he'd informed Louise that you could always tell by looking at a whore if she came from Eastern Europe. "It's only in the lowest classes that children aren't viewed as status symbols. Quite the contrary, they're sometimes perceived of as trash if you're unlucky enough to get pregnant, and then it's easier to get rid of the kid than struggle with some government caseworker about institutions and forcible removal."

Stig paused for effect and took a swig of his soda.

"After all, it's easier to dump a kid than take responsibility," he continued. "And the people we're talking about here certainly aren't the sharpest tools in the shed, so it's not really a surprise that they use the same place as a dump. That way they don't have to have a single original thought."

Louise had a hard time stomaching his tirade and thought about just walking out and leaving him to the others, but hung back when Stig continued.

"Do they know if the stillborn baby's mother was a drug user?" Stig looked from Louise to Lars.

Lars shrugged and looked over at the provisional report, which was in front of Louise.

She shook her head.

"We don't know yet," Suhr said and got up off the shelf.

"The baby's autopsy was yesterday," Louise reminded Stig. "The results from the blood tests won't be back until this afternoon or tomorrow."

"If this were my case, I'd be asking the crackheads and

hookers some questions, before I spent too much time on the mothers who've been dutifully going to their prenatal appointments and eagerly awaiting the birth of their babies. Those other women, though, you can certainly imagine that there might be some of them who aren't particularly eager to go through official channels with their pregnancies. Especially not if they already knew from the beginning that they were going to get rid of the kid," he concluded before disappearing off to his office.

Suhr stood there in the doorway, watching him go. "Actually, he might have a point," he said, resting an arm on the doorframe as a thoughtful expression came over his face. "Have a chat with the folks at the Nest and find out if they know anyone who had started to show but never turned up with a baby."

Louise sat there with her elbows on her desk and her head resting heavily in her hands. There was always someone who was good at putting other people to work. He could have offered to ask around himself, since he was out there anyway working on those two murder cases, but that would have been too much to expect.

* * *

Before Louise heard the sound, she felt the phone in her pocket vibrating. Anonymous caller, the caller ID said. She excused herself, assuming it must be a personal call, maybe her mother, who she had never called back over the weekend.

"Hi, it's Jakobsen," the crisis psychologist said, and Louise instinctively glanced at her watch. Camilla had had an appointment at nine fifteen that morning. It was eleven now. For a second she was afraid, thinking maybe he'd decided to admit her friend or drug her so heavily that he felt he ought to inform Louise.

"She never showed up," he said tersely, sounding irritated. He was already overbooked before they'd managed to convince him to squeeze Camilla in, so he was justified. "She didn't even call to cancel."

Louise stared out the window. Camilla had still been asleep when she left a little before eight, and she had assumed her friend would wake up on her own and make sure she got off on time.

"I tried calling your place, too, because I understood she had spent the weekend there, but no one's answering, and she doesn't answer the cell phone number I had for her, either."

"I don't get it," was all Louise could think to say. "I'll stop by home and get her. I'm really sorry. She must have overslept." She apologized and added that Camilla had been very tired since her experience out at the church. "I should have made sure she got up myself."

"Call me when you get a hold of her. We'll have to set up a new appointment." Jakobsen still sounded pissed.

Lars and Suhr were looking at her as she put her phone back in her pocket.

"Camilla just blew Jakobsen off," she explained. "I have to drive home and find out if she's OK."

Lars nodded, but she could tell that Suhr was about to lose it, given all the work they had ahead of them.

"It won't take long," Louise promised, pulling on her jacket. "And it's on the way to Stenhøj Church anyway."

30

At first, she couldn't find the alarm clock on the night-stand, so she propped herself up on her elbow and then spotted it down on the floor. Still half asleep, she reached for it and determined that it was almost ten.

Camilla had been up most of the night, but she must have eventually fallen asleep just before dawn. She hadn't heard Louise or Markus get up. He had slept on a mattress on the floor right next to her bed, and the whole time she was lying there awake, staring into the darkness, she had listened to his relaxed breathing.

She set down the alarm clock and after rubbing her eyes, spotted the note on the nightstand.

I LOVE YOU, MOM. MARKUS.

She read the sentence again and suddenly felt afraid and

let the affectionate note flutter down onto the comforter as she lay back down on the pillow. It occurred to her that she didn't feel anything. The warmth she usually felt in her heart when she read one of his little declarations of love did not come, nor the smile that always appeared without her even being aware of it, nor did she picture his face. And she didn't try to imagine him sitting in the kitchen writing it for her.

Again, it struck her that everything that was usually inside her was gone, and what scared her was the thought that it might be gone forever if even one of Markus's little notes couldn't make her happy. When she thought about it she realized mostly what she felt was apathetic.

She closed her eyes and lay there for a long time without moving. Kaj had kept appearing in her thoughts overnight. She thought about his life, which she didn't know shit about aside from the few details he'd shared with her, and at one point overnight she had cried because it was so unfair that she'd had to postpone his funeral. She realized she'd been looking forward to the funeral, to taking care of it, doing a little something for him, decorating with flowers and playing Johnny Cash for him.

She pulled the blanket up over her head and lay like that for a long time. She heard the phone ringing in the living room, but pulled the blanket in closer around her face and lay like that until it stopped. She'd turned off her cell phone the previous evening. It was on the nightstand, and she couldn't be bothered to turn it on. She was sure there would be at least one message from Høyer.

Suddenly she remembered Jakobsen and her appointment with him at National Hospital. She couldn't remember what time it was for—it was on a slip of paper in the kitchen—but she knew she was already too late.

She swung her legs out over the edge of the bed and wriggled a little on the mattress to reach the sweatpants she'd tossed on the floor the previous night. She kept on the T-shirt she'd slept in and went to the bathroom.

The phone rang again, but she closed the door behind herself and sat down on the toilet. She wasn't hungry and didn't need coffee, didn't have any needs. The only thing she could feel was an all-encompassing melancholy. All the same, she decided to go out and get a little air.

The sun was shining, and down on the street below people were walking around in shirtsleeves or lightweight jackets. She stuck her bare feet into a pair of Adidas sneakers Louise had sitting in her hallway and pulled a white sweater on over her head. She pulled her blond hair into a loose ponytail. Her Mulberry brand purse was the only thing that revealed that she was normally much more put together.

She walked all the way down Gammel Kongevej to Central Station. She wanted to go to the Plaza, where Kaj had reigned in the kitchen in his day, and she thought she might settle for a cup of coffee in the bar. The sun hurt her eyes. She'd forgotten her sunglasses, so she walked with her eyes squinted shut a little, heading into the bright daylight. It wasn't until she passed the Planetarium that it occurred to her that the Plaza had been sold many times since the legendary hotel magnate had owned it and turned it into something special. Several international hotel chains had owned it since, so there probably wasn't much of Kaj's spirit left. She decided to get her coffee from somewhere inside Central Station instead. There was also something appealing about the idea of sitting in there and being an anonymous face in the crowd. Blending in with all the other strangers who were just passing through.

She took a free paper from the holder on her way in and walked down through the high-ceilinged railroad station concourse with its shops and newsstands along one side and the stairways down to the train tracks on the other. There weren't very many people in the DSB café, so she tossed her papers on an empty table and went up to the window to get a coffee.

* * *

The Meat Baron. She didn't know what he looked like, had only seen his silhouette behind the steering wheel of the dark green Jaguar, and then she'd heard his story. But if she went down to the Meatpacking District surely someone would know who he was. She wanted to hear more about Kaj's time as a chef when everything had been different.

There were more people in the café; some of them knew each other and chatted briefly before they hurried on, Danish mixed with foreign languages. She watched lazily as people came and went.

After half an hour, she folded up her newspapers and drank the last of her cold coffee before getting up to go.

She walked down past the convention center along Kvægtorvsgade and past Rysensteen High School toward Halmtorvet. She had her eyes on the ground and didn't see the Audi or have a chance to react when a guy with dark hair said her name and grabbed her arm.

31

Louise ran up the stairs to her fourth-floor apartment. Putting her key in the lock, she thought about how she'd run up the stairs and was a little surprised she could do so without getting winded, especially since she hadn't gotten out to run much lately.

"Hello?" she yelled as she entered.

The guest room door was open, and both beds were unmade and empty. Louise went to the kitchen to see if there was a note and knocked on the bathroom door.

It didn't take her half a minute to determine that Camilla wasn't in the apartment. She saw Camilla's jacket still hanging on the hook but noticed that her purse was gone. She tried calling her again. A female voice had only just started to tell her that the number she'd called was not in service when she spotted Camilla's Sony Ericsson on the nightstand next to the bed, turned off.

She leaned against the doorframe for a second, wondering if she ought to start looking for Camilla. She decided it would be almost impossible to know where her friend had gone. The only obvious place was if she'd gone home to her own apartment for some clean clothes.

Louise tried Camilla's home number, but no one answered. Louise felt the touch of concern that had flitted through her mind now take a firmer hold on her. A glance at the clock showed that it was eleven thirty. She was going to have to drive if she were going to have time to stop and see Pastor Holm and be back to Police Headquarters by one o'clock as she'd promised.

She locked her apartment door behind her and found Flemming Larsen's direct number at the pathology lab. Even though he was probably down in the autopsy rooms working, she needed to try to get hold of him and ask about the blood tests. Visiting all the new mothers the hospitals had records of would be a waste of time if it turned out that the baby had been born to a drug addict. Or it would rule out a large percentage of the potential suspects. Stig had had a good point.

"They're not back yet," the secretary told her after checking for the blood test results. Then the woman explained that she didn't expect Larsen to be done until sometime between two and three that afternoon. "They've got a busy schedule after the weekend."

Louise thanked her and said that she'd call back later.

The trip out to Stenhøj Church took her ten minutes. Louise had called to let Henrik Holm know that she would be stopping by, and he didn't sound that curious, so she decided to wait and explain when she got out there.

He greeted her with a smile and thanked her again and

again for having watched Jonas. "He had a great time and thinks it's the coolest thing ever that you're a police officer," he said after they'd taken a seat in the kitchen.

"Ah yes. Well, that's actually why I'm here," she said, seizing the opportunity. "In my official capacity as a police officer, that is."

Henrik raised an eyebrow and cocked his head at her.

"The case of the deceased baby we found Saturday was officially assigned to us this morning," she said, adding that it had wound up on her desk specifically. Then she explained that they'd done the autopsy on the baby on Sunday. "The pathologist says he was stillborn. His lungs, heart, and other internal organs were fully developed, so the baby was viable. The cause of death was the chorioamnionitis, or a bacterial infection of the amniotic fluid."

Henrik's eyebrow was still raised.

"In the worst cases, it can kill both the mother and the baby."

He nodded, and his eyebrow finally returned to its normal position.

"Something else was discovered during the autopsy which is actually the reason the case was transferred to the homicide division. After the birth, one of the baby's pinky toes was removed. The pathologist is convinced that this was not a birth defect."

She decided to spare him the details and avoided telling him that Flemming had noted that this had been done with a knife, scissors, or pincers.

She saw the look in his eyes change. Henrik leaned back on the bench and looked at her, as if he didn't quite understand. An uncertain shadow flitted over his face.

"It is possible that the child had a defect in the toe,

so the parents removed it before they placed him in the church?" he suggested.

"In principle, yes," Louise consented, "but the fact that someone harmed the dead infant makes the act a criminal matter. As opposed to before, when we considered it a deeply tragic and sorrowful event, which is what it is when someone decides to abandon a stillborn baby."

"Some babies are stillborn," the pastor said absentmindedly. He looked through the living room, out at the tops of the trees in the yard. "As far as I can remember there were about 320 stillbirths in 2005."

He didn't say anything else, and they sat there for a bit before Louise explained that the Bellahøj precinct still had officers on the case, but she and her partner were now officially in charge.

"We have a couple of witnesses who saw a light green Fiat Regata parked here outside the cemetery early Saturday morning. Does that mean anything to you?" Louise asked. She was surprised when he nodded and made a face.

He ran his fingers through his wiry blond hair as if he needed to pull himself together before he got sidetracked. This left his hair somewhat tousled.

"If it's the people I'm thinking of, Otto Birch, my sexton, has had problems with them before," he said and then smiled a crooked smile. "It's a middle-aged couple, I'm guessing they're in their late forties or early fifties. We've caught them having sex in the cemetery several times. That's a bizarre thing to be turned on by, and Otto has thrown them out several times and forbidden them from coming here, but I've never heard yet of a person getting a restraining order against coming to a cemetery."

He laughed wryly.

"Now they've started coming at times when they don't think we'll catch them. It used to be mostly in the evening, as if this were part of their evening stroll."

He shook his head and stood up.

Louise had the sense he wanted to go back to what he'd been doing before she arrived, and she asked if he knew the couple's names.

"No, unfortunately I can't help you there. Otto just tried to scare them away. He threatened to report them to the police, but he never made a big enough deal out of it to ask their names."

Louise set her card on the table and said that he should just call if he had any questions or wanted to find out how the investigation was coming. She was almost out the door when she turned around and added that unfortunately there was no getting out of having the church in the spotlight again because of this.

"If my boss hasn't already called, I'm sure he will," she said and explained that Suhr wanted to appeal to the public in the hopes of finding witnesses.

Henrik nodded absentmindedly. Despite his previous concerns, it didn't appear to bother him that both of the big news broadcasts wanted to use his church in their broadcasts. At the last minute, it occurred to Louise that she probably should have said that the baby's pinky toe was something they wanted to keep confidential.

"We would prefer not to have that made public."

"Of course," he said.

32

"Camilla Lind."

He repeated her name twice before she turned to look at him. The glasses' metal frames were reflecting the sunlight, and her arm hurt. She tried to yank it back. She ought to have been feeling nervous but instead she felt a rage that only grew when he continued to hold her in a tight grip, like a vise being tightened around her bone.

"Let me go," she hissed, trying to break free again as he pushed her up against the wall of the building and held her with both hands. A bicyclist rode past, but looked away when she tried to make eye contact with him.

"We know you were the one who wrote the article about that wino, who saw a car like mine down on Skelbækgade. And we'd like to have a little chat with you," he said, receiving help from a second guy she hadn't noticed until he started pulling her over to the car, which was stopped with the motor idling out in the lane of traffic.

"I don't have anything to talk to you about," she said, but felt her rage withdrawing, making room for the fear that suddenly rushed through her with such force that her throat tightened.

Why hadn't it occurred to her that they might come after her the way they'd gone after Kaj? Finally, she felt something move inside her body, but they shoved her into the backseat so hard they knocked the wind out of her and then slammed the door shut.

A second later one of them got in behind the wheel and the other climbed into the back seat with her with a hand on her shoulder, which tightened its grip any time she made the slightest movement. The Audi started moving, she heard the automatic door locks engage and stared out the windshield as they drove across Halmtorvet.

What had she called it? A Balkan necktie, brutal payback for those who snitch on the perpetrators. She was breathing in such short jerky gasps that her chest was hardly moving.

The car continued down Sønder Boulevard and turned onto Enghavevej, past Enghave Square, and back to Istedgade.

"We didn't kill him," the guy sitting next to Camilla said. The driver kept his eyes on the road and seemed to be concentrating fully on his driving. "And we didn't kill the woman in the courtyard, either, even if that's what the police think."

Camilla closed her eyes as he spoke, didn't want to look at him or participate in what was going on around her right now.

The pain stabbed through her shoulder as he shook her. "Listen!" he shouted into her ear.

The driver was still staring straight ahead, but Camilla nodded.

"Go to the club," he ordered and the driver nodded and drove a little farther down Istedgade before turning onto Saxogade. She could tell they had Eastern European accents, but she couldn't narrow it down any more than that.

They passed Estlandsgade past Litauen Square and parked at the corner of Letlandsgade and Saxogade. She hurried to get out when the door on her side was opened.

* * *

Three steps led down to the front door, where a little sign said that they were entering an Albanian club. The basement space was larger than she had expected. The color of the walls was tired and sad and showed signs of the thick cigarette smoke, which hung densely in the space. There were a bunch of tables, each with four or five chairs around it. Men were sitting at four of the tables playing cards; each man had either a glass or a mug in front of him. It took Camilla a second to look around and determine that there was a single woman in the room. Along one wall there was a bar which appeared to be tended by an elderly man, who was changing the filter in a coffeemaker.

She was pushed through the room to a door at the back left.

"We're going in here," the man in the glasses told the bartender and received a nod back. No one reacted to the way they were holding her. Several of the men didn't even look up when they came in.

The room in back must have been some kind of combination office and storeroom, she thought. There was an old desk with a calculator and a couple of three-ring binders, and beer and soda crates were stacked along the wall.

"Sit down."

He gestured toward a worn-out armchair and then walked over and took a seat at the desk. The driver stayed by the door, and for a second Camilla wondered what would happen if she didn't obey but asked if she could leave instead. Would they hit her?

She went and sat down.

"We read what you wrote," he said and nodded at the guy by the door to make it clear that they'd both seen the article.

"That old fool didn't see shit," he continued angrily. "And if he did, then he was wrong."

He took a deep breath and she could tell that he was trying to curb his temper so the rage didn't subsume him.

"Or someone made him believe that story," the guy by the door said. That was the first time the driver had said a word.

The man with the steel glasses and the smooth hair nodded. "There is, of course, a third possibility. That someone paid you." He leaned over toward her menacingly. "Is that it? Did someone pay you to write all that crap?"

She shuddered when a little glob of spit hit her cheek. "No one paid me or asked me to write anything they didn't think was true," she said, deciding not to wipe her face, continuing to look him in the eye as she spoke.

He folded his hands behind his head and tipped his head back. He sat like that for a bit looking at the ceiling before he dropped his hands again and looked at her.

"We didn't do it," he repeated. "But someone really wants the police to think we were behind it." Now his tone was more subdued.

The man by the door was doing something with his phone, like he wasn't really involved with whatever was going on with Camilla.

"It's true that we were on Skelbækgade that night. I was also in the courtyard, but she was already lying on the ground when I got there with the blood pouring out of her."

He glanced over at the door before he continued. "I actually knew the girl, so I ran out to the car. Hamdi"— he nodded toward the door again, and the guy reacted when his name was mentioned, but then looked away again quickly—"and I drove down to Halmtorvet to look for the person who did it, but the police came quickly, so we pulled back."

Camilla gathered up her courage before she interrupted him, her voice steady and clear. "Why am I getting mixed up in all this? I don't want anything to do with this," she said, maintaining eye contact. Which was how she saw his rage return.

"I want you to go to the police and tell them it wasn't us. They need to lay off our asses and start looking at the people who did it. You got it?" His eyes were hard and they bore into her as he spoke.

Camilla took a deep breath and nodded. Even here, with her ability to think rationally paralyzed by fear, she knew her only option right now was to humor them. The fact that they wanted her to go to the police meant that at least they weren't planning to kill her.

"The police listen to you, and you're going to tell them to leave us alone and go after the right killer."

"I knew Kaj—not that well, but I knew him, and I know what happened to him in that courtyard."

Camilla was interrupted by Hamdi, who came over from the door to stand next to the desk.

"We weren't in that courtyard and we didn't touch him. Instead why don't you ask the police if they know why Ilana wasn't on the flight from Prague that day we went to the airport to get her. We know they were there, too, and if they haven't already talked to their Czech counterparts, then I suggest that they do."

The guy with the glasses nodded.

"Then they'll find out that she couldn't have taken that flight because she was found that same day in the apartment where she rented a room, her throat slit. They can also ask what the police have on that Serb we heard was seen in the building in Prague the day Ilana was murdered, because he was also in Copenhagen when the two murders took place."

"If he was seen, then I'm sure the police are already searching for him," Camilla said, watching him.

"No point in searching for him," he said, a smile rippling across his lips. "He's not the type who gets caught."

Again, she had that feeling in her throat. She didn't know how long she'd been in this back room, but she had no desire to know all the stuff she'd just been told. Mostly she wanted to go home to bed, so she could pull the covers up over her head and shut everything out.

"I don't know anything about a flight from Prague or some Ilana who didn't show up. I suggest you tell the police about this yourself, just the way you told me, if you think they know what's going on."

The arms were around her shoulders before she saw them coming and she was lifted up off the chair.

"We'll drive you over to the police now and then you will tell them what I just told you. And tell them they should leave us alone."

She was yanked toward the door. They quickly exited the premises, and Camilla felt like someone was holding the doors for her, so she flew through until she was sitting in the backseat of the car and listening to the motor start.

"If I'm going to talk to the police, you need to drive me to Police Headquarters. I know someone there, someone I can make listen to me."

Something had relaxed within her; the fear didn't seem quite as paralyzing to her thoughts anymore. On the other hand, she was fully aware that they would come after her again if she didn't do exactly as they said.

33

There was a printout of names waiting on Louise's desk when she returned from the pastor's residence. She exhaled slowly as she skimmed through the pages and counted about fifty women who had been due to deliver their babies during the period of time they were working on. There'll be even more once we track down the women who were past their due dates, Louise thought and glanced over at her partner.

"Should we just divvy the list up and work our way through?" she asked Lars.

He nodded and noted drily that of course calling the women wouldn't do any good.

"You're right about that." She undid her ponytail and shook out her hair before gathering it into a bun and wrapping the elastic around it. "The only way is the hard way," she said, mimicking Willumsen's brusque tone as she spread out the pages, "and if we're lucky, we'll be done by August."

"I suppose you're most interested in your local area, so why don't you take Herlev, Hvidovre, and Glostrup? Then I can do National Hospital, Gentofte, and Frederiksberg." She was interrupted by the phone on her desk ringing. It was the front desk informing her that a Camilla Lind was downstairs and wanted to talk to her. Would Louise come down and escort her in, or should they send her away?

"I'll be down," she said quickly. Lars gave her a questioning look.

"It's Camilla. Of course, she wasn't there when I went home. I have no idea what she's been off doing or why she blew Jakobsen off this morning. I was starting to get a little worried about her," Louise said and darted out the door.

Down in the courtyard, Louise stopped short when she spotted Camilla in the waiting area. The only sign of life on her was the red access badge she had clipped to the waistband of her loose gray sweatpants. Her face was pale and without any makeup at all, and her hair was flat. But what stopped Louise in her tracks most was something in Camilla's face, a tenseness that made Louise break into a jog for the last few steps before putting her arms around her friend.

They stood there for a moment, both stunned. Then Louise loosened her grasp and said that she was assuming Camilla wanted to come up to her office. Camilla nodded mutely and Louise saw that she'd begun to cry. She put her arm around Camilla again and then led her across the courtyard.

While she'd been down there, Lars had organized his

list of names by addresses and had already planned the order of his visits. He'd turned off his computer and was standing up, his denim jacket over his arm, clearly about to leave.

Camilla had stopped crying and dried her eyes on her sweater sleeves, but they still looked red. When they were still out in the hallway, she had started telling Louise about what the two Albanians had done to her. Now, in the office, she assured them both that she was only crying out of relief, that they hadn't actually harmed her.

"Have a seat," Louise ordered, pointing to the visitor's chair.

Lars tossed his denim jacket aside and offered to make a pot of coffee. Louise nodded to him, found a 10-kroner coin in her pocket, and asked him to stop by the vending machine in the lunchroom on his way and buy a bag of gummy candies.

"They didn't do it," Camilla said once the door had closed behind him.

Louise took a seat and studied Camilla before she even tried to understand what Camilla was talking about. Had she been drinking? Or what was wrong? She wasn't making any sense.

"They didn't do what?" she asked.

"Kill Kaj. Or that prostitute in the Meatpacking District. They admit that they were on Skelbækgade, but she was already dead when he went into the courtyard."

Camilla's words swirled past her and Louise asked her to hold on.

"You blew Jakobsen off this morning even though he moved around his whole schedule and canceled on another patient to make room for you," Louise said, trying to slow the pace down a little. "Did you do that so you could go play private detective?"

Camilla shook her head.

"I overslept." She apologized and promised to call Jakobsen and set up a new appointment if he was still willing to see her.

Lars pushed the door open with his foot and walked in with a thermal carafe, three cups, a bag of Eldorado, and a roll of chocolate cookies. Louise smiled at him and got up to close the door as he set everything down on the desk.

"Were they watching you out on the streets?" Louise asked after Camilla told her about her morning and her visit to Central Station.

"Yeah, I was on my way to Halmtorvet to see if I could find one of Kaj's old friends and I didn't hear the car stop," she explained and then blew on her coffee before taking a sip.

"What did the guys look like?" Lars asked to get the details squared away.

"The one who grabbed me had kind of smooth, shoulder-length hair and glasses."

Louise and Lars exchanged looks.

"So, it was Arian and Hamdi," Louise said, and Lars agreed. Camilla nodded when she heard the name Hamdi.

"God damn it!" Lars pushed his chair back against the wall, put his legs up, and rested his mug on his knee. "Well, then they've figured out that we're tailing them."

"Yeah, I'd say so," Camilla said with a sarcastic little smile. The first one Louise had seen since she spotted her downstairs. "But I was supposed to tell you something— aside from the fact that they claim that they didn't kill those two people. The guy you say is named Arian knew her and says that he's sorry she's dead and that he sped off to get the killer. That's where he was going when he came back out of the building."

"And what did they say that's supposed to convince us it wasn't them?" Louise urged, trying to get Camilla back on track.

"Something about how they were out at the airport waiting for a girl who never showed up. Evidently, you guys were there, too," she said, watching them until they both nodded in confirmation. "That girl was found dead in her room the day she was supposed to come. Her throat had been slit, and he recommended that you guys call your counterparts in Prague and ask about the Serb who was seen in the girl's building at the time of her murder. According to them he was in Copenhagen when the two murders here were committed."

Louise suspected that Lars thought this was a story they just came up with, as if the two Albanians were trying to hamstring him, and she had to admit she was leaning that way herself.

"We'll bust them for unlawful imprisonment," Lars said once Camilla was done. "How long did they hold you at the Club?"

"No, no. Please, don't bother," Camilla responded quickly. "But you're going to have to investigate if there's any basis to what they said, because otherwise they're going to come after me again."

"It's not our case anymore," Louise explained, watching a look of confusion come over Camilla's face. "But I can either pass this on, or you can talk to Toft and Stig yourself. It's their case now."

"What does that mean? You mean only two people are

working on it?" Camilla stiffened, looking at them in disbelief.

"Well, and Mikkelsen," Louise added.

"Two people were violently slain and there's only three men on the case? What the fuck's up with that?"

Louise wasn't sure why Camilla suddenly sounded so agitated. Camilla set down her cup and looked like she was getting ready for battle.

"Some folks from the downtown precinct will back them up when they need it," Louise said in an attempt to tone things down a little.

"Well, what the fuck are you two doing then, sitting around the office drinking coffee and eating chocolate cookies?" Camilla burst out, nodding toward the open roll of cookies on the desk. "The two people you suspect of flaying open two human beings just pushed me into their car and hauled me down to some basement room on Saxogade. What the fuck! You have to do whatever you can to catch these people!" she shouted frantically. "If what they said is right, that someone else did it, you're going to have to go find out who it was."

Camilla took a deep breath, down into her abdomen, and sank back in the chair. "I'm sorry," she said, rubbing her face to wipe the anger away. "It was just a huge shock to be detained like that. And in a way, I think they were telling the truth when they said it wasn't them. Why else would they have let me go?"

Since no one seemed to have an immediate response to her question, she now asked why they'd been taken off the case.

"We're investigating the stillborn baby you found in the church," Louise said, quickly trying to assess whether it was a good idea to tell Camilla what Flemming had discovered, but before she was able to decide, Lars was already doing it.

"It turned out the little baby was assaulted after birth, and we got the case because the injury occurred after death."

Camilla's face stiffened into an incredulous grimace. "Someone hurt him?" she asked, looking from Lars to Louise. Louise nodded.

"His pinky toe was amputated," she elaborated by way of explanation.

She watched the vacant look in Camilla's eyes, which suddenly seemed to focus on a point just to the left of the window. Camilla stared at that spot for a second, trying to reason her way through this labyrinth of new information.

Then Camilla seemed to snap out of it and she asked, "From which foot?"

"The right."

Camilla's farewell was rapid and happened before Louise even had a chance to stand up. But Camilla turned around in the doorway and looked at her.

"Make sure you check your information," Camilla urged before disappearing.

For a second Louise just sat there staring at the empty doorway, before she turned to her partner and shook her head a little despondently.

"Do you think it was wise to let her just leave after what happened to her?" Lars asked, concerned.

Louise shrugged and rolled her chair up to her desk. "I don't know. I mean, we can't put a man on her, and she's also not the kind of person who would accept a bodyguard, even after a frightening experience like that."

"But I guess it would be worth checking on whether the

woman they were waiting for really was murdered," Lars said.

Louise nodded.

"What was her name again? Ilana...but what was her last name?" Lars asked, flipping through the stack of papers in front of him. "Procházková. We'd better tell Willumsen what happened."

"Let's go tell Toft instead. Then he can contact Interpol or e-mail the police in Prague directly," Louise suggested, getting up. "Willumsen will just chew us out for not being done with the lists of all the mothers-to-be."

She quickly walked over to Toft and Stig's office first, which was two doors down from her own.

"A Serb? Well, there's quite a few of those," Toft exclaimed, scratching the thick, full beard he had grown over the winter, but which he already seemed to be rethinking now that the weather was warming up again.

"But, of course, it ought to be checked."

He crossed his arms in front of his chest and glanced over at the row of certificates and trophies he and Michael Stig had brought home from all their bowling tournaments, both in Denmark and abroad, as he contemplated.

"If I can find the Serb's name, I have a good relationship with the criminal investigations unit in Prague. She's won a bunch of bowling tournaments and for a while she played professionally, but went back to police work after a couple of years. She said she missed it."

Louise smiled.

"What do we know about this Serb?" Toft asked, pulling out a sheet of paper, but they had to disappoint him then.

"Nothing aside from that he was seen in the woman's building. We don't have a description, but the police down there apparently know who the Albanians were referring to. Or at least they told Camilla that asking for 'the Serb' would be enough."

Toft nodded and stuck his plastic cigarette in his pocket.

"Maybe we should go pick up those two Albanians and haul them in here and find out if they have any more to tell us instead of letting them steer this show!"

Stig had appeared in the doorway with two sodas and a piece of fruit in his hands, and Lars made room for him so he could enter.

"Yeah," Toft said. "There might be something to that, but let's just check if they're leading us off on a wild-goose chase or if what they're saying is true."

He was already looking through his address list to find the Czech criminal investigations unit.

"Well, at least we don't have to sneak around after them anymore, since they already know we're breathing down their necks," Stig said, using one cola bottle to pop the lid off the other.

"Here she is!" Toft exclaimed, pointing at his screen. "I'll write to her."

"Well, we'd better be off," Louise said, nudging her partner in the side.

34

There was no answer from the first doorbell Louise rang, but the next address on the list was only two blocks away.

"Copenhagen Police. I'm Assistant Detective Louise Rick. May I come in and talk to you for a second?" she asked over the intercom after the woman answered.

When she got to the second floor, there was a woman standing in the hallway with a belly so enormous it looked ready to burst.

Louise hurriedly smiled to allay the fear on her face, which people typically had when receiving a visit from the police. Then she apologized for bothering her and quickly explained why she was there. After the woman confirmed that her name was Gitte Larsen, Louise crossed her off the list and left.

Eight of the nineteen on her list lived in the four bridge

districts—the dense residential neighborhoods of Nørre-bro, Amagerbro, Østerbro, or Vesterbro, which had once been linked to central Copenhagen by gates through the old city walls—so she decided to cover them by bike. After that she would go back to Police Headquarters and check a squad car out of the garage.

It was almost eight p.m., and there were three women left on her list when she rang the doorbell at Maja Lang's place. She lived in a little row house in Gentofte, and a dog barked noisily as the doorbell elicited a melody in a scale of shrill tones.

This woman had neither a bulging stomach nor an expectant glow. To the contrary, her skin was so pale it almost seemed translucent or blue, and the veins in her temples were visible, making her face seem sensitive and exposed.

Louise explained why she was there and felt a pang when she saw how the woman pulled back as if she'd struck her.

"It's been almost three months since I lost her," she said, slumping a little.

Pictures of autumn trees in warm golden colors hung on the wall behind her, and in the living room there was a lap blanket on the sofa, as if she'd just gotten up. The candles were lit, and there was a quiet that suddenly seemed striking given that the row house was right off the heavily trafficked Lyngbyvej.

Maja Lang nodded toward a room that opened off the living room.

"We had everything all ready, but one morning suddenly I just couldn't feel her, and then I knew something was wrong. Really wrong."

She pulled back, sat down on the edge of the sofa, and pushed the blanket aside a little apologetically.

"Four days after that they induced the delivery, and we buried her the last Saturday in January."

She started crying and pointed to the armchair on the other side of the coffee table.

Louise quickly decided not to sit down and apologized profusely for having bothered her. On her way out, she swore to herself that Gentofte hadn't struck Maja Lang off their list of women who were due. Now she'd ripped open the woman's grief completely unnecessarily.

35

When Louise and Lars gave their status reports the next afternoon, they had to acknowledge that none of the women on the maternity ward lists seemed to have given birth outside the official health-care system. In the previous twenty-four hours, they'd been in touch with everyone who had been due during the right time period in Region H, or Greater Copenhagen.

Louise hadn't gotten home to her empty apartment until almost ten thirty the previous evening. Camilla had left a message on her kitchen table that she and Markus were spending the night at their own place, because he needed to get some of his schoolbooks and his gym clothes there anyway. Louise had briefly considered calling to make sure her friend had calmed down after her dramatic afternoon, but she didn't want to risk waking them.

At eight o'clock in the morning she was back at it, starting with a couple in their early thirties who were busy timing contractions.

Two women had been admitted that same day with preeclampsia and were going to be kept under observation until their labors started; four were having contractions, including the couple Louise had visited that morning. Everything had been the way it was supposed to with all the rest. They had opened their doors with their big bellies jutting out in front of them and had immediately been crossed off the list and given an apology for the disturbance.

Maja Lang and a very young girl that Lars had spoken to out in Glostrup were the only ones for whom things had not gone the way they should. The young woman had had an acute abortion as the result of a serious traffic accident she had been involved in a month earlier. When Lars visited her, she had just returned home from the hospital and assumed that was why the maternity clinic still hadn't been informed of what had happened.

Louise glanced over at the door in irritation when someone knocked three times, hard, and was about to ask whoever it was to go away and let her work when Toft came in and said he'd just received an e-mail from Jana Romanová.

"She's a detective at Bartolomějská Street, which is Prague's 'hard' police precinct," he explained, closing the door behind him. "She confirmed that last week Monday they found Ilana Procházková in an apartment just behind Václavská Street, where a lot of the city's prostitution takes place."

Louise reached for the half-empty roll of chocolate cookies and offered Toft one. Then she helped herself to one and pushed them across the desk to Lars.

"OK," she said, feeling the little hairs on her arm stand up.

"True enough, her throat had been slit. Jana's going to have the most important details from the pathology report and the crime-scene investigation results translated into English and promised to e-mail them ASAP."

Louise rested her head in her hands. This was starting to feel like a Sudoku in which someone had switched all the numbers around.

"Did you ask what she knew about the Serb?" Lars asked out of curiosity, taking a bite of his cookie.

Toft got a deep wrinkle in his forehead and nodded pensively.

"Yeaaah. She's guessing they might be referring to this guy named Bosko. They know him from the prostitution scene, but she hadn't heard that he had allegedly been seen in the area. They did have a couple of witness statements that said that a man with short hair and a leather jacket had been seen in the building, but he hadn't been identified yet."

"What else was she able to tell you about him?" Louise asked, taking another cookie. "I mean, it certainly sounds like she knows who he is."

"Nothing else. She seemed a little reticent about him, but maybe that's because she wants to look into him first and see if there's a connection. They're working on looking for a match for the fingerprints they found in the apartment and in the stairwell right now. The results aren't back yet. And she said there was a lot of blood around the body, which means that the jugular was severed and sprayed, and the murderer must have had a fair amount of blood on him when he left the site. And that doesn't match the description of the man witnesses saw leaving the building around the time of the murder."

"Well then, I guess you're going to have to get a hold of Arian and Hamdi and get them to tell you some more," Louise said. "If they think there's a connection, and if they want to get out from under the cloud of suspicion that's hanging over them."

"They're being picked up right now." Toft nodded and added that Mikkelsen and Stig were going to question the two Albanians. He would stay in touch with Jana so they could compare the technical findings from Prague with what they'd found at the murder locations in Copenhagen to help determine if the cases were connected.

"That's good, because that will let them know that Camilla held up her end of the agreement," Louise said to Lars after Toft had shut the door behind him.

* * *

Willumsen had asked them to turn in a report to him once they had finished going through the list. He nodded toward the conference table when they knocked and quickly gathered up the papers that were spread out in a little heap in front of him.

"Was there anything suspicious?" He stood up and came over to sit down across from them.

"Unfortunately not," Lars said. "But I suppose that would have been awfully lucky if it had been so easy."

The lead detective nodded and rubbed his chin as he thought about it. "Let's just compare with what Bellahøj found in their search for Baby Girl's mother." He added that it would surely take a couple more days, or maybe a week, before the boy's DNA came back.

"So I guess there's no way around it. We're going to have to appeal to the public and ask people to come forward if they noticed a woman walking around with a big belly but without a baby carriage since losing the weight. Obviously, we run the risk of offending someone by assuming that she might have been pregnant if she turns out to have only gotten a little fat, but that's a risk we'll just have to take," he said, looking as if it wouldn't bother him in the least to hurl an insult like that.

The lead detective got up and walked over to the stack of papers, which he hadn't had a chance to look at yet.

"Do the techs have anything on the towel he was wrapped in?" she asked, looking at Willumsen.

He shook his head absentmindedly as he flipped through the pages.

"Yes, here!" he exclaimed when he was almost through. "But all it says is that they can tell from the brand that it was made for the Føtex chain."

"That's the same type of towel Baby Girl was left in," Louise said with a start. "And the same color," she added with a level of enthusiasm that made Willumsen look at her eagerly.

"Are you sure?"

"A hundred percent! A dark blue terry cloth towel from Føtex. That's pretty damn interesting, wouldn't you say? There's no way that's just a coincidence."

Willumsen didn't say anything, but she could tell he was inclined to agree with her. "We'll have the two towels compared for prints and DNA," he decided, then walked back over to his desk and picked up his phone. "Oh, and Bellahøj picked up those two lovebirds with the green Fiat. Sure enough, they were in the cemetery from about four a.m. until about six or six thirty, but they didn't see or hear anything. People get turned on by the weirdest things these days," he said, then started dialing Frandsen's number.

36

It was just past six when Camilla and Markus ran across the courtyard in front of the pastor's residence. Markus was carrying the wine and the big bottle of soda, and Camilla was carrying the two bags from Meyers Deli. They were supposed to be there at six, but they'd had to wait in line to get the takeout, so the time had gotten away from them.

She stopped in surprise when she spotted the black women's bicycle with a basket on the handlebars parked at the base of the kitchen stairs. The kitchen door was slightly ajar.

"Just a sec," she called to Markus, who was already on the first step. "Maybe we ought to go to the front door if he has guests."

Markus looked from his mother to the bicycle, not understanding what she meant. "That's just the girl's," he said. "Jonas said she was going to do some cleaning and stuff."

Camilla looked at him in astonishment. "How do you know that?"

"He told me at school. She started yesterday."

They walked up and used the knocker.

"Come in." Henrik Holm took the bags and put them on the kitchen table.

Markus instantly disappeared upstairs, even though Camilla called after him that they were about to eat.

"How are you doing?" the pastor asked, looking at her with concern.

He really didn't need to ask, because it was perfectly obvious to anyone who looked that things were falling apart. She had finally worked up the energy to take a bath before Markus came home from school, and she'd also found some clean clothes in the very back of her closet, but she hadn't done much else. All the same, she appreciated his concern.

Someone ought to be showing some for him, too. It occurred to her that his cheeks looked hollower and his skin more ashen than when she'd last seen him, but she certainly hadn't been paying that much attention on Saturday that she would have noticed if the changes had already started by then.

She accepted the glass of wine he handed her.

"Markus says you have a housekeeper," she said, nodding toward the open kitchen door, where the bike was parked.

He seemed embarrassed and turned around to take the food out of the bags.

"Yeah," he said with his back to her. "After everything

that's happened in the last few weeks, I suddenly felt like it would be nice to have a little help on that front."

Camilla walked over and started to get out the plates. "I can certainly understand that," she said, then walked over to get the salad Henrik had made. "I could use a little help myself to make it through the day, you know, just from first thing in the morning until it's time for me to go to bed again."

Henrik smiled at her and refilled their wineglasses, without her really having noticed that she'd emptied hers.

"How often is she coming? Once or twice a week?" Camilla asked, trying to concentrate on tasting the wine instead of just chugging it down.

"I've taken her in as an au pair, so she's living here. Three months to start with. I'll just see if I can get used to that, and hopefully by then things will have settled down again in our lives. Right now, I'm being bombarded with messages from the parish council and parishioners who want to know what's going on."

Camilla nodded and put the plates out on the table.

"Plus, maybe this way I'll be able to spend a little more quality time with Jonas," he added with a little smile, as if he felt like he needed to find excuses to justify finally having accepted a little help.

Camilla nodded and abruptly turned toward the door to the living room, from where she'd suddenly heard the sound of a woman's voice. A tall, young woman walked into the room with her cell phone to her ear and her eyes on the floor, as if she were concentrating on the phone call and hadn't noticed that they were looking at her.

Camilla recognized the dark pageboy hair and the dark eye makeup right away. "Well, but then it looks like it ended up working out very nicely," Camilla said and greeted the woman, who smiled at them uncertainly before leaving the room again.

Henrik nodded and said that some things worked out on their own. He stopped Camilla when she offered to set another place, and explained that Tereza didn't eat with them.

"There's a little mother-in-law apartment in the attic," he explained, pointing toward the staircase. "It has its own bathroom and a little kitchenette, so she prefers to eat on her own."

I suppose that makes sense, Camilla thought. It probably suited Henrik best, too, that he and Jonas could continue to do things the way they usually did without having to involve a stranger.

"Boys!" Camilla yelled up the stairs, hoping that would be enough to get their attention.

"Would you rather have coffee or tea?" Henrik asked once they'd cleared the table. "I've given up drinking coffee in the evenings lately. It's no good to have it interfering with everyone's sleep."

There was still more wine in the bottle, so Camilla said she would stick to that.

"Have you had any thoughts about what you think we ought to do in terms of the funeral?" Henrik asked after sitting down across from her with a cup of tea in front of him. "I have it tentatively scheduled for Saturday."

If she were thinking about it, that would probably have been her choice. She set her hands on the table and looked at him.

"I'm going to have to back out of it and leave it to you, or you can leave it to other people. I can't do it anymore. It eats away at me night and day and I'm going crazy, so I've decided that I'll have to wait to say my good-byes to him, until after he's in the ground in whatever pauper's grave somewhere. Someday when the sun is out, like it was today, I'll go there with a bag full of beer bottles and a ghetto blaster and play 'I Walk the Line' for him. That'll be my way of doing it."

Henrik's tired eyes twinkled at her. "That's a good plan," he conceded and said he'd be sure to show her where the urn was interred.

Camilla took a deep breath and then changed the topic. "Did you hear that the case from last Saturday has been turned over to the Homicide Division?" she asked after she'd poured the last of the wine into her glass.

He nodded and said that Louise had stopped by.

"Do you think there could be a connection between the two cases after all, even though the police are investigating them separately?" she asked, swirling her wine around in the glass.

He shrugged, but then shook his head. "Obviously, I've been thinking about it a lot, but I don't see what they could have to do with each other," he said.

"But it is sick, isn't it, to abandon a stillborn baby."

She studied his face to find a reaction and then looked away when he looked up from his teacup and nodded with a deep furrow in his brow.

"That's one of the things that depresses me the most," he admitted. "Most people have no idea how many mentally ill people are left to their own devices. People who are lonely and unhappy cry out for help, but only a tiny number are ever actually heard. Only in the most glaring circumstances, when it turns into a shootout with the police or something, where the mentally ill person is doomed to lose from the beginning."

"Maybe abandoning the baby last Saturday was an attempt to get you to listen," Camilla said, after a couple moments of silence. She could hear the boys playing *World of Warcraft* up in Jonas's room, and based on the cheers she was guessing one of them had just made it to a new level. "I'm thinking about the thing with the toe," she added. She waited for his reaction, but when it didn't come, she continued, "Markus told me that Jonas is also missing a pinky toe."

She knew she was overstepping her bounds, trespassing on his privacy, and she watched him to see if he was taking it the wrong way. At first, he looked at her in surprise, as if he were surprised that she knew about that detail, but then he looked over toward the breadbasket, which was still sitting on the table, and looked lost in thought, in a way that made her not want to bother him.

"Obviously, I've thought about that," he said after a while. "But I don't see how those two things could be connected. My son has a congenital defect on his foot, which anyone who has seen him barefoot knows about, but otherwise it's not really something anyone would notice. If someone is trying to tell me something, I really hope they'll come forward so I can help them."

There was a look of resignation in his face, which Camilla interpreted as tiredness. It was a little after nine; she had to be getting home so that Markus wouldn't be too much of a basket case when he had to get up for school the next morning.

She smiled when he thanked her for bringing the food, and while he yelled up to the boys that Markus should come down, she got their jackets.

37

On the way down from the cafeteria, Louise spotted the interpreter. Igli was on his way to the monitoring room. She overtook a couple of the office girls, who were taking up most of the stairwell, chatting as they walked, and received a snide comment as she squeezed by.

She jogged to catch up to Igli and asked him if he had time for a cup of coffee. She knew that he'd worked for the police in Belgrade for years before moving to Denmark during the war in the former Yugoslavia.

He smiled at her in surprise and said that he thought she and Lars had been reassigned and weren't following the wiretaps that he was working on anymore.

"True enough," she hurried to say, as they started heading back up to the cafeteria together.

"Do you take milk or sugar?" Louise asked as the cashier rang them up.

"Sugar," he requested and added that he wouldn't mind a pastry to go with the coffee.

Louise pointed to the two last chocolate chip rolls on the plate and paid before carrying the tray over to the table in the back corner of the room.

"So, what is it you want?" Igli asked. He then apologized for having to leave his cell phone on while they talked, because his son was going to call when he left school. "He's just started taking the bus home by himself."

"That's fine," Louise said, passing him one of the rolls and mopping up the coffee that had sloshed over onto the saucer. "I want to find out if you know anything about a Serb named Bosko."

Igli's teaspoon stopped stirring for a minute as he watched her attentively. "That's really a very common Serbian name," he said and then kept stirring.

She nodded and thought, I suppose it is. "I'm talking about a person who is known to both the Czech police and the two Albanians whose phone calls you've been monitoring, and I imagine that might be the same guy they're talking about. Does that tell you anything?"

A gloomy look slipped over his face and a deep wrinkle formed on his forehead. "Well, then I have an idea who you're thinking of. Why do you ask about him?" Igli asked, as though she'd asked him to pull out a shadow from the past.

"Because his name has come up in connection with the Meatpacking District case. We don't know if there's anything to it, but I'd like to find out who he is."

She explained what had happened to Camilla and told Igli about the tip Arian had given them, which had turned out to be true.

"But when Toft tried to get information from his source with the police in Prague, she just wormed her way out of it and said that they hadn't heard he was in town. So he was obviously someone they were familiar with."

Igli nodded and leaned his head over his full coffee cup before admitting that Bosko was someone who was known throughout most of the Balkans.

"Personally, it's been my opinion that it's best to know as little about him as possible, but if you think you need to know, I'll be happy to tell you what kind of person he is."

Igli pushed the plate with the untouched chocolate chip roll away and leaned in over the table.

"I ran into him the first time when he was in his midtwenties. That was more than twenty years ago. He's from Belgrade and started his criminal career as a soccer fan of the Belgrade Red Star, the professional Serbian club, which recently received a big fine for violent riots during a league game. A policeman was attacked and seriously injured. Several of the club employees are suspected of having started the riots, so things haven't changed much over the years."

Soccer and league games were not something Louise knew much about, and she had to admit that she'd never heard of the Belgrade Red Star.

"He became the lead fan," Igli went on. "Then in 1992 he joined up with Arkan's Tigers; that was right after the election when Bosnia became independent, and he was behind some of the nastiest ethnic cleansing by the paramilitary unit, which caused thousands upon thousands of Muslim citizens to flee."

Igli gave her a very somber look.

Suddenly Michael Stig was standing at their table without Louise having noticed him walk up. He said, "You guys shooting the breeze?"

"I guess you could say that," Louise said, irritated, as Stig got ready to join them. "Igli was just telling me about Bosko." She asked Stig if they had gotten any more out of Arian or Hamdi during the questioning sessions the previous day. They'd still been going when Louise had left.

Stig shook his head and eyed Igli with curiosity, as if it hadn't occurred to him that Igli might know anything about the Serb. "They're not saying a word. Just keep repeating that we should check where Bosko was when the two murders took place. But then when we ask them to tell us any more about the Serb, they completely clam up, even when we try to explain to them that that makes it a little hard for us to get anywhere if they don't want to say anything."

Igli nodded as Stig spoke. "No one's going to talk if Bosko is involved. But is there any reason to think he's been in Copenhagen?" he asked.

Louise could see the anxiety in Igli's brown eyes.

"Just what those two say," Stig responded with a shrug of his shoulders. "And no one here seems to have heard of him before, not even Mikkelsen, who otherwise is familiar with most of the rumors going around in the neighborhood."

The interpreter shook his head again. "I haven't heard anything about Bosko starting to be active in Denmark," he confessed. "And I hope he doesn't decide to turn up, either."

"I interrupted you in the middle of something," Stig said, opening his soda bottle against the edge of the table. Louise nodded and asked Igli to continue what he had been saying.

The interpreter sighed and took a deep breath, as if he would have preferred not to finish what he was saying. He glanced at his cell phone on the table, which hadn't rung yet.

"He got his own military unit, weapons and trained people from the ultranationalist parties, who were interested in cleaning out the Muslims and claiming land for the Serbs. But that's not how I ran into him again."

Louise could tell that Stig didn't find Igli's old wartime memories particularly interesting and that he was hoping their chat would be more closely related to the case they were working on.

"Two years after the war broke out and was at its peak, Bosko realized how much money could be made if he used the situation to his own advantage. That was during the siege of Sarajevo, when Serbian forces created a blockade around the city and stopped all supplies from entering. Residents were short on food, and emergency supply convoys were having a hard time making it in. That's when Bosko started building up his smuggling business."

The look in Igli's eyes made it clear that the memories were painful.

"The Bosnian-Serb forces were shelling the city daily with mortars, and snipers were killing people in the streets, and they weren't distinguishing between civilian and military targets. It was in the middle of all that chaos, while the city was in a state of emergency, when Bosko made his first millions."

The plate of chocolate chip rolls remained untouched, and the coffee in Igli's cup had grown cold.

"We think he brought in the first war tourists in April 1994, but he may have started even earlier than that. The route ran from Moscow to Budapest or Sofia, and then from there they were brought to Belgrade by car and on to Zvornik, which is the border between Serbia and the Serbian part of Bosnia, which is now called the Republika Srpska," Igli explained. "From Zvornik, a team leader brought them to Pale, the little town up in the mountains, which has since become the capital of the Serbian territory. The town is about twenty kilometers from Sarajevo."

The cafeteria was empty by now, and the employees were sitting at the other end of the room having a cup of coffee. They didn't seem bothered that the last of the customers hadn't left yet.

"The war tourists were housed in some of the luxury hotels, which had been built for the Winter Olympics in 1984. We thought it was mostly the newly minted millionaires from Russia and Ukraine he was bringing in when he arranged what we started calling his human safaris. They were the ones who could afford to pay the big money for an adrenaline rush that they could hold on to long after they'd returned home again."

Louise was staring at Igli in disbelief but didn't interrupt, and Stig no longer looked like Igli's story was boring him.

"You bought a basic package, which covered the trip to Serbia, your room and board, and after that you could say the price depended on the level of danger or the size of the adrenaline rush you wanted.

"The trips were broken up like this:

"Tour Number One was the economy trip. Participants were allowed to fire mortars out over Sarajevo without a chance to see what they'd hit, or whether anyone was killed.

"Tour Number Two was more like coach. A guide would take you down into the city so you could follow the fighting and see where the mortars you launched had hit and how many people you'd killed.

"Tour Number Three was the exclusive one. Here, a personal guide and a bodyguard would take you down into the city with a sniper rifle so that you could shoot right at people."

Igli paused for a bit.

"Rumor had it that if you hit anyone, you got a discount on the price of the tour. But we never managed to confirm that, and the police only managed to figure all this out after the fact. We were just never anywhere near catching Bosko, even though he never hid the fact that he was the man behind the tours. People like Bosko are rarely caught, because men of that caliber are known by Serbs and Muslims, and there will always be someone willing to cover up for them."

For a second, Louise thought what she saw in Igli's eyes was respect, but then she realized that it was profound fear.

"I hope for your sakes and everyone else's that he hasn't come to Denmark. Bosko goes wherever there's a lot of money to be made, and he uses unscrupulous people to increase his fortune. Now I've heard that in the last few years of the war, he was trading in children, that he was trading in women and smuggling people over borders for big sums of money. But the truth is I want to hear as little news about him as possible."

The cell phone on the table rang, and Igli quickly looked at his watch before answering it and arranging with his son that the boy would call again once he was home. Then Igli excused himself and said that he was going to go down to the monitoring room and see what was on the computer so they could keep on top of it.

Louise and Stig sat there for a bit without saying anything before Louise cleared the table and then took the full tray over to the garbage area.

"It's not going to do any good for us to check the airlines' passenger manifests around the times of the killings," Stig said, once they were on their way back downstairs. "He can cross national boundaries freely by car, if he turns out to be the one who was here."

Once they got down to the second floor, where the Homicide Division offices were, Louise proceeded down the hall and cautiously knocked on the door to the monitoring room.

"Excuse me," she hurried to say, as Igli pulled his headphones off. "Do you think your old colleagues might have a picture of Bosko that they could e-mail us?"

Igli thought about that for a moment, but was interrupted by his cell phone ringing.

His son must have made it home and the father's shoulders noticeably relaxed. Igli folded his hands over his stomach and gave Louise a somber look. "I would really like to ask you to keep me out of this. I told you about Bosko because you sounded like you might need to know. But I'd rather not have any further involvement," he said, an urgent look in his eyes.

"Of course," she said quickly, taking a reflexive step back, surprised by the intensity in his voice.

"Don't misunderstand me. It's not that I subscribe to the idea that some people should be allowed to demand to be left in peace, but I swore to myself that I would never have anything to do with Bosko or his people ever again.

Both of my brothers worked for the police. They were the ones, along with a couple of other people, who figured out the war tourism thing. When Bosko learned that they'd detected his smuggling business, he went looking for the four men who'd been working on the case, he went to their homes, and gunned them down in front of their wives and children."

The pain was evident in his face as he gave a quick nod, as if to emphasize that that's what happened when you went up against a man like Bosko. Then he turned back around to face his computer and reached for his headphones without reacting to Louise's good-bye.

38

Louise stopped abruptly in the doorway to her office when she saw Camilla sitting there waiting for her with a mug of steaming tea in her hands.

Lars had already been out to a private birthing clinic in Østerbro before lunch to pick up a list of the names of pregnant women who were due to give birth or whose due dates had just passed. The manager there had not been favorably disposed toward handing over the list even though Lars had a court order, but it did seem to mollify her when he offered to come pick it up in person so there was no risk it would fall into the wrong hands.

"Hello," Louise said, noting that her voice sounded a little lackluster. She was still mulling over Igli's story and especially his own personal involvement in it. She took the electric water heater that had just boiled and got out a packet of green tea before she sat down to find out why Camilla had stopped by.

"Markus and I had dinner with Pastor Holm and Jonas last night," Camilla began slowly.

Louise tossed her tea bag into the trash, leaving a line of wet drips on the floor, before she swung around in her chair and told Camilla that of course it was nice of her to stop by, but that she and Lars were in the middle of a monumental assignment, since Willumsen had left it up to them to find the mother of the stillborn baby. She didn't have much time for tea parties.

"Did you know that Jonas is missing the pinky toe on his right foot?" Camilla asked, without paying any heed to Louise's attempt to send her on her way.

There was a pause, as they each held their mug of tea and looked at each other while their thoughts took over.

"No," Louise said, shaking her head. "I didn't know that."

"Henrik is totally convinced that the toe wasn't amputated, that it just happened to be like that, but I don't believe in that kind of coincidence. I just can't tell if he has noticed the similarity, or if he's really as clueless as he's acting."

Louise set down her mug. "What do you mean by that?" she asked, eyeing Camilla expectantly, hoping she would fill her in on whatever idea had occurred to her. Without question, it seemed too absurd for someone to cut the toe off a newborn baby just because they knew the pastor's son was missing a pinky toe, but Louise did agree that it didn't sound like a coincidence. Especially since it was the same toe.

"Maybe someone feels like he's let them down, or that

it's his fault their child didn't survive," Camilla suggested, shrugging her shoulders at the lack of an obvious explanation.

"But if that's the case then, whoever left the baby in the church must be someone who knows that Jonas has that defect," Louise said, picking up her phone and dialing Willumsen's extension.

"Yeah?" Willumsen said tersely.

Louise realized how tired she felt as she asked if he had time to stop by her office. "I thought you had enough work to keep you busy," he said sarcastically when he spotted Camilla in there, drinking tea.

Louise didn't even have the energy to explain, just motioned toward Lars's chair and asked Willumsen to take a seat.

Camilla smoothed back a tuft of hair, which had come out of her ponytail, and repeated what she'd just told Louise.

Willumsen grunted slightly, while the two women watched him to see what his assessment was.

"What does the pastor have to say about it?" was the first thing Willumsen asked, eyeing Louise. She had to shrug because she hadn't spoken with Henrik Holm about it yet. "If this isn't a coincidence, then it does kind of look like someone has decided to go after him. That there's a personal motive, at least behind that last event."

Camilla nodded. "But he's not saying anything," she said, watching Louise's boss.

Willumsen got up and paced back and forth a bit. Then he pointed to Louise. "You need to go talk to him. If it was someone trying to tell him something, then we're going to have to start a completely different kind of investigation."

Louise agreed. She contemplated calling the pastor's residence first, before she left, but decided to just hope he was home.

"I brought my car," Camilla said and offered her a ride out to the church. "It's not far out of my way, after all." They walked down toward Otto Mønsteds Gade. "But I'm not going in with you," she hurriedly added before they climbed into the car. "It's bad enough that I've been blabbing to you about his kid's toes."

39

Louise climbed the steps to the pastor's kitchen door and banged a couple of times with the doorknocker. She smiled shyly at the tall, dark-haired woman who opened the door a second later. Camilla had told her about the housekeeper on their way out there, but now she realized she was interrupting them in the middle of a conversation. There were three girls sitting around the table talking softly in a language Louise didn't understand. Now their conversation stopped, and they all looked down at the table a little uncertainly and avoided looking her in the eye.

"Could I come in to speak to Henrik Holm?" Louise asked in English.

The housekeeper pointed over to the church without saying anything, but her meaning was clear enough, so Louise smiled and thanked her before turning to walk back across the courtyard, where the sexton had just come into view.

"He's in the middle of a wedding rehearsal with a couple who's going to get married here this weekend," the sexton said, squinting slightly at the sun as he turned and looked at the clock on the church tower. "I think they'll be done soon."

"Oh, that's fine. Then I'll wait for him," Louise said and walked over to sit down on a bench in the sun. It was positioned such that she had her back to the whitewashed church wall and had a wonderful view of the cemetery, where the beech tree buds were just about to open.

It still didn't make any sense to her that someone would remove the infant's toe to harass or provoke Henrik Holm, but sometimes it didn't take much to make people act based on emotion. Often it seemed like a trivial matter to other people, but to the person who felt like they'd been wronged, a relatively simple occurrence could cause their world to fall apart.

A couple in their midthirties walked out of the church with the pastor. Louise watched them say good-bye and didn't get up until Pastor Holm started walking toward the residence.

"Hi," she called after him and apologized for coming by unannounced. "There was just one thing I wanted to discuss with you."

He turned around, surprised, and smiled when he saw her. "No problem," he assured her. "Let's have a seat," he suggested and they walked back over to the bench.

Instead of getting right to the point, Louise said she'd just met his new housekeeper. "What does Jonas think about her?"

"He hasn't said much," the pastor admitted. "But I think that's a good sign. Tereza told me yesterday that for the last month she's been the leader of a network that tries to help Eastern European women who've been forced to come to Denmark and work as prostitutes against their will. The network tries to help them get back home safely."

Louise listened with interest and thought about Pavlína. A network like that would be great for her.

"There are already a number of people involved, and I got the sense that there would be even more. So, I gave them permission to meet out here, where they can talk in peace and quiet," he said.

Louise sensed a new dedication in his voice and was sure it hadn't been there during her last visit. But his eyes seemed tired and kept darting around the courtyard anxiously and over toward the parking lot, as if he were having a hard time concentrating.

"If they're not already familiar with the Nest and Stop Trafficking in Women, they might like to talk to them," Louise suggested. "They also have some resources that can be used to help victims get back home, even with a little money in their pockets, so they can get by for a while and not be susceptible to being rounded up again right away." She could tell that this was all news to him, but that he was clearly interested.

Louise took a breath, which ended up being a little deeper than she'd been planning, and then turned to face him and changed the topic. "You should have told us that Jonas is missing his right pinky toe," she said, watching him to see what his reaction would be. When there was none, she continued: "It's certainly possible that that isn't significant, but that is a piece of information we're going to need to include in our considerations as we investigate the case."

Finally, he nodded and leaned forward so that his forearms were resting on his knees with his fingers interlaced. He nodded again but remained silent.

"It makes us think there might be a personal motive behind the event," Louise explained, watching his wiry hair flutter a little in the wind as he shook his head.

"I can't imagine there is one," he said, focusing intently on his fingers, which were moving in and out of each other. "I wouldn't have even given it a thought myself if Camilla hadn't mentioned it yesterday." Louise could almost physically feel his reluctance to talk any more about it.

Now she was forced to ask, "Are there many people who know about his little defect?"

The pastor slowly shook his head.

"Whether there's any connection or not, I'd like to ask you to make a list of the names of the pregnant women you have had any recent contact with for any reason," she requested. "And also, a list of names of anyone who has already scheduled a baptism or who had at least discussed possibly wanting to baptize a child in your church."

She hazarded a guess that having a pastor who was familiar from his media appearances might make people more interested in him.

"Maybe we should also consider whether you might have written something recently that might have triggered this action," she finally suggested.

He turned to her then, and to her surprise, she saw a look of profound irritation in his eyes, and she jumped slightly when he suddenly got up from the bench.

"I'm going to need to ask you to respect that as a pastor

I'm bound to keep certain things confidential. But having said that, I don't need to even think about it to know that there haven't been any episodes here in the church that could have triggered what you're thinking of."

Louise was about to tone things down a little, but she didn't have a chance to say anything before Henrik continued:

"If someone wanted to come after me because of the things I write, then I can pretty much promise you it would've happened a long time ago. But you're welcome to go through everything if you think it might have some significance. All my columns and commentaries are on my home page."

She hadn't meant to make him mad, and she was so surprised at his violent response that she just sat there staring at him as he walked back toward his kitchen door. Then she closed her eyes and turned her face to the sun and composed herself for a second with the back of her head resting against the wall.

She decided to cut through the cemetery and walked along, lost in her own thoughts, her eyes trained on the gravel, which was why it wasn't until she'd passed the young girl on the path that it occurred to her there was something familiar about her. Louise turned around, but then she wasn't sure it had been Hana. From behind it was only the long blond hair that confirmed her guess.

At the end of the graves, she exited through the gate and crossed the street before continuing on into Frederiksberg Park. When she reached the lake, she stopped abruptly and enjoyed the view of the white swans and coots walking along the shore. The mild spring weather reminded her that summer was on its way. Suddenly she felt an almost overwhelming urge to get out of town, to head for the fields and woods and water. She sat down on the bench closest to the ice cream stand, which wasn't open for the season yet, and pulled out her phone.

A quick glance at her watch told her that it was just past four when she sent Mik a text message inviting herself to go kayaking with him on the Holbæk Fjord. "If you have the kayaks ready in an hour, I'll pay for dinner at the harbor when we get back to shore," she wrote and smiled as she pressed Send.

The response came before she'd even had time to get up off the bench. "Great. See you soon."

40

Mik Rasmussen and Louise overslept. She'd planned to leave at about seven; now it was almost eight thirty. Of course, they'd ended up having Irish coffees when they got back to his traditional thatch-roofed farmhouse after they'd eaten soup, monkfish cheeks, and a "sumptuous symphony of chocolate," as the chef had elegantly dubbed the four different chocolate desserts that had been dusted with powdered sugar and served together in one square glass dish.

They hadn't gotten much sleep, but her body felt great and she was humming, "Wake up, it's a wonderful morning," as she backed out of the courtyard and blew him a kiss through the driver's-side window.

Once she was on the highway she turned on the radio and sang along to "Billie Jean," glad that P4 still played Michael Jackson.

She stopped in Frederiksberg to park her car and biked the rest of the way in to Police Headquarters. She was still humming as she biked along Gammel Kongevej with her sunglasses on and the wind in her long, dark curls. Out in front of Police Square she spotted Mikkelsen walking down the sidewalk.

"Hey!" she called, waving to him before swinging her leg over the saddle of her black mountain bike. "You want to walk up with me?"

He nodded, breathing a little heavily.

"Too many cigarettes and not enough exercise," he admitted honestly.

Louise was about to add "And too much barbecue" but managed to bite her tongue. It really wasn't any of her business.

"Are you guys meeting?" she asked Mikkelsen and nodded at the guy at the front desk as she showed her ID.

"Yeah," Mikkelsen grunted, still not quite having caught his breath. "We really want to find out where the Albanians are meeting with the girls now when they make their payments. They're not going to Central Station anymore."

"Could they have put their business on hold for a bit?" Louise suggested, but Mikkelsen shook his head, smiling.

"No, no way," he said. "That's the last thing they'd do, even though they know we're watching them."

She gave him a blank look.

"You have to keep in mind that even if they get caught and charged with pandering or in a worst-case scenario, trafficking in women, the penalty isn't that high. Considering what they make in a single day, it's not enough to scare them. It's no skin off their backs if they wind up in the slammer for a year or two, because they're raking in so much money when things are going well."

Louise listened with interest as he continued:

"Right now, human trafficking is the most lucrative crime. That's where they get the money to buy weapons and drugs!"

That last bit was a little dig, justifying why they still ought to take down the people behind the scenes, even if it was only for a year or two.

Louise stopped outside her office and watched Mikkelsen as he continued two doors farther down the hallway and knocked on Toft and Stig's door.

* * *

It was five to ten when she said good morning to Lars, who was facing his screen, but watched her as she took off her jacket and turned on her computer.

"Good morning," he teased, implying that he'd been working for several hours already and that he no longer really considered it morning.

"Yeah," she said apologetically. "I overslept. I should've called you when I woke up, but I didn't think about it."

He shook his head. "You didn't need to," he said quickly.

Suddenly she noticed something in his expression that she hadn't seen before. Louise sat down and looked at him. "Were you afraid something had happened to me?" she said.

His eyes were back on his computer, but after a second he nodded and admitted that the thought had crossed his mind.

She smiled. "You were worried about me," she said, and he looked embarrassed.

He mumbled something about given what had happened to Camilla it didn't hurt to pay a little extra attention...

"You shouldn't be apologizing. I'm just glad you care," she exclaimed, but was interrupted by a knock at the door. Toft stuck his head in and she saw Suhr standing behind him.

"Could we come in?" Toft asked.

She nodded, casting a quick glance at Suhr to see if he'd noticed that she'd come in late. If he had, she would have to apologize. If he hadn't, she didn't see the point in drawing his attention to it.

"We succeeded in getting a picture of that Serbian man, Bosko," Toft said.

Louise could tell right away that Suhr did not deserve any of the credit for this accomplishment. Toft, in his terrier-like style, had doggedly pursued and obtained the photo. "We sent the picture around to all the precincts last night, but so far no one has responded to it," Suhr reported. "But at least they have him up on their radar now, and the patrols have been informed."

Suhr stepped all the way into the office while Toft remained in the doorway, leaning against the frame.

"We would really like your assistance for the rest of the day," Suhr said. When he saw Louise's expression, he added that Willumsen had suggested it himself, that they put everything they could into confirming or disproving whether the Serb had been seen in or around Skelbækgade and Sønder Boulevard around the times of the two murders.

"We're going to make the rounds on Istedgade and the

rest of the neighborhood with this picture," he continued. "If it turns out that there aren't any witnesses who saw him moving around in the area, then we'll drag the two Albanians in and charge them with the killings and hope that that's enough to make them talk."

"We have had them in here for questioning for the last two days," Toft added, as if to justify this harsh-sounding decision. "They're not saying anything. Nothing at all. Except that they keep claiming it wasn't them. They also clam up completely when we ask them to tell us what they know about Bosko. They just shake their heads and repeat that we should find out where he was when the two murders took place."

"So that's what we're going to spend the rest of the day on," Suhr concluded. Then he corrected himself. "Of course, we'll also find out if anyone saw him during the interim between the two killings."

Louise was still happy it was spring, but some of the effervescence was gone, replaced by an expectant restlessness. It suited her just fine to go back to Istedgade, even though she was kind of hoping they didn't find him. Hard to tell what the consequences would be if an international criminal with a background like that set up shop in Copenhagen. She also knew that the reason she was looking forward to taking a little break from her own case so much was the way her conversation with Henrik Holm had ended the day before.

"We'll split the area up between you," Suhr said, adding that Mikkelsen was providing four people from the downtown precinct. "Willumsen will go with you, so there'll be five of us from here." He dropped the pictures on the table.

Louise pushed one over to Lars and took the other one herself. She didn't know what she'd imagined a man with so many human lives on his conscience would look like, but she was sure she'd seen him before, and she knew where, too.

41

Camilla had brought her comforter in to use on the sofa, and now she turned on the morning shows as soon as Markus left for school. She hadn't slept well at all. She shouldn't have told the police about Jonas's toe. The thoughts kept swirling around in her head, but she'd seen the pastor's reaction when she mentioned that she thought there might be a connection. It had been there, but then it was gone again. At three a.m., she'd gotten up and shaken six sleep-inducing valerian pills out into her hand, but they hadn't helped. The last time she looked at the clock it was a little past five. By that point there were just under two hours until she had to get up to see Markus off. Now she ought to do some laundry. Markus had been forced to wear a pair of sweats and a long-sleeved T-shirt whose arms were too short when she was forced to confirm that there was nothing else clean.

But instead of getting up and gathering the laundry, she took her thoughts back to that evening, when she'd been sitting in the pastor's kitchen. And suddenly a new thought struck her. What if the stillborn baby in the church wasn't related to the pastor, but to the son's mother? Then maybe that would explain why Henrik so categorically rejected that the two things had anything to do with each other.

That was a possibility that hadn't occurred to her before now, surely because she'd never known the boy's mother. She'd seen only one picture of her, a photo of the three of them at a dilapidated farm in Sweden where Markus had once spent Easter with them. Once in Laholm she had almost not been able to figure out the last bit of the way to the farm when it was time to go pick him up. Alice Holm smiled from the photograph on the bookshelf, and she guessed it was taken when Jonas was about three—one year before she died.

Camilla tried to remember what Henrik had said about his wife and their time in Bosnia. Camilla didn't know where they'd been stationed in the country as aid workers, just that the camp had been in a small town, which had been subjected to several brutal massacres in short succession.

Camilla tossed the comforter aside and went into the bedroom to get her laptop. It was Srebrenica, where the bodies from the brutal ethnic cleansings had been carted off to a huge mass grave outside of town.

She also searched Infomedia to see if the pastor had written anything about his experiences in the Balkans. She determined that he had. There were six articles. Camilla felt a little flutter in her stomach where she hadn't been feeling much of anything lately, but there turned out to be nothing to go on. They were all objective descriptions of the area, of the mood that weighed on the city like an overcast sky. He wrote that no one ever produced a concrete number of how many people had died in the brutal cleansing, but that it had affected all portions of the civilian population: men, women, children, the elderly. No one escaped. Maybe five, or eight, or ten thousand dead. Who knew? he wrote, and his point was that the correct number didn't mean that much to the residents who were left anyway. "The people are broken and humiliated. There couldn't be more sorrow, even if the tally went up."

He wrote well, Camilla observed, after she'd read all the way through. Gripping and clear. Even though the events were from fourteen years before, they got under her skin and gave her the sense of being a snotty-nosed, overprivileged dolt like the rest of the Danish population. No one here had experienced anything that came anywhere close to what the Muslims in the Balkans had suffered, and despite that many Danes still felt an inflated sense of arrogance toward the people who had been affected and had since come to Denmark to make a fresh start.

She suddenly sat up, alert, concentrating as if she were listening to something. She didn't move, trying to be sure, but then she realized she had no doubt that it had been there. Her cheeks pulled up and for a second she smiled, a smile no one saw, as to her great relief she noted that everything in her wasn't dead after all.

She felt indignation, rage at how ridiculously smug and egocentric people were. She was struck by it, and it made her want to write. Maybe it was a little late to be scolding people for the cold shoulder so many asylum seekers from the former Yugoslavia had been met with, but she yearned to do it. Over the last couple of weeks she'd totally written off ever feeling this way again. Apparently, she just needed to be prodded hard enough.

Camilla got up and went in to print out the six articles. Then she read them again, but aside from eliciting her compassion, there was nothing in what Henrik had written that seemed in any way related to his private life.

She did manage to figure out that they'd been sent by the Red Cross and that one of the people they'd shared their barracks with was Elsa Lynge. Camilla had run across her in connection with one of the big emergency-aid collection drives, so she knew Elsa was still somehow affiliated with the organization.

After a quick shower and reinvigorated, she sat down on the sofa and called the Danish Red Cross. She had to talk to only two people before she had Elsa Lynge on the line.

"I'm calling you about a personal matter," Camilla admitted right off the bat and asked if she should call back at another time.

"No, no, now's as good as any," Elsa responded. "But could I ask you to call me back on my cell in three minutes? Then I can just duck out and have a smoke."

Camilla smiled and jotted down Elsa's cell number on the back of one of the pages she'd just printed out.

"Henrik and Alice Holm," Elsa repeated after Camilla had her back on the line. "Yeah, I know him, although now of course it's mostly from the media, but I don't think I can remember her."

Camilla sank back in the sofa a little. "Can you think of anyone else I could try calling? Someone that you think might remember her?"

"I'm going to need longer than a smoking break to think

about that one," Elsa admitted after a moment's contemplation, during which Camilla could hear her puffing away heartily on her cigarette. "It was so long ago, and I've done so much traveling, but if you tell me what you need to know, then maybe that would make it a little easier for me to think of who you should talk to."

Very briefly and without going into too many details, Camilla explained that she had been the one who found the stillborn infant out in Henrik Holm's church and that she had reason to believe that there might be some connection between the baby in the church and the baby the Holms had while they were living in the refugee camp.

Camilla heard Elsa's lighter clicking and a hoarse cough as Elsa lit the next cigarette. "I can tell you one thing for sure," Elsa said once she finished coughing. "Which is that in the two and a half years I was there none of the aid workers in our camp had a baby. The conditions just weren't suitable for babies." Elsa cleared her throat when her voice became gravelly. "Of course, there were tons of kids and babies who had survived with their mothers, or who were left behind after the rest of the family had been wiped out." Again, she paused to take a drag off her cigarette.

Camilla thought for a moment before she asked her next question. "And when exactly were you there?"

"From the middle of '96 until the end of '99," Elsa said without stopping to think. "I had just come home when we celebrated the new millennium. But there was something about his wife getting sick, and as far as I can remember they left early."

Camilla could hear that Elsa had started walking. "And you're sure we're talking about the same pastor?" she asked, even though she knew the question was unnecessary.

"Yeah, there weren't any others," Elsa confirmed. "And then there was his wife's death. A few years after that and so tragic, to die at such a young age. I don't know where you got the idea that they supposedly had a child while they were there."

Camilla sat holding her phone in her hand long after the call was over. Maybe she wasn't finding her way back to her old self after all. On the contrary, maybe she was really losing it.

42

At Police Headquarters, Suhr had summoned Willumsen's investigative team to his office. Mikkelsen was just pulling the blinds to keep the sharp May sun out of their eyes, but he was listening attentively as Louise told them where she'd run into Bosko.

"He was coming out of the building on Valdemarsgade, the one that Miloš Vituk's apartment is in," Louise said. She was able to tell them that without a doubt it had happened on the Wednesday after Kaj Antonsen was murdered, because she'd looked up her report from her stakeout, and she now had it lying on the table in front of her.

She explained that the Serb had come out the front door while she was standing in the doorway across the street. "There was something about his eyes and the way he looked at me that gave me the sense that maybe we knew each other. But we didn't, and now I'm sure he was just being vigilant. He noticed that I saw him."

"Is this something you're totally sure of, or is there a chance you're confusing him with someone else?" Willumsen asked her, looking tense.

Louise smiled at him stiffly and noted how a few hairs on the back of her neck were standing up. Because she was completely sure that the man in the picture and the man she'd seen on Valdemarsgade were identical.

She just said, "I'm sure," and was struck by the tense silence that had come over the room. She looked at her partner and saw the anxiety in his eyes, the worry that made the blue in his eyes a shade darker.

"We made eye contact twice," she said. "Both when he left the property, and when he returned again a little later."

Suhr was sitting behind his desk with his hands folded, his thumbs circling each other, and Toft had taken out his plastic cigarette while his partner, Stig, was tipping his chair back perilously.

Louise caught Stig's eye; the chair's front legs hit the floor as he tipped back down, forward, and she asked him to help her explain what Igli had told them about Bosko.

They listened in silence, but Louise noticed with growing concern the looks that Suhr and Willumsen were exchanging as she and Stig talked, because it hit her that right now they were both trying to decide, on their own, whether Bosko was of such a caliber that they were about to hand the case over to the PET, the Security and Intelligence Service, Denmark's equivalent of the CIA. She noted how Willumsen moved to speak the instant they were done.

"We'll get a court order so we can start a wiretap on

Miloš Vituk as soon as possible," he decided, not even looking over at Suhr as he spoke.

Something inside Louise fell into place. Clearly, he didn't want to hand over a case that might be of international importance, and she respected him for that.

"Bring those two Albanians in for questioning again." Suhr looked at Mikkelsen. "This time don't let them leave until they've told us exactly what the fuck they know about Bosko. How did they find out what happened in Prague? Who saw Bosko? And where was he seen?" He slapped his desk with the palms of his hand, making a loud bang, and looked at them.

"What about the pregnant women?" Lars asked.

Willumsen looked at him, as if he'd just farted audibly. "To hell with the pregnant women right now. The baby was dead, so it's not like that case is going anywhere."

Louise and Lars looked at each other and Louise subtly shook her head. That hadn't really been his attitude when Willumsen put them on the case.

Suhr cleared his throat and waited until he had everyone's attention. "Two things," he began, hesitating a little.

Louise could tell that he didn't completely agree with Willumsen that they should race headlong after the clues the two Albanians had given them.

"First of all, we only have the two Albanian men's tip that we should be interested in this Serb, Bosko. OK, so far, they've been right, but I'm sure we can agree that this could still be an attempt to clear their own names. Their car was actually seen at the one crime scene and at the harbor."

"We don't have squat on those two boys," Willumsen interrupted, slicing through the air with both hands. "And you know that. Otherwise they'd have been in jail ages ago. Since when can we arrest someone because a stinking drunk alcoholic thought he saw an identical car? I'm just asking! And besides that, do you understand how many dark blue Audi A4s there are driving around in this country? We'll burst the prison if we stuff all the car owners in there!"

It was clear that Willumsen was in top form, so he must have believed they were close to a breakthrough.

"Second of all," Suhr continued impassively, "we don't know anything about why Bosko suddenly showed up in Copenhagen. We don't know if it's a coincidence that he came out of the building Miloš Vituk lives in."

Michael Stig made a face.

"And we don't know why he would be interested in murdering a prostitute," the homicide chief finally said.

"I can answer that last one for you," Mikkelsen said and took a step forward from his spot by the window. "If Bosko has set his sights on Vesterbro, then it's because he sees money to be made and is getting into the Danish prostitution market. Which would make several pieces start to fit together in my mind."

He hit himself on the temple to make the point.

"So far Arian and Hamdi have been doing pretty good business, and there's definitely no doubt that they've pretty much cornered the trade on the Czech girls. Iveta's murder out in the Meatpacking District took out one of their girls; the murdered girl in Prague was on her way here to work for them. The way I see it, the signs are extremely clear— if you want to clear the playing field and send a signal to the competition about what's coming."

"And Kaj?" Louise asked.

Mikkelsen shrugged apologetically. "Kaj was punished

for talking to the press, but it was probably mostly a sign for everyone else that that kind of thing just isn't done. When you're dealing with a person who's taken war tourists into a besieged city and been well remunerated for bringing them close enough that they could kill people just for the fun and excitement of it, well that shows you very clearly that human life doesn't mean much to him," Stig interjected and Louise was inclined to agree with him.

"Wait a second, though," Louise suddenly blurted out so loudly that everyone turned to look at her.

She grabbed her head. "God, Miloš Vituk—that bastard coming here with his sob story about the Albanians extorting him during his noble attempt to buy Pavlína's freedom from them! I'm sorry, but there isn't any other fucking thing to say if the Danish police get a reputation among shepherds for being the easiest to fool in Europe."

"Shepherds?" Toft repeated, cocking his head and raising his eyebrow at her.

"People who traffic in women," she explained succinctly. "He was obviously using that story about Pavlína to push those two Albanians into our search lights, to make room for himself."

Louise shook her head despondently; she was irritated that she hadn't seen it herself. They'd just bought his story and tried to help without checking into him. And when the theory had briefly been mentioned, they'd brushed it aside because Pavlína had been so convincing in telling her story.

"Couldn't you just spell this out for those of us who are a little dim?" Toft asked, clearly confused by her excited outburst.

But Louise could tell Mikkelsen was with her. "Miloš Vituk works for Bosko," Louise said. "And I'm betting he was the one Miloš borrowed money from when he wanted to buy Pavlína's freedom the first time. Which was how Bosko got his claws into him, and since then he's been part of Bosko's network. When Miloš went to borrow money from him, Bosko took advantage of the situation to make his debut in the Danish marketplace. The money he paid to free Pavlína was chump change compared to what he could earn on the women."

Louise paused for a second, trying to put all the pieces together.

"I'm sure that's right, that it was a coincidence that Pavlína specifically was their way into the Danish market. I believe her story, but he took advantage of her when she asked for help, and by buying her freedom he simultaneously bought her loyalty and tied her to him."

"And then maybe Arian and Hamdi tried to respond by sending young Hana on a little tour of the harbor?" Willumsen suggested, looking like he was starting to understand how it all fit together.

"But those two guys are surely just a couple of loogies. If Bosko decided to take over the market, then they were done," Stig said thoughtfully after a little pause. "And without question, they knew that. That's why they ratted him out to us."

"But if they didn't do the two murders, then they could have just come in and told us what they knew. They didn't have to send Camilla Lind in," the homicide chief said hesitantly, as if he still couldn't get everything to fit together.

Mikkelsen nodded, and a smile brought out the laugh lines around his eyes. "Of course they sent her. They would never dare to blab directly to us. If it turns out that this is all how it fits together, then that's also why they're not saying anything when we have them in here. I'd bet that we won't get them to talk, either. No one wants to wind up wearing a Balkan tie," he added, and now his smile was gone.

"Well, then I guess we're going to have to find out if it was Miloš or Bosko holding the knife at the two crime scenes," Suhr said after contemplating the unexpected turn the case had taken.

"I'd be really surprised if Arian and Hamdi realized who they were up against in the beginning," Mikkelsen said, as everyone started getting up. "They probably thought that Miloš was on his own, but at some point they realized that he has one of the Balkans' most notorious criminals behind him, and then they start shrinking back into their shells. And that fits quite well with Bosko coming to Denmark again after the episode down at the harbor."

Louise nodded and explained what had happened to Igli's brothers when they started figuring out how Bosko's business in Sarajevo worked. "They were gunned down in front of their families," she said. "He obviously doesn't like it when people get all up in his business."

"I want a tail on Miloš Vituk," Willumsen rumbled, unnecessarily loudly, and then looked at Michael Stig. "The wiretap should be up and running today, and if there are any problems getting a warrant so quickly, have that idiot at the preliminary hearing come see me."

He was looking at Mikkelsen now. "Find out if Pavlína and Hana are working for them," he said without waiting for Stig to respond. "We need to find out how many girls they have working for them. There must be a pattern, right? Like with the Albanians?"

"That's not how it works if they have the girls work in

a brothel," Mikkelsen objected, explaining that that was a possibility since they hadn't seen Pavlína or Hana on the street.

"Well, but you haven't been looking for them, have you?" Willumsen asked him irritably.

"No," Mikkelsen admitted. "But now you are."

Willumsen looked at Louise and Lars. "Find those two girls and keep an eye on them." Finally, he looked over at Toft. "And you bring in those two Albanians, and don't let them leave until they've told us what they know. And take whatever time you need at it."

Toft nodded calmly.

Now Willumsen looked around the room, from one person to the next. "Ladies and gentlemen," he said with hard-won calm, "I'm sorry, but this means we're going to be working over the weekend. You need to be able to account for every step Miloš Vituk makes. Find out who saw Bosko while he was in town. We're going to get him this time, that jerk. Who does he think he is, pushing us around as it suits him?"

Willumsen's face was coppery-red as he stood up and adjourned the meeting.

43

Camilla had been to Føtex to stock up her fridge. The cupboards had been bare, and she threw out what little was left based on the looks of it. She had the washing machine going out in the bathroom, and she'd also pulled herself together enough to change her sheets and air out the apartment a little.

Now she was back on the sofa, sitting cross-legged and with an open-faced sandwich on rye bread in one hand. Her thoughts raced through her mind, jockeying for attention.

It had been ten years, she thought. Elsa Lynge might be remembering wrong, but if you spent a long time with a person who later became a well-known media personality, as was the case with Henrik Holm, then you'd remember the time you had spent with him.

On the other hand, she had no doubt that you would remember it if someone had a baby while you were living in a primitive barracks with them. There was something about crying babies and lost sleep overnight that people just didn't forget. As long as she was willing to trust Elsa Lynge's memory. But maybe the timing was just a little off, she thought, brushing off the crumbs that had landed on her blouse.

If she now imagined Alice Holm getting sick because of her blood disease, then maybe she was in a hospital for treatment. After that they might have been moved to a new camp to continue their work, and maybe Elsa didn't necessarily even know about that.

She didn't know, and she thought she probably shouldn't get mixed up in it, since Henrik didn't seem to want anyone stirring up the past.

Nonetheless Camilla reached for her phone, which was on the coffee table. She pulled her laptop over to her and went to www.cpr.dk, the site of Denmark's Central Office of Civil Registration, to look up the number. She called, then waited patiently until a woman's nasally voice said, "Ministry of Social Affairs," and put her on hold for the switchboard.

"Office of Civil Registration, please," Camilla said to the switchboard operator, then waited again. Her call was eventually transferred to their legal staff.

Camilla explained that she was a reporter working on a story about a Danish citizen, and she wanted to learn a little more about the procedure for a Danish couple who had a child abroad. What happened when they came home again? How did the child acquire Danish citizenship and get assigned a social security number?

"We mostly just need a birth certificate that documents that both parents are Danish citizens," the helpful woman told her. She read a list of criteria that had to be met before the child could be issued a social security number. "This is all described in the Danish Civil Registration Act, which you can find on our home page. It's in Annex 1 of Act No. 1134."

"And the documents you need from the hospital where the child was born—do you need to have a physical copy, or is it enough for someone to write the information down and send it to you?" Camilla asked.

"No, we need all the relevant paperwork and copies of the parents' birth certificates before the child can be registered," she replied. "But in the case you mention, we would also go in and record that the parents returned to Denmark. You see, the Danish government keeps track whenever a Danish citizen is employed or stationed abroad, and it is recorded in someone's file when they've left the country—and then, of course, that needs to be changed if they come back again with a baby."

"OK," Camilla said. She asked if it were possible to find out if the couple in question had had a baby abroad and brought it back to Denmark with them after having been outside the country for a couple of years.

It didn't surprise her to learn that this was considered confidential personal information. After all, she had been a journalist for some time, but she had been one long enough to know that you could sometimes get someone to tell you how you could obtain the information even if they wouldn't actually give it to you.

"Under Paragraph 42 of the act, the standard information for regular citizens is accessible to anyone," the friendly woman said. Camilla had been lucky to wind up talking to her. "If you can identify the person you want information on, either by name and address or name and social security number, then you can certainly get the basic details confirmed—although that won't really get you very far. We wouldn't be able to tell you if they had a child or where or when it was born, for instance."

"I understand," Camilla hurried to say, but she confirmed that someone would be able to see the child's birth date and the date the couple returned to Denmark if someone had access to the Civil Registration database.

"Yes, all the information is in there," said the woman. Camilla was betting the woman was about her age; she had used herself as an example, saying that someone could easily tell she had had a son in 1998 as well as in what city. "But that is considered family information, and we can't give you that."

Camilla thanked her profusely for being so helpful. Before she hung up, she asked if the police had access to all the information.

"Yes, they have full authorization," the woman confirmed. When Camilla thanked her again, she replied, "You're welcome."

44

Pull over!" Louise cried immediately after they turned the corner from Absalonsgade onto Sønder Boulevard.

It was almost seven p.m., and they'd spent the day driving through the neighborhood at random looking for the girls. They were in Louise's old Saab 9000 to avoid drawing attention to themselves by using one of the police's unmarked cars. Oddly enough, people always seemed to recognize those even though they really were totally unmarked.

Lars braked, causing the empty soda bottles on the floor of the car to slide forward.

"Drive up to Skelbækgade and turn around, so we can get closer," Louise ordered. She pointed across the planting strip with bicycle parking in the middle of the street over to the big Borch building, which was on the corner across the street.

Two girls were standing on the corner talking. One was skinny with dark hair and the other had long blond hair. Louise had straightened up and was now leaning forward a little. They hadn't seen hide nor hair of them until now, but she was sure it was Pavlína and Hana.

Her partner turned the Saab sharply to the right and just then Louise saw a silver-gray Citroën hatchback pull over to the curb at the corner across from them. Both girls walked over to the car and leaned up to the passenger-side window, but the dark-haired one quickly jumped in next to the driver, and the one Louise was pretty sure must be Hana moved back and leaned against the wall with her hands in the pockets of her short jacket, which stopped just above her waist, right over her tight jeans.

They drove up to Skelbækgade, turned around, and drove back just in time to see the girl's long hair disappearing into a little black Peugeot. She pulled the passenger-side door shut, and the car pulled away at high speed.

"There are obviously plenty of customers," Louise noted drily. She nodded as Lars pointed across the street where a parking spot had just opened up.

"We can wait there, then we can see them if they come back here," he suggested.

Louise nodded, thinking they would certainly come back. It wasn't that late, it was a lovely, warm spring evening, and there was no soccer game on TV that night.

Lars parked and they settled in to wait. They were both prepared for it to be a long wait, until the girls' workday was over, but they were determined to find out where Hana went after work.

"They did a study that showed that the younger a man is the first time he has sex with a prostitute, the greater the chances that he'll be a lifelong customer," Louise said, breaking the silence.

Her partner nodded and said that he'd looked into it and found out there were about seven hundred brothels in Denmark, 120 of which were in Copenhagen.

"Well, I suppose there's your proof that quite a few young men must have picked up the habit," Louise remarked, looking across the street, where the girls had returned and a new car had just stopped. She noticed the little pat Pavlína gave Hana's shoulder before she climbed into the car.

"Prostitutes can buy in at a brothel for somewhere between 800 and 1,800 kroner a day, depending on how nice the place is," Lars continued, his eyes following Pavlína. "For that price, they get ads in the print and online editions of *Ekstra Bladet* as well as condoms and maybe phone privileges—and then of course it covers their rent, electricity, and heat."

Louise looked at him, surprised.

"I called the Nest," he hurried to explain.

"How much do they get per trick?" Louise wanted to know.

"Between 500 and 1,500 kroner, again depending on how exclusive the place is and what the johns want," Lars guessed. "But out here on the street the girls sell themselves for between 100 and 300 kroner. These are the foreign women and the drug addicts, who would go down on a dog. The latter just need enough for a fix, and once they've made their 1,000 kroner, they stop. But the women with pimps are on the street until they've made whatever their pimps demand. If they go down to South Harbor with the tricks, then they can only turn one an hour, but if they take them down to Club Intim, they can do three. Down at the Nest several people have overheard witnesses in Copenhagen's Municipal Court testify that some of the young foreign women supposedly service twenty-five to thirty men a day—seven days a week—before their pimps leave them alone so they can get a little food and be allowed to sleep."

Just then the car came back and dropped Pavlína off.

"I was under the impression that it's mostly addicts, foreigners, and the mentally ill who turn tricks down here," he continued. "The rest stick to the brothels and clubs, and many are single mothers who can't make ends meet."

Louise eyed him skeptically. "Isn't that an old wives' tale, invented by the men?"

Lars shook his head. "Picture a single mother with two kids and a job as a cashier, or maybe she's getting unemployment. How's she supposed to get the finances to work out if she has to pay rent, utilities, and day care or after-school care, and if she also wants to give her kids a new cell phone or some cool clothes so they don't get teased at school?"

Louise shrugged.

"If you don't have that much else, it gives you status, so you can easily imagine that the material things suddenly become important, and maybe she even wants to take her kids on vacation?"

Louise was going to object, but she knew that there were quite a few people living on what was basically the poverty line if they were sole providers on welfare.

Her eyes wandered back over to the girls on the street corner. Hana was back now, too, and Louise saw how she was laughing as she pulled her cigarettes out of her pocket.

Based on her arm gestures, she guessed Pavlína was telling some story that had gotten Hana laughing even harder.

There was something about her feigned laid-back attitude that made Louise think about survival. They had to keep the tone cheerful to get through it, because Louise didn't believe the myth of the "happy whore." That came exclusively from the way men wanted to see it. The same men that drained the household budget and pretended they were doing a good turn by spending a 500-kroner note on a whore, so she received some of the family's wealth, too.

In principle, Louise didn't have anything against men visiting prostitutes, if the girls were acting of their own free will and there was no pimp waiting in the shadows to cash in on the day's earnings.

"It's just so bizarre that the men who come here are the same ones who dutifully donate to the Red Cross and the SPCA, when they have fund-raisers," she said. "They kiss their wife and pet the dog when they leave for work, but they turn a blind eye when they pick up a woman who's the victim of sex trafficking or a young Roma girl who's been forced onto the street by her family. It's enough to make you puke."

* * *

Seven hours later they were still parked there. It was two a.m., and the girls had averaged about one or two johns an hour. Louise was trying to read their body language, but there was nothing that gave away how they were doing. In between johns they stood around, relaxed and chatting, but they paid a lot of attention to the cars that drove by, and they reacted right away when a big four-wheel-drive vehicle with white plates already started blinking its lights from a distance. They both moved over to the curb and were ready when the car pulled over a second later.

Louise couldn't see over the car's roof, but when it drove away again, both of the girls were gone.

"Two thirty in the morning and there are still customers," she noted a little later, starting to feel the need to sleep. She yawned out loud and jumped at the offer when Lars suggested that she go home and go to bed. He would stay in the car and follow Hana when the girls decided to go home.

"We have to find out where she moved," he said.

"If you follow her when she leaves here, you can text me the address. Then I'll go out there tomorrow morning and keep an eye on it, see if she goes to meet anyone to pay up. But with the hours they work, they must stay in bed until sometime after noon, otherwise they wouldn't be able to keep this up," Louise added, as yet another yawn overcame her, and her own night without much sleep caught up to her.

45

The apartment was out behind Enghave Square. The text message was waiting for her on her cell when she got up.

Heavy winds were blowing through the streets, and even though the sky was still clear, it wasn't hard to spot the dark clouds that were gathering out past the Valby Hills and rapidly approaching.

Maybe a raincoat would have been a good idea, Louise thought, warming her hands on the grande drip she'd gotten to go on her way out here. She looked up at the windows in the building Hana had gone into, not knowing which one was for the apartment where Hana was sleeping.

Lars had texted that the girls had gone home around four, almost immediately after Louise herself had left. He'd followed them down past the apartment on Valdemarsgade, where Pavlína went, while Hana had unlocked a bike and ridden it the last portion to the outskirts of Vesterbro.

It wasn't even ten in the morning yet, but Louise didn't want to risk Hana having a chance to leave the apartment before she arrived. She should have brought an extra jacket along, it occurred to her, because the temperature had dropped a few degrees.

She shivered slightly, finished the coffee, and was looking around for a trash can when the front door suddenly opened and Hana walked out and leaned over to unlock a bicycle. Her hair was in a tight braid that had been wrapped up into a bun. She was wearing the short-waisted jacket but with loose-fitting, casual pants.

Louise deposited her empty coffee cup in a stranger's bike basket before turning her bike around and following Hana down Enghavevej and out toward Vesterbrogade. She kept a good distance as they approached Pile Allé, and she dropped back even farther when she guessed where Hana was going.

She let Hana park her bike by the gate and walk all the way past the graves before following.

Her pulse was racing as she sat down on the bench, where she couldn't be seen from the kitchen window, and after a deep breath, she slowly exhaled again to calm her heart rate down again. It had come as a shock, but she shouldn't have been so surprised that the network met early in the day, before anyone was interested in what the girls were up to. Later in the morning it was probably harder to slip out without being discovered.

It had been good to sleep. The worst of the fatigue had left her body, and the unexpectedly quick departure from

Enghave Square had removed the last of the sluggishness that remained.

Louise quickly hid behind the wall of the church when Hana came back a little later, moving toward her bicycle. Hana walked past with her eyes on the ground, pale and tired. Louise thought she looked younger than eighteen. She still was just a big kid, even though there wasn't much that was childish about the life she was living.

Louise waited until Hana was almost to the gate before she started walking down the neatly tended gravel paths, and she caught a glimpse of the girl's hair over the church wall as Hana got onto her bike and headed back toward Enghave Plads.

* * *

"She's still in the apartment," Louise confirmed when Willumsen called at five p.m. A couple hours earlier, Lars had stopped by with a sandwich, and they'd swapped so that she had the car, and he had taken her bike over to Valdemarsgade to keep an eye on Miloš Vituk and Pavlína. It had been nice to come in and sit, even though something in the heating system had broken, so it either blew maximally hot or ice-cold air into the cabin. There was no longer anything in between.

"I did a little digging into young Hana," Willumsen said with more dedication than Louise had heard in him for a long time. "Would you believe, it turns out she's actually registered as a prostitute. The same goes for the twenty-two-year-old Pavlína Branková."

"You're kidding!" Louise exclaimed, thinking that was smart of Miloš, because then the police didn't have anything to get them on. But it didn't make her look any less forward to the questioning session they were planning to drag him and the girls in for after the weekend was over. Hopefully they would have a pattern to present him with.

Her thoughts slid back to that day at Police Headquarters and all his rubbish about how Pavlína had become his girlfriend. Maybe she was, but she was certainly back out on the street all the same.

"What about the questioning session?" Louise asked, turning off the car's engine once the heat had finally become too much.

"We're tapping the numbers Miloš gave you, both the cell phone and the landline, but there hasn't been much so far; only three calls. Either nothing is happening, or he has another phone that we don't know about."

That sounded most likely, Louise thought, fascinatedly watching a young guy with a bandana wrapped around his head that was so dirty it was almost black. He was staggering his way toward the front door of a building with his key out in front of him, as if he were on horseback, jousting and holding a lance in his hand. A big black dog with an equally dirty bandana around its neck was trotting along behind him.

"Mikkelsen and his people rounded up a bunch of the women who work for Arian and Hamdi last night. They caught them with their pants down, literally, and none of them had their prostitution paperwork in order, so they were slapped with the 500-kroner fine and, as Mikkelsen put it, the admonition not to let it happen again. Oddly enough, not one of them knew anything about the two Albanians. But Mikkelsen is making plans to wake them all up early tomorrow and drag them to the downtown station.

Then they'll put them through their paces again and hope that something comes of it."

Louise heard a quick laugh before Willumsen rounded off the conversation by saying that their colleagues from Halmtorvet had also learned that the Albanians were now meeting their girls at a pizza place on Istedgade to collect their money.

"You'll be relieved by someone from the downtown precinct around eight, then you'll be on again tomorrow."

Louise nodded toward the windshield, where the bandana-wearing pair had finally managed to make it in the door.

46

The foam was thick and dense on the top of the Czech pilsner that had just been set on the table in front of Camilla. Svejk just wasn't the same since the ban on indoor smoking had gone into effect for all pubs over forty square meters. It was certainly easier to breathe inside, but a little bit of the pub atmosphere that she so enjoyed had been lost. Two musicians were setting up their instruments, but otherwise there was only one other couple in the bar aside from herself. She looked at her watch: it was only just after eight, so there were two hours until the music started.

She'd spent most of her day lying on her sofa, staring up into space. Her boss had called and left a couple of messages, but she'd just listened as he asked how she was doing. She couldn't even muster up the wherewithal to pick up the receiver and get the conversation over with, but she was prepared for the fact that he would try again.

The psychologist from National Hospital had also called and left a message that he'd had a cancellation for Monday, which he would hold open for her. If he didn't hear otherwise, he would plan to see her at 10:15. She'd written it down on a slip of paper and stuck it on the refrigerator door, but at the moment Monday felt so far in the future, because she still had her hands full getting by one day at a time.

Markus was at Jonas's place, and she didn't need to pick him up until tomorrow morning, so Camilla had called and asked Louise if she wanted to get a beer when she got off work.

Camilla looked up as Louise walked in the door and greeted the owner, who was manning the bar, before she headed for the table in the back of the room where Camilla was sitting. It would be the quietest corner once people started arriving. On the other hand, there was a permeating odor from the urinal cakes in the men's bathroom.

Camilla asked for another beer when Louise ordered and ignored the look aimed at her half-empty glass.

"Light or dark?" the waiter asked.

"A tall light," Louise said.

"Henrik and Alice didn't have a child while they were at the camp," Camilla began without any sort of lead-in once the beers arrived at their table. She didn't elaborate until she saw the confused look on Louise's face. Then she explained that she'd called and talked to a woman at the Red Cross who'd lived with them at the refugee camp in Bosnia.

"She was totally sure that Alice Holm was not pregnant and did not have a newborn during that period," Camilla emphasized. She added that the woman had even lived in the same barracks with them. But the woman had thought there was something about Alice getting sick at one point.

Camilla was a little irritated that Louise wasn't really paying attention. She knew the police had new clues in their quest for the culprit behind the two murders, but she was just so preoccupied with the news Elsa Lynge had provided. She was feeling more and more certain that there was a connection between that dead baby in the church and the pastor's own son.

"There's something wrong," Camilla said. "Something he doesn't want to say."

Louise raised one eyebrow, and Camilla was distracted for a second by a group of people who had just walked in and sat down at a table close to the bar. They looked like they were in their forties and could easily have been co-workers closing out their week with a night on the town.

Camilla turned back to Louise and looked at her earnestly, raising her voice a little to make herself heard over the music. "They didn't have a child. Not one on the way, not one in their arms, during the period when he claims his wife gave birth to Jonas. They left the camp at the end of the summer in 1998, and according to him his son was almost one when they returned home in August."

Camilla pushed her beer aside a little and leaned in over the table.

"I called the Office of Civil Registration," Camilla said. "But, of course, they can't pass on confidential personal information to unauthorized civilians."

Louise shook her head, but Camilla could tell that she finally had Louise's full attention.

"What was that about Alice Holm getting sick and them leaving the camp?"

Camilla shrugged. "That was obviously the excuse they gave when they cut their stay in the camp short. But Henrik hasn't mentioned that his wife got sick and they had to go home early."

"Maybe they just switched camps. That's possible, right? Maybe your source just got something mixed up?" Louise suggested.

"No. I read some of the articles Henrik wrote while they were there, and they clearly state that he was in Srebrenica the whole time. But I haven't asked him directly. He just talked about their great joy when they discovered that his wife was pregnant, even though they had started to think they might never get pregnant. I mean, that didn't exactly make me start to have doubts about the case."

"Of course not," Louise said.

"But it's not true, and I have a theory about how it all might fit together."

"*Out!*" they suddenly heard someone shout from the bar. It was the owner, yelling so loudly the glasses were clinking. "*That's it! You're out of here!*"

Camilla and Louise smiled at each other and turned to look at a dark-haired, heavyset woman from a big group of people, who were standing by the bar. The woman had a frightened expression and was trying to appease the owner.

"'Shooby Dooby Doo-Wop,'" Camilla suggested, and Louise nodded.

Anyone who knew the least thing about Svejk knew that you would be kicked out immediately if you were dumb enough to request "Shooby Dooby Doo-Wop." If the woman had wanted to hear something by Herbert Gröne-meyer, by contrast, she would have received an appreciative nod, but there was no way she could have known that.

Now it appeared that she was mercifully being allowed to stay if she behaved properly.

Suddenly Camilla laughed and shook her head at the bartender's quirks. That was exactly what she loved about this place. The place was so liberatingly chic, and the owner did what he felt like.

"You should go in and see what the civil registry says," Camilla said once the patrons had settled down again.

Louise appeared to be thinking, but she didn't protest as Camilla had feared she would.

"My guess is," Camilla said, leaning even farther forward, "that they adopted Jonas right after they returned home from Bosnia, and for some reason or other they didn't want to admit that they're not his biological parents, and therefore they put together this story that he was born while they were away."

"But why?" asked Louise, her eyes fixed on Camilla. "Why would the pastor and his wife come up with a story like that?"

Camilla shrugged. She looked around the room, which had really filled up. "I don't know," she admitted, feeling the wind slowly starting to go out of her sails. She wanted to go home and go to bed.

"I'll check him in the registry," Louise promised when they were standing out on the sidewalk unlocking their bikes. "But don't let it go to your head if I let you read over my shoulder, because it's still confidential personal information, but obviously, I'll let you take a peek..."

"Say no more," Camilla stopped her tiredly.

Whenever they got involved in each other's professional lives, they always had some iteration of this conversation. It would never end.

"As long as you find out if this has some connection to Jonas. I'm afraid for him. I couldn't bear it if something happened to him. Or Henrik Holm, for that matter," Camilla added, and she flipped on the headlight she had strapped to her handlebars.

47

Camilla found the boys at the big dining table in the kitchen when she arrived at the pastor's home the next morning. They were sitting across from each other in total silence, each with a plate in front of him and a cup containing cocoa that had once been hot.

The breadbasket was full of fresh morning rolls, but it looked like they'd hardly touched it. Suddenly she noticed how quiet it was in the house. There were no voices, no footsteps, and she could tell from looking at the boys that they'd been sitting at the table for a long time in this oppressive silence.

Earlier that morning Louise had called and woken her. She was calling from Police Headquarters, where she was going to assist Toft in questioning Arian and Hamdi, but she had just looked Henrik Holm up in the civilian registration database. When she sank back into her bed after their conversation, Camilla had a hard time deciding whether she was filled by relief or disappointment.

According to the information in the database, Alice Holm had given birth to a son at the hospital in Sarajevo on June 14, 1997, while the couple was stationed in Bosnia. There was a birth certificate from the hospital to document it. It also said that they returned to Denmark in August of that same year, just as the pastor had said. Shortly thereafter, once all the documents had been approved, the Danish civil registration database recognized Jonas Holm as a Danish citizen and issued him a social security number.

It took Camilla rather a long time to make it out of bed after that call, because once the information sank in, she realized that it was mostly for her own sake that she had been hoping the explanation lay somewhere in the past.

However egocentric it was, it really just came down to the fact that she needed an explanation in order to move on. An explanation that gave some sense to everything that had happened, even though it was far from clear that she had the mental capacity to understand it.

While she'd been lying in bed with her arms under her head staring at the ceiling, she'd felt profoundly grateful that she hadn't voiced her suspicions to the pastor. She could easily have had doubts and started opening up old wounds pertaining to his dearly departed wife. As soon as she'd had her chat with Elsa Lynge, she'd wanted to confront him with what his former colleague had said, and she hadn't been concerned with whether Elsa might have been wrong or not.

"Did you guys have an argument?" Camilla exclaimed, helping herself to a poppy seed bun out of the basket. "What did you do to your dad and the housekeeper?"

She was watching Jonas and when he slowly looked up, she immediately dropped the chipper tone and set down the bun before leaning over and putting her hand on his arm.

"What happened?" she asked, worried, casting a quick glance at her son, who she had an easier time reading.

"Where's your dad?" she repeated.

"Over in the church," Jonas finally said, turning his face toward her.

She suddenly felt afraid and wasn't able to hide it so the boys wouldn't notice. "And Tereza. Did something happen?" Her voice was higher pitched now and sharper than it should have been, and Jonas pulled his arm back.

"They had an argument," Jonas said so softly that she almost couldn't hear him. "Dad got really mad."

"And then he threw her out," Markus continued, "and then he got all her things and threw them out after her—"

Markus stopped abruptly when his friend very quietly started sniffling.

"Why were they arguing?" Camilla asked, not really knowing if she ought to put her arm around Jonas or if he would rather be left alone.

Both boys shrugged, but neither of them said anything.

"Is he still over there?" Camilla asked and then got up, heading for the kitchen door.

They both nodded.

"Well, then I think I'm just going to go over there and talk to him. Meanwhile, you guys just go back up and play," she suggested.

They both got up right away and disappeared up the stairs.

48

At first, she couldn't see him, but she heard the quiet sobs and when she walked up toward the altar, she spotted him in the front pew, where he was sitting with his face hidden in his hands. His shoulders were moving softly in time to the rhythm of his sobs.

She quietly walked over and sat down next to him. She started out not saying anything, just sitting there in the silent church listening to his breaths, as he tried to get himself under control. She knew he could tell she was there, but he hadn't looked up.

Five, maybe ten minutes passed before he wiped his face and straightened up. He didn't turn to face her, but looked like he was about to say something, and she hurriedly beat him to it.

"I really owe you an apology," she began and was met by his confused stare, as he hurriedly turned his head to her.

She heard him swallow, and she cringed a little when she saw that his face was filled with despair and something she interpreted as fear, but which could also have been anger.

"What on earth for?" he asked hoarsely and cleared his throat, trying to ward off whatever crying was left in his body.

She said that she'd called Elsa Lynge and explained how she'd doubted him when she couldn't get things to add up. Without looking at him, she admitted that she'd passed the information on to Louise and had asked her to check whether he and his wife had brought Jonas home with them when they came back from Bosnia.

She looked down at the wide grooves between the stones in the church floor. "Please forgive me for being so nosy. I was confused and thought you were keeping something to yourself, something that might give the rest of us some kind of explanation for what happened out there." She nodded in the direction of where she'd found the still-born baby. "But obviously, you weren't, it was just me..."

When she tried to recall the sound later, she had a hard time saying whether it was a dull laugh or a dry sob that spontaneously emerged from Henrik's chest. But the expression in his eyes was unmistakable as he slowly turned and looked her in the eye.

Camilla collapsed onto the pew when she realized she was sitting next to a man who'd lost everything.

He reached for her hand and gave it a squeeze, and she saw that he was trying to pull it together so that he would be able to say something.

"You're certainly entitled to try to find out what happened," he began. "I would never hold that against you, especially not since you and Markus were so involved, and I'm so sorry that I've only just now really put together how the events all fit together."

He pulled his hand back and rubbed his forehead hard, as if he were trying to gather up his strength to keep going. Then he took a deep breath and leaned back in the pew.

Camilla could almost see his thoughts slipping back through time.

* * *

"Alice and I started dating when we were eighteen. We were married two years later, and we started trying to have a baby from day one. I had just started my theology program and she was going to nursing school. We dreamt of having a big family and a parsonage in Jutland."

The little laugh Henrik emitted now was unmistakable, but it was for the memories and seemed very remote from the present moment.

"Five years later we were still dreaming. There was still no sign of any kind of expansion to our family, and we started to concede that the doctors were right when they blamed it on the blood disease Alice had been treated for since she was very little. So, we decided we would adopt our children instead. We went to visit an adoption agency and started the process of getting preapproved as potential adoptive parents. But we didn't even make it through the first phase because of Alice's disease—even though her doctor at National Hospital wrote to the agency that it was extremely likely she would live with the disease until she died of old age. But back then people didn't take any chances. Since then they've eased up on the requirements some. Nowadays single people can be approved, so maybe they would also accept that a father could handle a child on his own in the unfortunate event that his wife up and died on him."

He cleared his throat and took another deep breath, while Camilla sat very still so as not to interrupt.

"For a while, right after they rejected us, Alice really took it hard. It was the first time her illness had really impacted her life. Up to that point it really hadn't limited what she could do; it had only lurked in the wings like a dark shadow she was forced to live with. Now it was preventing her from becoming a mother, and for a long time we were really depressed about it—Alice more than me. But one night after dinner, she asked if I wanted to come with her if we got permission to work in a refugee camp. She had made up her mind that she really wanted to go and do something to help the people who had lost everything. That was right after the Dayton Agreement was signed in Paris, the peace agreement that was supposed to put an end to the war—but far from that, the war went on from one day to the next."

He stopped for a moment and looked at Camilla, as though he were looking right through her. Then he slumped a little and sighed heavily.

"Clearly, it was escapist of us, a way of getting away from the life we'd fantasized about but would never have. But I guess we were also hoping that by going someplace where people had suffered real loss, it would help us see that the loss we were suffering really wasn't so bad in comparison."

Camilla nodded, shifting slightly on the hard bench, and feeling like she understood.

"As I told you before, it was both a wonderful and a painful time. Never have I seen people in such torment, and never have I seen people fight so hard for their right to live, even though everything around them should have broken them down. Of course, there were many people who couldn't handle it, and some of them went over to the darkest sides of the human mind, where evil takes over and overshadows everything else.

"A year, almost a year and a half," he corrected himself, doing the math quickly, "went by with the camp as our world, and we no longer dreamt of the life we had hoped to have. We lived in the barracks with the youngest of the children, the ones whose parents had been killed in the war or who had been forced to abandon them for other reasons. So our desire to be around little kids was really fulfilled. Every once in a while, a stranger would come and knock on our door with a baby in their arms who had been left alone in one of the surrounding villages. When they brought us little ones like that, it was always done in the cover of darkness, and it was never something anyone discussed. We took them in without asking too many questions. Srebrenica was predominantly a Muslim area, but the villages around it were mixed, and no one wanted to have anything to do with a Muslim baby in a Serbian area. A baby like that had no chance of survival if it wasn't brought to us."

"But how could anyone tell the baby was Muslim?" Camilla couldn't help but ask.

For a second the pastor seemed to snap out of it, but he flew back in time again before he answered.

"The same man came to us many times with toddlers or infants who he'd saved from Serbian areas, and eventually we got to know him and he became our friend. Bosko was a Serb; he moved around in the villages and told us about the Muslim families who had been victims of the ethnic cleansing his fellow countrymen had been subjected to. After the peace agreement, many of the Muslim families came back to reclaim their houses and possessions. But they didn't get anything back. Instead they were gunned down and left lying in the streets."

Henrik sighed, and Camilla saw that he had to pull himself together before he could continue.

"One night he brought a bottle of slivovitz with him, and I guess all three of us had had a little too much by the time we started talking about the little kids who were sleeping in the big room next to ours. Some were just infants, others toddlers, but none of the ones living in our barracks were older than three.

"We told him why we were working in the camp, about Alice's disease, and about our dream of becoming parents and how the adoption agency had rejected us. At some point in the conversation he leaned in over the table a little and asked if we hadn't considered taking one or more of the children who didn't have any future in Bosnia anyway back to Denmark with us and giving them a proper life far from the aftermath of the war.

"'You could give them a life of love and security and a good education,' he said, and he reminded us that there was nothing for them where they were now. No one wanted them, and they were going to grow up and live their daily lives in an orphanage if they ever made it out of the camp.

"'That's not a real life. If you really want to help these children, then help make sure they get out of here and help them find a good home with parents like you, who dream of having a child but aren't able to themselves.' That's how he said it," Henrik remembered.

"And at that point it sounded totally right. We saw the little children every day, we sat with them, fed them, and comforted them, but everyone knew that one day they would be on their own. It was unbearable, and the only way you could deal with that was to try not to think about it. Luckily, it also happened fairly regularly that a mother or father would come to the camp looking for their child, and sometimes they found each other. But the very littlest ones...no one ever came looking for them. They were there because their parents were no longer alive."

He swallowed one time before continuing.

"The next night he brought Jonas. We guessed he must have been about a year old, based on the number of teeth he had. But he was small for his age, and he was totally silent, just lay there in a big blanket and watched us with his brown eyes, and he had a big bandage around his right foot.

"Bosko told us that he was the son of a young married couple from outside Srebrenica who had found their home burned to the ground with everything they owned inside it. All they had left was the garage, and when the man went to pull the car out, they were attacked and shot at close range. The mother was holding Jonas in her arms when she was shot, and the bullet had sliced his pinky toe right off."

Henrik emitted a grunt, which was a mixture of laughter and a statement of fact, before he proceeded.

"I knew it was already too late when he set the boy in Alice's lap. Still, I tried to explain that we couldn't just take the child home to Denmark with us illegally. At that point, my wife was ready to stay in Bosnia if it meant she could keep him."

Henrik ruffled his hair so it was sticking up in the air, while he reported the agreement they entered into on that night; that first time they met their son.

"Back then you could pay to get any kind of paperwork or document made. We never heard about that side of things here in Denmark. There was a big problem with driver's licenses being issued to people from the former Yugoslavia even though they'd never had so much as one hour's worth of driving lessons. When they came to Denmark, they would just send a picture and some number of German deutschmarks home to a contact person, and one month later they received their Yugoslavian driver's license with whatever issue date they wanted, and they could just walk in to the department of motor vehicles and swap it for a Danish one. Easy-peasy. The same for birth certificates. We paid Bosko ten thousand marks to get a certificate that said Alice gave birth to Jonas on June fourteenth the previous year at a hospital in Sarajevo."

The tears overwhelmed him before he managed to choke them back, and he sat for a moment with his eyes closed until he appeared in control of them again, and slowly shook his head.

"It's not so much that we paid and broke the rules. I could certainly live with that. The only thing in the world we wanted was to have the little baby, and the alternatives for him weren't even worth thinking about. But I can't forgive myself for not realizing that it wouldn't end there. I was so naïve in my joy at our wish for a child finally becoming a reality. And I believed Bosko was helping us for the sake of the child. I try and justify that with the fact that we were just so over the moon with our own happiness, when we made the agreement with him, that we would help other infertile couples and orphaned children find new homes in Denmark."

He took a deep breath.

"A couple of months earlier, I had received a message that I could start my post as pastor of Stenhøj Church in September of that same year. By that point, I had almost forgotten that I'd applied for it, but that fit just fine with the agreement we made with Bosko. There was no exchange of money between us, aside from what we paid him for the forged birth certificate. I suppose that was also one of the reasons we still believed that he was doing it for humanitarian reasons, that he wanted to help the children have better lives. If we'd known he was planning to do it to earn money, a lot of money, we wouldn't have agreed to it.

"According to the agreement we were not supposed to be involved in bringing the children illegally into Denmark or finding families who wanted them. Our only obligation was to be a way station when they arrived in the country, and it always transpired like that, that they would be left in the church early in the morning. We didn't know who brought them, and didn't want to know, either, and later that same day the new family would come pick up the baby. They handled the paperwork themselves; we weren't involved with that. It seemed so innocent to see the same joy in other childless couples that we had experienced ourselves.

"The agreement was that we would help find new homes for three babies. But it kept going. Every time we made a new agreement, he broke it, and we couldn't stop it. If we hadn't accepted the falsified birth certificate, we could have severed our ties to him whenever we wanted. But the way it was, he had something over us. If we didn't do what he said, we would lose Jonas."

"Yes, and you would probably also have lost the reputation you had built up in the media if the story about an illegal baby came out."

"Oh, whatever, I wouldn't have cared about that!" Henrik exclaimed. "But we were not going to risk having Jonas taken away from us and sent back to Bosnia. We had gotten trapped in Bosko's web and we were stuck, no matter how hard we wriggled. Things went on like that for several years, and then suddenly we stopped hearing from him. You can probably imagine what an incredible relief that was when we realized it was over."

He watched Camilla, who didn't have time to nod before he continued. "But then everything with Alice happened, and suddenly there was only me and Jonas left. At that point I obviously should have told him how everything fit together. Alice and I talked about that many times, why we'd done what we'd done, but then when she died I just couldn't get myself to do it. His mother's death was just so hard on him, that wasn't the right time to tell him that she and I weren't his biological parents. Then he was missing her so much, it still wasn't the right time. And now it almost feels like it's too late. I know I should have done it, but it just never felt like it was the right time."

Henrik shook his head and ran his fingers through his hair despondently.

"And if I'm being honest, it's not something I've really given much thought to since. In my heart he's my son, and it doesn't make any difference to me if we gave birth to him. But I know that it might mean something to him, that he doesn't know about his heritage. In the last few days I've also become horribly aware that I'm risking his turning against me, because I haven't told him the truth. The question is if it will even be enough anymore to explain how much we loved him from the first moment we saw him and how right it felt to make him our child."

"Do you need to tell him that now?" Camilla asked after a bit. She had to clear her own throat to get her voice to work properly.

Henrik nodded. "This is never going to end. I don't want to keep going anymore, and I don't want to lie anymore. I haven't heard from Bosko in so many years, and I refused to believe there was a connection when the boys found that little girl in the church. It wasn't until you found the little dead one who was missing a toe that I started to suspect what was coming."

He smiled sadly. "I also didn't get that he was the one who had sent Tereza the first time she rang the bell and asked for work. Even though that happened the same evening. I turned her away the second time she came, too, even though she brought a letter with her. It just didn't occur to me that he might send me a housekeeper."

Camilla was concentrating, but it was hard for her to get everything to fit together so that all the events made sense.

"After I turned her away again, still without understanding what it was all about, he cut the toe off that little boy, and then there was no longer any mistaking his message."

"But how does Tereza fit into the picture?" Camilla asked, confused.

"I didn't figure it out until now, either. He needs to stash her somewhere where the police won't be watching her."

Camilla raised one eyebrow, still not understanding.

"I was supposed to employ her in my home. In the beginning, I didn't like the idea, but when she told me about the network I was glad to help. Then it dawned on me that it wasn't really a question of my generosity, but rather that the girls should have free access to my home. It wasn't until this morning, when I overheard a conversation, that the chips fell into place. I had just gotten back from the bakery and was about to put breakfast on the table for the boys, and Tereza obviously hadn't heard me come in."

Henrik looked at Camilla, as if he were ashamed of himself.

"They're prostitutes," he said, slowly and clearly. "And Tereza is some kind of madam. Every day the girls meet to hand over the money they made the previous night. One of the girls is only fourteen. And you can call the police and tell them that they don't need to look for Baby Girl's mother anymore. It's Tereza's baby. Bosko's people took it from her the second it was born. She never got to see her and only knows her daughter from the pictures on TV."

Camilla's mouth hung open as she pictured the little baby in her mind. A deep desperation hit her when she realized that the circumstances that had separated the mother from her infant were far more unbearable than what she had imagined.

"And quite right, that little boy was stillborn. His mother is from Romania, but she works as a prostitute in Malmö. Bosko trafficked her, too."

"How do you know all this?" Camilla whispered.

"I asked Tereza to pack up her things and get out of here when I realized what she did and what she was using the pastor's residence for. Initially, she was all tough and threatened me, because she knew the whole story on Jonas. But I decided that I wasn't going to let myself be threatened anymore. I yelled that she could go right ahead and tell Bosko that it was done, and that I wanted her out of here right away. When she realized I meant it, she completely broke down and told me about her baby, which he'd taken from her. In exchange for that she no longer had to turn tricks herself and just collected the money from the other girls instead. She was more than willing to pay that price."

Camilla slumped, suddenly noticing the cold had crept in under her skin while the pastor was talking.

"She was afraid and she swore that Bosko would come after me when he heard that I'd kicked her out."

"Will he?" Camilla asked, and Henrik nodded.

"I have no doubt. I see now that I'll never be free of him if I don't stand by what's happened."

"What about Jonas, then? Isn't there a risk that you'll lose him if the truth comes out?"

The pastor nodded with a sad smile. "Yeah, and that's why he and I need to leave. This will never end so long as I remain in Denmark. Bosko will always be able to find me. We're going to have to start all over again, establish ourselves somewhere else under new names. I have no doubt that that business with the toe was his way of saying that if I don't do what he says, then it will be Jonas next time. Our only chance for escape is to run away."

Camilla nodded, feeling the tears running down along her nose, because she knew he was right.

"I've decided to tell the police everything I know about Bosko and his business undertakings in this country, but once they get my version of events, I will have already left."

"Where are you going?"

He shrugged and seemed to be avoiding looking her in the eyes. She could tell he'd made a decision, and he wasn't going to tell her what it was.

49

Arian ran his fingers through his shoulder-length black hair and looked at Louise over his steel-rimmed glasses.

She couldn't read anything from his expression, but knew that he was lying to their faces when he repeated that, yes, he did know a few of the girls from the Istedgade neighborhood, but that he didn't have the foggiest idea what they did for a living.

He shrugged his shoulders exaggeratedly.

"I don't know anything about their working as prostitutes. That kind of thing goes against my religion," he repeated, holding out his hands as if it were an affront that they might even consider his being involved in such a thing.

Toft had been through the same thing all morning. Louise had joined him after lunch, after she finished wait-

ing for Hana outside the apartment by Enghave Square.
She hadn't gone anywhere else, which was what Louise
had expected. On the other hand, Tereza had suddenly
gotten out of a cab with two big bags, clearly nervous
that someone would see her. She'd looked around several
times before quickly walking over and ringing the bell as
she again surveyed the street and waited to be buzzed in.
Pavlína came by a little before eleven and rang the bell several times. She had seemed angry or upset, Louise thought
as she watched Pavlína walk out into the street and look up
at the windows before walking back to the door and ringing
the bell some more. She spent fifteen minutes doing that
before she gave up and left again.

Toft had started with Hamdi, but as he explained to
Louise, Hamdi had pretty much not even opened his
mouth. He sat in complete silence, shaking his head in response to every question.

When she biked back to her office and was on her way
down the back side of Central Station, her thoughts kept circling around Miloš Vituk, Bosko, and the Czech girls. She
agreed that they were only going to have one shot at it when
they decided to haul Miloš in, and if they struck too soon
he'd pack up his whole business, he and Bosko would be
long gone, and the case in the Meatpacking District and Kaj
Antonsen's murder would end up in the unsolved-cases file.

But when would they have enough?

Her train of thought was interrupted as the cell phone
in her jacket pocket started ringing. She thought she'd explained herself clearly when she declined Camilla's dinner
invitation by saying she was probably going to have to work
late. But Camilla had just said that she'd have the food
ready at six. She added that it was important that Louise

come, because there was something Camilla had to tell her about the pastor and all the business out at the church.

Louise had shaken her head as she waited for a red light, then set the phone down in her purse, which was in her bike basket.

Up in the division, she went to the kitchenette and got two pieces of crisp bread, which she quickly scarfed down as Toft filled her in on what they had gotten out of the questioning sessions so far.

"It's not like we've really gotten very far," Toft admitted, before they walked into his office, where Arian had been asked to wait.

The Albanian had been politeness itself and obligingly answered all their questions as long as they didn't have anything to do with the business they suspected him of being behind. Arian willingly admitted that for a while he had been going to Central Station every morning.

"I drink a cup of coffee and read the free papers," he explained.

"Who are the girls who walk up to you?" Louise wanted to know.

Once again, Arian's shoulders took up a defensive posture, but after a little contemplation he ended up admitting that he knew a couple of them.

"But you haven't received money from any of them?"

He shook his head apologetically, as if he were sorry he couldn't be of more help to her.

Toft had remained silent after Louise took over the questioning session, but now she saw him take out the surveillance pictures of Arian meeting with the girls. Toft pushed them across the desk one at a time.

"Then just explain to us what's going on here." Toft

added that to his eye it looked like the girls met him daily to pay him. "You can see the dates in the corner of the pictures. These were taken over the last few weeks."

Arian took the pictures and it looked as if something suddenly occurred to him. "Now I remember!" he exclaimed, flipping through the photographs without really looking at them. "I loaned a bunch of those girls money and they came by to return it."

"What did you loan them money for?" Toft asked.

"Food, or clothes if they were short. Back where I come from we help each other. If I talk to the girls it's to make sure they're doing all right. It's friendliness. I'm just looking out for them."

Toft gave Louise a look and changed the topic. He pulled out the lists with the phone calls, and with a nod Arian confirmed that it was for his cell phone.

"We have a number of calls made on that phone," Toft began. Arian gazed at him with his accommodating look and nodded interestedly, as if it didn't really have anything to do with him.

"A lot of the calls go to the phones of the six girls named, whom we've identified as the girls you met with at Central Station. At the moment, all six of them are down at the Halmtorvet police station telling our colleagues how they're connected to you and Hamdi."

Suddenly, his hands flew up into a defensive position, and an expression came over his face that said that they were subjecting him to a great injustice. "Well, if they really are prostitutes, as you say they are, then they'll just tell you what their pimps force them to say. But it's not true, I don't have anything to do with their work."

His hands fell back down to rest on the edge of the desk,

and Louise saw the little curl around his mouth that was supposed to show that he didn't have anything to hide even if someone claimed otherwise. But she also saw the flutter in his eye.

Toft ignored his vehement outburst and kept on calmly. His plastic cigarette was lying next to his pad of paper. Now he picked it up and sucked it a couple of times, before carefully stuffing it in his pocket, as if he had all the time in the world, as if Arian could just take all the time he needed to answer the next question.

"It is also still your contention that you don't know any of the girls, even though you're in daily telephone contact with them, multiple times per day?"

Toft popped a menthol in his mouth and watched the Albanian, who didn't show any sign of response with his face but did sit for a long time, contemplating.

"As you know I go to the Albanian club on Saxogade every single day," he began, looking from Toft to Louise. "We don't have a phone down there, and when I'm there, my cell phone is almost always plugged in, recharging, and while it is there are a lot of people who could use it."

"We've listened to calls in which you threatened the girls that you'll send the police after them if they don't pay. We hear you say that you're cooperating with the police so the girls have to do what you say, what you command, and that the money they pay goes to the police so the girls will be left alone."

Louise felt a sharp sting of irritation at the way he was trying to shirk any and all responsibility and not even trying to hide it. She asked him how he would explain that.

"I've never said anything like that. Someone borrowed my phone," he replied curtly.

"Well, then give us some names," Toft asked patiently while Louise tried to keep her irritation from turning into rage because he thought it was so easy.

The Albanian shrugged yet again. "I don't keep track of who, but anyone could use it and I don't know who they call."

Louise sighed: it was money they'd borrowed, the girls were paying it back, the cell phone could have been used by anyone. It was inconceivable that he could even get himself to say all this shit without their detecting the least bit of uncertainty in his eyes.

They gave up on getting anywhere with the cell phone right now and confronted Arian instead with the fact that they knew where and when his car had been driven. He shrugged again, as if he didn't feel like that was something he needed to answer for.

"Anyone in the club can use the car. When I'm there, my keys are on the desk. I don't know who takes it out for a drive or where they go."

Louise took a deep breath, but then let it slowly seep back out again. It was no use getting all worked up; that wouldn't make him talk.

"That's a pretty nice car you drive. It doesn't worry you that you don't know who's using it?" Toft asked, receiving only a shrug in response.

"Your Audi is less than a year old and cost about 400,000 kroner," Louise said, taking over again. "I'm a little curious to know how you can afford such an expensive car since you're on public assistance."

"I borrowed money from my uncle," he replied without blinking.

The phone in front of Louise rang, and Mikkelsen said

briefly that all six of the girls they had brought in for questioning had confirmed, to a one, that they made their livings as prostitutes, but they all claimed that they did it of their own free will and that they didn't give anyone money.

"One of them was dumb enough to say that she didn't pay anyone except for the money she gave the police to leave her alone," Mikkelsen said with a dry laugh.

There was a long silence after Louise hung up. They had agreed in advance that they would draw the questioning session out until they heard from Mikkelsen and knew whether the girls had said anything they could use. They hadn't been expecting them to talk, but they wanted to be sure before they changed tacks.

Toft got up and asked if Louise or Arian wanted him to bring them a cup of coffee.

Louise nodded and looked at Arian. He had very obviously been expecting that he would be allowed to leave once they'd run through their questions. Now for the first time he looked slightly uncertain, but nodded and asked for milk and sugar.

* * *

When Toft returned, setting a little brown wooden tray on the desk, they started again. It was obvious that Arian still felt like he was getting off scot-free and wasn't prepared for the change in tactics that arrived along with the coffee.

"We've heard that you received rather a lot of money from Miloš Vituk to let him buy one of your girls, one by the name of Pavlína."

Louise didn't phrase it as a question, just as a statement. She ignored him as he began to make objections and told him instead how Miloš had come to them and told them his story.

"He was the one who suggested that we start keeping an eye on you and your partner. He also helped by pointing out where you were meeting the girls for them to pay up."

The Albanian leaped up out of his chair and leaned over the desk to make her stop, but Toft quickly got him back in his seat again.

"The police have no doubts that you and Hamdi are earning a great deal of money off several of the Czech girls who work as prostitutes around Skelbækgade. Your car has been seen down there daily, as either you or Hamdi drive around keeping an eye on the girls. But it surprises us that you have not chosen to do it as professionally as Miloš Vituk. He, for example, has made sure that his girls' paperwork is in order so we have to let them go again if we stop them. And he also covers his tracks, so it's very hard for us to prove what he's up to."

Louise saw the provocation hit home, but Arian took his time before he said anything.

Instead, he clenched his teeth together so hard that his jaws jutted out like two rock formations. And when Toft took over and turned the topic to Arian's knowledge of Bosko and the police's suspicions—that Miloš Vituk was working for the notorious Serb, and that Miloš and Bosko were working on pushing Arian and his business out of the market—Arian seemed to shut down completely, his eyes hard.

Toft was starting to maneuver in his patient fashion, and even though Louise was betting they had a one in a million chance of getting this pimp to talk, she watched with interest as the game played out between the two men. When she felt her cell phone vibrating in her pocket, she quietly walked over to the window to answer the call without disturbing what Toft was up to.

"I'd bet 1,000 kroner that Bosko just picked up Miloš Vituk out here on Valdemarsgade," Michael Stig yelled into her ear to drown out a truck that was driving past him right then.

"Did you see him?"

"Just from the side, through the car window, but I'm almost positive. He was driving a big Volvo with Swedish plates. Unfortunately, I didn't get the license number, because it didn't occur to me that it might be him until Miloš hopped into the front seat."

Louise bent over and picked up her purse.

"Hurry up and pack your makeup bag and get out here so you can confirm it's the Serb if they come back."

She didn't bother scolding him for the way he was ordering her around, since she was the only one who'd seen Bosko and could say for sure he was the one with Miloš.

"I'm off," she told Toft, noticing Arian following her with his eyes as she got up. He was on the edge of his chair, and it was obvious that he was dying to know what was going on.

She gave him a quick nod before disappearing out the door. Then she took the stairs down to Otto Mønsteds Gade, where her bike was parked.

50

Michael Stig pulled a piece of chocolate out of his backpack and offered it to her once she'd parked her bike. Even though the sun was shining, it was cool in the doorway, where big graffiti tags overlapped each other, leaving hardly ten centimeters of contiguous, untagged concrete wall between all the faded colors.

She quickly glanced up at the window on the second floor, but the curtains were closed, so there was no indication of whether anyone was in the apartment. Stig thought that Pavlína must still be up there; at least he hadn't seen her leave after she came back from Enghave Square.

Louise let the chocolate melt in her mouth while Stig told her about how the big Volvo XC90 had pulled over to the curb and then left again immediately thereafter.

"He honked the horn one time, and two seconds later

Miloš came out the door. It was obvious that they must have arranged for him to be ready."

"Any sign of calls on Miloš's phones?"

Stig shook his head and smiled. "No, so that means he has a number we don't know about."

"What about Pavlína?"

"Nope, her either. Aside from the calls she made to Hana's number a little after ten, but they weren't answered, so they couldn't have set up the meeting that way."

It didn't surprise Louise that Miloš was using a cell phone they didn't know about.

There had been surprisingly little activity on his phones, so of course he was using a prepaid cell phone for calls he didn't want to risk the police being able to trace.

"Well, then I guess there isn't anything else for us to do but wait," she said and leaned back against the doorway. "What does Willumsen have to say?"

"He asked Mikkelsen to keep some guys ready in case we need to tail them by car if they show up again. My car is parked down here." Stig indicated a silver station wagon with a tip of his head. "I'll follow him when he leaves here, but it definitely seems like a good idea to have a succession of people ready to help out with tailing him so we're not too obvious."

Louise nodded and looked over at her bike. Maybe she should have brought one of the police vehicles, but it was often quicker to get through town by bike, so she hadn't even thought about it when Stig called.

"The downtown precinct people are also on standby in case Miloš and Bosko make a move on foot. At some point or other Pavlína and the other girls will probably go to work, too."

"I'm supposed to relieve Lars Jørgensen at Enghave Square around five or six tonight," Louise said, looking at her watch.

Stig gave a wry laugh.

"I'm pretty sure your partner is going to have to bail on Saturday night dinner with the wife and twins, because I'm not so sure you'll be getting out of here in time to relieve him."

Sometimes it was clear that Michael Stig lived alone, and that he had only scorn for anyone who was tied down by family life and its obligations, but sometimes Louise also suspected that there might be a touch of envy or longing. She'd never called him out on it, and she bit her tongue now, too, thinking that given the trouble Lars was having at home these days Stig really couldn't be more wrong. Lars would probably be just as glad to have to work late.

"Don't worry your pretty little head about Lars," Louise replied snidely and added that her partner was never the kind of person who went home early because he had to stir the sauce or watch a soccer game.

That last comment was a little dig at Stig, because at least once a month he was so busy with his bowling tournaments that he was forced to trade shifts with someone.

But then all the comments on dinner obligations made Louise realize she'd better call Camilla, who was surely not going to be happy to be stood up.

"It's just not going to work out for us to have dinner tonight," Louise began the second Camilla answered. Before Camilla had a chance to get a word in, she continued, "We believe the Serb we suspect of being behind the murders of Iveta and Kaj is in town. Michael Stig thinks it was Bosko who came and picked Miloš Vituk up an hour ago, so now we're waiting for them to come back. We're going to have to have our talk another day."

"Bosko," Camilla repeated softly. And for a second Louise could hear Camilla breathing. Then she hung up on Louise.

Louise figured Camilla was either pissed off or disappointed or both, and sighed, but she pulled herself together when she realized that Michael Stig was watching her. She took a breath to defend herself, because he knew perfectly well that Camilla wasn't working right now, so he didn't need to worry about scolding her for telling a journalist about Bosko.

Camilla was very involved in the case and besides, the homicide chief trusted her, damn it. "How's she doing?" Stig asked in an unexpectedly friendly tone, causing Louise to instantly forget her anger.

She studied him for a second. His gray-blue eyes, which usually made people keep a certain distance, looked concerned and intense. Louise nodded slowly and realized that even though she'd been working closely with Stig for several years, she still couldn't quite figure him out. This wasn't the first time he'd surprised her with one of his infrequent expressions of concern. The last time had been for her after a case that had ended rather dramatically down in Roskilde, and now it made her wonder if he had a hidden nurturing side, which he didn't reveal unless he was really concerned that the person he was talking about might be losing it.

"She's doing better," Louise said, half-expecting the arrogant look to return to Stig's eyes.

But Stig just nodded and turned back to survey the street and then look up at the apartment.

51

For a second, Camilla felt paralyzed. She'd turned off her phone but was still holding it in her hands, all the thoughts in her head having come to a standstill. It hadn't been more than two hours since she and Markus had come home from the pastor's residence, and Henrik seemed to expect Bosko to react quickly. But not that he'd be in Copenhagen already.

She wanted to call and warn Henrik. Her fingers felt stiff, as she found the number for the pastor's residence in the phone's memory, and anxiety coursed through her body with her blood as the phone rang and rang and eventually started beeping in her ear. She let it ring out one more time before she got up and went to the front hall to find her wallet.

Markus asked her several times if there was something wrong. He watched her, not understanding that she had no mental capacity left for anything besides the thoughts Henrik Holm's story had left in her mind. But she hadn't been able to bring herself to tell him that his best friend had to leave and was never coming back.

Now he was standing in front of her again with a frightened look, watching her as she feverishly rooted around in the outermost pocket of her wallet where she stuffed all her old receipts.

"Please go to your room," she said.

She found the little torn-off scrap of paper on which Henrik had written his cell number, ran into the living room, and grabbed the phone. For a second she felt a wave of panic as the cell phone went straight to voice mail, and she could tell the phone was turned off. She ran back to the entry, snatched her jacket from the hook, and checked to see that her car keys were in her pocket.

"I have to run out," she yelled to Markus, who was lying on his bed with his face to the wall.

For a second she stood there, looking at the rejection of his skinny back, before she turned around.

"I'll be back soon," she promised as she turned the lock.

If the police had stopped her, they would have confiscated her license on the spot, but she carefully avoided looking at the speedometer as she darted down Nordre Fasanvej.

From the second she got home from the pastor's residence, part of her had really been pushing for her to go down to Police Headquarters and tell them what the pastor had confided in her so they could head out there and protect him. At the same time, another part of her forced her to keep her promise and give him the head start he was going to need in order to get himself and Jonas to safety.

His car was gone, she noted with a little sigh of relief as she pulled into the parking lot and turned off her engine. There weren't any other cars, either. The only thing she could see was the sexton's bicycle, which was propped against the wall of the church. There wasn't a person in sight.

She inhaled all the way down to her diaphragm and let it out again slowly before walking across the courtyard, then stopped to listen for a second. No movement, no voices, nothing.

Even in the car she'd decided to hightail it out of there if there were the slightest indication the Serb was out there. Then she'd have to call the police and let them take over, but mostly she just wanted to make sure that Henrik and Jonas had managed to get away, then she would tell Louise afterward why Henrik had fled.

Now she was feeling rather sure that Henrik had already left, and if this was where Bosko and Miloš Vituk had been coming, they must have already left again.

The sun was reflected in the kitchen window as she walked up and let the door knocker fall. For a second she stood there waiting, then leaned to the right and peered in the window. The basket of morning rolls was still sitting on the table. Things looked pretty much as they had when she and Markus had left.

Camilla walked down the stairs and around the building before continuing out into the yard. Over by the patio door she put both hands up against the window and peered into the living room. It was hard to see if he'd packed anything, but she did note that the laptop wasn't sitting on the desk anymore.

Again, a sense of relief caused some of her tension to dissolve.

She scanned the road leading to the cemetery for the sexton to find out if he knew when they'd left. She walked down and around the shed, by where the wheelbarrow and watering can were, and where she'd occasionally seen the sexton enjoying a cheroot when the weather permitted it.

Finally, she walked up toward the church and hesitated slightly before walking in. But the floor was bare; there weren't any more newborns there. On the other hand, there was an open box of white candles on the bench next to a yellow plastic watering can.

She walked over and opened the door from the entry-way into the main body of the church, calling to him to avoid startling him in the event that he was in there finishing something up.

The blood was the first thing she saw. The light from above, from the broad windows in the roof of the church, cast reflections down, making it shine on the dark stone floor.

The door slammed shut behind her as she ran forward without giving even a thought to the fact that maybe she should have been running out instead of in.

52

His eyes were closed. He was lying on his side with his torso half up on the kneeling pillows in front of the altar, and the blood had dyed his light summer jeans and shirt dark red, where it had spread through the material in big splotches. It spread across his chest all the way out over the shoulder and left arm, which was resting on the floor, and there were colored areas on both knees, like two oval patches with frayed edges.

Camilla instinctively stepped back and sank down into a squat. She inhaled deeply a couple of times to keep herself from hyperventilating before she eventually got up to put a finger on the sexton's wrist. If there was any beat at all, the pulse was so weak that her inexperienced fingers couldn't find it.

She managed to tell the dispatcher clearly and precisely what she'd found once she'd gotten through to emergency services, but she couldn't answer the question of whether or not he was still alive.

"I think he was shot. He's bleeding from both knees and his chest."

As she was talking she got up and in uncertain steps started backing away through the church, her eyes trained on the sexton's powerful body. She should stay with him until the ambulance arrived, she thought, but she didn't dare. She knew that if Otto Birch were still alive, he might need her, but her fear that Bosko would return trumped that thought. She was almost out the door when she suddenly stopped.

"Is he still breathing?" the dispatcher's voice calmly asked into her ear.

"I don't know," she answered hoarsely, and cleared her throat before repeating herself a little louder.

The thought *It's too late to be a coward* flashed through her head. The only thing that made her consider trying to run away was the image of Markus, lying in bed at home with his back to her. But that wasn't enough given that there was a man lying on the floor in front of her, a man who was dying if he hadn't already.

"Feel his throat and see if he has a pulse," the man's voice urged. He added that the ambulance was on its way.

Camilla ran back up to the altar and dropped down onto the floor next to the seemingly lifeless body.

"Take two fingers and hold them gently against his throat. Don't press," he instructed her.

"I think there's a pulse," Camilla whispered, closing her eyes to concentrate.

"Find something that you can press against the wound on his torso and hold it there until the ambulance arrives."

There was no acceptable way to tell the dispatcher that

she didn't know if she would be sticking around that long, and as she tossed her jacket aside and pulled off her cardigan, she felt a strange sense of calm belaying the fear that a moment earlier had been on the verge of making her flee the scene.

She unbuttoned his shirt and determined that the gunshot wound was in his chest, and she put some muscle into it as she leaned over him and pressed her cardigan against the bloody opening.

In a relatively calm voice she started talking to the wounded man. If he could hear her, it might help him to know the ambulance was on its way. If he couldn't hear anything, repeating those same words made her feel calmer, and she promised that she would stay until the EMTs got there and took him to the hospital.

The words sounded like pebbles, but she understood the last part and straightened up a little.

"I told where the house is," he whispered, still with his eyes closed, and she had a hard time telling if he was still conscious.

With her free hand, she pulled her cell phone out of her jacket, which she'd tossed on the floor when she took her cardigan off.

Louise's number appeared after three quick taps.

"Just shut up for a second," Camilla hissed into the phone, turning her head away from the injured man, as Louise started to object. "I'm sitting out in Stenhøj Church. The sexton is lying on the floor next to me. He's been shot at least three times. The ambulance is on its way. I'm trying to keep the blood from gushing out of him until they get here."

At last, Louise was starting to listen, and Camilla told

her how she'd arrived at the church and found Otto Birch on the floor.

"While you've been standing around waiting, Bosko has been out here assaulting this poor, elderly man, and I know why, too. He's looking for Henrik Holm and Jonas, and we have to get to them before Bosko finds them."

"What do you know about Bosko?" Louise asked, astonished.

Camilla felt like she could almost see inside Louise's head, where the pieces were not all quite fitting together.

"Just get out here now; then you can find out," Camilla implored, concentrating the whole time on pressing her cardigan against the wound. "It goes back to when the pastor and his wife were in Bosnia."

53

The ambulance and the EMTs pulled up in front of the church just as Michael Stig drove into the courtyard and parked.

Camilla came running out of the church toward them and pulled open the back door of the police car.

"We're going to Sweden," she yelled with her jacket over her arm, getting in. "I think Henrik Holm might have driven up to his house there and I'm afraid Bosko is right on his heels."

Louise hadn't been able to tell Stig much as they had stood in the doorway and Louise suddenly ordered him to scrap the stakeout and drive out to the church, aside from that there was a seriously wounded man, and that it sounded like that might be where Bosko and Miloš Vituk had gone.

On the way to her colleague's car, Louise had called

Willumsen, who had just been notified of the shooting victim by the central duty desk, but it was news to him that Camilla Lind was at the church. Louise told him Bosko was after the pastor. He did not want to obey Camilla's request, though, and wanted to bring Lars and Toft out to the church instead of Louise and Stig.

"Are you sure it was Bosko and Miloš?" Stig asked, looking at Camilla in the rearview mirror as she slammed the car door shut.

She nodded.

He watched her face in the mirror and listened as she started her story—in hectic snippets—which was news to the two policemen.

Camilla desperately brushed a couple of long strands of hair out of her face before she continued.

"This morning he told me the whole thing. He said he had to disappear, and the man in the church, Otto Birch, said that he'd told him where the house is. So, I'm guessing that he went up to the summerhouse to start with, to gain a little time. He had no way of knowing that Bosko would react so fast."

* * *

The gravel flew around the tires as Michael Stig put the car in gear and backed up to where he could turn around; it flew up and hit the underside of the car as he accelerated and navigated his way out of the narrow driveway into the courtyard.

Louise looked at him in surprise. It was one thing that Louise knew Camilla well enough to know that her friend was serious about this, but Louise was taken aback that

Stig didn't ask any more questions before he started obeying Camilla's orders.

Camilla sat there breathing deeply for a bit as they sped down Stenhøj Allé. Then she leaned forward between the front seats and started to tell them, in more or less coherent sentences, why Henrik Holm had been forced to flee.

Louise listened intently while trying to figure out who they ought to contact with the Swedish police to request assistance, so they could have a patrol sent out to the pastor's summer home and also get permission to drive into Sweden.

"Afraid I can't help," Camilla said, resigned, when Louise interrupted her to get the address and then recommended that Stig get it from central dispatch. "I don't know the address. It's a numbered road, a little forest service road, and they use some idiotic system that doesn't make any sense to people like us who are used to roads with names and houses with numbers. But I was there over Easter and could certainly recognize the place. We just head up toward Helsingborg to start with and then on toward Laholm."

"We'll take the Øresund Bridge over to Malmö in Sweden; that way we won't have to wait for the ferry," Stig decided, pulling onto the highway heading toward the airport.

Eventually Camilla's breathing settled down some, and she told them about the forged birth certificate that ended up being the lifelong shackle Bosko had on the pastor, and how that had forced Henrik Holm into his decision earlier that day.

"They forced Otto Birch to tell them where the pastor and Jonas had gone. And, fuck," she exclaimed vehemently and said that she hadn't been able to get a hold of Henrik even though she'd tried many times. "His cell phone is off."

A desperate note had snuck into her voice, but she tried to tone it down.

"Well, we don't know how much Otto told them," Louise said, turning to look at Camilla.

"No, but he told them where the house is, and that's enough," Camilla responded, closing her eyes.

Louise received a text from Lars in which he wrote that he was just getting in touch with Otto's next of kin and that he would go to National Hospital later and try to talk to him if he was conscious. Right now, he was on the operating table.

Camilla shook her head and sank into the backseat as they zipped past Kastrup Airport, where a large KLM plane was slowly taxiing out to the runway. They continued on over the bridge that linked Denmark to Sweden.

With a sudden jolt, Camilla sat up and slapped her hands to her face. "Markus!" she cried so loudly that Michael Stig slowed down for a second. "He's all alone at home, waiting for me. I told him I'd be right back."

Choking up, she took out her phone but ended up passing it to Louise and asking her to call Tobias and ask if he could go over and stay with their son until Camilla came home.

Louise found his number and explained as little as possible, but added extra emphasis when she said that it was a life-or-death matter and that she was the one who forced Camilla to come. Actually, that was a little unfair, because Tobias didn't usually put up a fuss over getting a little extra time with his son, but every now and then he did accuse Camilla of being too disorganized. Once that was all arranged, Louise passed the phone back over the headrest.

"But you've pretty much got to assume that an elderly man says what he knows if a couple of guys show up and shoot his kneecaps to smithereens," Stig said, getting back to Louise's conclusion as they drove through the Øresund tunnel. "I'm guessing they shot before they asked their questions to show that they were serious and then he told them what he knew."

"But he did have the last word," Camilla admitted, as they had water on both sides of them.

Michael Stig nodded.

"Bosko doesn't leave witnesses."

Louise sighed and thought it was no wonder that Mikkelsen had been so concerned about the violent trend he'd seen beginning to show up on the scene a few weeks earlier. The kind of brutality they'd seen recently was unheard of—beyond even the knifings that got citizens and politicians so upset, even though they were standard fare in Copenhagen.

* * *

As they approached the tollbooth, Louise spotted the Swedish police cars. She'd been notified that an APB had gone out in Sweden; Bosko was heavily armed and considered extremely dangerous, but if he'd made it over the sound more than forty-five minutes ago, then he'd have gotten away before they had started watching the border. That would have been true of the crossing from Helsingør also, where officers had been stationed at both ends of the Scandlines ferry route to Helsingborg.

Willumsen had ordered two men from the Nordsjælland police department to go to Helsingør and review the surveillance tapes from the ferry terminal; two of Mikkelsen's guys were doing the same thing at the bridge's control center, but Willumsen had reached out to Louise to let her know that it would take a couple of hours before they knew if a man matching the picture of Bosko the police had circulated had crossed the border.

As they pulled away from the tollbooth on the Malmö side, Stig pulled over and quickly jumped out to greet their Swedish counterparts, who were ready to follow them the rest of the way. Once he was back behind the wheel a second later, he announced that while the Swedish police had been there, two Volvos of the model they were interested in had gone by, but neither of them with a driver of the nationality they were looking for.

"One was a woman, and she was Danish. I don't know, I might consider moving to Sweden if I could afford to buy a car like that over here," Stig said getting back onto the highway.

As they drove toward Landskrona, Camilla again started telling them how the pastor had discovered early that same morning that the network he thought his housekeeper was working with didn't have anything to do with helping women from Eastern Europe.

"To the contrary," she said indignantly. "The reason for the lively traffic in young women at his house was that they had to go out there to deliver their earnings. And Henrik wasn't going to put up with that. There was no way he was going to let himself or his church be pressured into helping exploit young women like that."

Suddenly things added up for Louise. Now everything

fit, but she wasn't sure if she would have been able to put it all together, even though she'd been studying the pattern closely for several days and would have continued to do so.

Louise thought about Hana and the other young women, who had passed her with their eyes on the ground, and of her conversation on the bench with Henrik Holm, whose eyes had kept flitting to the door whenever someone approached. But it hadn't occurred to her that he had been under so much pressure, and she didn't doubt that at that point he still believed in the network's and Tereza's good intentions. Otherwise he wouldn't have spoken to Louise so passionately about it.

Michael Stig kept up the rapid pace and the light greens of Skåne County in the springtime flew past. Louise glanced at the speedometer and saw he was doing about 150 kilometers an hour—but even so she had a niggling knot in her stomach that told her it was too slow. The tense silence made her reach over and flip on the radio, but after two verses she shut it off again and sighed, then leaned back and closed her eyes.

"He's not coming back," Camilla finally said, breaking the silence. "Not even if you succeed in catching Bosko."

Louise thought about Jonas, who sometimes seemed both shy and a little withdrawn.

Still, he had opened up that weekend he'd stayed with her.

She was assuming he knew the truth by now. Henrik would have a hard time explaining that they weren't going back to the pastor's residence without telling him why.

Who even knew how much Jonas would understand? Louise thought, feeling a pang in her heart that everything the boy had considered part of his secure, everyday life was gone, just like that. But he was a great kid, and she was sure that with time he would adjust to the situation his parents had gotten him in.

They were driving the last little way up E6 toward Laholm when Willumsen called and said that a Volvo XC90 with Swedish plates had been spotted at the harbor in Helsingør.

"The car was rented from Avis in Malmö by a man named Hendrich Müller with an address in Hamburg, but there's no trace of anyone by that name, so now I'm sending some techs up so they can look at the car."

"So he's still on board as a pedestrian, or someone picked him up at the ferry terminal, or he had another car waiting," Louise said, looking over at Michael Stig, who nodded to show that he'd understood the latest development.

"Miloš Vituk returned to his apartment half an hour ago," Willumsen continued. "He came sauntering down from Vesterbrogade but was dumb enough to have a Smith & Wesson .38-caliber in his inside pocket. What an idiot. He's being questioned by Toft as we speak."

He gave a little, satisfied chuckle. "Where are you guys?" he wanted to know.

"We'll be there in about fifteen minutes," Louise said, glancing back at Camilla, who nodded in affirmation. "Ten minutes," Louise corrected herself as she noted her colleague had sped up, even though they'd left the main road.

54

The woods closed in around them, and the roads got smaller. Stig had been forced to ease up a little on the speed and was now working to avoid the worst of the potholes in the poorly maintained asphalt.

"We turn right up by that big farm," Camilla ordered, pointing toward a forest road, which was almost hidden behind a high pile of logs.

The pavement turned into gravel, and the speedometer was down to twenty as Stig coaxed the car along the uneven road.

None of them said anything, and aside from Camilla's brief instructions to turn or go straight, there was an oppressive silence that became more and more intense the thicker the trees got around them and the closer they got to the pastor's house in the woods.

Their Swedish colleague was still right behind them,

and the agreement was that they would stop a couple hundred meters away from the house.

"We're going to go down around that little lake, and then there's an old, dilapidated tractor where we turn off to his house."

The sun had dipped behind the tall treetops, and an early twilight sent a light bluish gray through the narrow openings between the trees and onto the forest road.

"The house is in there," Camilla said, pointing toward a thick copse with yet another high pile of cut logs. Only a little white mailbox revealed that someone lived behind the densely growing trees.

Stig signaled and then slowed down.

* * *

Camilla stayed in the backseat while Louise and Stig got out of the car to talk to their Swedish colleagues before they approached the house. She had rolled down her window, and aside from the police voices, it was completely quiet. Not a sound made it in here, no car engines, no noise. The only sound came from the birds flying low between the branches.

Most of all, she wanted to run to the house and get the pastor and Jonas so they could get out of there, but she had been ordered to remain in her seat until they told her they were ready to go in. The two Swedish officers were armed, unlike Louise and Stig, and would approach the house first.

As they started walking, Camilla got out of the car and immediately noticed the scent of freshly chopped pine. A little farther in, the forest road ended and turned into a narrow path that led into a jungle of toppled trees—a relic from the powerful storms that had claimed large portions of the forest several years earlier.

Her fear impeded her movements, but when they waved to her from the driveway, she slowly started following the others. At first a little hesitantly, but then her footsteps became more confident and finally she was jogging. Even from a distance she spotted Henrik's black car, which was parked in front of the red-and-white wood house, and she saw the light in the kitchen window and the smoke curling up from the chimney from the woodstove in the living room.

The two Swedish officers came around from the back of the house and nodded, as Louise signaled that they were going to enter.

"There's no one visible in there," one of the Swedes said, glancing up at the house's second floor, where a window was ajar. "There's no sign of a confrontation. Everything looks peaceful."

After a quick knock on the front door, Louise waited for a second before pressing the door handle down and pushing the door open. She stood in the doorway listening before she took the first step into the front entryway.

Camilla stood in the driveway watching her. She was still afraid and her muscles were stiff, her heart pounding, and her hands clenched, her fingernails cutting into her palms. At the same time, she felt like they'd made it in time. She filled her lungs with fresh forest air and slowly exhaled, feeling slightly dizzy.

Through the window, she watched Louise walking into the kitchen. The others had gone upstairs. Camilla watched Louise walk toward the living room, which they knew was empty. Camilla's shoulders relaxed since the Swedish officers had already peeked in all the windows on the whole ground floor.

The wind pulled at her hair, blowing it over her face as she turned around and started walking around behind the house and over the large lawn, which had been left wild and natural. She sat down at the table by the fire pit and for a second enjoyed the silence and the scent of the thick carpet of pine needles that formed a natural carpet under the tall trees.

* * *

Louise was puzzled by a sound from the room at the back of the house and slowly walked forward through the living room, past the woodstove. She spotted Camilla out in the yard by the long, wide picnic table, which was made of a split tree trunk resting on two stumps.

Camilla had described the layout of the house. On the ground floor, along with the kitchen, bathroom, and living room, there were two guest bedrooms, which were mostly used for storage. Upstairs there was a second bathroom, three bedrooms, and a little attic room.

There was the sound again. Louise stood still and listened until she realized it was the ceiling creaking as her colleagues walked around upstairs.

She put a hand on the dining table and stood there for a second to let her heart calm down. She didn't know what she'd expected, and she decided that most of all she was trying to avoid expecting anything.

She heard the others coming down the stairs, and Stig came over and opened the door of the woodstove, which was burning briskly. A big log was still going strong even though it had obviously been in the stove for a while.

"Well, there's just no telling," Stig said after he shut it again. "They could be absolutely anywhere, but it must be somewhere they can get to on foot. What about neighbors? Are there any?"

Camilla had told them about the Jønssons, who had a farm on the other side of the band of pines, which ran through this stretch of woods like a belt.

"About a kilometer away, through the woods," Louise said, but she didn't know if Camilla knew the way. She walked over to open the lock on the patio door and call to Camilla when she saw Camilla suddenly jump up and start running toward the woods bordering on the backyard.

The lock jammed and wouldn't budge despite Louise hitting it. She watched Camilla disappear into the edge of the woods. Louise ran through the kitchen and had just gotten to the corner of the house and around into the backyard when the screams ripped through the silent forest.

Louise ran through the tall grass past the table, past the fire pit, but stopped suddenly when Camilla came staggering back from the edge of the woods with her hands clenched together over her head in helplessness, as she ran, tears streaming, shrieking. Then Camilla collapsed, her violent sobs filling Louise with fear.

Stig and their Swedish colleagues were right behind Louise as she went farther into the woods where a small, narrow path wound its way between the pine trees.

Henrik Holm was lying on his stomach with one arm over his head and the other out to the side. Killed from behind by one shot in the back of the head and two more in his back.

Louise gasped for air and doubled over, as though she suddenly had a terrible stitch in her side. The others kept going past her and kneeled next to the body.

Louise didn't need to go all the way to know that the pastor was dead. Liquidated. She was also experienced enough to know that he had been shot at close range. He hadn't had a chance to get away and was still lying in the place where he had been shot.

Camilla's sobs sliced through her bones. It went black before her eyes, and she didn't have enough air to stand back up and walk back to her. Instead, she sank even more and let herself fall onto the forest floor, where she sat with her back against a tree and ignored the sharp pine needles that pierced her knit sweater.

They felt for a pulse, looked at his face. The bullet exited where his mouth had been.

Louise looked away, into the darkness between the tree trunks, as she heard the Swedish officers on their cell phones, both calling for backup.

55

It was his eyes she noticed first. They found her through the dense branches. There were several rows of trees between them. Still, she could see his face quite clearly.

Stig had stayed on the footpath, while the other two ran back to the house.

Louise was slowly crawling her way forward on her knees, squeezing her way between the trunks. When she got there, Jonas's face was hidden in his hands and he was sitting perfectly still. Louise put an arm around him and pulled him to her. Squeezed him and felt his face against her shoulder. He wasn't crying. He wasn't making a sound. She could hardly feel him breathing.

Tears streamed down her cheeks and landed on his hair, but otherwise she felt nothing. The sound of Camilla's deep sobs didn't penetrate this far into the woods, nor did the piercing tones of the first sirens. Not even Stig's gentle voice, talking to her right before he grasped her elbow and started helping her out, while she was still holding the boy in her lap.

Jonas kept his head buried in against her shoulder, until they were out on the path. Then Stig lifted him up into his arms and carried him to the house, with Louise walking right next to him.

As they reached Camilla in the grass, she slowly got up onto her knees and took the hand Louise held out to her. Together they walked up to the house, where the first responders' flashing lights made the place feel too crowded. The ambulance and police cars were parked in a long line down by the driveway. None of them had driven all the way up to the house, since the driveway had already been cordoned off.

Louise followed Stig into the living room and let Camilla collapse into the room's only armchair, in front of the woodstove, which no longer showed a glow behind the soot-covered glass door. Louise sat down on the sofa, as Stig let Jonas slowly slip down next to her.

"Do you think it would be better if we put him to bed until we leave here?" her colleague asked, searching her face to see what she thought.

"Just let him lie here," Louise said and swallowed a couple of times in quick succession when she saw how the boy curled up into a fetal position and hid his face in a cushion.

A weak shiver ran through him as she carefully placed a hand on his shoulder and then quickly pulled it back again; she couldn't even fathom the misfortune this eleven-year-old boy had suffered in just one day, and now he may have just witnessed his father being gunned down, as well.

The silence in the living room was oppressive.

Jonas was still curled up into a tight ball, breathing so quietly that occasionally Louise feared he'd stopped.

Camilla sat in the armchair staring straight ahead. She was pale and staring off into space. Every so often, she reacted as an almost invisible shiver ran through her, and she mindlessly clasped her hands together hard, as if a sharp pain were jabbing through her.

Stig had gone out front and was talking to Willumsen by phone. From what she could hear, Louise was going to take Jonas and Camilla back to Denmark in the car after the Swedish police questioned them, knowing full well that the boy was definitely too deep in shock to be able to tell them anything. Jakobsen would be waiting at National Hospital to receive them so Jonas could get emergency crisis counseling.

* * *

Darkness had fallen outside, and Louise counted about six or eight CSI techs from the Swedish crime lab working both in front of and behind the house. Three were leaning over the tire imprints in the driveway and preparing to take plaster molds.

Louise held Jonas's hand as they walked out to the car. As expected, the boy hadn't been able to tell the police anything about what happened, so they decided to wait and have him try to talk to them when their own expert crisis psychologist could be present.

Louise noticed Stig standing and watching them as she carefully turned his car around on the narrow forest road and slowly started driving back through the darkness, avoiding the biggest of the potholes.

56

The murder of the popular pastor Henrik Holm filled all the newspapers' front pages on Monday morning. Only a little bit of the story had leaked to the public, but it was enough to leave people in shock about the brutality of his killing.

The investigative team was gathered in Willumsen's office. No one had slept more than a couple of hours since Louise had arrived at National Hospital late Saturday night with Jonas and Camilla, who were both admitted to be treated for shock. Louise had sat with them until Sunday morning, going directly from the hospital to Police HQ.

"Miloš Vituk pleaded guilty to the four killings," Willumsen began, eyeing them with tired eyes, his face unshaven.

"Four?" Louise and Stig exclaimed simultaneously.

"Otto Birch died overnight," Willumsen informed them

sadly. After a moment of silence as that news sank in, he returned to the topic of Miloš Vituk. "We searched the cell phone we found on him when we arrested him and, sure enough, it had a different number from the ones we knew about. Igli is just compiling all the numbers. He'll bring a list as soon as he's done."

He signaled he was changing subjects by taking a gulp of his coffee. "Late last night Lars spoke briefly with Otto Birch."

Willumsen nodded to Louise's partner to have him take over.

"He was very confused about what had happened. He went into the church and was swapping out the candles in the candleholders when two men came in. They asked for the pastor and an instant later his legs exploded in pain, and he collapsed onto the floor. One man walked right up to him and held a big revolver to his forehead, demanding to know where they went. So, Otto told him about the house in Sweden and gave them the address. Then that man disappeared—we're assuming this was Bosko—while the other one, who had stayed in the background, stepped forward and aimed at him."

"Is there any evidence that Bosko was there?" Louise wanted to know. She had asked that same question many times since Sunday morning, but Willumsen had shaken his head each time.

"Miloš Vituk was brought before a judge yesterday at two o'clock, and after confessing was sentenced to jail for four weeks."

"But he wasn't the one behind the murders," Toft said, without removing the plastic cigarette from his mouth. He'd been sitting with the Serb ever since his arrest Saturday afternoon right up until they had escorted him down to see the judge for his preliminary hearing.

Willumsen shook his head. "That's not what we're trying to prove here. Frandsen has had his CSI techs working all night, and he called twenty minutes ago to say that he was on his way over from Slotsherrensvej. But obviously, he has to make it through morning rush hour traffic before he'll be here." Willumsen pulled the printout of an e-mail out of the stack he had in front of him on the table.

"We received a report from the DNA lab. They confirm that the same DNA was found on the girl murdered in the Meatpacking District and Kaj Antonsen. And," he said, drawing it out a little, "the murdered prostitute in Prague. They sent the results to the international database, and we have a match with Bosko. He's been charged multiple times for violent assaults, but they've had to let him go each time because of a lack of evidence. We don't have anything on Miloš Vituk. We ran the fingerprints the techs found in the big Volvo in Helsingør through our own automated fingerprint ID system, but we didn't get any hits.

"However, Interpol did find a match when they ran it through their system. Helsingør also sent us prints from the surveillance footage from when the ferry disembarked in Helsingborg."

He pushed two pictures out onto the table. "Bosko!"

The Serb was walking purposefully down the hallway, making no attempt to hide his face. To the contrary, he was looking right up into the camera in one of the pictures. In the corner, the time stamp read 3:07 p.m.

"He had a car waiting on the other side, and we were standing on Valdemarsgade at that time," Louise calculated. She looked over at Stig, who was clicking the pen he was holding in his hand. There was a half-empty cola on the table in front of him, even though it wasn't nine a.m. yet. He might have slept even less than she had. He had stayed behind in Sweden so that he would be available to the Swedish police during the first few hectic days of the investigation. They had found the pastor's computer and the letter he'd written to them but had not had a chance to send.

Everything matched what Camilla had repeated to their Swedish counterparts and then again at National Hospital. It had also been confirmed that Baby Girl was Tereza's daughter. The baby was still at Skodsborg Orphanage, and Toft had brought the mother out there that same afternoon so that she could sign the necessary paperwork now that they had the mother's permission for the baby to be put up for adoption.

"What about the father?" Louise asked, her eyes drifting over toward her partner.

"Bosko," he said. "The first time she met him, he raped her in a little apartment in Malmö. After that he forced her to work until a week before she gave birth. He sent her to Denmark the day before the birth, and she stayed in the apartment out at Enghave Square. Miloš Vituk was with her when she gave birth, and he was also the one who immediately took the baby and left it in the church."

Louise sighed, then took a deep breath when Toft added that the little stillborn baby boy had been born in Malmö and the mother didn't know what had happened to it after Bosko's men had taken it.

* * *

Frandsen didn't knock before he walked in and quickly greeted everyone around the table. "Bosko was in the church," he began without any introductions. "We also have evidence that he was at the crime scenes in the Meatpacking District and in the courtyard off Sønder Boulevard, but there are no traces of Miloš Vituk in any of these locations."

Frandsen looked over at Willumsen, who just nodded.

"The three bullets that hit the sexton were not fired from the same weapon. The two bullets in his knees were fired from a pistol and match the casings from a Glock 9mm that our people found in the church, while the shot in the chest was fired from a revolver, which in all likelihood was identical to the Smith & Wesson you confiscated from Miloš Vituk when he was arrested. And," he continued, glancing around, "the pistol is the same as the one that shot and killed Henrik Holm up in Sweden, which occurred while Miloš Vituk was in custody being questioned by you guys."

He tossed his report onto the table in front of Willumsen and looked over toward the door as Igli knocked and stepped in.

The interpreter apologized and asked if he were interrupting. Willumsen shook his head and waved him into the office.

"Miloš Vituk still insists that he was responsible for all three shots even though he can't explain what happened to the other weapon," Toft confirmed.

Igli stood against the wall, ready to distribute the copies he'd printed out of the numbers from Miloš's "secret" phone. Once everyone had a copy, he cleared his throat.

"You're not going to get Bosko," he said softly and sounded sure. "Miloš Vituk will continue to claim that he was responsible for the whole thing and doesn't know anything about Bosko. In return he will be well looked after for the rest of his life. That's how it usually goes. I'm guessing that Bosko has already been back in Serbia for ages by now, and a man like him won't be caught there."

Louise was lost in her own thoughts when Lars tapped her on the shoulder and pointed to the door. Suhr had stuck his head in and waved for her to come out. She spotted Jakobsen behind him with his silver-gray hair, appearing all business yet with a concerned look in his eyes.

Out in the hallway, Suhr took her by the elbow and led her down to his office. The somber look in his eyes kept her from saying anything as he asked her to take a seat and pointed to a chair for the psychologist, who must have come straight over from National Hospital.

"We're going to have to talk about Jonas," Suhr began once he'd taken his own seat behind the desk. "There's no reason to doubt the information the pastor gave us. According to the civilian registration database, there is no next of kin either in the pastor's family or that of his deceased wife."

Louise nodded. That matched what Camilla had said Henrik had told her about his wife's death.

"That leaves Jonas Holm all alone. Without a family or any next of kin, and we're going to have to concede that it will be darn near impossible for us to try to track down any potential biological family members in Bosnia, since no one knows his parents' identities."

"I've talked a bit with the boy." Jakobsen took over now, watching Louise with his clear, penetrating gaze. "Jonas is still in a state of deep shock, but he did say that he was walking around at the edge of the woods gathering some kindling for the fire, when his dad suddenly ran out of the house. Almost at the same time he heard a car door slam and the stranger came running along behind his dad. He crouched down and hid only a few meters from where his father was gunned down."

Louise's throat constricted.

"I sat with him a long time last night," Jakobsen continued. "This is a tough period he's going to have to make it through, and this trauma will be with him for a very long time. I tried to talk to him a little about the fact that—along with his input, of course—we're going to have to find him a new family that he can move in with and live with."

"How is that going to happen?" Louise asked, leaning forward.

Jakobsen looked at her, a serious expression on his face. "Normally the social welfare authorities would find a foster family for him or maybe even a family that wants to adopt him. In his case, of course, they will have to keep in mind that it might be best if they live nearby so Jonas can keep going to the same school and stay in touch with his friends."

"Normally," Louise repeated, watching Jakobsen. "What do you mean by normally?"

Jakobsen folded his hands together in his lap and leaned back a little in the chair. "In some cases, the child expresses a desire to live somewhere in particular." He added slowly, "And Jonas Holm would very much like to live with you."

Louise stood up and turned away as Suhr took over.

"Do you even know this boy?" her boss asked.

Her eyes wandered to the window, watching a bird fly past before heading farther up into the sky, where there was no limit to how far it could go. Then she nodded.

"It's a very big responsibility and no one expects you to—"

He hadn't finished when Louise spun around and walked out of the office.

Once out the front door, she started walking down the street, heading away from HQ. Her thoughts were racing. Sitting down on a concrete wall, she looked over at the main library and Iceland's Quay across the water. She watched the bicycles zoom past and a few boats sail by. She concentrated, recalling that fortune-teller who had once very convincingly told her that when a woman had a child, it was because the child had chosen her to be its mother. Now Louise's number seemed to have come up— she'd been chosen by a big, eleven-year-old boy.

Life sure is weird and unexpected, she thought as she jumped down and started walking again.

ACKNOWLEDGMENTS

From my very first publication and onward, I've been a stickler for thorough research, which is essential if the goal is storytelling that is believable, authentic, and realistic. I've had enormous help along the way. Special thanks go to my now old friends at Copenhagen's Police Headquarters, without whose help the framework around Louise Rick wouldn't hold. A big, fat, massive thank-you to Tom Christensen, Flying Squad, who has been with me all along the way, and has generously contributed with talk and details as the book developed. Deep gratitude for your time and compassion.

Heartfelt thanks go, as always, to my brilliant friend, forensic expert Steen Holger Hansen, who is there to help out when a plot needs to be spun together. Without you there would be no books.

Great thanks to my talented Danish editor, Lisbeth

Møller Madsen, and to my publisher, People's Press. It's a pleasure to work with you.

A billion thanks to my wonderful, super-smart American editor, Lindsey Rose, and to the spectacular, endlessly committed team at Grand Central. It is a thrill, an honor, and an enormous joy to work with you all. I appreciate every single effort you've made on my behalf. So happy to be here.

Thank you so very much to my fabulous and savvy American agent, the unparalleled Victoria Sanders, who works magic for me, and to your incredibly wonderful associates, the lovely and talented Bernadette Baker-Baughman and Jessica Spivey, whose great work, all around the world, leaves me filled with gratitude and aware of just how fortunate I am.

Thank you to the clever and tireless Benee Knauer, who knows what I am thinking and what I mean, and how to capture it perfectly. It means so much to know you are there, to have you beside me.

I want to express my heartfelt appreciation of the American crime-writing community, and to my dear American readers. I cannot sufficiently convey how much your warm welcome has meant to me; you have made my dream come true. I love this country so much and am delighted to call it my second home.

My warmest thanks must go to my son, Adam, whom I love with all my heart, and who has traveled every step of the way with me on this indescribable journey.

*If you enjoy Sara Blaedel's Louise Rick
suspense novels,
you'll love her new Family Secrets series.*

**An unexpected inheritance from a father she hasn't
seen since childhood pulls a portrait photographer
from her quiet life into a web of dark secrets and
murder in a small Midwestern town . . .**

PLEASE SEE THE NEXT PAGE FOR
AN EXCERPT FROM *THE DAUGHTER*.

AVAILABLE NOW.

1

"What do you mean you shouldn't have told me? You should have told me thirty-three years ago."

"What difference would it have made anyway?" Ilka's mother demanded. "You were seven years old. You wouldn't have understood about a liar and a cheat running away with all his winnings; running out on his responsibilities, on his wife and little daughter. He hit the jackpot, Ilka, and then he hit the road. And left me—no, he left *us* with a funeral home too deep in the red to get rid of. And an enormous amount of debt. That he betrayed me is one thing, but abandoning his child?"

Ilka stood at the window, her back to the comfy living room, which was overflowing with books and baskets of yarn. She looked out over the trees in the park across the way. For a moment, the treetops seemed like dizzying black storm waves.

Her mother sat in the glossy Børge Mogensen easy chair in the corner, though now she was worked up from her rant, and her knitting needles clattered twice as fast. Ilka turned to her. "Okay," she said, trying not to sound shrill. "Maybe you're right. Maybe I wouldn't have understood about all that. But you didn't think I was too young to understand that my father was a coward, the way he suddenly left us, and that he didn't love us anymore. That he was an incredible asshole you'd never take back if he ever showed up on our doorstep, begging for forgiveness. As I recall, you had no trouble talking about that, over and over and over."

"Stop it." Her mother had been a grade school teacher for twenty-six years, and now she sounded like one. "But does it make any difference? Think of all the letters you've written him over the years. How often have you reached out to him, asked to see him? Or at least have some form of contact." She sat up and laid her knitting on the small table beside the chair. "He never answered you; he never tried to see you. How long did you save your confirmation money so you could fly over and visit him?"

Ilka knew better than her mother how many letters she had written over the years. What her mother wasn't aware of was that she had kept writing to him, even as an adult. Not as often, but at least a Christmas card and a note on his birthday. Every single year. Which had felt like sending letters into outer space. Yet she'd never stopped.

"You should have told me about the money," Ilka said, unwilling to let it go, even though her mother had a point. Would it really have made a difference? "Why are you telling me now? After all these years. And right when I'm about to leave."

Her mother had called just before eight. Ilka had still

been in bed, reading the morning paper on her iPad. "Come over, right now," she'd said. There was something they had to talk about.

Now her mother leaned forward and folded her hands in her lap, her face showing the betrayal and desperation she'd endured. She'd kept her wounds under wraps for half her life, but it was obvious they had never fully healed. "It scares me, you going over there. Your father was a gambler. He bet more money than he had, and the racetrack was a part of our lives for the entire time he lived here. For better and worse. I knew about his habit when we fell in love, but then it got out of control. And almost ruined us several times. In the end, it did ruin us."

"And then he won almost a million kroner and just disappeared." Ilka lifted an eyebrow.

"Well, we do know he went to America." Her mother nodded. "Presumably, he continued gambling over there. And we never heard from him again. That is, until now, of course."

Ilka shook her head. "Right, now that he's dead."

"What I'm trying to say is that we don't know what he's left behind. He could be up to his neck in debt. You're a school photographer, not a millionaire. If you go over there, they might hold you responsible for his debts. And who knows? Maybe they wouldn't allow you to come home. Your father had a dark side he couldn't control. I'll rip his dead body limb from limb if he pulls you down with him, all these years after turning his back on us."

With that, her mother stood and walked down the long hall into the kitchen. Ilka heard muffled voices, and then Hanne appeared in the doorway. "Would you like us to drive you to the airport?" Hanne leaned against the doorframe as Ilka's mother reappeared with a tray of bakery rolls, which she set down on the coffee table.

"No, that's okay," Ilka said.

"How long do you plan on staying?" Hanne asked, moving to the sofa. Ilka's mother curled up in the corner of the sofa, covered herself with a blanket, and put her stockinged feet up on Hanne's lap.

When her mother began living with Hanne fourteen years ago, the last trace of her bitterness finally seemed to evaporate. Now, though, Ilka realized it had only gone into hibernation.

For the first four years after Ilka's father left, her mother had been stuck with Paul Jensen's Funeral Home and its two employees, who cheated her whenever they could get away with it. Throughout Ilka's childhood, her mother had complained constantly about the burden he had dumped on her. Ilka hadn't known until now that her father had also left a sizable gambling debt behind. Apparently, her mother had wanted to spare her, at least to some degree. And, of course, her mother was right. Her father *was* a coward and a selfish jerk. Yet Ilka had never completely accepted his abandonment of her. He had left behind a short letter saying he would come back for them as soon as everything was taken care of, and that an opportunity had come up. In Chicago.

Several years later, after complete silence on his part, he wanted a divorce. And that was the last they'd heard from him. When Ilka was a teenager, she found his address—or at least, an address where he once had lived. She'd kept it all these years in a small red treasure chest in her room.

"Surely it won't take more than a few days," Ilka said. "I'm planning to be back by the weekend. I'm booked up at work, but I found someone to fill in for me the first two days. It would be a great help if you two could keep trying to get hold of Niels from North Sealand Photography. He's in Stockholm, but he's supposed to be back tomorrow. I'm hoping he can cover for me the rest of the week. All the shoots are in and around Copenhagen."

"What exactly are you hoping to accomplish over there?" Hanne asked.

"Well, they say I'm in his will and that I have to be there in person to prove I'm Paul Jensen's daughter."

"I just don't understand why this can't be done by e-mail or fax," her mother said. "You can send them your birth certificate and your passport, or whatever it is they need."

"It seems that copies aren't good enough. If I don't go over there, I'd have to go to an American tax office in Europe, and I think the nearest one is in London. But this way, they'll let me go through his personal things and take what I want. Artie Sorvino from Jensen Funeral Home in Racine has offered to cover my travel expenses if I go now, so they can get started with closing his estate."

Ilka stood in the middle of the living room, too anxious and restless to sit down.

"Racine?" Hanne asked. "Where's that?" She picked up her steaming cup and blew on it.

"A bit north of Chicago. In Wisconsin. I'll be picked up at the airport, and it doesn't look like it'll take long to drive there. Racine is supposedly the city in the United States with the largest community of Danish descendants. A lot of Danes immigrated to the region, so it makes sense that's where he settled."

"He has a hell of a lot of nerve." Her mother's lips

barely moved. "He doesn't write so much as a birthday card to you all these years, and now suddenly you have to fly over there and clean up another one of his messes."

"Karin," Hanne said, her voice gentle. "Of course Ilka should go over and sort through her father's things. If you get the opportunity for closure on such an important part of your life's story, you should grab it."

Her mother shook her head. Without looking at Ilka, she said, "I have a bad feeling about this. Isn't it odd that he stayed in the undertaker business even though he managed to ruin his first shot at it?"

Ilka walked out into the hall and let the two women bicker about the unfairness of it all. How Paul's daughter had tried to reach out to her father all her life, and it was only now that he was gone that he was finally reaching out to her.

2

The first thing Ilka noticed was his Hawaiian shirt and longish brown hair, which was combed back and held in place by sunglasses that would look at home on a surfer. He stood out among the other drivers at Arrivals in O'Hare International Airport who were holding name cards and facing the scattered clumps of exhausted people pulling suitcases out of Customs.

Written on his card was "Ilka Nichols Jensen." Somehow, she managed to walk all the way up to him and stop before he realized she'd found him.

They looked each other over for a moment. He was in his early forties, maybe, she thought. So, her father, who had turned seventy-two in early January, had a younger partner.

She couldn't read his face, but it might have surprised him that the undertaker's daughter was a beanpole: six feet tall without a hint of a feminine form. He scanned her up and down, gaze settling on her hair, which had never been an attention-getter. Straight, flat, and mousy.

He smiled warmly and held out his hand. "Nice to meet you. Welcome to Chicago."

It's going to be a hell of a long trip, Ilka thought, before shaking his hand and saying hello. "Thank you. Nice to meet you too."

He offered to carry her suitcase. It was small, a carry-on, but she gladly handed it over to him. Then he offered her a bottle of water. The car was close by, he said, only a short walk.

Although she was used to being taller than most people, she always felt a bit shy when male strangers had to look up to make eye contact. She was nearly a head taller than Artie Sorvino, but he seemed almost impressed as he grinned up at her while they walked.

Her body ached; she hadn't slept much during the long flight. Since she'd left her apartment in Copenhagen, her nerves had been tingling with excitement. And worry, too. Things had almost gone wrong right off the bat at the Copenhagen airport, because she hadn't taken into account the long line at Passport Control. There had still been two people in front of her when she'd been called to her waiting flight. Then the arrival in the US, a hell that the chatty man next to her on the plane had prepared her for. He had missed God knew how many connecting flights at O'Hare because the immigration line had taken several hours to go through. It turned out to be not quite as bad as all that. She had been guided to a machine that requested her fingerprints, passport, and picture. All this information was scanned and saved. Then Ilka had been sent on to the next line, where a surly passport official wanted to know what her business was in the country. She began to sweat but then pulled herself together and explained that she was simply visiting family, which in a way was true. He stamped her passport, and moments later she was standing beside the man wearing the colorful, festive shirt.

"Is this your first trip to the US?" Artie asked now, as they approached the enormous parking lot.

She smiled. "No, I've traveled here a few times. To Miami and New York."

Why had she said that? She'd never been in this part of the world before, but what the hell. It didn't matter. Unless he kept up the conversation. And Miami. Where had that come from?

"Really?" Artie told her he had lived in Key West for many years. Then his father got sick, and Artie, the only other surviving member of the family, moved back to Racine to take care of him. "I hope you made it down to the Keys while you were in Florida."

Ilka shook her head and explained that she unfortunately hadn't had time.

"I had a gallery down there," Artie said. He'd gone to the California School of the Arts in San Francisco and had made his living as an artist.

Ilka listened politely and nodded. In the parking lot, she caught sight of a gigantic black Cadillac with closed white curtains in back, which stood first in the row of parked cars. He'd driven there in the hearse.

"Hope you don't mind." He nodded at the hearse as he opened the rear door and placed her suitcase on the casket table used for rolling coffins in and out of the vehicle.

"No, it's fine." She walked around to the front passenger

door. Fine, as long as she wasn't the one being rolled into the back. She felt slightly dizzy, as if she were still up in the air, but was buoyed by the nervous excitement of traveling and the anticipation of what awaited her.

The thought that her father was at the end of her journey bothered her, yet it was something she'd fantasized about nearly her entire life. But would she be able to piece together the life he'd lived without her? And was she even interested in knowing about it? What if she didn't like what she learned?

She shook her head for a moment. These thoughts had been swirling in her head since Artie's first phone call. Her mother thought she shouldn't get involved. At all. But Ilka disagreed. If her father had left anything behind, she wanted to see it. She wanted to uncover whatever she could find, to see if any of it made sense.

"How did he die?" she asked as Artie maneuvered the long hearse out of the parking lot and in between two orange signs warning about roadwork and a detour.

"Just a sec," he muttered, and he swore at the sign before deciding to skirt the roadwork and get back to the road heading north.

For a while they drove in silence; then he explained that one morning her father had simply not woken up. "He was supposed to drive a corpse to Iowa, one of our neighboring states, but he didn't show up. He just died in his sleep. Totally peacefully. He might not even have known it was over."

Ilka watched the Chicago suburbs drifting by along the long, straight bypass, the rows of anonymous stores and cheap restaurants. It seemed so overwhelming, so strange, so different. Most buildings were painted in shades of beige and brown, and enormous billboards stood everywhere, screaming messages about everything from missing children to ultracheap fast food and vanilla coffee for less than a dollar at Dunkin' Donuts.

She turned to Artie. "Was he sick?" The bump on Artie's nose—had it been broken?—made it appear too big for the rest of his face: high cheekbones, slightly squinty eyes, beard stubble definitely due to a relaxed attitude toward shaving, rather than wanting to be in style.

"Not that I know of, no. But there could have been things Paul didn't tell me about, for sure."

His tone told her it wouldn't have been the first secret Paul had kept from him.

"The doctor said his heart just stopped," he continued. "Nothing dramatic happened."

"Did he have a family?" She looked out the side window. The old hearse rode well. Heavy, huge, swaying lightly. A tall pickup drove up beside them; a man with a full beard looked down and nodded at her. She looked away quickly. She didn't care for any sympathetic looks, though he, of course, couldn't know the curtained-off back of the hearse was empty.

"He was married, you know," Artie said. Immediately Ilka sensed he didn't like being the one to fill her in on her father's private affairs. She nodded to herself; of course he didn't. What did she expect?

"And he had two daughters. That was it, apart from Mary Ann's family, but I don't know them. How much do you know about them?"

He knew very well that Ilka hadn't had any contact with her father since he'd left Denmark. Or at least she assumed he knew. "Why has the family not signed what should be signed, so you can finish with his...estate?" She set the empty water bottle on the floor.

"They did sign their part of it. But that's not enough, because you're in the will, too. First the IRS—that's our tax agency—must determine if he owes the government, and you must give them permission to investigate. If you don't sign, they'll freeze all the assets in the estate until everything is cleared up."

Ilka's shoulders slumped at the word "assets." One thing that had kept her awake during the flight was her mother's concern about her being stuck with a debt she could never pay. Maybe she would be detained; maybe she would even be thrown in jail.

"What are his daughters like?" she asked after they had driven for a while in silence.

For a few moments, he kept his eyes on the road; then he glanced at her and shrugged. "They're nice enough, but I don't really know them. It's been a long time since I've seen them. Truth is, I don't think either of them was thrilled about your father's business."

After another silence, Ilka said, "You should have called me when he died. I wish I had been at his funeral."

Was that really true? Did she truly wish that? The last funeral she'd been to was her husband's. He had collapsed from heart failure three years ago, at the age of fifty-two. She didn't like death, didn't like loss. But she'd already lost her father many years ago, so what difference would it have made watching him being lowered into the ground?

"At that time, I didn't know about you," Artie said. "Your name first came up when your father's lawyer mentioned you."

"Where is he buried?"

He stared straight ahead. Again, it was obvious he didn't enjoy talking about her father's private life. Finally, he said, "Mary Ann decided to keep the urn with his ashes at home. A private ceremony was held in the living room when the crematorium delivered the urn, and now it's on the shelf above the fireplace."

After a pause, he said, "You speak English well. Funny accent."

Ilka explained distractedly that she had traveled in Australia for a year after high school.

The billboards along the freeway here advertised hotels, motels, and drive-ins for the most part. She wondered how there could be enough people to keep all these businesses going, given the countless offers from the clusters of signs on both sides of the road. "What about his new family? Surely they knew he had a daughter in Denmark?" She turned back to him.

"Nope!" He shook his head as he flipped the turn signal.

"He never told them he left his wife and seven-year-old daughter?" She wasn't all that surprised.

Artie didn't answer. *Okay*, Ilka thought. *That takes care of that.*

"I wonder what they think about me coming here."

He shrugged. "I don't really know, but they're not going to lose anything. His wife has an inheritance from her wealthy parents, so she's taken care of. The same goes for the daughters. And none of them have ever shown any interest in the funeral home."

And what about their father? Ilka thought. *Were they uninterested in him, too?* But that was none of her business. She didn't know them, knew nothing about their relationships with one another. And for that matter, she knew nothing about her father. Maybe his new family had asked about his life in Denmark, and maybe he'd given them a line of bullshit. But what the hell, he was thirty-nine when he left. Anyone could figure out he'd had a life before packing his weekend bag and emigrating.

Both sides of the freeway were green now. The landscape was starting to remind her of late summer in Denmark, with its green fields, patches of forest, flat land, large barns with the characteristic bowed roofs, and livestock. With a few exceptions, she felt like she could have been driving down the E45, the road between Copenhagen and Ålborg.

"Do you mind if I turn on the radio?" Artie asked.

She shook her head; it was a relief to have the awkward silence between them broken. And yet, before his hand reached the radio, she blurted out, "What was he like?"

He dropped his hand and smiled at her. "Your father was a decent guy, a really decent guy. In a lot of ways," he added, disarmingly, "he was someone you could count on, and in other ways he was very much his own man. I always enjoyed working with him, but he was also my friend. People liked him; he was interested in their lives. That's also why he was so good at talking to those who had just lost someone. He was empathetic. It feels empty, him not being around any longer."

Ilka had to concentrate to follow along. Despite her year in Australia, it was difficult when people spoke English rapidly. "Was he also a good father?"

Artie turned thoughtfully and looked out his side window. "I really can't say. I didn't know him when the girls were small." He kept glancing at the four lanes to their left. "But if you're asking me if your father was a family man, my answer is, yes and no. He was very much in touch with his family, but he probably put more of himself into Jensen Funeral Home."

"How long did you know him?"

She watched him calculate. "I moved back in 1998. We ran into each other at a local saloon, this place called Oh Dennis!, and we started talking. The victim of a traffic accident had just come in to the funeral home. The family wanted to put the young woman in an open coffin, but nobody would have wanted to see her face. So I offered to help. It's the kind of stuff I'm good at. Creating, shaping. Your father did the embalming, but I reconstructed her face. Her mother supplied us with a photo, and I did a sculpture. And I managed to make the woman look like herself, even though there wasn't much to work with. Later your father offered me a job, and I grabbed the chance. There's not much work for an artist in Racine, so reconstructions of the deceased was as good as anything."

He turned off the freeway. "Later I got a degree, because you have to have a license to work in the undertaker business."

They reached Racine Street and waited to make a left turn. They had driven the last several miles in silence. The streets were deserted, the shops closed. It was getting dark, and Ilka realized she was at the point where exhaustion and jet lag trumped the hunger gnawing inside her. They drove by an empty square and a nearly deserted saloon. Oh Dennis! The place where Artie had met her father. She spotted the lake at the end of the broad streets to the right, and that was it. The town was dead. Abandoned, closed. She was surprised there were no people or life.

"We've booked a room for you at the Harbourwalk Hotel. Tomorrow we can sit down and go through your father's papers. Then you can start looking through his things."

Ilka nodded. All she wanted right now was a warm bath and a bed.

"Sorry, we have no reservations for Miss Jensen. And none for the Jensen Funeral Home, either. We don't have a single room available."

The receptionist drawled apology after apology. It sounded to Ilka as if she had too much saliva in her mouth.

Ilka sat in a plush armchair in the lobby as Artie asked if the room was reserved in his name. "Or try Sister Eileen O'Connor," he suggested.

The receptionist apologized again as her long fingernails danced over the computer keyboard. The sound was unnaturally loud, a bit like Ilka's mother's knitting needles tapping against each other.

Ilka shut down. She could sit there and sleep; it made absolutely no difference to her. Back in Denmark, it was five in the morning, and she hadn't slept in twenty-two hours.

"I'm sorry," Artie said. "You're more than welcome to stay at my place. I can sleep on the sofa. Or we can fix up a place for you to sleep at the office, and we'll find another hotel in the morning."

Ilka sat up in the armchair. "What's that sound?"

Artie looked bewildered. "What do you mean?"

"It's like a phone ringing in the next room."

He listened for a moment before shrugging. "I can't hear anything."

The sound came every ten seconds. It was as if something were hidden behind the reception desk or farther down the hotel foyer. Ilka shook her head and looked at him. "You don't need to sleep on the sofa. I can sleep somewhere at the office."

She needed to be alone, and the thought of a strange man's bedroom didn't appeal to her.

"That's fine." He grabbed her small suitcase. "It's only five minutes away, and I know we can find some food for you too."

The black hearse was parked just outside the main entrance of the hotel, but that clearly wasn't bothering anyone. Though the hotel was apparently fully booked, Ilka hadn't seen a single person since they'd arrived.

Night had fallen, and her eyelids closed as soon as she settled into the car. She jumped when Artie opened the door and poked her with his finger. She hadn't even realized they had arrived. They were parked in a large, empty lot. The white building was an enormous box with several attic windows reflecting the moonlight back into the thick darkness. Tall trees with enormous crowns hovered over Ilka when she got out of the car.

They reached the door, beside which was a sign: JENSEN FUNERAL HOME. WELCOME. Pillars stood all the way across the broad porch, with well-tended flower beds in front of it, but the darkness covered everything else.

Artie led her inside the high-ceilinged hallway and turned the light on. He pointed to a stairway at the other end. Ilka's feet sank deep in the carpet; it smelled dusty, with a hint of plastic and instant coffee.

"Would you like something to drink? Are you hungry? I can make a sandwich."

"No, thank you." She just wanted him to leave.

He led her up the stairs, and when they reached a small landing, he pointed at a door. "Your father had a room in there, and I think we can find some sheets. We have a cot we can fold out and make up for you."

Ilka held her hand up. "If there is a bed in my father's room, I can just sleep in it." She nodded when he asked if she was sure. "What time do you want to meet tomorrow?"

"How about eight thirty? We can have breakfast together."

She had no idea what time it was, but as long as she got some sleep, she guessed she'd be fine. She nodded.

Ilka stayed outside on the landing while Artie opened the door to her father's room and turned on the light. She watched him walk over to a dresser and pull out the bottom drawer. He grabbed some sheets and a towel and tossed them on the bed; then he waved her in.

The room's walls were slanted. An old white bureau stood at the end of the room, and under the window, which must have been one of those she'd noticed from the parking lot, was a desk with drawers on both sides. The bed was just inside the room and to the left. There was also a small coffee table and, at the end of the bed, a narrow built-in closet.

A dark jacket and a tie lay draped over the back of the desk chair. The desk was covered with piles of papers; a briefcase leaned against the closet. But there was nothing but sheets on the bed.

"I'll find a comforter and a pillow," Artie said, accidentally grazing her as he walked by.

Ilka stepped into the room. A room lived in, yet abandoned. A feeling suddenly stirred inside her, and she froze.

He was here. The smell. A heavy yet pleasant odor she recognized from somewhere deep inside. She'd had no idea this memory existed. She closed her eyes and let her mind drift back to when she was very young, the feeling of being held. Tobacco. Sundays in the car, driving out to Bellevue. Feeling secure, knowing someone close was taking care of her. Lifting her up on a lap. Making her laugh. The sound of hooves pounding the ground, horses at a racetrack. Her father's concentration as he chain-smoked, captivated by the race. His laughter.

She sat down on the bed, not hearing what Artie said when he laid the comforter and pillow beside her, then walked out and closed the door.

Her father had been tall; at least that's how she remembered him. She could see to the end of the world when she sat on his shoulders. They did fun things together. He took her to an amusement park and bought her ice cream while he tried out the slot machines, to see if they were any good. Her mother didn't always know when they went there. He also took her out to a centuries-old amusement park in the forest north of Copenhagen. They stopped at Peter Liep's, and she drank soda while he drank beer. They sat outside and watched the riders pass by, smelling horseshit and sweat when the thirsty riders dismounted and draped the reins over the hitching post. He had loved horses. On the other hand, she couldn't remember the times—the many times, according to her mother—when he didn't come home early enough to stick his head in her room and say good night. Not having enough money for food because he had gambled his wages away at the track was something else she didn't recall—but her mother did.

Ilka opened her eyes. Her exhaustion was gone, but she still felt dizzy. She walked over to the desk and reached for a photo in a wide mahogany frame. A trotter, its mane flying out to both sides at the finish line. In another photo, a trotter covered by a red victory blanket stood beside a sulky driver holding a trophy high above his head, smiling for the camera. There were several more horse photos, and a ticket to Lunden hung from a window hasp. She grabbed it. Paul Jensen. Charlottenlund Derby 1982. The year he left them.

Ilka didn't realize at the time that he had left. All she knew was that one morning he wasn't there, and her mother was crying but wouldn't tell her why. When she arrived home from school that afternoon, her mother was still crying. And as she remembered it, her mother didn't stop crying for a long time.

She had been with her father at that derby in 1982. She picked up a photo leaning against the windowsill, then sat down on the bed. "Ilka and Peter Kjærsgaard" was written on the back of the photo. Ilka had been five years old when her father took her to the derby for the first time. Back then, her mother had gone along. She vaguely remembered going to the track and meeting the famous jockey, but suddenly the odors and sounds were crystal clear. She closed her eyes.

"You can give them one if you want," the man had said as he handed her a bucket filled with carrots, many more than her mother had in bags back in their kitchen. The bucket was heavy, but Ilka wanted to show them how big she was, so she hooked the handle with her arm and walked over to one of the stalls.

She smiled proudly at a red-shirted sulky driver passing by as he was fastening his helmet. The track was crowded, but during the races, few people were allowed in the barn. They were, though. She and her father.

She pulled her hand back, frightened, when the horse in the stall whinnied and pulled against the chain. It snorted and pounded its hoof on the floor. The horse was so tall. Carefully she held the carrot out in the palm of her hand, as her father had taught her to do. The horse snatched the sweet treat, gently tickling her.

Her father stood with a group of men at the end of the row of stalls. They laughed loudly, slapping one another's shoulders. A few of them drank beer from a bottle. Ilka sat down on a bale of hay. Her father had promised her a horse when she was a bit older. One of the grooms came over and asked if she would like a ride behind the barn; he was going to walk one of the horses to warm it up. She wanted to, if her father would let her. He did.

"Look at me, Daddy!" Ilka cried. "Look at me." The horse had stopped, clearly preferring to eat grass rather than walk. She kicked gently to get it going, but her legs were too short to do any good.

Her father pulled himself away from the other men and stood at the barn entrance. He waved, and Ilka sat up proudly. The groom asked if he should let go of the reins so she could ride by herself, and though she didn't really love the idea, she nodded. But when he dropped the reins and she turned around to show her father how brave she was, he was back inside with the others.

Ilka stood up and put the photo back. She could almost smell the tar used by the racetrack farrier on horse hooves.

She used to sit behind a pane of glass with her mother and follow the races, while her father stood over at the finish line. But then her mother stopped going along.

She picked up another photo from the windowsill. She was standing on a bale of hay, toasting with a sulky driver. Fragments of memories flooded back as she studied herself in the photo. Her father speaking excitedly with the driver, his expression as the horses were hitched to the sulkies. And the way he said, "We-e-e-ell, shall we...?" right before a race. Then he would hold his hand out, and they would walk down to the track.

She wondered why she could remember these things, when she had forgotten most of what had happened back then.

There was also a photo of two small girls on the desk. She knew these were her younger half sisters, who were smiling broadly at the photographer. Suddenly, deep inside her chest, she felt a sharp twinge—but why? After setting the photo back down, she realized it wasn't from never having met her half sisters. No. It was pure jealousy. They had grown up with her father, while she had been abandoned.

Ilka threw herself down on the bed and pulled the comforter over her, without even bothering to put the sheets on. She lay curled up, staring into space.

3

At some point, Ilka must have fallen asleep, because she gave a start when someone knocked on the door. She recognized Artie's voice.

"Morning in there. Are you awake?"

She sat up, confused. She had been up once in the night to look for a bathroom. The building seemed strangely hushed, as if it were packed in cotton. She'd opened a few doors and finally found a bathroom with shiny tiles and a low bathtub. The toilet had a soft cover on its seat, like the one in her grandmother's flat in Bagsværd. On her way back, she had grabbed her father's jacket, carried it to the bed, and buried her nose in it. Now it lay halfway on the floor.

"Give me half an hour," she said. She hugged the jacket, savoring the odor that had brought her childhood memories to the surface from the moment she'd walked into the room.

Now that it was light outside, the room seemed bigger. Last night she hadn't noticed the storage boxes lining the wall behind both sides of the desk. Clean shirts in clear plastic sacks hung from the hook behind the door.

"Okay, but have a look at these IRS forms," he said, sliding a folder under the door. "And sign on the last page when you've read them. We'll take off whenever you're ready."

Ilka didn't answer. She pulled her knees up to her chest and lay curled up. Without moving. Being shut up inside a room with her father's belongings was enough to make her feel she'd reunited with a part of herself. The big black hole inside her, the one that had appeared every time she sent a letter despite knowing she'd get no answer, was slowly filling up with something she'd failed to find herself.

She had lived about a sixth of her life with her father. *When do we become truly conscious of the people around us?* she wondered. She had just turned forty, and he had deserted them when she was seven. This room here was filled with everything he had left behind, all her memories of him. All the odors and sensations that had made her miss him.

Artie knocked on the door again. She had no idea how long she'd been lying on the bed.

"Ready?" he called out.

"No," she yelled back. She couldn't. She needed to just stay and take in everything here, so it wouldn't disappear again.

"Have you read it?"

"I signed it!"

"Would you rather stay here? Do you want me to go alone?"

"Yes, please."

Silence. She couldn't tell if he was still outside.

"Okay," he finally said. "I'll come back after breakfast." He sounded annoyed. "I'll leave the phone here with you."

Ilka listened to him walk down the stairs. After she'd walked over to the door and signed her name, she hadn't moved a muscle. She hadn't opened any drawers or closets.

She'd brought along a bag of chips, but they were all gone. And she didn't feel like going downstairs for something to drink. Instead, she gave way to exhaustion. The stream of thoughts, the fragments of memories in her head, had slowly settled into a tempo she could follow.

Her father had written her into his will. He had declared her to be his biological daughter. But evidently, he'd never mentioned her to his new family, or to the people closest to him in his new life. Of course, he hadn't been obligated to mention her, she thought. But if her name hadn't come up in his will, they could have liquidated his business without anyone knowing about an adult daughter in Denmark.

The telephone outside the door rang, but she ignored it. What had this Artie guy imagined she should do if the telephone rang? Did he think she would answer it? And say what?

At first, she'd wondered why her father had named her in his will. But after having spent the last twelve hours enveloped in memories of him, she had realized that no matter what had happened in his life, a part of him had still been her father.

She cried, then felt herself dozing off.

Someone knocked on the door. "Not today," she yelled, before Artie could even speak a word. She turned her back to the room, her face to the wall. She closed her eyes until the footsteps disappeared down the stairs.

The telephone rang again, but she didn't react.

Slowly it had all come back. After her father had disappeared, her mother had two jobs: the funeral home business and her teaching. It wasn't long after summer vacation, and school had just begun. Ilka thought he had left in September. A month before she turned eight. Her mother taught Danish and arts and crafts to students in several grades. When she wasn't at school, she was at the funeral home on Brønshøj Square. Also on weekends, picking up flowers and ordering coffins. Working in the office, keeping the books when she wasn't filling out forms.

Ilka had gone along with her to various embassies whenever a mortuary passport was needed to bring a corpse home from outside the country, or when a person died in Denmark and was to be buried elsewhere. It had been fascinating, though frightening. But she had never fully understood how hard her mother worked. Finally, when Ilka was twelve, her mother managed to sell the business and get back her life.

After her father left, they were unable to afford the single-story house Ilka had been born in. They moved into a small apartment on Frederikssundsvej in Copenhagen. Her mother had never been shy about blaming her father for their economic woes, but she'd always said they would be okay. After she sold the funeral home, their situation had improved; Ilka saw it mostly from the color in her mother's cheeks, a more relaxed expression on her face. Also, she was more likely to let Ilka invite friends home for dinner. When she started eighth grade, they moved to Østerbro, a better district in the city, but she stayed in her school in Brønshøj and took the bus.

"You *were* an asshole," she muttered, her face still to

the wall. "What you did was just completely inexcusable."

The telephone outside the door finally gave up. She heard soft steps out on the stairs. She sighed. They had paid her airfare; there were limits to what she could get away with. But today was out of the question. And that telephone was their business.

Someone knocked again at the door. This time it sounded different. They knocked again. "Hello." A female voice. The woman called her name and knocked one more time, gently but insistently.

Ilka rose from the bed. She shook her hair and slipped it behind her ears and smoothed her T-shirt. She walked over and opened the door. She couldn't hide her startled expression at the sight of a woman dressed in gray, her hair covered by a veil of the same color. Her broad, demure skirt reached below the knees. Her eyes seemed far too big for her small face and delicate features.

"Who are you?"

"My name is Sister Eileen O'Connor, and you have a meeting in ten minutes."

The woman was already about to turn and walk back down the steps, when Ilka finally got hold of herself. "I have a meeting?"

"Yes, the business is yours now." Ilka heard patience as well as suppressed annoyance in the nun's voice. "Artie has left for the day and has informed me that you have taken over."

"*My* business?" Ilka ran her hand through her hair. A bad habit of hers, when she didn't know what to do with her hands.

"You did read the papers Artie left for you? It's my understanding that you signed them, so you're surely aware of what you have inherited."

"I signed to say I'm his daughter," Ilka said. More than anything, she just wanted to close the door and make everything go away.

"If you had read what was written," the sister said, a bit sharply, "you would know that your father has left the business to you. And by your signature, you have acknowledged your identity and therefore your inheritance."

Ilka was speechless. While she gawked, the sister added, "The Norton family lost their grandmother last night. It wasn't unexpected, but several of them are taking it hard. I've made coffee for four." She stared at Ilka's T-shirt and bare legs. "And it's our custom to receive relatives in attire that is a bit more respectful."

A tiny smile played on her narrow lips, so fleeting that Ilka was in doubt as to whether it had actually appeared. "I can't talk to a family that just lost someone," she protested. "I don't know what to say. I've never—I'm sorry, you have to talk to them."

Sister Eileen stood for a moment before speaking. "Unfortunately, I can't. I don't have the authority to perform such duties. I do the office work, open mail, and laminate the photos of the deceased onto death notices for relatives to use as bookmarks. But you will do fine. Your father was always good at such conversations. All you have to do is allow the family to talk. Listen and find out what's important to them; that's the most vital thing for people who come to us. And these people have a contract for a prepaid ceremony. The contract explains everything they have paid for. Mrs. Norton has been making funeral payments her whole life, so everything should be smooth sailing."

The nun walked soundlessly down the stairs. Ilka stood in the doorway, staring at where she had vanished. Had she seriously inherited a funeral home? In the US? How had her life taken such an unexpected turn? What the hell had her father been thinking?

She pulled herself together. She had seven minutes before the Nortons arrived. "Respectful" attire, the sister had said. Did she even have something like that in her suitcase? She hadn't opened it yet.

But she couldn't do this. They couldn't make her talk to total strangers who had just lost a relative. Then she remembered she hadn't known the undertaker who helped her when Erik died either. But he had been a salvation to her. A person who had taken care of everything in a professional manner and arranged things precisely as she believed her husband would have wanted. The funeral home, the flowers—yellow tulips. The hymns. It was also the undertaker who had said she would regret it if she didn't hire an organist to play during the funeral. Because even though it might seem odd, the mere sound of it helped relieve the somber atmosphere. She had chosen the cheapest coffin, as the undertaker had suggested, seeing that Erik had wanted to be cremated. Many minor decisions had been made for her; that had been an enormous relief. And the funeral had gone exactly the way she'd wanted. Plus, the undertaker had helped reserve a room at the restaurant where they gathered after the ceremony. But those types of details were apparently already taken care of here. It seemed all she had to do was meet with them. She walked over to her suitcase.

Ilka dumped everything out onto the bed and pulled a light blouse and dark pants out of the pile. Along with her toiletry bag and underwear. Halfway down the stairs, she remembered she needed shoes. She went back up again. All she had was sneakers.

The family was three adult children—a daughter and two sons—and a grandchild. The two men seemed essentially composed, while the woman and the boy were crying. The woman's face was stiff and pale, as if every ounce of blood had drained out of her. Her young son stared down at his hands, looking withdrawn and gloomy.

"Our mother paid for everything in advance," one son said when Ilka walked in. They sat in the arrangement room's comfortable armchairs, around a heavy mahogany table. Dusty paintings in elegant gilded frames hung from the dark green walls. Ilka guessed the paintings were inspired by Lake Michigan. She had no idea what to do with the grieving family, nor what was expected of her.

The son farthest from the door asked, "How does the condolences and tributes page on your website work? Is it like anyone can go in and write on it, or can it only be seen if you have the password? We want everybody to be able to put up a picture of our mother and write about their good times with her."

Ilka nodded to him and walked over to shake his hand. "We will make the page so it's exactly how you want it." Then she repeated their names: Steve—the one farthest from the door—Joe, Helen, and the grandson, Pete. At least she thought that was right, though she wasn't sure because he had mumbled his name.

"And we talked it over and decided we want charms," Helen said. "We'd all like one. But I can't see in the papers whether they're paid for or not, because if not we need to know how much they cost."

Ilka had no idea what charms were, but she'd noticed the green form that had been laid on the table for her, and a folder entitled "Norton," written by hand. The thought struck her that the handwriting must be her father's.

"Service Details" was written on the front of the form. Ilka sat down and reached for the notebook on the table. It had a big red heart on the cover, along with "Helping Hands for Healing Hearts."

She surmised the notebook was probably meant for the relatives. Quickly, she slid it over the table to them; then she opened a drawer and found a sheet of paper. "I'm very sorry," she said. It was difficult for her not to look at the grandson, who appeared crushed. "About your loss. As I understand, everything is already decided. But I wasn't here when things were planned. Maybe we can go through everything together and figure out exactly how you want it done."

What in the world is going on? she thought as she sat there blabbering away at this grieving family, as if she'd been doing it all her life!

"Our mother liked Mr. Jensen a lot," Steve said. "He took charge of the funeral arrangements when our father died, and we'd like things done the same way."

Ilka nodded.

"But not the coffin," Joe said. "We want one that's more upscale, more feminine."

"Is it possible to see the charms?" Helen asked, still tearful. "And we also need to print a death notice, right?"

"Can you arrange it so her dogs can sit up by the coffin during the services?" Steve asked. He looked at Ilka as if this were the most important of all the issues. "That won't be a problem, will it?"

"No, not a problem," she answered quickly, as the questions rained down on her.

"How many people can fit in there? And can we all sit together?"

"The room can hold a lot of people," she said, feeling now as if she'd been fed to the lions. "We can squeeze the chairs together; we can get a lot of people in there. And of course you can sit together."

Ilka had absolutely no idea what room they were talking about. But there had been about twenty people attending her husband's services, and they hadn't even filled a corner of the chapel in Bispebjerg.

"How many do you think are coming?" she asked, just to be on the safe side.

"Probably somewhere between a hundred and a hundred and fifty," Joe guessed. "That's how many showed up at Dad's services. But it could be more this time, so it's good to be prepared. She was very active after her retirement. And the choir would like to sing."

Ilka nodded mechanically and forced a smile. She had heard that it's impossible to vomit while you're smiling, something about reflexes. Not that she was about to vomit; there was nothing inside her to come out. But her insides contracted as if something in there was getting out of control. "How did Mrs. Norton die?" She leaned back in her chair.

She felt their eyes on her, and for a moment everyone was quiet. The adults looked at her as if the question weren't her business. And maybe it was irrelevant for the planning, she thought. But after Erik died, in a way it had been a big relief to talk about him, how she had come home and found him on the kitchen floor. Putting it into words made it all seem more real, like it actually had happened. And it had helped her through the days after his death, which otherwise were foggy.

Helen sat up and looked over at her son, who was still staring at his hands. "Pete's the one who found her. We bought groceries for his grandma three times a week and drove them over to her after school. And there she was, out in the yard. Just lying there."

Now Ilka regretted having asked.

From underneath the hair hanging over his forehead, with his head bowed, the boy scowled at his mother. "Grandma was out cutting flowers to put in vases, and she fell," he muttered.

She felt their eyes on her, and for a moment everyone was quiet. The adults looked at her as if the question weren't her business. And maybe it was irrelevant for the planning, she thought. But after Erik died, in a way it had been a big relief to talk about him, how she had come home and found him on the kitchen floor. Putting it into words made it all seem more real, like it actually had happened. And it had helped her through the days after his death, which otherwise were foggy. Helen sat up and looked over at her son, who was still staring at his hands. "Pete's the one who found her. We bought groceries for his grandma three times a week and drove them over to her after school. And there she was, out in the yard. Just lying there."

Now Ilka regretted having asked.

From underneath the hair hanging over his forehead, with his head bowed, the boy scowled at his mother. "Grandma was out cutting flowers to put in vases, and she fell," he muttered.

"There was a lot of blood," his mother said, nodding.

"But the guy who picked her up promised we wouldn't be able to see it when she's in her coffin," Steve said. He looked at Ilka, as if he wanted this confirmed.

Quickly she answered, "No, you won't. She'll look fine. Did she like flowers?"

Helen smiled and nodded. "She lived and breathed for her garden. She loved her flower beds."

"Then maybe it's a good idea to use flowers from her garden to decorate the coffin," Ilka suggested.

Steve sat up. "Decorate the coffin? It's going to be open."

"But it's a good idea," Helen said. "We'll decorate the chapel with flowers from the garden. We can go over and pick them together. It's a beautiful way to say good-bye to the garden she loved, too."

"But if we use hers, will we get the money back we already paid for flowers?" Joe asked.

Ilka nodded. "Yes, of course." Surely it wasn't a question of all that much money.

"Oh God!" Helen said. "I almost forgot to give you this." Out of her bag she pulled a large folder that said "Family Record Guide" and handed it over to Ilka. "It's already filled out."

In many ways, it reminded Ilka of the diaries she'd kept in school. First a page with personal information. The full name of the deceased, the parents' names. Whether she was married, divorced, single, or a widow. Education and job positions. Then a page with familial relations, and on the opposite page there was room to write about the deceased's life and memories. There were sections for writing about a first home, about becoming a parent, about becoming a grandparent. And then a section that caught

Ilka's attention, because it had to be of some use. Favorites: colors, flowers, season, songs, poems, books. And on and on it went. Family traditions. Funny memories, role models, hobbies, special talents. Mrs. Norton had filled it all out very thoroughly.

Ilka closed the folder and asked how they would describe their mother and grandmother.

"She was very sociable," Joe said. "Also after Dad died. She was involved in all sorts of things; she was very active in the seniors' club in West Racine."

"And family meant a lot to her," Helen said. She'd stopped crying without Ilka noticing. "She was always the one who made sure we all got together, at least twice a year."

Ilka let them speak, as long as they stayed away from talking about charms and choosing coffins. She had no idea how to wind up the conversation, but she kept listening as they nearly all talked at once, to make sure that everything about the deceased came out. Even gloomy Pete added that his grandmother made the world's best pecan pie.

"And she had the best Southern recipe for macaroni and cheese," he added. The others laughed.

Ilka thought again about Erik. After his funeral, their apartment had felt empty and abandoned. A silence hung that had nothing to do with being alone. It took a few weeks for her to realize the silence was in herself. There was no one to talk to, so everything was spoken inside her head. And at the same time, she felt as if she were in a bubble no sound could penetrate. That had been one of the most difficult things to get used to. Slowly things got better, and at last—she couldn't say precisely when—the silence connected with her loss disappeared.

Meanwhile, she'd had the business to run. What a circus. They'd started working together almost from the time they'd first met. He was the photographer, though occasionally she went out with him to help set up the equipment and direct the students. Otherwise, she was mostly responsible for the office work. But she had done a job or two by herself when they were especially busy; she'd seen how he worked. There was nothing mysterious about it. Classes were lined up with the tallest students in back, and the most attractive were placed in the middle so the focus would be on them. The individual portraits were mostly about adjusting the height of the seat and taking enough pictures to ensure that one of them was good enough. But when Erik suddenly wasn't there, with a full schedule of jobs still booked, she had taken over. Without giving it much thought. She did know the school secretaries, and they knew her, so that eased the transition.

"Do we really have to buy a coffin, when Mom is just going to be burned?" Steve said, interrupting her thoughts. "Can't we just borrow one? She won't be lying in there very long."

Shit. Ilka had blanked out for a moment. Where the hell was Artie? Did they have coffins they loaned out? She had to say something. "It would have to be one that's been used."

"We're not putting Mom in a coffin where other dead people have been!" Helen was indignant, while a hint of a smile appeared on her son's face.

Ilka jumped in. "Unfortunately, we can only loan out used coffins." She hoped that would put a lid on this idea.

"We can't do that. Can we?" Helen said to her two brothers. "On the other hand, if we borrow a coffin, we might be able to afford charms instead."

Ilka didn't have the foggiest idea if her suggestion was even possible. But if this really was her business, she could decide, now, couldn't she?

"We would save forty-five hundred dollars," Joe said.

Forty-five hundred dollars for a coffin! This could turn out to be disastrous if it ended with them losing money from her ignorant promise.

"Oh, at least. Dad's coffin cost seven thousand dollars."

What is this? Ilka thought. Are coffins here decorated in gold leaf?

"But Grandma already paid for her funeral," the grandson said. "You can't save on something she's already paid for. You're not going to get her money back, right?" Finally, he looked up.

"We'll figure this out," Ilka said.

The boy looked over at his mother and began crying.

"Oh, honey!" Helen said.

"You're all talking about this like it isn't even Grandma; like it's someone else who's dead," he said, angry now.

He turned to Ilka. "Like it's all about money, and just getting it over with." He jumped up so fast he knocked his chair over; then he ran out the door.

His mother sent her brothers an apologetic look; they both shook their heads. She turned to Ilka and asked if it were possible for them to return tomorrow. "By then we'll have this business about the coffin sorted out. We also have to order a life board. I brought along some photos of Mom."

Standing now, Ilka told them it was of course fine to come back tomorrow. She knew one thing for certain: Artie was going to meet with them, whether he liked it or not. She grabbed the photos Helen was holding out.

"They're from when she was born, when she graduated from school, when she married Dad, and from their anniversary the year before he died."

"Super," Ilka said. She had no idea what these photos would be used for.

The three siblings stood up and headed for the door. "When would you like to meet?" Ilka asked. They agreed on noon.

Joe stopped and looked up at her. "But can the memorial service be held on Friday?"

"We can talk about that later," Ilka replied at once. She needed time to find out what to do with 150 people and a place for the dogs close to the coffin.

After they left, Ilka walked back to the desk and sank down in the chair. She hadn't even offered them coffee, she realized.

She buried her face in her hands and sat for a moment. She had inherited a funeral home in Racine. And if she were to believe the nun in the reception area laminating death notices, she had accepted the inheritance.

She heard a knock on the doorframe. Sister Eileen stuck her head in the room. Ilka nodded, and the nun walked over and laid a slip of paper on the table. On it was an address.

"We have a pickup."

Ilka stared at the paper. How was this possible? It wasn't just charms, life boards, and a forty-five-hundred-dollar coffin. Now they wanted her to pick up a body, too. She exhaled and stood up.

ABOUT THE AUTHOR

Sara Blaedel's suspense novels have enjoyed incredible success around the world: fantastic acclaim, multiple awards, and runaway number one bestselling success internationally. In her native Denmark, Sara was voted most popular novelist for the fourth time in 2014. She is also a recipient of the Golden Laurel, Denmark's most prestigious literary award. Her books are published in thirty-seven countries. Her series featuring police detective Louise Rick is adored the world over, and Sara has just launched her new Family Secrets suspense series to fantastic acclaim.

Sara Blaedel's interest in story writing, and especially crime fiction, was nurtured from a young age. The daughter of a renowned Danish journalist and an actress whose career included roles in theater, radio, TV, and movies, Sara grew up surrounded by a constant flow of professional writers and performers visiting the Blaedel home. Despite a struggle with dyslexia, books gave Sara a world in which to escape when her introverted nature demanded an exit from the hustle and bustle of life.

Sara tried a number of careers, from a restaurant apprenticeship to graphic design, before she started a publishing company called Sara B, where she published Danish translations of American crime fiction.

Publishing ultimately led Sara to journalism, and she covered a wide range of stories, from criminal trials to the premiere of *Star Wars: Episode I The Phantom Menace*. It was during this time—and while skiing in Norway—that Sara started brewing the ideas for her first novel. In 2004 Louise and Camilla were introduced in *Grønt Støv* (*Green Dust*), and Sara won the Danish Academy for Crime Fiction's debut prize.

Originally from Denmark, Sara has also lived in New York, but now spends most of her time in Copenhagen. When she isn't busy committing brutal murders on the page, she is an ambassador with Save the Children and serves on the jury of a documentary film competition.